DATE DUE

NOV 15 2010 NOV 28 2010		
2/11 MAR 15 2011		
AUG 31 2011		
NOV 27 2011		
JAN 31 2014		

W9-BYF-754

The Blood
of Lorraine

The Blood of Lorraine

Barbara Corrado Pope

PEGASUS BOOKS
NEW YORK

THE BLOOD OF LORRAINE

Pegasus Books LLC
80 Broad Street, 5th Floor
New York, NY 10004

First Pegasus Books cloth edition 2010

Interior design by Maria Fernandez

ISBN: 978-1-60598-098-0

10 9 8 7 8 6 5 4 3 2 1

Printed in the United States of America
Distributed by W. W. Norton & Company, Inc.

For Daniel and for Stephanie, a true *avocat*

Acknowledgments

THANKS MUST FIRST GO TO my wonderful writers group who offered consistently incisive criticism and support throughout the piecemeal creation of this book: Elizabeth Lyon, Geraldine Moreno-Black, Mabel Armstrong, Carolyn Kortge and Faris Cassell. At the midpoint of the novel, I also benefited greatly from the critiques given in a seminar led by Cai Emmons with Llew Wells, Kari Davidson and Shannon Pool. I am deeply grateful (and touched) that readers of an early draft, George Wickes, Richard Stein and Linda Frederick, were not only willing to give me their invaluable suggestions, but did it, graciously, on very short notice. I also owe much to the time and effort that my editor, Jessica Case, and agent, Mollie Glick, put in to making this a better book.

Thanks, too, go to Ray Birn for sending me to Nancy; Dorothy Anker for her last-minute guidance in Yiddish and Lisa Wolverton for hers in Latin; and to Mary Signer for leading me to the Bible passage from Numbers, and for much else. *Merci aux vrais Nanciens, Jeanne et Philippe Rousseau, pour leur précieuse amitié.*

Last, and far from least, I thank my husband, Daniel Pope, for his technical, critical, moral, and life support. I am continually amazed and gratified that he has so wholeheartedly championed my life's dream of becoming a writer.

The Jews of Alsace and Lorraine had to proceed step by step from village to nearby town, from town to city; from small trading, to big shops, to high commerce. . . . It took time, patience; finally they stirred up the great affair—the war [of 1870–71]—and twenty years later Nancy has become the little Jerusalem of thousands and thousands of Jews from Lorraine, Alsace, Poland and Russia.

—Abbé François Hémonet,
Nancy-Juif (Jewish Nancy), 1892–93.

The Blood
of Lorraine

Historical Preface

ON 22 DECEMBER 1894, A CLOSED-DOOR military tribunal convicted Captain Alfred Dreyfus of treason and sentenced the first Jewish Army officer in the French General Staff to a life of solitary confinement on Devil's Island. In 1898, the increasingly contested issue of his guilt or innocence erupted. The famous Dreyfus Affair tore the country apart. As evidence mounted that Dreyfus was not the officer who had passed on military secrets to the Germans, his supporters claimed that what was at stake was the very survival of France as a nation of rights, justice and equality.

Dreyfus was as much a victim of prejudice as he was of a kangaroo court. Fueled by scandal-mongering journalism and Edouard Drumont's runaway bestseller, *La France Juive* (Jewish France), a virulent new anti-Semitism took hold among certain segments of the population during the last two decades of the nineteenth century. This hatred was aimed at less than one per cent of the nation's inhabitants.

French Jews (or Israelites, as many preferred to be called at the time) had always been concentrated in a few pockets across the country. The most populous traditional Jewish community lived in Alsace-Lorraine, most of which was ceded to the Germans in 1872. Nancy, the largest city remaining in French Lorraine, became its capital, its artistic, commercial and administrative center. By November 1894, when this novel opens, it was also the center of Jewish life in the region, even though only 2,000 Israelites inhabited the rapidly growing city of approximately 90,000 people.

1
Friday, November 16

THE CITY OF NANCY, 1894. Twenty-four years after France pro-
claimed itself a republic in the midst of war. Twenty-three years
after the humiliating defeat, occupation and concession of the
ancient territories of Alsace and part of Lorraine to the new powerful Germany. And only two years after examining magistrate
Bernard Martin transferred from Aix-en-Provence to this elegant
capital in the truncated northeastern corner of his beloved country.

Martin stood stacking his papers into piles, preparing for the
weekend. His white-walled chambers were already growing cold. The
black pot-bellied stove that sat in one corner no longer glowered with
half-hidden flames. All that came from its mouth now was a soft,
amber glow. As the muted footsteps of officials and clerks beckoned
through Martin's ground-floor windows, he swelled with what was
still for him an unexpectedly joyful contentment. He was going home.

Suddenly the door to his chambers flew open, and his colleague, David Singer, came rushing in, breathless and disheveled. "You've got to take this case off my hands," he said, almost shouting.

"Singer, you didn't knock?" The question slipped out before Martin could stop himself. He did not intend it as a reproach. He was quite simply shocked. Singer was the most proper person in the court-house, the one least likely to commit any breach of etiquette. And yet here he was before Martin, unannounced, panting, his frock coat open, his cravat askew, and his close-cropped black hair sticking up in shaggy crags as though he had been attempting to tear it out. Martin gestured toward the wooden chair beside his distraught colleague. "Please sit down."

Singer ignored him. "I've been thinking about it all afternoon. I'm sure they gave it to me as a joke. This is their chance to catch me out."

Martin approached his friend to take a closer look. One of Singer's well-manicured hands was locked into a fist, the other clutched a rolled-up newspaper. "Please, sit," he repeated, trying to remain calm. Singer's demeanor was beginning to put him on edge.

When his colleague did not respond, Martin took the precaution of walking around him to close the door. Although he was almost certain that other judges and clerks had already left the Palais de Justice for the weekend, he wanted to make sure that no one else saw Singer in such a state.

"What is wrong?" Martin insisted.

"Presumably," Singer said in a strangled whisper, "it's a case of 'ritual murder.'"

"What?" His confusion churning into dismay, Martin returned to his desk to face his friend.

"A ritual murder." Louder this time. "An accusation that a Jew has killed and mutilated a Christian baby."

"But that's preposterous. These things don't happen——"

"Were you about to say 'any more'?"

"What do you mean?" Martin could not for the life of him understand why Singer was being so prickly with him, of all people.

"These things don't happen *any more*. Not in 1894. Not in the third decade of our glorious French Republic."

"No, no, not at all." Martin feared that soon he, too, would be shouting.

"I tell you, they gave the case to me as a joke, a trap."

"I don't understand."

"You don't understand," Singer responded sarcastically. "My name is *Singer*. David Singer."

"Well, I never thought that mattered—"

"I'm sure you never did," Singer interrupted as he took a step back from Martin's desk. "Will you take it? That's all I need to know." He laid the newspaper down and began to fidget with his collar and cuffs, putting himself back together.

Martin stared at his fellow examining magistrate. Somewhere in the back of his mind he had known that Singer was an Israelite. But it had never occurred to him that this held any particular significance. They had been friends from the day, shortly after Martin's arrival here, when Singer was kind enough to show him around the courthouse. They were alike in age, middle thirties; in height and weight, medium in every way; and both passionately republican in their sympathies and ideals.

Most of all, Martin was grateful for Singer's reaction—or lack of it—to the early revelation that Martin, unlike the other magistrates, was not a man of means and that he had married a teacher. Instead of looking down upon him, Singer had volunteered to help the Martins find an inexpensive place to live, which he did, in the very center of Nancy, near the Palais de Justice and Clarie's school. An apartment, Singer had boasted with a smile, that even had running water, an essential aid for the working woman. If it had not been for his colleague's excessive formality, Martin would long ago have started calling him by his Christian name.

But of course, Martin thought with a start, David was not Singer's *Christian* name.

Singer fingered his coal-black mustache, which rose ever so slightly to a peak on either side of his mouth. "It won't be hard," he continued. "Working-class man and his wife bringing the accusation. Only witness, the wet nurse. They're all lying."

Singer's beard fell to a point so precise, he must have trimmed it every morning. Always well-tailored, respected, treated with utmost civility by everyone in the courthouse, there was no reason for him to be so sensitive. Yet without realizing it, Martin found himself scrutinizing Singer's nose, which was not remarkable in any way.

Their eyes met and Singer stiffened. "I can get the file to you first thing Monday morning. It won't take much of your time."

"It's not that," Martin murmured.

"What, then?" Barely containing his frustration, Singer grabbed the newspaper again.

How could Martin make the cowardly admission that what he felt at this moment was something like fear, that Singer's outbursts had set off memories of another case he had been urgently called upon to solve at the very beginning of his career. The case that had made him an outcast among the police and judges in Aix-en-Provence. The Vernet murders. He shook his head slightly, hoping to vanquish the vision of all those dead bodies.

"You're saying no? After all our talks about justice. Perhaps this is a kind of injustice you don't recognize." Singer moved toward the door.

Martin sighed. "Wait. Surely this is something I will have to take up with the Proc." That's the way everyone referred to the *Procureur*, the prosecutor who assigned cases to the examining magistrates for investigation.

"Surely," Singer concurred. "And as soon as possible."

"Perhaps I'll see him tonight—"

"I wasn't invited. Never have been." Singer cut him short.

"Well, it's only our first time, and I'm not exactly looking forward to it." It had taken the Presiding Judge almost two years to invite Clarie and him to a formal dinner party. Martin struggled to remember how long Singer had been at the court at Nancy.

"Nevertheless, I've been here two years longer than you have," Singer said, as if reading Martin's thoughts.

Martin shrugged his shoulders in exasperation. "I've never thought of you as other than a Frenchman, a good republican—"

"A French Jew *is* a Frenchman and a republican." At least Singer had stopped his retreat and was again approaching Martin's desk.

"Yes, I know."

"You know? Do you read Edouard Drumont's newspaper, *La Libre Parole?*"

Martin raised his hand, fending off any suggestion that he would bother to pick up Drumont's anti-Semitic rag. *La Libre Parole,* "the free word" indeed.

"Perhaps you would find it instructive." Singer unrolled the paper he had been carrying in his right hand. "This is the weekly version, fully illustrated."

Martin had no choice but to examine the cover of *La Libre Parole Illustrée,* dated the previous Saturday, November 10. A drawing of a bearded man took up most of the page. He stood beside a stack of books. Martin squinted. He could make out the first title, Drumont's fabulously successful best seller *La France Juive,* the scurrilous "Jewish France." Martin sucked in a breath. "So this is Drumont."

"Yes, and this," Singer's finger pointed to the little man crawling at the bottom of the page, a caricature of a Jew with a gigantic hooked nose, wearing the helmet of the Prussian army. Drumont held a long prong with which he had grasped this miniature soldier by the seat of his pants. "You know who this is, of course," Singer persisted.

"Singer, I can read," Martin said impatiently. The caption made it all too clear what the cartoon was about: "*A propos of Judas Dreyfus.* Frenchmen, I've been telling you this every day for eight years."

"First, *La France Juive*, now his newspaper," Singer exploded. "You know that Drumont is the one who broke the story of Dreyfus's treachery. He's having a field day with it."

Martin nodded, still staring at the caricature. Alfred Dreyfus was in all the newspapers, accused of having sold military secrets to the Germans. Martin wondered what the real Dreyfus looked like. Surely, if he had managed to become a member of the Army's elite General Staff, nothing like this ugly caricature.

"Don't you see," Singer pleaded, "they are going to use Dreyfus to try to prove that all of us are traitors and cheats."

Martin made one last attempt to calm down his friend. "Even if it's true that Dreyfus did have contact with the Germans, he's only one man, not an entire race. Surely. . . ." He did not finish. *Surely, what?* If Drumont and his ilk kept beating the drums against Dreyfus, wasn't there a danger that they could incite the mob against the Israelites? Martin eased himself into his chair.

"I think you need to read *La France Juive*," Singer pressed on. "You have no idea of the kind of noxious slime Drumont has spread about us. And now in his newspaper, he slanders us, drags us through the mud, every day. Every single day. You are fortunate that you do not have to care about these things."

Martin could feel the heat rising in his face. Why was *he* being subjected to this barrage? Again and again he had proved himself to be a true republican. When he was barely out of school, he had given up on the Church, in part, because of the anti-Semitic sermons of his parish priest. Martin did not deserve this harangue. He began, again, to straighten out the files on his desk.

"I'm sorry," Singer said as he drew nearer, demonstrating a belated recognition that Martin did not count among the bigots and rabble rousers. "I'm upset. I just came back from seeing the body of that poor child. You can't imagine what some people will do to prove that we are beasts." He paused. "Bernard, you are the only one I can turn to, the only one I can trust."

It was the appeal to their friendship that did it, the use of Martin's first name, breaking through the formalities imposed by profession and Singer's punctilious sense of comportment.

Martin pressed his lips together and nodded. "I'll try." After all, what did he have to lose? If Singer was right, and it was a case of false accusation easily cleared up, then it was not at all like the Vernet case.

Or was it? Martin sank back into his chair, remembering. Of all the dead bodies in Aix, there was one that Martin could never allow himself to forget, the pallid figure of his oldest friend Jean-Jacques Merckx laid out on the gray slab like an anarchist Christ with four holes drilled into him. Not by nails, but by bullets. A friend he had let down because he hadn't agreed with his radical ideas, a friend who was killed, in part, because Martin had been indecisive, half-hearted, neither really helping him to desert from the army nor insisting that the two of them obey the law and Merckx go back to face his terrible punishment. A friend who, just as Singer had done, accused him of complacency, of not understanding what he was going through. Martin gave his head a hard shake to bring himself back to the present. This situation was entirely different. There was nothing dangerous or unpatriotic about Singer's views. He did not dream of destroying the state as Martin's boyhood friend had. No, Singer, like Martin, was a builder. They both believed in the French Republic and strived together to make it stronger and better, less corrupt, more just. They were alike in so many ways. In all that really mattered.

Singer stood above him, waiting for assurances. Martin nodded. "I'll do everything in my power to corner Didier tonight. First, though," he added, trying to lighten the mood, "I need to get home."

"Yes, of course." Singer took in a breath. "But I strongly advise you go to the Faculté to see the body right away. You need to know what you are getting into. I've asked Dr. Fauvet to wait for you."

Before Martin could object, his companion continued as he retreated for the second time. "I'll prepare the orders so that all three of the so-called witnesses will be at the Palais on Monday morning, waiting for you." Reaching the door, Singer bowed slightly. "Please give my regards to Mme Martin." His return to form accentuated, rather than covered up, the fact that Singer's self-pitying outburst had been completely out of character. And, Martin sincerely hoped, just as completely unwarranted.

As the door closed, Martin threw a pencil across his desk and watched as it bounced off onto the floor. Why did he have to go off tonight and examine the body of a mutilated baby? Why was he always the stranger, the new man in town, the one that others came to with their grisly cases? *Now there's self-pity for you!* At least this time he had a reason: Singer.

Martin got up with a sigh and followed the rolling pencil to the foot of his *greffier's* desk, which stood near the wall in a position that allowed his clerk to face both judge and witnesses while taking down the official record of their conversations. After a moment's hesitation, Martin placed the pencil beside Guy Charpentier's inkwell. This was almost a malicious act. His clerk was rather officious for his young years, and his small, orderly workplace stood as a constant rebuke to the clutter on Martin's much larger and more luxurious mahogany desk. Smiling to himself, Martin retrieved his bowler and long woolen coat from the coat rack in the corner.

Clarie would understand his being late again. Best to get the worst of it over with.

Martin exited through the main entrance of the Palais de Justice which lay on the southern edge of the sedate and dignified Place de la Carrière. He loved the "Carrière" because it expressed in greenery and stone everything he believed in his heart, that progress, equality and justice were possible. Part of the oldest section of the city, the stately elongated public square had once been a feudal playground for military parades and jousting, rimmed by palaces inhabited only by men of title and privilege. In the last enlightened century, the good Duke Stanislas had changed all that, harmonizing the façades of surrounding buildings, acquiring some of them for governmental functions, and transforming the central strip into a park open to all, graced by straight rows of clipped linden trees, stone benches, and elegant statuary. On most evenings before heading home through the town's Arc de Triomphe, Martin would pause and contemplate all this with gratitude. Grateful that he was leaving the cares of his work behind at the courthouse, grateful that he no longer led a lonely existence in sleepy, pretentious Aix.

But this was not a usual evening. Holding his hat over his face to protect it from a gust of cold wind, he hurried past the Place de la Carrière and Arc de Triomphe to the busy rue Saint-Dizier to catch the horse tram to the Faculté de Médicine.

Hanging onto an overhead strap in the single crowded car, Martin watched ruefully as it paused at the head of the street that led to his apartment and to Clarie. Unaccustomed to public transport, he anticipated each clanging stop and influx of last-minute shoppers with growing impatience. What if Dr. Fauvet had given up on him and gone home? The jostling reached its peak at the open-air market, which was folding up for the night. Bustling, chattering women knocked him about with their sacks filled with paper-wrapped packets of fresh fish, bread, and dangling vegetables. It was only after the tram passed through an archway of the ancient porte Saint-Nicolas, a massive stone gate leading out of the old city, that Martin breathed easier. The crowd thinned and the broad-backed draft horse, relieved by the lighter load, clopped along the parallel iron tracks at a faster pace. When Martin spotted the steeple of Saint Pierre, it was his turn to ring for a stop. The Faculté de Médicine was only a block away from the church, which was at the center of one of Nancy's newer, less densely populated neighborhoods.

As soon as he extricated himself from the tram, Martin broke into a run. When he got to the Faculté, the morgue in the basement was locked and dark. After a quick search of the main hall, he saw a block of light on the floor, which led him to Lucien Fauvet's office. He rapped on the clouded-glass window that formed the top half of the oaken door and was invited in.

Martin was greeted by the gray-blue haze and pleasant aroma of tobacco.

"Ah yes, *Monsieur le juge*, good to see you. I've been waiting." Lucien Fauvet looked up from a pile of books and put down his pipe. He had the straw-blond hair and blue eyes of a true northerner and the enthusiasm of a schoolboy. Which he almost was. His beard and mustache, attempts to age and dignify his pudgy face, were still touchingly scanty.

"Sorry—"

"No need, no need," Fauvet said as he got up from his cluttered desk. "I've just been reading up to make sure that my conclusions are correct. Come. Let's get this over with and send you home to dinner." He left his pipe on the ashtray and his jacket hanging on his chair. The young professor of physiology obviously was not done for the evening.

"Quite an interesting case, very interesting," Fauvet muttered as he led Martin back downstairs.

As Martin walked behind the young doctor, a quiver of trepidation rose in his chest. Fauvet had a reputation for delighting in the grotesque.

After opening the morgue with one of the keys that he carried in a brass ring in the pocket of his gray trousers, Fauvet pulled a cord to activate the electric bulb hanging over an iron table. Its light fell upon a small bundle covered with a white cloth. Fauvet rolled up his shirt-sleeves and pulled the sheet back only far enough to reveal the head. Martin steeled himself not to react. The greenish face was more ghastly than he had imagined. The dead child had taken on the appearance of a toothless, wizened old man. Under the naked bulb, the fine strands of blond hair on the baby's skull shone white against the mottled, darkened skin.

Fauvet lifted the lid of one of the baby's eyes.

"See these little red specks?"

Martin leaned forward and peered into the dead baby's blue-gray eyes. He nodded as he fought down the bile rising in his throat.

"Signs of asphyxiation. But," Fauvet raised a triumphant finger, "*not* by strangulation. No bruising on the neck. Could have been suffocation. A pillow, a diaper. However, the nose was intact, and one does have to ask," he pronounced as he tore off the sheet with a flourish, "why this?"

The preternaturally thin little body was more shocking than the head. The torso had collapsed inward, toward a central jagged gash that ran from the child's throat to the place where his genitals would be, if they had not been cut off. This time Martin stepped back against the cold stone wall for support and covered his mouth to hide his gasp.

"Gutted him. Hinders my work a bit. But at least, you may have noticed, cleaning out the innards saved us from the smell."

Martin hadn't noticed, although once Fauvet mentioned it, he knew he could start breathing hard without getting sicker. It took him a moment to get out a question.

"Why do *you* think someone did that?" he rasped, echoing Fauvet's rhetorical question with disgusted disbelief.

"Suffocation is still a possibility, but my best guess is that he swallowed something, a stone, a piece of meat, and they tried to cover it up."

"But this?" Despite the sickening sour taste gathering in his mouth, Martin could not take his eyes off the body.

Fauvet shrugged. "Perhaps the wet nurse was afraid of an accusation of neglect. He was only about seven months old. He should not have been eating anything hard. From what I've seen in my lab, we really need to outlaw the practice of sending babies off to the country. It's impossible to regulate all the women who hire themselves out as wet nurses."

"But I thought that's hardly done any more, sending infants away."

"Except for the working classes. When women go back to the factories. . . ."

"Yes, of course." Martin paused as he tried to draw a picture of the probable sequence of events. "Why would the parents accept this bizarre story?"

"Ignorance. Old wives' tales about Jews. My own mother used to tell them to me."

"I never heard them."

"You didn't grow up around here. Your parents probably didn't come from one of the villages where Israelites and Christians lived cheek by jowl. Most of these villages are gone now, to Germany, of course."

Fauvet was speaking of the provinces lost in the last war, and the villages in which most of the Jews of France had lived. Or, at least, the poorer Jews—the horse traders, tinkers and peddlers. As far as Martin knew, this world of forests, goblins and legends was fast disappearing. It certainly was not part of Nancy, the only major city of Alsace-Lorraine still on the French side of the border. Or, at least, not the Nancy he knew.

"Do you have children?" Fauvet asked.

Martin shook his head.

"I only asked because you appear a bit—"

Did he seem all that squeamish? "My wife is pregnant," Martin said, using Clarie's condition to ward off Fauvet's insinuations.

"Ah, well, if I were you, I would not describe any of this to her. You know that pregnant women suffer certain mental imbalances."

"I have no intention of saying anything about this." Even if, as some medical experts asserted, women were prone to hysteria because of their physiology, Martin knew this was not true of his Clarie. Still, this was a delicate time and, more than ever, he wanted to protect her.

"So you told Singer that you thought the baby might have swallowed something," Martin said, changing the subject.

"I told him I could not be absolutely sure. Since they cleaned him out, I have no idea what he might have choked on."

"You keep saying *they?*"

"They, he, she—just about any adult with normal strength could have cut through the kid's middle. The cartilage is still pretty soft at this age."

They, he, she? No idea what the baby choked on? If, indeed, that's what had killed him. Or had someone smothered him with his own diaper? The gruesome journey to the morgue had not gotten Martin very far—except to see why Singer had been so shaken. Martin stared at the tiny mutilated corpse as he heard himself ask if Fauvet had explained his hypotheses to Singer.

"I tried to. He insisted on seeing the body, to find out, so he said, if his worst fears were confirmed. And when I showed it to him, he kept repeating, 'How dare they. They say a Jew did this, a bloodthirsty Jewish peddler. How dare they.' And on and on in that vein. I could not get through to him that anyone could have done it. Not necessarily even a man, for that matter. So when he declared that he should not be involved, I had to agree since he was not being at all rational. Rather hysterical really. That's when he asked me to wait for you."

Martin considered "hysterical" to be a harsh and disrespectful judgment, even though he had witnessed Singer's agitation. But he did not want to argue with the smug young professor. He just wanted to leave.

"Have you found anything at all that would help us identify who mutilated the baby?" This was a crucial question. If the child had died by accident there might be no crime. However, in the atmosphere created by the news of Dreyfus's alleged treachery, a false accusation of this type could be explosive. Martin needed to nip it in the bud.

"If we could find a knife, perhaps we could match it to these marks," Fauvet said, as he retraced the long, jagged line with his finger. Then mercifully he pulled the sheet over the body. "If they were smart, they would have dumped the knife in the river or cleaned it up very carefully."

Of course. The police would be lucky to find the knife. Even so, Martin would order them to try to do just that, first thing on Monday morning. Fingers fumbling, he began to button his overcoat. "It's important that we not let any of this out, until we are certain about what happened. We don't want this to get in the press."

Fauvet nodded in agreement as he rolled down his sleeves. "No need to upset some people more than they already are."

Was Fauvet, who had a perverse love of dead bodies, referring to the public, or to the weak stomachs of Martin and Singer? Regardless, before he made his escape Martin shook Fauvet's hand and thanked him. Then he began the short walk home, praying that he would have time to compose himself before seeing his very pregnant wife.

2

THE DIN OF FRIDAY EVENING traffic on the busy rue des Dominicains penetrated even third-story windows shut tight against the cold. Clarie Martin didn't mind. She had grown up in the center of the southern town of Arles. She liked hearing the clatter of horses' hooves and carriages and the shouts and laughter of shoppers. These were the sounds of life, of home. If only she could lie back in the armchair, close her eyes, and drift with the shadows spreading across her sitting room. How she longed to catch just a bit of sleep before facing the ordeal of a formal dinner. But she had a guest. And getting Madeleine Froment to leave without hurting her feelings was an arduous and delicate task.

Madeleine had arrived in Nancy four weeks ago to take Clarie's place at the Lycée Jeanne d'Arc during the last two months of her pregnancy. Today, once again, Madeleine had appeared right at tea time, ostensibly to talk about new lesson plans for history, geography and literature. Clarie suspected, however, that her companion had really just come to talk.

Clarie shifted in her chair, trying to make herself more comfortable. Winters were so dark in the north. In the sunlight, the sitting room was the most cheerful place in the apartment. Now Clarie could barely make out the delicate sprays of pink and yellow roses that decorated the wallpaper. She was about to suggest that Madeleine turn up the gas lamp on the table beside her armchair, when the baby kicked. Putting her hands on her bulging middle, she waited for another blow. How she loved the new tautness of her belly and the vigor of the being that was growing inside her! This was the life, the home that she and Bernard were making together.

"You're not listening."

"I'm sorry, the baby moved."

"I suppose I should understand; they do say that pregnant women get all dreamy."

Spoken with the true bitterness of an old maid, which, at forty-four years of age, Madeleine surely was. She had ceased fluttering to the rhythm of her latest enthusiasm—some article in the Catholic news-paper *La Croix* about the "miraculous" conversion of a prominent French Jew—to sit straight up and glare at Clarie. With her dark piercing eyes, sharp little nose, graying hair, and the flat black hat she wore for visiting, Madeleine looked for all the world like a scrawny little bird.

Clarie bit her lower lip. Poor thing, she thought, as she tried to smile away this uncharitable image. "Please go on."

"All I was saying, my dear, is that if they all became Catholics, it might solve the problem."

"Umm," Clarie managed a nod to show she was listening.

"Although perhaps not, given the way they are." Madeleine pursed her lips and thrust her chin upward, as if restraining herself from saying more.

Clarie sighed. She knew how much Madeleine wanted her approval, her agreement, when all Clarie could give was her sympathy. She was tired of hearing about how, according to Madeleine, the Jews, the Protestants, and the Freemasons were responsible for all of France's woes. It was hard to believe that the two of them had been trained to teach enlightened principles in the new public high schools for girls. Still, Clarie had to be kind. She owed so much to Madeleine, not least the very fact that she had come to Nancy to take over Clarie's classes.

Clarie smoothed over the hard round mound of her stomach, pondering the different paths their lives had taken. Eight years ago, when Clarie entered the experimental teacher's college at Sèvres, she had been so frightened. She had known nothing and felt everything: her inexperience, her loneliness, her lack of style and money. Worst of all, she had arrived in a state of emotional turmoil because she had stuck to her dreams and left Bernard Martin, her judge, her sweet young judge, in Aix-en-Provence.

Back then Madeleine, an older student who had taught in private schools, took Clarie under her wing, guiding and consoling her. Now it was Clarie's turn to be understanding. The intervening years had not been kind to Madeleine. She had never found a permanent position, in part because she returned to Bordeaux to care for her father. He died suddenly in 1889 after discovering that he had just lost what remained of his small fortune in the catastrophic failure of the Panama Canal Company. Clarie frowned, knowing all too well that the story did not end there. A few years later, the tabloid press uncovered the bribery scheme that had kept the Company's dire financial straits a secret from its investors. Although the ensuing scandal engulfed an entire political class, the anti-Semitic press gleefully emphasized the role that a few prominent Israelites had played.

That's when Madeleine had begun to blame her misfortunes on the Jewish people.

Madeleine cleared her throat.

"Sorry," said Clarie, "guess I was dreaming." As if to make up for this harmless lie, Clarie began to push herself up from the chair. "Are you chilly? Perhaps I should stoke the fire." She had given Madeleine the armchair by the marble hearth, because the older woman always complained of the cold.

"Please, my dear, don't bother. I'll be leaving any minute."

Clarie sank back and tugged her maroon wool shawl more tightly around her shoulders and chest, wondering what tack Madeleine would use to prolong the conversation. *Where is Bernard?*

"Before I go, my dear, I need to ask you again," Madeleine said as she began to put on her gloves. "Don't you think you and the judge should think of moving?"

That old question. Clarie could never decide whether Madeleine's main criticism of their living quarters stemmed from some notion that a *juge d'instruction* should have a more elegant address or because the Martins lived above a Jewish shop. She clenched her jaw and patiently explained, again, how much they liked being in the middle of things—close to the Palais and to the school, on a street so beloved by the city's inhabitants they always simply called it the rue des Dom.

"But this place is so small," Madeleine objected.

"And it took all we had to furnish it and hire Rose, our day woman. I suppose that in a year or so we'll have to move across the railroad tracks to one of the new neighborhoods. But for now, we're quite happy," Clarie said, hoping that would put an end to it.

"Here? Above one of your students? Having her father as your landlord?"

"Rebecca Stein is very respectful. She always asks before she visits. And she's a sweet girl." Clarie reached over to the plate that lay on the end table by her chair and picked up a small ginger biscuit. "She brought these to me this morning, with the excuse that she had made too many for her family. I think she just wanted to show she was thinking of me."

Clarie began to chew on the sugary biscuit to hide her irritation.

"That's because she worships you. They all do. They must find me a very poor substitute."

"Oh Madeleine, you mustn't think that way," Clarie said, exasperated, even though there were times she suspected her companion was not a very popular teacher. "Think of all the things you taught me, I was such a country bumpkin—"

"That was a long time ago." Madeleine concentrated on buttoning her gloves as she spoke.

This time Clarie did manage to push herself up out of the armchair. If only there was something she could do for her friend. She was about to reach out to her when she heard the key rattle in the door. Both of them turned and watched as Bernard came into the foyer. As soon as he saw them, he took off his bowler. "Madame Froment," he greeted Madeleine with a slight bow of his head.

"Monsieur Martin." Madeleine nodded. She seemed quite aware that Bernard did not like her.

Clarie went over to him, although she knew he would not kiss or embrace her. Not in front of a guest. Not even in front of the maid. Her judge was so reserved. Still he smiled at her, before frowning.

"Sorry I'm late. I know we have to get ready. I was held up."

"That's right," Madeleine said, "I've been keeping you. You need to get properly dressed."

"Oh, I'm in no hurry," Clarie smiled. "In my condition you don't have to worry about being too fashionable, thank God. Bernard," she turned to her husband, "will you fetch Madeleine's coat? And you," she took Madeleine's two hands in hers, "don't worry so much. By this time next year I'm sure you'll find a good position." Clarie pressed until she felt her grasp being returned.

"My dear," Madeleine said as she pulled away, "I do hope you enjoy yourself tonight."

Clarie shook her head. "Neither of us is looking forward to it, I can assure you." She said this for Madeleine's benefit, so that she would not envy them this occasion, and because it was true.

The empty crib—and the images it evoked of the baby in the morgue—added to Martin's apprehensions as he and Clarie maneuvered around their cramped bedroom, getting dressed for their first formal dinner in Nancy. He knew that Clarie had been dreading this occasion from the day of their arrival more than two years ago. Being a shy man from a relatively humble background, Martin was just as uneasy about social duties. Especially tonight. If only he had not promised Singer that he would find a way to talk to the prosecutor. Still the courthouse was his world, not Clarie's, and his first duty was to set his fretting, pregnant wife at ease.

"You know they are going to think I am unnatural, too ambitious to be really womanly, just because I chose to work for a living," Clarie said as she closed the armoire and threw her woolen cape on the bed beside him.

"I am sure they will know you are quite womanly. You're beautiful. And you are obviously about to be a mother."

"And awkward, too, like a goose," she grumbled as she moved over to the dresser. "A big blue goose," she added referring to the satin dress that she and Rose, their day woman, had hastily put together for the occasion.

"More beautiful than ever," Martin murmured as he pulled up his silk stockings and slipped into his shoes.

Clarie fell into silence as she put on sparkling blue earrings and stuck a matching pin into the coil of hair she had wound at the back of her head. She picked up the heavy silver-and-sapphire pendant her mother had left her. "Help me with this?" she asked.

"With pleasure." Martin tried to maintain the jocularity in his voice as he got up and took the necklace from her. After he fastened the clasp, he kissed the fragrant spot on her neck where she had just applied her perfume. He looked up to see her smiling in the mirror. How could he not love his passionate Arlésienne? Compared to her, he was an unobtrusive presence in the world—grayish blue eyes, brown hair and beard already flecked with gray, everything about him plain and ordinary. Clarie, with her mass of black hair and great almond-shaped brown eyes, made a mark everywhere she went. He watched as she began to finger her pendant. The mischievous glimmer in her eyes dimmed.

"I know you wish your mother were alive for this," he said softly.

"And you, your father." Spoken like the brave girl she was.

But it was different for her. Although they had both lost a parent, Martin was sure that at a time like this a woman must need her mother. Besides, Giuseppe Falchetti, Clarie's father, had become a second father to him. As for his mother, she had never forgiven him for choosing a blacksmith's daughter over a rich cousin from an influential family and, consequently, had never taken to Clarie. Martin kissed his beautiful wife again. "At least we have each other."

"You never told me why you were delayed today," she said, giving him a playful push to break the mood.

Martin crossed to the armoire to get his silk cravat. "Just a case that Singer wanted to discuss with me," he said, facing the closet to avoid looking at her. This was foolish, of course. The image of the grotesquely maimed baby was not etched across his forehead.

"And?" Clarie always took a lively interest in his work.

"And nothing. Boring technicalities." He closed his eyes, assaulted by guilt. He had never kept anything from her before. Would he feel more terrible if he told her the truth about what he had seen at the morgue? He could not do that. Not now. He took a deep breath and turned to her. "I'd wager that your conversation with Madeleine was much more exciting."

21

"Not likely." Clarie shrugged. "More of the usual: the poor king in exile, the Church under siege, the godless Republic corrupted by power-mongering Protestants and Jews. Mostly the Jews, of course." She rolled her eyes and gave him a crooked ironic grin.

Martin yanked at his cravat as he tried to tie it. He was well aware of Madeleine Froment's reactionary opinions, but he had forgotten her particular animus against the Israelites. Did he need another reminder that he had more to do at dinner than get Clarie through it?

"I can see you are annoyed."

"No, not at all," although he was. "It's just too bad that you have to spend so much time with her. You should be resting, enjoying yourself."

"You men are so silly. I've got plenty of time on my hands. And it costs nothing to listen to the poor dear."

Poor *insufferable* dear, Martin thought as he peered in the mirror and angrily botched the knot again.

"Don't tell me you're as nervous as I am," Clarie laughed. "Let me do that for you, or we'll never get out of here."

He gladly submitted to her ministrations. Although Martin was a man of medium height, Clarie was almost as tall as he was. Her hair tickled his nose as she concentrated on his tie. Having her so near, smelling her scent, feeling her warmth restored his good humor.

"There," she stood back, "you look very handsome."

"Hardly." But what did it matter? Clarie had told him he was, and was laughing.

"We'd better hurry," she warned. "I don't walk as fast as I used to."

"Right you are." Martin picked up Clarie's cape and wrapped it around her. After he had thoroughly shielded her against the cold, he kissed the slightly upturned tip of her long, thin nose. "Courage!" he whispered. They would both need it.

Clarie prayed that no one would demonstrate any curiosity about her or her pregnant state until after dinner, when the men separated themselves from the women in order to smoke and "talk business." The introductions in the gas-lit drawing room, to seven of Bernard's colleagues and six of their wives, passed smoothly enough. One only had to smile politely and sip on the champagne offered by the liveried servants. But as soon as she entered the rectangular dining room, with its dark walls hung with crimson-colored embossed paper, Clarie began to feel closed in. Illuminated only by huge ornate candelabras, the room's opulence gleamed at her from all directions: from sideboards covered with dishes filled with steaming food, to the heavily framed portraits hanging on the wall, to the long dining table, where each setting held a daunting surfeit of shining silverware and gold-rimmed plates. Worse, as first-timers, she and Bernard were given seats of honor, he by the hostess at the foot of the table, she by Charles du Manoir at its head.

Mercifully, as the Presiding Judge of the Court at Nancy, du Manoir enjoyed holding forth and ignored her most of the time. When he did give her his attention, he proved to be a solicitous host, exchanging innocuous pleasantries, and tacitly guiding her through the proper order of things by being first to pick up the appropriate utensil for each course. Clarie began to breathe more easily as the paté, the bisque, the turbot, and the roast beef succeeded each other.

Her particular purgatory did not ensue until the white-and-black-uniformed maids began to offer the tray of cheeses. The mistress of the house, Albertine du Manoir, could no longer suppress her curiosity.

"So, Madame Martin," she began, almost shouting from the opposite end of the table, "you teach?"

"Yes," Clarie said as she glanced at her husband through the branches of the candelabras.

"The upper grades?" Mme du Manoir spoke even louder this time, encouraging her prey to do the same. Her neck craned upward from her portly body. Clarie could clearly see all the white curls her elderly

high-born hostess had so carefully arranged around her stern, pow-
dered face.

"Yes, at one of the new public high schools for girls." Clarie got it
out quickly. Her heart began to pound. She had said it. She was
working in a place that was "new" and "public," certainly not the way
the wife of a judge should spend her time. Perhaps all these facts run
together would shock them into silence, at least for the moment.

It did. And the silence was unnatural. The clink of silver on plate
had ceased. So had the murmur of conversation. Clarie took a sip of
wine; her mouth was running dry.

"And how, my dear, did you learn to do *that*?" Mme du Manoir was
not about to let her off the hook.

"I was trained at a boarding school, at Sèvres, just outside of Paris."
Clarie put down her knife and fork. She had no need for more food,
and she certainly was not going to eat when all eyes were on her. If
only she were sitting beside Bernard, he'd do something reassuring.

"You went off to Paris on your own?" asked the prosecutor's wife,
who sat directly across from her. She was younger than most of the
other guests, perhaps in her thirties. A pretty brunette with an oval
face, which expressed surprise, but, Clarie hoped, not disapproval.

Clarie nodded and looked down at her plate.

"How extraordinary."

Clarie was not even sure who had interjected this comment, which
was not meant as a compliment.

"Yes, it was extraordinary. Very competitive," Bernard intervened,
leaning over the table to get the attention of the diners.

"Still, a young woman, alone, allowed to roam the city with other
young women. I understand there were no restrictions on travel."
Clarie could have sworn that Mme du Manoir's jowls were shaking in
disapproval. Her large diamond earrings quivered and shimmered in
the candlelight.

"Only the restraints of a very strict morality. A Kantian morality, to be specific. I can tell you," Bernard continued, "that I was more nervous about asking the headmistress for Clarie's hand than her father. Mme Favre was much more exacting about who could court her students."

"You actually asked the headmistress's permission?" The prosecutor's wife smiled in amazement. Clarie's chivalrous defender had won at least one of them over.

"I did not drop to my knees," Bernard paused before adding, "but let me tell you, I felt I should have."

This even drew appreciative titters.

"Still," Mme du Manoir laid her hand on Bernard's as if to forestall more frivolity, "one wonders, what kind of woman would pursue such a difficult profession." She stared in Clarie's direction, waiting for an answer.

Clarie's felt a rush of blood spreading across her cheeks and forehead. How could any of them possibly know how difficult it was? First there was the uncertainty about finding a place. And when you found one, facing all those eager girls, expecting you to teach them everything under the sun. Staying up until the early morning hours, preparing, almost crying with fatigue. "Actually," she said trying to keep her voice as even as possible, "the students at Sèvres come from all walks of life."

Mme du Manoir raised her eyebrows. "Surely not."

Was this the point where Clarie was supposed to admit that her own father was an immigrant and a blacksmith, and Bernard's had been merely a clockmaker? She held her hands tight under the table to keep from trembling. She was becoming a spectacle.

"Albertine," Monsieur du Manoir came to Clarie's rescue, "if our republican government has decreed that young women deserve a secondary education, who better to give it to them, a nun or someone who will become a wife and a mother?"

"Hear! Hear! Let's raise a glass to that!" cried out Alphonse Rocher, the senior examining magistrate, whose face was already ruddy with drink. A dozen diners, in various stages of reluctance and bewilderment, lifted their glasses. Relieved at the distraction, Clarie again refused the cheese plate. After the anemic toast, the table dissolved again into the sharp clink of silverware and the soft murmur of private conversations. Still flustered, Clarie surveyed the scene under lowered eyes. When she saw the servants arranging ices and cakes on the sideboard, she let her hands slip apart and breathed a sigh of relief. It was almost over.

Martin touched the tips of Clarie's fingers with his own as he passed her on his way to the library with the other male guests. This was his unspoken apology. He didn't like having to leave her at the mercy of "the ladies," but there was nothing to be done about it. As soon as he consulted with Théophile Didier, the prosecutor, Martin had every intention of getting Clarie away.

Martin paused at the entrance to the library and took a deep breath. Unless there was some truth to Singer's assertions, this should be easy. If the Proc refused to let him lead the investigation, then Martin would explain to Singer that he had done his best. If Didier agreed to hand the case over to Martin, a much more likely possibility, then he would begin to concentrate on formulating a plan of action. Either way, Martin told himself as he pulled down his dinner jacket and forged ahead, a definitive decision should help him get through the weekend without seeing flashes of that little corpse in his mind's eye.

The rest of the men were gathered around du Manoir's gargantuan mahogany desk, where the servants had set out the cigars and cognac. Big as it was, the desk was dwarfed by a room lined with books reaching up to a very high ceiling. The Presiding Judge had even installed a movable ladder so that he, or his servants, could reach the top shelves. Martin doubted that this device was used much. Du Manoir had never struck him as a very deep thinker.

Martin refused a cigar and picked up a snifter of cognac, planting himself at the edge of the conversation, waiting for his chance. When Didier broke off from the rest of the smokers to peruse a shelf of books, Martin immediately approached him.

"Singer came to see me this afternoon," he began.

"Oh, really?" Didier arched his eyebrows and took a sip from his tiny round glass of cognac. He was a tall, thin man with curly, close-cut sandy hair. He usually wore the severe expression appropriate to his calling on his clean-shaven face. Even in this social situation, he demonstrated one of his many well-known tactics, forcing the witness to fill in all the details and, possibly, to stumble.

"He was upset about the case you just handed him, the mutilated baby and the accusation of ritual murder." Martin lifted his glass to his lips, although it hardly sheltered him from Didier's unflinching blue-eyed gaze.

"And?" the prosecutor asked.

"And, he'd like me to take it over." There, now it was Didier's turn. Martin took a gulp of the warm amber brandy.

But instead of responding, Didier whispered a warning. "I think Rocher is heading our way."

There was a general, unspoken disdain around the courthouse for the portly Alphonse Rocher, Nancy's senior examining magistrate, who somehow had blustered his way to the top. Reluctantly, Martin stepped aside, allowing the man who had offered the clumsy toast to Clarie to join their circle.

"What's this? Talking business?" Rocher asked, before sucking contentedly on his cigar.

"You might say that." Didier's smile went up one side of his face as he gave Martin an expectant look.

"Well, let's hear it then!" Rocher exclaimed, the dinner's drink having made him even more voluble than usual.

"It's nothing," Martin muttered as he took another sip and tried to step back further from both of them.

"Well, I'm not so sure about that. I bet it is something." With his rosy cheeks, walrus mustache and generous mane of white hair, Rocher could have been any child's jolly grandfather. But he wasn't supposed to be indulgent and jocular. Judges were supposed to be serious about their duties and their responsibilities. Martin had no desire to discuss Singer's request with him.

"It's the case I offered to you and that you urged me to give to Singer," Didier said, casting a significant glance toward Martin. The wily prosecutor's few words had economically delivered two messages: that he did not feel the case would be hard to solve, or he would not have given it to Rocher, and it had been Rocher who had suggested that Didier assign it to their Jewish colleague.

"Yes, yes, yes, that one," Rocher said as he began puffing on his cigar with pleasure.

"Why Singer?" Martin asked. He would have liked very much to wipe that stupid, merry expression off Rocher's face.

"Now, now, don't get your dander up," Rocher said as he laid an unwelcome hand on Martin's shoulder. "We just wanted to see what he would do. And besides, it's about his people. We thought it would be best if he handled it." Rocher winked at Didier, who remained stone-faced.

"The Republic is for all people. I believe we have held to that principle since 1789."

Rocher laughed and glanced at Didier. "Oh my, a history lesson yet."

"All right. Sorry," Martin said. Somehow whenever he began to speak about the things he held most dear, he ended up sounding like a prig. Still, he didn't appreciate being mocked. He took a swallow of his cognac, letting its warming effect fortify him before going on. "So," he said, turning to Didier, "since the case has gone from one judge to another, I assume it doesn't matter if I take it over."

Didier pursed his lips and nodded.

"Yes, take it if you must," Rocher intervened, even though it was no longer his call. He blew a circle of smoke before bending toward Martin and adding, "That is, if you consider yourself a friend of the Israelites—"

"I don't know what you are talking about." Martin could barely conceal his anger.

"Did you know," Rocher asked, "that the Singer family 'opted' to come to Nancy when the Germans took over the other half of Lorraine?"

Although Singer had never told him, Martin was not surprised. After France lost Alsace and half of Lorraine to the Prussians in 1871, many Frenchmen chose to become refugees in their own country rather than remain under German rule.

"I don't think he understands," Rocher remarked to Didier, as if Martin were a schoolboy failing a lesson. "They are," the old man insisted, raising his voice slightly, "taking over. It's not enough that the city was flooded with them in the seventies. They're even coming from Russia. Beggars all."

Martin could hardly believe his ears. He was torn between a desire to show his senior colleague what he thought and extricating himself as expeditiously as possible. Because of his experiences in Aix, where his involvement in the Vernet case had turned most of the courthouse against him, he knew he needed to tread carefully. He glanced at Didier, who had chosen to observe rather than take sides.

"You've noticed, haven't you," Rocher continued, "how many children they are having. Singer has three of his own already. You, my boy, are only working on your first. How will we keep up?"

"How, indeed?" Martin seized the opportunity offered by the fool's last, maddening remark, "It's good you've reminded me, Rocher. It must be very late. I should be getting my wife home before she gets overtired."

Didier's only response was a crooked, mirthless smile. But Rocher, drunk as he was, couldn't stop talking. "Yes, go to her," he said to

Martin, waving his cigar as his voice trailed off. "Charming woman, that one, charming. . . ."

Martin backed away with a slight bow. "Gentlemen, until Monday," he said, as he left to seek out his hosts to say his good-byes. And to calm down.

Mme du Manoir repeated her offer to rouse the driver of the family coach, until Clarie finally convinced her hostess that the walk home would do her good. Warmly wrapped and much relieved, the Martins escaped at last into the cold autumn night, exiting onto the northern corner of the Place de la Carrière. As he listened to Clarie's complaints, Martin hoped their midnight stroll would remind his dear Provençal girl of the things she loved most about Nancy. Arm in arm they scuffed through the hoary leaves glistening gold under the flickering gas-lit street lights.

"They suspect," she said, "that I will bear a monster because I've overheated my brain by using it too much."

Martin suspected, in turn, that Clarie was exaggerating. "Come," he said, as they passed the Palais de Justice, which lay at the southern end of the block, "let's take a peek at the park." He turned the corner towards the gate to the Pépinière, the vast public park which had once been the private hunting grounds of the nobility. The Martins had often strolled through its gardens, imagining their own child there, playing ball or pointing with delight at the animals in the zoo.

"It's cold. I would rather not." Clarie shrank away from him, still mulling over her time with the other women. She kept walking straight ahead toward the Arc de Triomphe.

"All right, then. But remember, this is the only formal dinner we have had to go to in two years," he said as he hurried to catch up, "and by the time you have to go again you will have a beautiful baby to brag about." Even though her head was turned away from him, he knew he had made her smile. "Besides," he continued as they entered the Place

Stanislas, "we have all this. The theater, the opera, the cafés, the shops, the gallant officers flitting about, flirting with the ladies."

They paused for a moment at one of the gilt-edged wrought-iron gates that opened upon the central jewel of Nancy. She took his arm again, as they looked across the sparkling fountains and statues toward the broad Hôtel de Ville. This was the side of the last century that Clarie liked best: its wit and its charm, even though the uniformed soldiers who frequented the nightlife were a reminder of their own time and the fact that the German border was only twenty-five kilometers away.

"Is there something wrong?" Clarie peered into his face. "You don't usually wax poetic about our armed guards."

"No," he shook his head as he led her homeward, across the darkened square. "Just trying to—" he shrugged without ending his sentence. Trying to what? With a sudden pang he realized that he needed cheering every bit as much as Clarie. As his eyes followed the silhouette of his wife and their unborn child preceding them on the gas-lit cobblestones, Martin knew more than ever that he could not tell her about the troubling and gruesome details of his new case.

3

Saturday, November 17

"WHAT A WONDERFUL CHANGE FROM last night," Clarie sighed as she leaned back toward the mirrored wall to survey the half-empty Café Stanislas. Martin had proposed they stop for an early supper after a long afternoon stroll. They had spent the day as he intended, remembering—and forgetting.

Clarie had never looked more beautiful, her great brown eyes shining and cheeks still red from the cold. Although she had declared that she would never be hungry again after being "force-fed" by the du Manoirs, she had voraciously consumed her grilled trout. On her plate lay a perfect fish skeleton, exposed and picked into a translucent shadow of its former self. As she took another sip of Riesling, she wrinkled her nose in distaste at the wreckage of Martin's choucroute. "I told you that was too much after last night. No dessert for you," she added brightly.

Martin grunted as he forked through the clumps of pungent sauerkraut and potatoes and overturned a sausage. His distractions had sapped his appetite. When he reached for his beer stein, Clarie placed her hand on his.

"So now, you must tell me what this is all about."

"What do you mean?" Martin feigned innocence.

"All this. Spending the afternoon going past all our favorite haunts, reminiscing about how we met, bringing me to this café. What is bothering you?"

"You mean I can't take my pregnant wife on a romantic walk and buy her a dinner? Soon we won't have such freedom."

Clarie slumped back and stared at Martin. "Are you nervous for me?"

Of course he was, a little. Martin could not bear the thought of his beloved Clarie in pain or in danger. But she was young and strong. And brave, of course. "No," he lied, aware that it was a husband's duty to reassure a pregnant wife. "Everything is going to be fine, I'm sure of it."

"Then, what?"

"Today was beautiful and clear, and as I told you—"

"Were you trying to make up for last night's torture?"

She was exaggerating again, and teasing him. She had always seen through him. From the first moment at her aunt and uncle's restaurant in Aix, she had understood his shyness. When he had to hide his best friend from the police, she had, without asking why, given him food, and worried. Days later, when he did tell her about Merckx, and what he had gotten her involved in, all she had cared about was him. Certainly he would tell her about the mutilated baby, and Rocher and Didier. But later, as with Merckx, when it was over and she was safe.

"Well?"

"Yes, the horrible, terrible dinner," he said with a wave of the hand. "I wanted to wash that out of your mind with some fine wine and fond memories."

"Humph." Clarie put down her glass, unconvinced. "Well, at least now I know what you are dealing with at the courthouse. Du Manoir was nice, if a bit pompous. Didier," she widened her eyes, "was rather scary, despite that nice young wife. And Rocher," she shook her head, "where did he come from?"

"He's been around a long time," Martin mumbled as he gave his plate a definitive shove toward the side of the table.

"And why wasn't Singer there? I was looking forward to meeting him. You've talked so much about him and what a fine man he is."

Martin shrugged and hoped that Clarie would not notice the blush he could feel rising up toward his forehead. Without knowing it, she had hit upon the very source of his distraction. Why hadn't Singer been invited? And what had he gotten Martin into?

Fortunately, at that moment, the waiter came to clear their dishes and ask if they wanted more. The café was beginning to fill up. Behind him Martin could hear the murmur of recently arrived diners and the great coffee urn behind the bar begin to hiss. Clarie, of course, ordered the *tarte*, Martin asked for coffee.

"You could have one too," she remarked as soon as the white-shirted waiter left them.

"So you could eat mine?" he teased back.

It was her turn to shrug and blush a little. She had a passion for the local Mirabelle plums. "Anyway, perhaps even before the baby comes, we should have the Singers over. After all, he is the one who put us in contact with the Steins. You know all the teachers. I should know your friend."

The truth was, and they both knew it, that the Martins were much more comfortable with the teachers and their husbands, and even with their landlords, who owned the drygoods store in their building, than with the coterie at the Palais de Justice. Two of Clarie's colleagues were married to teachers who taught at the boys' lycée, the third to a carpenter. Their clothes, their language, their concerns, their lack of wealth and connections echoed the social strata from which Clarie and Martin had come, even though Martin, being a judge, had presumably risen above it.

But maybe David Singer, the only colleague with whom Martin discussed troubling cases, the courthouse and politics, was different. Maybe he would not find anything amiss in the Martins' more humble way of life.

"You're right. Of course, you must meet him," Martin said as the waiter placed a glistening triangle in front of Clarie. He smiled as she became quite engrossed in the decorative criss-crossing of the rosy-gold plums before, once again, digging in.

4

Monday, November 19

THERE WERE TIMES IT SEEMED that Monday morning would never arrive. The Martins spent the gray, cold Sunday confined to their apartment. Mercifully, Clarie had stopped asking questions about Singer and the courthouse. Instead, she spent most of her time in front of the fire, stitching tiny clothes or staring into space, long periods of quiet broken only by inexplicable spurts of dusting or fluffing up pillows or fussing over the crib that sat beside their bed. Clarie seemed to be in another place, a waiting place. Martin longed to be there with her, but every time he tried to think or talk about the arrival of their child, he was assaulted by the memory of the baby in the morgue. He had to rid himself of that grotesque image. The only way to do that was to get the case behind him by finding out exactly what had happened in the wet nurse's cottage. That's why, early on

Monday, he left for the courthouse as soon as he could without rousing Clarie's suspicions.

By the time he entered his chambers, he was ready to interrogate, to threaten, to wait out the suspects, to do whatever it took. He was in no mood for unforeseen obstacles.

"*Monsieur le procurer* wants to see you right away." Guy Charpentier, always excessively formal, stood up to greet him. Martin noted that his fastidious clerk had already ejected the errant pencil from his desk, and his notebooks were open and dated in anticipation of the day's work. Charpentier had also donned a new outfit, a deep blue frock coat with a matching silk cravat. His thick auburn hair was parted in the middle, forming two drooping wings around his forehead. His dark brown eyes shone with the obscene curiosity he always showed when there was a possibility of conflict in the Palais. It was all very irritating.

"You've heard, then," Martin murmured as he unwound the woolen scarf from around his neck. "We're to carry out a minor investigation this morning. Did you get the dossier from Singer?"

Charpentier shook his head. "Monsieur le juge Singer just left. He told me to tell you that Monsieur le procurer Didier asked to see it again and wanted to hand it to you himself."

"I see." Martin took his time hanging up his coat, methodically fastening each button. As long as his back was to Charpentier, his clerk could not see how much the Proc's interference troubled him. Usually Didier assigned cases without comment. What was different this time?

He turned to Charpentier. "Do you know if the witnesses have arrived?" Martin asked, in part to indicate to his clerk that he felt neither cowed nor rushed by the Proc's request to see him.

"The inspector said that they are waiting for you downstairs in a cell."

"All three?"

"Yes. Monsieur le juge Singer said that since they've already got their lies in order, it would do no harm to keep them together." Charpentier could not repress a smile. He loved to watch witnesses flail and stew in their own juices.

"Well, then," Martin said, in as light a tone as he could muster, "I'll go see what Didier has to say."

The Palais de Justice occupied one of the most elegant old mansions on the Carrière. Although the building was a complicated interlocking of former private chambers, servants' quarters, and large salons, Martin had a direct route to the Proc via the polished wooden staircase directly across from his chambers. Annoyed and apprehensive, Martin took his time trudging up to the second floor. Didier's office was well situated near the head of the stairs, close to the great hall, a former ballroom, where the most important trials took place. Before knocking on his door, Martin took a moment to pull himself together. If he were to suffer a reprise of Friday night's idiotic encounter, he'd have to find a way of staying calm. He rapped hard and went in.

Didier was at his desk in shirtsleeves and a gray vest. When he saw Martin, he lifted the pince-nez from his nose and set it down on top of the document he had been reading. He stood up to hold out his hand. With his long reach, from behind his mammoth desk, the prosecutor seemed to tower over Martin, an illusion fostered by Didier's Cassius-like thinness.

The handshake was perfunctory, but Martin could not tell if the greeting was cooler than usual. At the courthouse the Proc was all business. He did not even invite Martin to sit; instead, without taking his steely blue eyes off his visitor's face, Didier asked Roland, his greffier, to leave the room.

Roland, who had been sitting at a desk every bit as cluttered as Didier's, wiped off his ink pen and departed, closing the door without a sound. The stooped, white-haired, ever-discreet Roland was the clerk that any of the examining magistrates would have liked to have in their employ. But he was Didier's, and it seemed quite fitting that the formidable prosecutor should have acquired the most diligent and subservient greffier in the courthouse.

It was equally fitting that Didier inhabited the largest office at the Palais de Justice and that it was painted a grim olive green. The long rectangle led from Didier's desk on one end to a gray marble fireplace on the other. Roland occupied the desk near the fire, perhaps to warm his aging bones. Didier's half of the room always seemed chilly, which never seemed to bother the prosecutor, a man of unbounded energy, accustomed to generating his own heat.

After staring at Martin for another moment, Didier went to a window which gave onto a small cobbled courtyard below. The tall, lanky prosecutor crossed his arms and positioned himself at an angle to observe the comings and goings on the Place de la Carrière. Martin found himself tapping his foot in time with the ticking of the black lacquered clock above the fireplace.

"Martin," Didier began, "do you know who lives on the Carrière? That is, besides President du Manoir?"

"Many—"

"Ah, yes, many," Didier nodded and gazed out the window as if he were considering the answer that he had not even allowed Martin to articulate. "Many, but who is particularly relevant to our conversation of Friday night? Which," he hastily added before Martin could respond, "you left in a rather precipitous fashion."

"What do you mean?" Martin's pulse began to race. Was he about to be toyed with as if he were some common criminal?

Didier walked over to his desk and grasped it with both hands as he leaned toward Martin. "I just want us to be very clear about why it will be important to handle this case with discretion and dispatch."

"Who, then?" It was obvious that Martin had no choice but to play along. He would have his chance to tell Didier what he thought later. "Who lives on the Carrière?"

"The commander, of course. The commander of the garrison. The commander of the garrison that is protecting us all from the Huns, who are a mere twenty-five kilometers away, waiting, guns fully loaded at the border. The commander of the garrison who is here to see that Germany takes nothing else away from us."

"And?" Martin crossed his arms and waited, for it was obvious the man accustomed to leading juries by the nose was just hitting his stride. Martin could barely stand still as he waited for the coup de grâce.

"The Nanciens love their army. Many of them are old enough to remember the Prussian occupation. Others came here as refugees. And now that army is under threat. People are uneasy. All because of a traitor. Captain Alfred Dreyfus, the first Israelite admitted to the inner sanctum of our most precious military secrets."

That was it! Just as Martin had feared, another broadside against the Jews. His arms fell by his side, taut, his hands locked into fists. "Dreyfus is one man," he insisted heatedly, "not an entire people. And furthermore he has not even been brought to trial." How can everyone be so sure that it was Dreyfus who had sold secrets to the Germans? For God's sake, Martin thought angrily, everyone in this building is supposed to be devoted to the efficacy of the court system.

"True. Not yet. But the military court is very likely to convict him, and we wouldn't want anyone to think that we are being soft on the Israelites. Nor, on the other hand," a long, bony finger went up to stave off interruption, "would we want to have politicians at the courthouse finding a way to use this case for their own ends, for some campaign against the Jewish inhabitants of our fair city. When I say 'we,'" Didier's voice gathered in volume and speed any time Martin deigned to open his mouth, "it is because I know that du Manoir fully agrees with me. We discussed the problem just yesterday. I interrupted his Sunday to do so."

The two most powerful men in the courthouse putting their heads together. And Singer had said it would be so simple: a wet nurse and two workers, all poor, all lying, all trying to cover up the death of one miserable little child. "I can see no possible connection between what is happening in Paris with an army officer and a trumped-up charge in Nancy."

"Neither do I!" Didier pounded his desk in the best prosecutorial manner. "Neither do I! But others might see the connection or try to *make* the connection." His sandy red eyebrows went up as if he were urging Martin to get the point. "Do you think our friend Rocher is exceptional?" he asked, with no intention of giving Martin a chance to answer. "There are a lot like him out there. Influential men. Even men, like our esteemed senior colleague, who dare to call themselves republicans. Men willing to arouse the rabble. And," he added darkly, "of course, there is the rabble itself."

"Then why did you—?"

"Assign the case to Rocher?" Didier had anticipated this obvious question and threw up his hands in mock surrender. "I made a mistake. I'll admit it. I like to give the easy cases to him and thought this would be one of them."

"Surely you must have known how he felt about the Israelites." Heart pounding with impatience, Martin had to bite his tongue to keep from adding, *and what a moron we all know Rocher to be.*

"No, I didn't know. I don't talk to him any more than necessary," Didier said, his lips pinched together as if he had just bitten into a sour lemon.

"So how did the case get to Singer?" At least Didier was not hiding his contempt for Rocher. Martin relaxed a little.

"Our senior examining magistrate had the nerve to confide that he had picked up a few recent issues of Monsieur Drumont's *La Libre Parole* and doesn't find it half bad." Didier snorted before continuing. "I realized then that Rocher might well make a mess of things, perhaps even enjoy getting his name in the papers by reporting the possibility of a 'ritual murder' to the local press. So when Rocher suggested giving the case to Singer, as a joke, I took him up on it. With alacrity, I might add, because I thought Singer, above all men here at the Palais, would be motivated to get rid of it as soon as possible." Didier paused. "Instead, I find, he pawned it off on you."

"You are saying, then, that you do not hold to Rocher's views?" Martin wanted to be absolutely certain about what he was getting into.

"I assure you I do not. I, like you, understand that our revolutionary tradition calls us to uphold the equality of all men. However, if you are wondering about why I let him go on and on Friday evening, I thought you might find it instructive."

"Instructive? What am I, a schoolboy?" There was no way to avoid the red blush of anger that was heating up his face.

"Please, Martin, don't take this as an insult. Take it as a warning. Get rid of this case as soon as possible."

Martin was tempted to slap away the bony finger which was once more pointing at him. Instead, he said, through clenched teeth, "I can best do that if there is no interference." After all, he had his own reasons for wanting to complete the investigation quickly, reasons that had nothing to do with politics or Jews or the machinations of the courthouse. He wanted to get on with his own life and forget what he had seen in the morgue.

But that was exactly why the prosecutor and the President were looking over his shoulder, as Didier made clear.

"This case, as you must well know, is not really about the death of one unfortunate child. It's about mutilation, about the accusation of ritual murder. An accusation that could send this town into a frenzy, particularly in light of what we are all reading about Dreyfus. We need to avoid that. So you need to find out exactly where our accuser got his ideas. What political rallies he attended, for example." Didier nudged a thin folder toward Martin. "When you catch a whiff of the father's breath, you will see how easily he could come under the influence of a stirring Jew-baiting campaign speech."

"Or an old wives' tale." Why assume that politics had anything to do with it?

"Or a priest."

"Or a priest," Martin echoed in resignation. Politics, the Church, the Army. It was enough to make his head spin.

Having made his point, Didier sat down and set his pince-nez back on the bridge of his nose.

"And if none of this has to do with politics or the Church?" Martin asked as he picked up the thin paper folder, making sure his hand held firm.

"Then, we can assume, the case will go the way of other sordid lower-class dramas. A flurry in the scandal sheets, then a nice evaporating fizzle." Didier retrieved the document he had been reading when Martin walked in, signaling that their interview was over. Disgusted, Martin started for the door.

"Good day, Martin," Didier shouted after him. "Remember, the integrity of the courthouse is in your hands."

Or the integrity of someone's political ambitions, Martin thought as he fought the impulse to slam the door. Everyone knew that, if he played his cards right, the brilliant, ambitious Didier might one day get the call to Paris or even to a Prefecture.

The sight of Roland, sitting meekly on the bench outside Didier's office, almost made Martin jump. "Pardon," the clerk whispered as he got up to return to his master. As soon as Martin was alone, he sank down on the same hard wooden bench. Stinging from the hail of condescension that Didier had rained upon him, Martin needed to calm down before facing the ever-curious Charpentier.

He leaned back, still clutching the file. If Didier was right, the case could blow up in Martin's face. At least they were on the same side. Against the likes of Rocher, who—Martin's fist tightened so hard, he almost bent the file in two thinking of it—who had hoped to play a joke on Singer. Martin sighed. He was just as irritated that somehow he had gotten caught in the middle of courthouse politics: Didier intent on proving he can keep the peace in his own district; Rocher being stupid;

David Singer being oversensitive. After a moment, he straightened up and stared at the blank cardboard in his hands. At least it was not Aix all over again, not a life-and-death situation for his friend, as it had been for Merckx. Not life and death, except—Martin flipped open the file and fingered its two pages—except for one tiny little boy. That's what they all should care about. He took a deep breath and began to read.

Today, Thursday 15 November 1894 at 17:45, Pierre Thomas, twenty-six years of age, a tanner residing at rue Drouin 6bis, came to the Palais de Justice at Nancy, Meurthe-et-Moselle, with an accusation that his child, seven-month-old Marc-Antoine, had been murdered and mutilated by a stranger passing through the village of Tomblaine. M. Thomas, who was in a state of obvious inebriation, carried the body of said child in a dirty, torn blanket. He was accompanied by his wife, Antoinette Thomas, twenty-eight years of age, a weaver at the Ullmann factory, and by the widow Geneviève Philipon, thirty years of age, of the village of Tomblaine, whom they employed as a wet nurse.

M. Thomas claimed that the murderer of his child was a "wandering Jew" who had visited the cottage of Philipon.

Mme Philipon testified that late in the afternoon of Wednesday 14 November a tinker, whom she had never seen in the village, came to her door. She asked him to fix a pot. The stranger had a large hooked nose, thick lips, black hair and a beard. He wore tattered clothes. He smelled "funny" and spoke with a strange accent. He did not remove his black hat even after entering the cottage. At that time, two of her daughters, ages ten and seven, were playing in the garden. Her youngest, a daughter, eighteen months old, and the Thomas boy were in the cottage. She observed that the tinker displayed a suspicious interest in Marc-Antoine, even asking if he was a baptized

Christian. As soon as the stranger left, she called her older children inside the cottage and locked all the doors.

The next morning when she awoke she found the door wide open and Marc-Antoine gone. She was sure the tinker had used his tools to break the lock and steal the child. She called to her neighbors for help and they hunted frantically for the boy, only to find him near a stream in the woods, cut open and drained of all his blood. She then walked into town to find Pierre and Antoinette Thomas. They returned with her to the village and retrieved the body of their son.

Pierre Thomas interjected at this point by shouting that we should find the ritual murderer who was probably an Israelite butcher disguised as a tinker.

Two police officers calmed Thomas down and accompanied him to the morgue at the Faculté de Médicine, where the child will be examined.

Michel Jacquette, Inspector of Police

That was it. A grieving father voluble with drink and grief. A fairy-tale version of the lone bloodthirsty Jewish male stalking the home of a widow and her children. Singer was right. They were all lying. But who created this particular lie? Martin scanned the report again. And where was the grieving mother in all this? Jacquette was a good man. If she had anything to say, he would have reported it. Yet she was silent. Dumbstruck by the loss of her child? Or by the clumsy scheming of those around her?

Calmed by the absurdity of the fabrication, Martin closed the file and started down the stairs, holding on to the banister, taking one slow step at a time. All he needed was to get one of them to tell the truth, and it could all be over today or, at most, tomorrow. An ignorant, talkative woman was likely to be the weakest link in the chain of lies. It should be easy. He would interrogate Geneviève Philipon first.

5

MARTIN'S CHAMBERS WERE NOT AS commanding as Didier's. Yet if you were accused of a crime or had lied to the police or simply happened to be numbered among the unschooled poor, crossing the threshold from the little vestibule into the spacious office with its hard wooden chairs, document-laden desks, and austere white walls had to be nerve-racking, for you were about to encounter an examining magistrate who had the right to question you endlessly, jail you indefinitely, search your home and belongings at will, interrogate everyone near and dear to you, use the words of your enemies against you, and, finally, by a legal logic well beyond your ken, decide what crime to charge you with and what court to send you to. If he chose the big one, the *cour d'assises*, well, then, you could be facing years of hard labor, or even the guillotine.

No wonder the wet nurse could barely move her feet. Although he never undermined his authority by showing it, Martin usually sympathized with the more humble suspects that were hauled into his chambers. Not today. Didier had made it abundantly clear that any of the crimes Geneviève Philipon had allegedly committed—neglect, murder, the brutal disgorging of an innocent child—had repercussions that reached far beyond her little village because of the story that she had invented to cover up her deeds. Repercussions for the courthouse, for the city, for Martin. He needed to find out the truth about what had happened to little Marc-Antoine Thomas before Philipon had a chance to spread her dangerous lies.

While the police officer led Geneviève Philipon into the room, Martin made a show of studying the papers on his desk in order to reinforce the frightening impression that he was in the midst of making important, mysterious, even fatal decisions. Martin fully recognized in her slow, shuffling steps the sound of one resisting her fate. When he looked up, he was not surprised that she was trying to shield herself by hiding her sallow face with the threadbare brown woolen shawl she wore over her head. Gripping it at her neck, she glanced furtively at both Martin and Charpentier as the police officer placed a hand on each of her shoulders and pressed her into the chair.

Although she was a pitiful little creature, Martin glared at her in stony silence for a full minute before introducing himself. Her black shoes and patched green dress, each too thin to ward off the wintry cold, were as drab and worn as she was. Aware of his scrutiny, the wet-nurse lifted the shawl from her head and brought it down to her shoulders, clutching it with both hands across her bosom. Was she possibly hiding the fact that the breasts she was supposed to be using to feed the little victim had dried up? If so, her attempt at subterfuge encouraged Martin to draw out the silence. When she began to breathe through her mouth, almost gasping for air, he could see that her teeth, like the strands of hair on her head, were dingier and sparser than they should be. An unpleasant fetid odor, a potent mix of malnutrition and fear, emanated from her open mouth. Martin drew back in his chair. How had this unhealthy creature come to be a wet nurse? Wealthy families examined their live-in nannies from head to foot before employing them, even counting and pulling at their teeth, as if they were horses or cattle. Obviously, Martin thought, poorer families had fewer choices. Or had Marc-Antoine's parents simply cared less? This is one of the things that Martin needed to find out. Had little Marc-Antoine died by intention, or neglect?

By the time Martin took up his pen, Geneviève Philipon's hands were visibly shaking. As if on cue, Charpentier, who had been mirroring the relentless severity of his superior, flipped open the notebook that would contain the official version of the interrogation.

Judge and clerk always began with the preliminaries of identification and background—Where were you born? Where have you lived? How much schooling do you have? What is your work? How much property do you own? Whom did you marry, and when, and why? And, of course, have you ever been in trouble with the authorities? First-time suspects were often puzzled, even visibly annoyed by these drawn-out preliminaries. So many questions, and for what? An examining magistrate knew exactly what: he was building a portrait of the witness, in order to understand her motives and gauge what punishments to mete out. And if it drove a suspect a little mad, that was fine. The better to get her to blurt out an incriminating response. The wet nurse, being humble and puzzled, mumbled her responses to dozens of questions as her eyes darted back and forth between Martin, the inquisitor, and Charpentier, his recorder.

It turned out that hers was an all-too-common tale of woe. Born into an impoverished family of eleven children in the town of Tomblaine, married to a dirt farmer at the age of seventeen, widowed by a freak accident when pregnant with her third child, Geneviève Philipon had always been in desperate straits and was sinking fast.

Offering herself as a wet nurse had been her way of getting enough money to hire a man to help her with the planting and harvesting.

"So this is the first time that you have cared for another's child?" Martin asked. Up to this point, he had tried to lull her into talking freely by maintaining a calm and matter-of-fact demeanor.

Geneviève Philipon nodded, as her lips stretched into a painful grimace. Tears and sobs followed as she let go of her shawl and hid her face in her trembling hands.

Martin shifted in his chair, waiting for her to calm down. Now that they were getting to it, she could not hide her despair. But he had to remain hard. Get this damned case over with.

"Then why did the Thomases hire you? Surely you were not the most qualified." He didn't like to think about how dispensable the children of the poor were, and felt blessed that Clarie was insisting that she would breastfeed their child herself.

The wet nurse wiped her nose with the back of her hand. She lowered her eyes, focusing on the floor. Martin could almost read an "if only" in them, if only she hadn't been the one caring for the child. Then she wouldn't be here now. Everything would be different! His chambers reverberated with the hard-luck stories of those who swore that if it had not been for an unexpected twist of fate, they would have never done wrong.

"I knew Antoinette." This came out in a whisper.

"How? How did you know her?"

"She's from my parts. We were in school together."

Martin glanced at his notes. Geneviève Philipon had only had six years of schooling, so the women had known each other since childhood.

"She went to the city, hoping for a better life. But," the wet nurse looked up at Martin, "she got started in that factory. I don't think she wanted any kids until. . . ."

"Until?" Martin raised his eyebrows. The fact that Antoinette Thomas did not want a child might be important.

"Until Pierre made enough money so she could quit."

"And that didn't happen?"

Geneviève Philipon shook her head. "He drinks too much."

Martin leaned forward. "And you? Were you still able to feed the child from your own breasts when he died?"

Her eyes widened with fear as she folded her arms over her sterile bosom and slowly began to shake her head. "But," she pleaded, "I gave him everything I could. By the name of Mary the Most Holy Virgin I swear it. I even took the cow's milk from my own children's mouths to feed him."

"And what else did you feed him?"

The woman shrank back in her seat. "Nothing. Nothing, truly. He was not ready. I knew that."

"You know that. Well—" Martin made a show of searching through the mounds on his desk. Although Fauvet had not yet submitted his report, any piece of paper would do. "This," Martin said, holding up an official-looking document, "is from the doctor who examined young Marc-Antoine Thomas, and he reports that the poor child died from asphyxiation. Either smothered or choked to death on a piece of bone or meat or, even, a stone." He paused before continuing. "Do you know why we don't know what killed him? Why we don't know what he might have choked on?" He stared at her until she met his eyes. "Do you know why? Because," he said in a loud voice, "someone cut him open and gutted him!"

Her gasps came out in a series of low croaks. Martin was not sure whether they echoed her inconsolable sorrow, or guilt and naked fear.

"And," Martin pressed on, "I believe that you are the one responsible for the death of this unfortunate little boy and that you are the one who heartlessly and savagely took out his insides."

Her eyes grew wide. She gulped, then declared, "Oh no sir, no. 'Twasn't me. Or my kids. 'Twasn't any of us. It was that man. That Jew."

"I don't believe you."

"But I told the policeman, and he wrote it all down. It was that man. I swear. It was the Jew."

"There was no man. There was only you and your children."

"No, no," she wailed. "We wouldn't do that. We loved Marc-Antoine more than—"

She stopped short, not daring to go on. It was one of those moments that occurs in so many interrogations, when the sudden silence is so palpable that you could reach out and clutch at it and will it to speak to you. Instead, Martin merely grasped the arms of his chair and leaned forward. "More than who?" he asked slowly and quietly. *The mother or the father?*

"No one, I didn't mean. . . ." She brought the shawl over her face again, as if that would be enough to fend off Martin's questions.

Martin glanced over to Charpentier and nodded. This was their signal that the clerk should be ready to take down a spurt of uninterrupted testimony. Charpentier responded with a cocksure smile. This was the part of any interrogation he liked best, the moment when a suspect either began to confess or, even better, got tangled up in a web of lies. He never wasted any sympathy on the poor and the ignorant.

"Very well, then," Martin said, settling back in his chair again, "if what you say is true, I want the whole story from beginning to end of everything that happened on Wednesday afternoon and Thursday morning. Speak slowly so that Monsieur Charpentier can get it all down in the official record." And, Martin thought, please tell the truth. All of it. Now.

Geneviève Philipon opened her mouth, but nothing came out.

"Please begin," Martin said, as he clasped his hands together across his stomach and pursed his lips, making it evident that he was utterly comfortable in what was, after all, his command, and could wait her out, no matter how long it took.

The wet nurse swallowed hard before reciting a story that did not differ one iota from the account in Jacquette's report. She had rehearsed it well. Despite his show of ease, tension rippled at the back of Martin's neck and down his spine as she talked. She was lying. Yet from everything he had seen, Martin sensed she was incapable of making up such an elaborate story all by herself. He had to find out who had put her up to it.

The fingers in his clasped hands were gripping together so tightly that his knuckles were turning white. But his hands were below the wet nurse's vision. All Martin hoped she saw was his stern, impassive stare. When she finally began to squirm, he pounced. "I don't believe you."

"It's the truth, I swear it." She tried to sit up straight, as if putting her rectitude on display.

Martin had seen it all before, the obvious fabrications, followed by righteous denial. But this poor woman, who for so many years had been bent over with work and cares, made only the most pitiful attempt at stubborn defiance. His body relaxed. He had her. "You must know that if you are caught lying to a judge, he can imprison you and sentence you to hard labor. For years."

Her mouth trembled. "I . . . I . . . I . . . ."

"Did you make up this lie? Or did someone else put you up to this? Pierre Thomas, for example?" This was Martin's first opportunity to get at a motive behind the anti-Jewish slander.

"No, not him!" she blurted out, then covered her mouth. She had answered too quickly.

"Then was it Antoinette Thomas?" Martin shouted. He meant to frighten Geneviève Philipon, and he succeeded.

"No . . . Yes." She began gasping for air again. "Maybe the two of us."

"Why?" Martin was still shouting.

"Because," the woman cringed, "because she was afraid to tell Pierre about what happened. She thought he would blame it on her. She wanted it to seem like he was murdered."

"Marc-Antoine? Then he wasn't murdered by a stranger? Is that what you are saying?" Martin lurched toward her with mock surprise.

She nodded and huddled down into the chair, as if she feared he was going to strike her.

"Then, if you have been lying, we must start all over again. With that afternoon. You must tell me everything you know about why Marc-Antoine died and why he was mutilated. Telling the truth now is the only chance you have to not go to prison for a very long time." Martin sat back and gave himself leave to scratch the beard under his high collar. He was itching from the anxious sweating that a crucial interrogation always brought on. They were almost there.

Geneviève Philipon stared into space for a long moment, then, speaking as if she were in a trance, gave a very different account of little Marc-Antoine's death. She had often left him in the charge of her two older daughters while she worked in the field. That afternoon, she heard cries for help. When she ran to the cottage, the seven-month-old was already blue and stiffening. Her older girls were hysterical. Their little sister was wailing in the corner. Apparently the baby had crawled over to the hearth while no one was watching and stuck a stone or piece of ash in his mouth. After ordering her children to wait inside the cottage until her return, she took the boy's body up into the attic loft and left it where neither her cow nor pig could get at it. Then she ran to the factory to find Antoinette Thomas. Antoinette came and took the boy. She was the one who opened him up, gutted him and left the body by the river for Geneviève and the men from the village to discover the next morning.

"It was an accident," the wet nurse whimpered and repeated over and over again.

An accident. Martin had seen enough of Geneviève Philipon to be predisposed to believe her. *An accident,* not a crime. But one that had caused a child's death and incited an incendiary lie. A lie that could set off a lot of mischief in the wake of all the panic about Dreyfus's treachery, dangerous mischief; a lie that could be humiliating to Israelites like David Singer and his family. Martin had to squelch the story before it got out. He had to get all three of them to confess.

When she stopped sniveling, Martin asked, "Whose idea was it to make up the story about the Jewish tinker?"

Geneviève Philipon shrugged. "I can't remember."

"But surely you can," he insisted. "You remember everything else. You probably spread the story to the whole village. *Whose idea was it to blame a Jew?*" he asked again, giving emphasis to each word.

He watched as her mouth opened and closed a number of times before she finally told him, "Antoinette. The Jew was her idea."

The wet nurse's hesitations, more than her words, indicated that she was telling the truth. "Why would Antoinette Thomas invent such an elaborate lie?"

Geneviève Philipon shook her head, not daring to look at him. "I don't know," she whispered.

"Surely you must know. You said you were friends. Where would she get these ideas?" Martin leaned forward and glared at her, waiting.

"Maybe from a priest?" she finally offered.

"When? How?"

"A sermon, maybe, a sermon, about them, you know, the Jews."

Her replies were barely audible. But their impact was explosive. Martin didn't want to tangle with the bishop over the behavior of one of his priests. "Which priest?" he asked.

Geneviève Philipon shrugged her shoulders. "Her priest? I don't know. I'm not saying nothing more. I can't. I told you everything!" She wrapped her arms around her chest in a final gesture of defiance. She was biting down on her lips and breathing hard. Tears were trailing down her sallow cheeks. She had just betrayed her friend. She was through talking.

"Very well." Martin suddenly rose from his chair. She had to get a taste of the consequences of her lies and her stubbornness, at least until he corroborated her testimony. "Charpentier, go get a policeman to accompany Mme Philipon to the jail. We'll hold her until somebody decides to tell us the entire truth."

"No, no, please." The woman fell on her knees.

Without a word, Charpentier brushed past her on his way to the door. He could barely conceal the smirk on his face.

"Let me go home," she pleaded. "My children. Someone has to be with them."

"I will send Inspector Jacquette to see how your children are doing. I will also order him to question them about what happened."

"No, sir, please. I didn't do nothing wrong. It wasn't my fault. It wasn't their fault either."

Martin turned his back on her. He could mete out mercy later, after he found out how a mother could tear open her own child and start a slanderous rumor, and who had put such a dangerous idea in her head in the first place. If it was a parish priest, Martin would have to move quickly to quash the slander before it spread.

6

"IT WAS THE JEW THAT did it," Antoinette Thomas shouted as soon as she spotted Martin as she entered his office.

Martin watched with wary fascination as the uniformed officer pushed her forward. Her feet stuttered, just as Geneviève Philipon's had. But not because she was timid or scared. Her scowls and expletives indicated that her resistance stemmed from defiance rather than fear. The veteran policeman sighed with relief when he finally shoved her into the witness chair in front of Martin's desk. Antoinette Thomas promised to be a tough customer.

"It was him, I tell you," she said again, her green eyes flashing, daring Martin to call her a liar. She did not flinch even as he made a show of scrutinizing her face. She sat straight up, arms crossed, returning his disapproving stare.

Antoinette Thomas was taller than Geneviève Philipon, and healthier. In less dire circumstances, she might have been considered an attractive woman, even seductive. Her thick dark brown hair stood out on each side of her face, the tangle of unruly curls bristling with electric energy. An angry ruddiness colored her cheeks, and some hidden store of pride stiffened her carriage. As she held back her head waiting for Martin to respond to her ridiculous accusation, she lifted her firm square chin and thrust her chest forward. Her breasts were not limp and dry like the wet nurse's.

Yet these breasts had not nourished her son. If what the wet nurse had told Martin were true, Antoinette Thomas had not been a mother at all, beyond giving birth to the unfortunate Marc-Antoine. How could any true mother disembowel her own baby? Martin shuddered as he remembered the greenish-gray corpse lying in the morgue. And then, equally unbidden, came the image of his own dear wife, with her great belly, waiting eagerly for the day that she would nurse a child at her breast. Martin squeezed his eyes shut, for to think of Clarie as he looked upon Antoinette Thomas seemed almost a sacrilege.

Martin stayed very still for a moment, clearing his mind to prepare himself for battle. With a hard case like Antoinette Thomas, it might take all manner of threats and manipulation to get her to confess to what she had done and why, and, most important of all, to tell him who had incited her to make up her inflammatory little fable.

"The Jew," she repeated, filling up a silence broken only by Charpentier clearing his throat at the little desk to the left of Martin and the muted sound of footsteps through the window behind him. Her voice was quieter and less confident. She crossed her arms over her chest again, protectively this time.

Martin leaned back in his chair, trying to effect a casual pose, even though his stomach was churning with disgust. "Madame Thomas," he began, "before we get to your"—he paused to underline his skepticism—"your *accusations*, we need information for the official record. Please answer truthfully and slowly so Monsieur Charpentier can write everything down with utmost accuracy."

Martin heard another cough, and much shuffling of papers behind him. Charpentier had caught on. Martin was about to grind the witness down by asking in slow, excruciating detail about her past and present life. He would make her spell out every name, every address, every date. And drive her a little mad in the process.

This should not have been difficult. Martin's refusal to respond to her provocations seemed to have put her in a state of animal-like alertness. Although she maintained her pose, straight as a statue before him, the way she clutched her shawls together with white-knuckled fists gave her away.

Still, instead of answering Martin's simplest questions, she hurled demands and invective at him and his clerk.

"Tell me why I am here! Ain't it your job to find the Jew that killed my boy and took out his guts? Don't you know about them, what they do? You bring in a poor, grieving mother, when they are out there right now finding more innocent children to use in their wicked ceremonies."

She caught her breath and smiled for just an instant, as if she had surprised even herself with the last inventive flourish.

It was enough to get on anyone's nerves. Nevertheless, Martin kept his voice low and steady. "Please spell your full name, maiden and married," he repeated.

And repeated. Until she began to respond. Until she understood that this was a game she could not win. Martin proceeded, stony, methodical, and relentless, gathering both useful and useless information about her life. He wanted to make her squirm with impatience and annoyance. At the same time, he hoped that the routine triviality of his questions would lull her into a state of compliance, so that when they got to what she had done and why, she would blurt out her answers without thinking.

Once he got her started, she was quite forthcoming. As long as she could pour scorn on other people.

Geneviève Philipon "had always been a stupid cow. Kept behind in school, she was. That's how I met her," Antoinette Thomas explained. "It was me that had to help her with her numbers."

When asked about her employer, she informed Martin that she worked at a factory owned by a "rich dirty old Jew. Working us to the bone to make his money."

She was hardly kinder to her husband, who was "the one who wanted a kid." The one "who comes home smelling of drink and dead animals' blood and shit." Her nostrils flared out with distaste. "He promised to get me out of the factory, then got me pregnant. The pig."

"Then why did you marry him?" The question slipped out, unplanned. But, Martin thought, it might offer him an opening. If the husband felt the same contempt for his wife, Martin could turn them against each other. He shifted in his chair, eager to see what she would have to say.

"I married him because they paid us. They said we should be 'wed in the eyes of God' because we were *co-habiting*," she sneered as she pronounced the fancy word, which evidently had been pressed into her limited vocabulary from some higher source. "What difference did it make to me?"

"Who paid you?"

"Them snooty ladies who like to stick their noses into everyone's business."

"The Saint Regius Society," Martin mumbled. A charity propagated by those having too much time on their hands. Rich women who believed that they could turn the Antoinette Thomases of the world into pious bourgeois housewives despite the poverty and brutality of their lives. What cruel foolishness.

"Yeah, that one. And they would have paid me to nurse my kid too, but I couldn't do it."

"Couldn't?" Martin asked, thinking of the proud, full breasts, which she had managed to keep well within his view. If only she knew how much her spite and hardness repulsed him, then maybe she would just relax back into the seat and stop trying to be provocative.

"How were we going to eat if I didn't keep going to the factory, making that Jew rich?"

Well said, thought Martin, only barely restraining himself from shouting at her. Blame your predicament on the Israelites. Yet who *was* to blame? Fauvet had reminded him that mill women often sent their children to the country in order to keep on working. Many, if not most of them, including the vixen who sat in front of him, had no choice. He sighed. "And you chose Geneviève Philipon because . . . ?" he asked

"Because," she leaned forward and screwed her mouth into another sneer, "she still had her last one at her breast and I knew she was desperate after her husband kicked the bucket. Because," she added as she sat back, "she'd take anything I gave her."

"Let's talk about you and Mme Philipon," Martin said, clasping his hands around his stomach. His gaze roved slowly over every facet of Antoinette Thomas's face, stopping at exactly the point where his eyes bored into hers. They had finally come full circle. To the pitiful dead body of little Marc-Antoine. To Antoinette Thomas's blatant lies and ridiculous accusations. Back to what the wet nurse had told Martin.

After almost two hours of questioning, Antoinette Thomas was becoming restless, apprehensive. The bosom that she had so proudly thrust at him was taking in shorter and shorter breaths. The tense stillness of his own body made Martin's chin prickle under his beard. He rubbed it with a slowness that he hoped would keep her on edge, while he considered the next step. If he began the most critical part of the interrogation by accusing her of mutilating her own son, he might set her off, either in a stream of denials or, if she cared anything about the little boy, a sudden flood of remorse and grief. Because he needed answers, not hysteria, he decided to save any talk of that gruesome scene by the stream in Tomblaine for last.

"Mme Philipon told me that it was *your* idea to accuse a Jewish tinker of killing your son."

Antoinette Thomas shook her head in denial, jangling her curls, before thrusting out her chin and proclaiming, "She's lying." Antoinette Thomas stared straight into Martin's eyes without so much as a flinch.

Martin persisted. "She even suggested that you might have gotten the idea that a Jew would do this to your son from a priest."

"A priest!" Antoinette Thomas arched her eyebrows in surprise. The idea seemed to amuse her. "I haven't been in a church since my first communion. Why should I bother? They're for the rich too."

"You just told me you got married——"

"Oh, yes, that. And you see what good it did me. Married." She turned her head in disgust as she spat out the word. "No, no. Geneviève's the one who listens to them and goes to confession and does what they say. A priest. The cow," she scoffed.

"Then where did you get such a preposterous idea? From a political speech? Or your husband?" Antoinette Thomas's assertion that the Church supported the rich had not escaped him. It suggested some acquaintance with anti-clerical politics.

She fell back in mock surprise. "Why do I need someone to tell me what everybody knows?"

Everybody! A pulsating tension streamed down the side of Martin's head from his temples to his jaw. Everybody! Did she mean all the tanners and factory workers and shopgirls living in the hovels that lined the river? The drunks trading insults and fisticuffs in working-class cafés, who would never dream of setting foot inside a church, as well as the pious and sober, like Geneviève Philipon, who, for all Martin knew, might hang on every word uttered by an ignorant country priest. Everybody! And she did not even know the half of it, the upper crust, the writers, the politicians, even those entrusted with dispensing justice, like the court's own Alphonse Rocher.

"And what exactly is it," Martin asked as his own breath became short and labored, "that everybody knows about the Israelites?"

Her eyes got wider than ever, as if she thought him quite daft. "What *is* it?"

"Yes, what is it that *everybody* knows? Tell me please."

She hesitated. He nodded encouragement. She shrugged. And then she spewed it all out. They ran everything. From the Rothschilds and their banks in the big cities to the local shopkeeper who cheats poor people like her. They're money-hungry. They stick together. Except they also want to be like us. If it weren't for their noses, and their smell, Antoinette Thomas averred with the air of a schoolgirl concluding a successful recitation, we'd never be able to tell them apart. And, of course, she added hastily, suddenly mindful of her own circumstances, their religion encourages them to kill Christian babies and use the blood in their ceremonies.

It was quite a list. Things he would have never dreamed of saying about anyone, or reading, or hearing without objection. The kinds of things that undoubtedly drove Singer up the wall, Singer for whom dignity and decorum were so important. What was it that he had told Martin last Friday? "You are fortunate that you do not have to care about these things." Not any more. Not if Martin was going to be a real friend to Singer or, for that matter, a principled republican judge. It was a distasteful business, one he had never thought he would have to confront. And here he was in the middle of it. He looked up to see Antoinette Thomas staring at him, waiting. Charpentier cleared his throat and shifted in his chair, also waiting. It was time.

"I see," Martin said, hoping to communicate his disdain. "You believe all these slanders, do you? Is this why you made up that story about a Jewish peddler?"

"What story?" Her impudence knew no bounds. It was time to cut her down to size.

"The slander that an Israelite killed your child and cut him open. Your friend Geneviève Philipon has already told us that little Marc-Antoine choked to death. She told us it was you who decided to cover up the accident with this slander. You who gutted and castrated your own son." His voice grew louder with every word, reaching a shouting, angry crescendo.

"She's lying," she brazenly repeated. But Antoinette Thomas had begun to shrink away from him. He had finally gotten to her.

"Lying?" Martin said with mocking skepticism. "She's lying? My inspector is in Tomblaine right now getting testimony from the children. I doubt if they will lie."

"They're little idiots. They'll say anything you tell them to." She was hugging her shawls around her again, rocking from side to side. Scared but not surrendering.

"It will be much better for you if you tell me what happened. If you did not kill the child, if you covered it up for your own reasons, I want to know why." It felt good to let out the heat that had been building up inside of him.

"I've lost my baby and you are going to let them get away with it." Her voice was trembling now. He even saw a tear run down her cheek. But he had no way of knowing whether its source was remorse or fear.

"Confess. It will be better for you in the end. I may not even charge you. I'm not sure our Code has a name for the crime you have committed, mutilating your own dead child," he said with contempt. "But we can and will indict you for slander, unless you stop telling these lies." Did the Code have a name for the crime of slandering a whole race? Martin did not think so. But he counted on her ignorance to put the fear of God into her.

"It was the Jew! I told you!" He had forgotten. She had no God. There was only one remedy: a filthy cell, a few days on gruel to soften her up. But he had no intention of putting her in the same place as the spineless Geneviève Philipon.

Martin swung his chair around to face his clerk. "Charpentier, get the officer. Tell him it's time to escort Mme Thomas to solitary confinement."

He should not have turned his back on her, for in an instant she was on her feet. Seeing her fury and her hands spread out like angry claws at the front of his desk, he instantly understood what it was like between her and her husband, the smacking, hurling and screaming. But he had no time to absorb this lesson. Afraid that she was going to find something on his desk to use as a weapon, Martin grabbed hold of his heavy ink bottle and ordered her to sit down.

Charpentier scurried for the door, as Antoinette Thomas loomed over Martin's desk. "What do you think people will say about a judge who persecutes a mother and lets the Jews off scot-free?"

What indeed? All Martin cared about at this moment was getting her out of his office. He could think of nothing more demeaning than being forced to come to blows with a woman.

Fortunately, the uniformed officer had been standing guard outside. Martin sighed with relief as the policeman took her in tow and began to drag her away. She kicked and flailed all the way out the door, which Charpentier closed with a loud slam. Then he turned to Martin with a gleeful glimmer in his eyes. "She forgot to say that Jews were Christ killers."

Martin was stunned, as he often was, by the callowness of his young clerk. He hoped Charpentier was only mocking the suspect and that he didn't believe any of the myths about the Israelites. In any case, Martin was too tired to care, and too hungry.

"We've both had a long morning. Let's go to lunch."

The clerk's face fell. "Yes, Monsieur le juge," he answered as he slipped back to his desk. It had been a joke. Martin managed a wan smile as he turned and gave a nod of recognition. "See you at two, then?"

He was too distracted to do more to salve Charpentier's feelings. He needed to get away. Far away. He didn't want to run into Didier, or Rocher, or Singer. He could not face Clarie, because she was sure to sense his disquietude.

Martin got up and took his coat from the rack. As he wound his scarf around his neck, he considered what would give him comfort. He'd find an anonymous café, put his foot up on a brass rail, eat a sausage, and drink a beer like any sensible Lorrainer. A sensible lunch for a sensible man. Fortification for what lay ahead.

It should have been over that afternoon. Case solved. Liars repentant and convinced of their wrongdoing. A dossier sent to Didier with an addendum on ways to track the propagators of this particular anti-Israelite slander. Martin should have been home before supper, sitting across from his beloved Clarie, she and their child his only care. Should have.

After all, minutes after Martin returned from his brief repast, Inspector Jacquette arrived from Tomblaine with the heartening news that the two older girls had verified the wet nurse's story. He recommended that Martin release Geneviève Philipon before nightfall so that the "little ones would have someone to tend their fire."

Martin readily agreed. He had no desire to punish the ignorant, foolish woman. He would send her home with a stern warning to tell the truth about the incident, if asked, and otherwise keep her mouth shut.

Should have. All Martin needed to do was to confront Pierre Thomas with the wet nurse's confession and his wife's blatant lies, and the tanner was bound to see that he had been duped. Then with two of them coming clean, he would force a confession out of Antoinette Thomas.

But what should have been did not take into account the mule-like obstinacy and slow-wittedness of Pierre Thomas. Big, blond and lumbering, the tanner came into Martin's chambers bearing the unmistakable odor of animal shit and blood, and an inexhaustible load of grievance. Against the rich. Against the state. Against the Jews. Against any God that had the audacity to let "them" at his son. His only son. The child he had always wanted. The child he had been so proud of.

Remarkably, his list of grievances did not include his wife, who, he testified, wailed in grief like a banshee when she first laid eyes upon her mutilated child. He described her as an admirable woman, a good wife, a mother who would have quit the factory and saved their child if it weren't for his fecklessness.

"Your wife's friend, Mme Philipon, confessed. Her children were thoroughly grilled by my inspector. Why should they lie?" Martin repeated.

Thomas shrugged, blue eyes stupidly blank over his grizzled unshaven face. He did not know why any of them should lie. He only knew what his wife had told him. And he knew what the Jews were capable of.

Martin sat back with a sigh and glanced at Charpentier, who was working hard to repress a sardonic grin as he bent over his notes. It was obvious to both of them. Pierre Thomas was so besotted with his wife that no appeal to reason was going to penetrate his thick skull. He wasn't even willing to try to save his own neck. How does a man get that way, besotted? As Thomas sat before him kneading his thighs with his strong, restless hands, Martin guessed how. The electric attraction of Antoinette Thomas. The animal passions. For some men, something more powerful than reason. Martin pictured the two of them, coupling on a filthy straw mattress, grunting and sweating, hungrily grabbing at what little pleasure life had to offer. It was too bad that the guileless laborer had paid such a high price for that pleasure, and would continue to do so. But Martin had no choice. After ordering Pierre Thomas to give him a list of the political rallies he had attended, he informed the tanner that he would remain in prison until he made a solemn vow not to repeat any of his wife's lies and fabrications.

What happened next was exactly as Martin expected. It took two policemen to drag Thomas out of his chambers, crying out that Martin and all like him were bastards. Martin set his face into an impassive mask during this violent exit, hiding the turbulence inside. At moments like this, he was always torn between his duty to enforce the law and his fear that he was committing an injustice. As the guards forced Pierre Thomas out of his chambers, Martin felt that his heart was hardening into a great stone, weighing him down. He knew the tanner had just lost his son. He had committed no crime. At least, not yet. And if Antoinette Thomas and Geneviève Philipon had committed one, he was not sure what he would call it. Was there a crime for hatred? For blind stupid prejudice? For blaming someone else for the tragedies that all too often befall the destitute?

Falling completely under the thrall of a seductive and manipulative woman was not a crime. Where was the justice in imprisoning Pierre Thomas in the hope that somehow he would come to see the error of his ways? Especially if Martin was doing it in order to "protect the integrity of the courthouse"?

Martin dropped his head into his hands and rubbed his aching eyes. If he was a bastard, he was more aware than ever that he was a lucky one. He and his Clarie did not have to worry about tomorrow's bread or limit themselves to pleasures stealthily and greedily consumed. Together they were building a life guided by a higher morality, dedicated to vanquishing ignorance and superstition. He could not imagine a time or circumstance when Clarie would betray that trust. Or what he would do about it if she did.

7

CLARIE STOOD IN THE CRAMPED foyer next to the coat hooks, her hands trembling as she tore open the thin blue envelope. As soon as she unfolded the telegram, she glanced at the name of the sender. "Papa." Her eyes raced over the message:

ARRIVING BY TRAIN TOMORROW AFTERNOON STOP STAYING
AT THE HOTEL DELANGLETERRE STOP LOVE STOP PAPA.

"Is it bad news?" Madeleine got up from her favored chair in the Martins' living room and tiptoed up to Clarie.

"Oh, no." Clarie folded the fragile blue message before turning and smiling at her friend. "No, it's the best of news. Papa is coming. He'll be here tomorrow."

"Oh." Madeleine retreated to her place by the fire. "I see."

Madeleine's curt response induced a familiar pang which Clarie had begun to recognize as loneliness. Except for Madeleine, the other teachers were all mothers who hurried home to their children at the end of the day. Clarie missed them and her students. Ever since she stopped teaching, there were times when she desperately felt that she needed a real friend, someone with whom to share her woman's joys and sorrows. Someone who would respond with unalloyed sympathy and spontaneity. Someone beside the devoted and obsequious Rose Campion, who came every day to help her with the apartment. Sadly too, Clarie frowned as she eased herself back into the chair, someone beside Bernard, who seemed more and more absorbed in his work, and for some unknown reason, very secretive.

"Isn't it early for your father to come? Isn't the baby a month away?" Madeleine asked, obviously still chewing over the news in the telegram.

Clarie sighed, *And certainly someone beside Madeleine who would do well to soften that critical tone in her voice.* "Christmas is next month," Clarie explained evenly. "Perhaps Papa will stay in town for the holidays. He'll be here, with me, waiting. . . ." Clarie bit her tongue before going on. There was no reason to be unkind. Madeleine was lonely, too, and more alone than she'd ever be. Clarie was only too well aware that Madeleine thought that *she* was the one helping her through the anxious, hopeful waiting for that wonderful, fearful day when she would deliver her child. Besides, Papa could ill afford to stay away from his work that long.

"Then you are happy to have your father here. He won't make you nervous. That is very good, my dear." Madeleine took a sip of her tea and replaced the rose-decorated china cup on the saucer in her lap. "I hope I will get to meet him," she added, with a smile that seemed rather forced.

"Of course you will," Clarie replied. Sometimes Madeleine sounded like a friend. Clarie knew that Madeleine did not want to feel displaced, and Clarie would try to see that she didn't. Still, Papa coming now, early. Clarie lifted her chest over her big hard belly, refusing to suppress her joy. She had been so unaccountably restless these last few days, and Bernard had been so distant and silent. Papa would wrap his strong blacksmith arms around her to comfort her. He'd put his stubby finger under her chin and tease her worries away. She was still his little girl. His grown girl. The person he doted on most in the world.

"I assume that he and Bernard get along." Madeleine hated being left out of Clarie's thoughts.

"Oh, yes, very well."

"A judge and a. . . ."

"A blacksmith," Clarie reminded her. A big, generous bear of a man. He would sit at the dinner table and point his fork at her dear republican husband and lecture Bernard on why he should have become an *avocat*, who defends the exploited, instead of a judge who punishes them. And Bernard would defend the laws. And they would spar and laugh because deep down they agreed with each other and adored each other. And soon, perhaps she would be bringing forth a little man to join them. And when she held her baby in her arms, how could she be lonely any more? Or restless? Or fearful?

"I'm very happy," she remarked to Madeleine. "He's good for Bernard. Papa always seems to make him less serious."

Madeleine lifted her eyebrows with surprise and once again raised her teacup, considering her response.

Clarie knew she could never explain to her the things that Bernard and her father, a judge and a blacksmith, had in common, so she tried another tack. "And, of course, you will meet Bernard's mother. She'll come right after the baby is born and—"

"She's knows about the names?"

"That the girl will be named after my mother, and a boy will be Henri-Joseph."

"Yes."

"No, we haven't told her yet, unless Bernard wrote without my knowing."

Madeleine laid her cup on the saucer and placed it carefully on the table. She folded her hands on her lap, as if preparing to deliver an important pronouncement. "I just found out that it is an Israelite custom to name a child after a recently deceased relative. That's one of the ways they perpetuate the tribe."

"Really? That seems like a nice custom. How *do* you find these things out?" This came out more tartly than Clarie had intended, but she was angry. How dare Madeleine sap the joy out of this moment?

"I read about them."

What does she read, Clarie wondered, besides *La Croix*? Drumont? Something even worse? Clarie's heart began to race, it was so upsetting to think of what her friend was becoming. Or had she always been that way? Clarie wasn't in the mood to speculate, or to argue, or to back down, so she explained, "Our little boy will only be half-named after a dead relative, Bernard's father. The Joseph is for my father, Giuseppe."

Madeleine's mouth formed into a round O, undoubtedly remembering that Clarie had once been Falchetti, and her father was Italian. And a blacksmith to boot. Was that almost as bad as being a Jew? There were times when Clarie felt that that's what Bernard's mother thought.

Then Henri-Joseph or Marie-Rose kicked and wheeled its tiny legs, reminding Clarie of all the things she had to celebrate. And of what she intended to say when Madeleine interrupted her. "You are going to be such a help when Bernard's mother comes. You know she has never really accepted me. So I'm depending on you to spend time with her and convince her that I am a good wife to Bernard."

This was true and kind, and a little naughty. For Bernard had put it very differently last week, when he said that Madeleine would be the perfect companion for his mother because they could go into some corner and together bemoan the defeat of the monarchy and the irreligion of the young. Then, he concluded, giving Clarie a peck on the cheek, Madeleine Froment, who had been consuming their tea and sympathy for over a month, would finally earn her keep by taking his mother off their hands.

"Of course, my dear," Madeleine said with enthusiasm, happy to be assigned a role in the great event.

Clarie put her hand on her belly and sank into her chair, her good humor restored by remembering that Bernard did have moments of impish wickedness. The baby was kicking, her father was coming, her husband would eventually tell her what was bothering him. Her pique receded into the contemplation of all the good things in her life.

8

Tuesday, November 20

THE STORY BROKE THE DAY Clarie's father arrived. Martin picked up
the afternoon edition of *Le Courrier de l'Est* at a kiosk in Place Stanislas
and stood under the flimsy protection of the vendor's flapping awning,
skimming the headlines. MYSTERIOUS MURDER OF WORKER'S CHILD IN
TOMBLAINE appeared just below the fold.

Martin closed his eyes and groaned. Why had he even bothered to
hope that the press would stay out of it?

"Are you all right, sir?" the paper-seller asked.

"Yes, yes, of course," Martin answered before turning his back on
the man while he read on, fighting the cold north wind as the story bil-
lowed up toward him.

The reporter had not talked to Geneviève Philipon or her children.
Or, at the very least, they had obeyed Martin's orders and refused to

talk to him. The main informant was a certain François Mouton, one of the local men who had searched for the baby and become troubled by the fact that no one had been arrested. This led the reporter to the jailhouse, where he discovered that the little boy's parents were under arrest. The writer concluded with a question: Were the people of Nancy about to learn of a singular abomination perpetuated by the mother and father, or were we witnessing, once again, a miscarriage of justice by an overweening judiciary? Bernard Martin was prominently mentioned as the investigating magistrate.

Martin's first instinct was to crumple the paper into a ball and throw it away. Then he thought better of it. He'd show it to Singer. Yes, Martin wanted to hear what Singer would have to say about it, Singer who had gotten him into the whole mess. Martin knew very well how Didier was going to react: another dressing-down, demands to make the obdurate Thomases confess, and an insistence that Martin somehow get to the bottom of a presumed anti-Semitic plot.

The bottom! Martin thought, as he marched back to the Palais de Justice. As far as he could tell, there was an endless well of hatred and idiocy to sink into. Fortunately, by the time he rang the bell for the doorkeep, he was calmer. Surely Singer, who had lived in Lorraine all his life, could offer some advice or, at the very least, some consolation. Especially now, when Martin wanted so desperately to keep Clarie out of it.

As soon as the door swung open, Martin rushed past the guard, taking the polished wooden stairs two at a time, only to find Singer's chambers locked up for the night. Martin stood before the thick oaken door for a moment to collect himself, before slowly retracing his steps. He stopped at his office to drop the paper on his desk. If only it were that easy to shed his frustrations, he thought, as he wrapped his scarf around his neck. From the moment he entered his apartment, he was going to have to play the role of the cheerful host and proud expectant father. Martin grinned in spite of himself. Maybe that's exactly what he needed, forced relaxation.

His spirits lifted as he strode through the gay, busy Place Stanislas for the second time. After all, he rationalized, it would all end soon enough. Little Marc-Antoine had not been murdered, so there would be no scandalous trial. Most importantly, the newspaper had made no mention of an alleged ritual murder. Perhaps Didier's and Singer's fears had been entirely overblown. All Martin had to do was to keep a lid on the situation until he got Antoinette Thomas to make a full confession.

By the time he opened the door to his apartment and took in the welcoming warm aroma of steaming tomatoes and garlic, Martin was convinced that there really was nothing to worry about. Until he saw a glower in the eyes of the barrel-chested Giuseppe Falchetti, who had hurried over to greet him in the foyer.

"What have you gotten into, my boy?"

Martin couldn't tell whether his father-in-law was condemning or teasing him. Then a smile broke out between the bushy white mustache and beard as Giuseppe shook his head and murmured, "The wrong side, I keep telling you, the wrong side."

"It's more than that—"

"Oh, I'm not the one who needs the explaining. It's your wife."

"You showed her—" Martin did not know whether to be angry or apprehensive.

"Of course. I picked up the paper at the railroad station. How could I miss seeing my son-in-law's name, more than once, right on the front page?"

The railroad station. Martin should have realized that Giuseppe Falchetti, a devoted socialist, would have spent time there, reading all the headlines before choosing a newspaper.

"Come." Giuseppe took Martin's bowler and helped him off with his coat. "Come. And don't worry. I remember how her mother got that last month. It will pass."

Will it? Martin thought. He had never kept anything from Clarie before. He tiptoed with trepidation to meet her eyes and her fury.

She was already sitting at the round wooden table that took up most of their tiny dining room. After Martin and Giuseppe squeezed in, she asked Rose to serve the pasta and Martin to open the wine. Clarie spoke in a monotone, staring straight in front of her, not even offering Martin a nod of greeting. As if on notice that orders had better be obeyed without delay or comment, Rose, their short, broad, middle-aged day woman, scurried to the kitchen to retrieve a steaming bowl of spaghetti bolognese. She set it near Giuseppe, who leaned over, took a sniff, and sighed with pleasure. For the Italian, food was sacred; the dish that he had taught Clarie's mother, and then Clarie, was a family sacrament that called for heedfulness, gratitude and joy. Clarie knew this. So did Martin. Yet, save for the glances he cast toward Clarie, who continued to ignore him, Martin dared not move a muscle.

Undeterred, the old Italian doled out the pasta, tucked his napkin in his collar and dug in, drawing the strands of red spaghetti into his mouth with noisy enthusiasm. Clarie merely nibbled, slowly picking up and examining each strand of spaghetti before depositing it in her mouth. Martin, for his part, twisted normal portions of the reddened pasta around his fork, but found it harder and harder to swallow. Giuseppe broke the silence.

"This is delicious, my sweet. So you finally succeeded in getting Rose not to overcook the spaghetti."

"Yes, Papa," Clarie said as she scrutinized another strand.

"Clarie—"

She snubbed Martin and turned to her father. "Did you know, Papa, that I am married to a man who calls himself a rationalist, yet believes that something terrible will happen to his pregnant wife if she hears about certain crimes?"

"No, Clarie—"

"Oh, that's not it?" she said, her beautiful almond-shaped eyes glaring at Martin. "Perhaps it's even worse. Perhaps you are afraid that if you told me what you had seen, our son would be born with a scar down his front, just like that poor, little baby left by the river? Perhaps after all your talk about progress and women's rights, you are secretly that superstitious."

"Clarie—"

"Well, I am not," she said as she threw her napkin on the table and, using both her hands, pushed herself up. "And I am not feeling well, so I am going to bed. Rose will clear when you are done. Good night, gentlemen."

"Clarie!" This time Martin rose, about to run after her.

Giuseppe stuck out a stout, strong arm to stop him. "Sit. Eat. Let her be for a while."

Martin stood for just a moment before sinking back into the chair.

"Even though Clarie's mother had borne six sons for her first husband," Giuseppe said as he filled Martin's wine glass, "she still had the nerves during her last month with our little Clarie. And then, after our beautiful baby came, it was all smiles."

"I know. That's why. . . ." Martin stopped himself. The white-haired Giuseppe Falchetti was a fine man, a lovable man, but he could not possibly know what it was like to carry the gory images of dead bodies around in your head or realize that, once again, you had been handed a career-threatening case. That it could be Aix-en-Provence all over again.

"We should eat," said Giuseppe as he tore a piece of bread and used it to wipe around the rim of his bowl, "we should drink, and then we should take a walk."

Martin fingered his fork, listening for any sounds from the bedroom. Sobs? Slamming? Shoes being thrown on the floor? Nothing.

"Eat while it's hot. She loves you. She worries about you, that's all." Giuseppe imbibed another mouthful and grunted with pleasure.

"That's all?" Then why the empty chair, the chastened Rose, the two men left alone in front of a rapidly congealing feast?

Giuseppe leaned toward Martin. "She asked me to get you to walk me back to the hotel tonight. She wanted us to try to talk about what is bothering you."

The kind-hearted, burly Giuseppe was a second father to Martin. He knew that even when the Italian pounded the table and roared out his opposition to the oppressive laws that Martin was charged with upholding, he did it with good humor and love, as a way of engaging and embracing the son he'd never had. Nevertheless, Martin was not in the mood to spar with him tonight.

"Clarie and I should not involve you in our quarrels," Martin said, as he concentrated on twirling the spaghetti round and round on his fork.

"But I *am* involved!" Giuseppe stretched out his arms and then thumped his heart with his right hand. "I am. After all, I was the fool who brought the paper home."

"And she asked you after she read—"

"No, before. Clarie's too smart a girl not to notice that something's wrong."

Before. Martin deposited the forkful of pasta into his mouth and began to chew. Even before she saw the newspaper, she had asked her father to get involved. And Martin thought he had been protecting her. He was a fool.

Giuseppe set Clarie's half-full bowl inside his and pushed them aside. "So you see, my boy, we're both under orders."

Giuseppe insisted that they stop for a drink as they headed down the hill toward the railroad station. They chose a dimly lit café, with only a scattering of customers, and took a corner table near the window. Martin stared at the red-and-white checked table cloth in sullen silence as Giuseppe ordered two cognacs. Neither said another word until the blacksmith's patient expectant gaze resigned Martin to the inevitable.

Yes, Martin admitted, he was keeping the weaver and the tanner under lock and key. Yes, he was under pressure to do this. "But," Martin whispered, "there may be a great deal more at stake." Giuseppe nodded sagely when Martin asked if he was aware of the upcoming trial of Captain Dreyfus in Paris. Then the old man shrugged.

"Who cares about the army? Who can trust any of them? It's the last bastion of the nobles, of the elite. They'll fire on the workers if it comes to that. They're worse," his hazel eyes twinkled as he shook a stubby finger at Martin, "worse even than the magistrature."

"That may be so," said Martin, suppressing a smile as Giuseppe made the obligatory poke at his profession. "But what if people use Dreyfus's treachery to punish all Jews?"

"Maybe they deserve it!" Giuseppe's fist fell upon the table, rattling the short, thick glasses. "The Rothschilds, the Perriers, their banks, their railroads, their exploitation."

The working man's plaint against the Israelites. The ignoramus Pierre Thomas had blurted out similar accusations. Martin took a gulp of the brandy. It seared a burning path down his constricted throat. He'd never dreamed that Giuseppe would be an anti-Israelite. The subject had never come up between them.

"Surely you don't read *La Libre Parole*?" Martin took in a breath while he waited for the answer.

"Oh no." Giuseppe grimaced with disgust. "You don't need to read Drumont's rag to know that the Rothschilds have too much power."

"Not all Jews are Rothschilds," Martin said, thinking of Singer. "Not all of them are rich," he murmured, as a vision of his landlords, the Steins, formed in his mind. There probably weren't any Israelites in Arles. And if Giuseppe did not know any Jews, he might not see how the Steins were like them, like Martin's dead father, who had barely eked out a living from his clockmaking, and like the blacksmith himself. Kind, decent, hardworking people. He shook his head, pulling himself back to his father-in-law. He had to press his case. As he gathered his thoughts, he realized that what he was about to say might be preparation for a new role. Instead of arguing that someone had committed a crime, he might have to prepare himself to exonerate an entire race from the crimes—real or imagined—that they stood accused of. "Should all the Israelites be hated and persecuted because some are very rich, or one may be a traitor, or because they are not Christians? Should we allow mobs to threaten all of them?"

"Do you think that could happen?"

"It has. In the past."

Giuseppe pursed his lips in thought, giving Martin an opportunity to go on. "They are in all walks of life. Among the bakers and shoe-makers and shopkeepers. Probably even among the workers," he added, appealing to his father-in-law's "red" sympathies. Martin's heart began to pound, he wanted so much to get Giuseppe on his side.

For the next few minutes, Giuseppe countered Martin's insistence that the Thomases' lies posed a danger to the city with a recitation of the many ways the rich, especially the Rothschilds, exploited workers, not only in France but wherever their banks and their companies oper-ated, for money, always for money, and the power money gave them.

"But that's not true of all Israelites," Martin insisted. Even though Singer, Martin's only real friend at the courthouse, was the reason he had been put into the position of defending French Jews, he did not mention him to his father-in-law. It was not only because they had never met. Martin guessed that his father-in-law would not have liked his fellow judge. Singer's excessively formal demeanor would have come off as a kind of snobbishness, an exemplar of everything Giuseppe accused the courts of being. This is why Martin clinched the argument by speaking of the Steins. "You've met our landlords," he said. "Who would they plot with? What other care do they have except running their store and passing it on to their children and grandchildren, just as you are passing your smithy onto your stepsons?"

"So," the old man said as he scratched his full white beard, "to blame all workers because one of them commits a crime, or all Italians because . . . is like blaming all Jews just because a few are Rothschilds!"

Giuseppe grinned. "I knew that, my boy, or, I should have known that. I just wanted to get you going. I know it's not right."

That was always the most important thing for Giuseppe Falchetti. What was right. What was just. If all men were as good and generous as Clarie's father, Martin thought as a familiar warmth flooded his body, he would not have to worry. How he loved this man!

But all men were not like Giuseppe Falchetti. This is why Martin had to proceed with care through the thickets of prejudice and court-house politics. Making sure that no one was listening, Martin continued in a low voice, "So I need to hold the Thomases until they come around to telling the truth, so as not to start a panic."

"Well, I hope it won't be too long." Giuseppe pounded his fist on the table again, lightly this time, and grumbled, for the sake of argument, "That's not right either."

Martin leaned back and smiled as the man he considered his second father found a way to come back to the old argument that Martin should be defending workingmen instead of persecuting them. Only this time, Martin realized, as he tilted his glass and peered at the amber liquid, something was missing. Clarie, eyes sparkling, laughing, shaking her head in delight as her "two men" sparred. What a fool he'd been. Of course she would not be afraid or superstitious because he had seen a mutilated, dead baby. Of course she'd condemn a slander against the Israelites. She believed in republican ideals every bit as much as Martin. That's why she had taken the radical step of training to be a teacher in a public girls' high school. She had struggled, was still struggling to do something so few of her sex had done. And he had not trusted her.

"Bernard," Giuseppe tugged at Martin's sleeve. "She'll get over it. I know my girl."

"Of course," Martin mumbled. She would. He would see to it. Even if she turned her back on him tonight, pretending to be asleep, they'd talk tomorrow. He'd cajole and beg and explain until she understood what a loving fool he was. They had time. A lifetime.

Giuseppe got up and slapped Martin on the back. "Let's go. We've got to get you back to my daughter."

They descended into the cold, clear night, linking arms in silence as they fought against the wind blowing up from the railroad station, feeling comfort in each other's presence and in the knowledge that their night would end in something more important than words— pressing together, heart to heart, in a manly embrace.

Yet this was not to be. For when they strolled into the hotel's lobby, they spotted Rose, trembling, waiting for them by the counter.

"The crisis has begun. Monsieur Stein has gone to fetch the doctor, and Madame is staying with her. You must come, both of you quickly." For just an instant Martin could not move, his limbs rooted into the wooden planks of the hotel floor, as his mind repeated, over and over, *It is too early*. And then he flung the door open and ran up the hill.

9

Tuesday–Wednesday, November 20–21

MARTIN GASPED FOR AIR AS he reached the entrance to his building. Leaning against the wall to catch his breath, he frantically fumbled through his coat pockets for his keys. He needn't have bothered. Like magic, the door slowly crept open.

"Monsieur Martin, Monsieur le juge?" a timid voice called out.

"Yes, yes," he said impatiently pulling the door hard from the hands of the Steins' younger daughter, Rebecca. She huddled out of the sight of anyone who might be passing in the street, a trembling sentry in thin, red cloth slippers, a wooly blue nightcap, and a white flannel bathrobe, which she grasped with both arms across her waist.

"Maman says everything is going to be fine." Her dark eyes, wide with concern, and her hair, a crinkly black mass let down for bedtime, accentuated the pallor of her face. The poor girl seemed every bit as frightened as Martin. She loved Clarie, as all of her students did, as anyone in their right mind would.

Martin managed to smile, and to lie. "I'm sure your mother is right. No need to worry. Mme Martin is very strong. And now. . . ." Martin lifted his chin toward the stairs and squeezed his eyes shut. *If there is a God in heaven, please let it be true that Clarie is fine, that the baby is fine, that Clarie knows how much I love her.*

As soon as the girl realized that she was blocking his path, she scuttled to the side and flattened herself against the pockmarked beige wall. "I'm waiting for the doctor, too," she called out as he barreled up the rickety, narrow staircase.

Although the door to his apartment was ajar, he waited to slow his breathing before lightly pressing it open with his fingertips. At the very least, he had to appear to be calm, for Clarie's sake. Alert to every sound, he slipped into the foyer and was startled by an ominous silence. Then from the bedroom, he heard a moan, followed by a whimper—"Where is Bernard? Why isn't he here yet?"—answered by a murmur of assurance. Before he could suppress it, a selfish joy inflated his chest. She wanted him above all others. She understood how insignificant their quarrel was, how much he loved her. Martin threw off his bowler and overcoat and flung his scarf on the nearest chair. He blew on his hands to warm them and, rubbing them together, hurried to the bedroom.

He found Clarie stretched out on the bed like a medieval saint about to meet her martyrdom, her hair forming a dark halo around her damp, reddened face; eyes closed, mouth clenched, desperate fists clutching at the blue woolen blankets. Their landlady, Mme Stein, was sitting by her side, patting one of Clarie's arms. Martin made a slight bow with his head. "Madame Stein." "Monsieur le juge," she said as she stood up from the chair and swept her hand across her forehead, wiping away a strand of gray hair. She had the same dark eyes and thick, wrinkled hair as her daughter, but not the same fright. She smiled as she repeated, undoubtedly for the hundredth time, "It will be all right."

Even so, Martin fell to his knees beside the bed and whispered, "Clarie, I'm here. Clarie, my love, I'm here."

"Come, come, Monsieur Martin, sit here." Mme Stein offered him her chair. "Sit, I'll go see that there is water for the doctor. But it is going to be a while yet."

"Papa?" Clarie opened her eyes as Martin moved to the far side of the bed and sat down. He gently unfolded one of Clarie's hands from the blanket and kissed it.

"He'll be here soon." How could he, at this moment, feel a pang of jealousy for Clarie's father? Face heated with shame, he kissed her hand again. It was Clarie, the baby, that he should be thinking of.

Clarie smiled weakly. "You're here."

No longer able to hold in all the emotions that had carried him to her, the words tumbled out. "Clarie, I love you. I'm sorry. I should have told you. I should have known, you above all women, would not be afraid. You—"

Clarie squeezed his hand with an iron grip and moaned again, in little, pitiful grunts.

Thank God, Mme Stein had not left the room. She leaned over to Clarie and whispered, "Relax, try to let them come. It will be better."

"Hah," a last breath came and Clarie's eyes opened wide. "Gone," she panted. "Gone for now."

"And in between," Mme Stein continued as she wiped Clarie's brow with a handkerchief, "know that your husband is right here and the doctor is coming soon."

"Yes," Clarie nodded, so desperately and submissively that it almost broke Martin's heart. It was not like his passionate, strong-headed girl to obey, to give in so readily.

"Tell her, keep telling her, how everything is going to be fine," Mme Stein ordered Martin in the gentlest of voices before leaving the room. He rasped out a thank-you, although what he really wanted to say was "Please don't leave. Not now. Not yet."

How long does it take to bring a child into the world? As the night lengthened into the dawn, and the dawn stretched out its fingers, releasing from its bountiful palette only the meager ashen blue of a wintry day, it seemed to take a lifetime. At least to Martin, who stayed by Clarie's side every moment, and to Giuseppe, who paced and sat and paced again in the tiny living room, pausing only to listen hard for every sound, to suffer with every moan, to pierce his heart with every cry.

But it was not a lifetime.

Not to Dr. Jean-Louis Pinot, whom the loyal Ernest Stein had tracked down at the hospital, delivering a sickly babe into the harsh realities of the city's charity ward. Because Stein's account of dire emergency had been so convincing, the good doctor did not even take off his bloody apron before rushing to the Martin apartment, where he was consigned to spend the entire night drowsily offering his assurances, and waiting.

Not to Esther Stein, who had borne two daughters of her own and kept busy, dividing her time between peeking in the bedroom to see if she was needed and keeping Giuseppe company.

Not to the widow Rose Campion, who was well past the age of childbearing and had two overgrown, ungrateful sons to show for it. After an hour's worry about her young mistress, during which she tossed and turned (insofar as one could toss and turn in the narrowest of beds, covered by the thinnest of blankets, in an ice-cold attic room), the Martins' day woman blessedly fell into that stupor which is the special gift granted to the overworked and careworn.

Not to Mme and Monsieur le juge Singer, who had been through it all three times before, and had happily given themselves over to a deep sleep after performing the act that would add one more child to their brood.

Not even to Madeleine Froment, who upon imbibing her third

spoonful of the opium-based *Elixir pour les femmes* (tranquility guaranteed) sank into her big goosefeather pillow, quite contentedly dead to the world.

What really mattered, of course, was whether it seemed like a lifetime to Clarie. Martin was sure it did, and that she was suffering a thousand times more than he. After all, he had only one small part to play: as Clarie's bulwark, her port in the storm, the voice of reason and hope, repeating a few stock, pious phrases over and over again. "Darling, it will be all right." "Dearest, it will be over soon." "My brave girl, you are doing so well." Until at last, the end of the ordeal approached, and he had to implore more than once, "Please, please, darling, try to do as the doctor said."

Not that Clarie heard him. She seemed to be obeying some ancient inner voice that drove her from one persona to another, beyond reason, sometimes beyond hope. From the piteous, suffering maiden praying for it to be over, to the silent, strong, brave woman; from the concerned mother, bemoaning the fact that her baby was coming too soon, to the fierce resister insisting "I can't, I can't do it." Until at last she could do it, and she lifted herself on her two strong arms, screwed her face into a mask of monumental effort and pain and, with the anguished, triumphant roar of a wounded Amazon, delivered Henri-Joseph Martin into the world.

Martin turned his head away as the blood-and-muck-covered creature slithered out of Clarie's body. He stared wordlessly as the tiny infant, whose outsized genitals boldly announced his sex, hung from Dr. Pinot's hands. He did not react to the first cry. He said nothing as the doctor held the baby against his chest, scrutinized him, then handed him to Esther Stein to wash in a basin of warm water. Martin did not reach out when his landlady brought his son, wrapped in a pure white towel, to Clarie. Martin's brain had gone mute, incapable of giving voice to the turbulent amalgam of repugnance and awe, fear and joy, humility and pride, storming through his entire being.

The women, on the other hand, responded as if everything that was happening lay well within the bounds of normal, human experience. Mme Stein smiled and kissed Clarie's damp brow. Smoothing away the wet curls of hair from Clarie's cheeks and forehead, their landlady murmured, "He's beautiful." And Clarie, in turn, ran her fingers over the strands of dark hair plastered to the baby's forehead, and unfolded the towel to examine his hands, and his feet, and the knot on his stomach. "Henri-Joseph Martin," she whispered, "you are perfect. But," her head shot up toward the doctor in alarm, "he's so tiny."

"He's not so tiny. My guess is he's a good three kilos, quite big enough," Dr. Pinot mumbled as he finally untied his bloody apron and wearily threw it on the floor. "Quite big enough," he repeated as he came by Clarie's side to watch as the infant jerked his arms and legs, and opened his empty little red mouth, gearing himself up for another squawking cry.

The unfamiliar, desperately anticipated little voice rang out more loudly than before, and soon they heard a light tapping on the bedroom door.

"That's your grandfather," Clarie said, speaking to the creature cradled in the crook of her arm. "Someone," she said to no one in particular, "tell Papa he can come see his grandson."

Numbly, Martin stumbled around the bed, stepping over the doctor's apron, and invited Giuseppe Falchetti in. Even the old man knew what to say.

"Oh, my sweet, brave girl, you did it. And," the new grandfather said as he admired his wriggling grandson, "he's beautiful just like you."

Martin leaned in closer. He wasn't sure who this big-nosed pink creature looked like or if he was beautiful or perfect. But it began to dawn upon him in a glow of joyful, radiant light: he had a son. This frail little thing *was* Henri-Joseph Martin. Suddenly, Martin laughed and bit his lip and laughed again. Finally, tears running down his cheeks, he kissed his wife and spoke: "Yes, if we have any luck at all, he will grow up to look exactly like you."

Rose arrived early the next day to take over the bedside watch from Martin. She clapped her hands with joy and relief when she heard the news and promised that she would make sure that Clarie got some rest. They didn't have to worry about Giuseppe. After building a fire, he had fallen into the nearest chair, where he still lay, head back, mouth agape, filling the living room with his rhythmic, resonant snores. Before he ventured out into the world, Martin covered his father-in-law with a coat and tiptoed into the bedroom for one last look at his beloved little family. Martin planned only to be gone long enough to send a telegram to his mother and to fulfill an important mission at the courthouse.

Amazingly, he was not at all weary. His limbs moved lightly and smoothly through the Place Stanislas, which had never seemed more beautiful despite the grayness of the day. He delighted in the smell of coffee emanating from the cafés. He loved the gold-topped gates, the cobblestones, the vendors, the passers-by. He loved everyone! *I am a father! Clarie is well!* He had a son. He felt like a king.

Didn't kings hold power over life and death? Wasn't a good king merciful, especially on the day when he was blessed with an heir? Today, Martin was that benign and merciful king. And for better or worse, he was about to pardon and release the grieving father and Jew-hater Pierre Thomas.

10
Sunday, November 25

CLARIE KNEW SOMETHING WAS WRONG. But she could not get anyone to listen. Sunday morning, and they were still insisting that what she needed was rest.

Clarie squeezed her eyes shut and pressed her lips together in an attempt not to start weeping again. She hated lying in her bed, in this perpetually darkened room, helpless, while the lot of them huddled in the living room and talked in hushed tones. If she didn't act so worried, maybe they would stop treating her like an invalid.

Yet how could she help herself? Little Henri-Joseph was not getting enough to eat, she was sure of it. She felt, and she did not know how she knew this, that the baby was not sucking hard enough, even though her breasts were hard and full and sore. When he did manage to get any of her milk, so much of it gurgled out of his sweet little mouth. And yet all they did, the whole pack of them—Bernard, Papa, Madeleine, Bernard's mother—was to tell her that everything was, really, all right. Frustrated, Clarie beat the covers with her fists. Confinement, that's what they called it, for good reason. Left alone, in a room, where every fetid smell, every tiny cry and gasp reminded her that she had never seen her little son smile or tug with voracious joy at her breast.

She pushed herself up on her side and looked down into the crib beside her bed. The baby was so rosy, like a ripe peach, as he lay there sleeping. She watched him breathe, steadily in and out. Except for one errant tiny arm that he had somehow wriggled free, he was covered by a blanket almost up to his neck. His head was protected by the blue woolen cap she had so lovingly knit for him. She reached over and maneuvered his arm, and his surprisingly warm little hand, under the soft woolen blanket. Then she sank back into the bank of pillows her father had fluffed up for her moments before. Oh, how she wanted to believe them. Babies cry, mothers worry. That's what they kept saying. Along with the eternally irritating "Try to get some rest, dear."

But she couldn't. If there was something wrong, it had to be *her* fault. She and the other teachers, and certainly everyone at Sèvres, scoffed at the books doctors wrote about women's "nature." But what if those doctors were right? What if ambition, intellect, and study sapped you of your womanly strength? What if, with all her learning, Clarie had lost some innate knowledge of the most important thing of all, how to be a mother? What if she was starving her baby? She had to do something. He began to cry again.

"Bernard!"

"Yes, dear. I heard him." The opened door brought light into the room and the sound of tinkling forks and spoons. They were eating breakfast. Bernard hurried around the bed and reached into the crib to pick up his son. She could not believe that her husband still had that silly smile on his face. She'd have thought the constant presence of his mother and Madeleine would have done him in by now, to say nothing of the sleepless nights he had spent walking the baby.

"I don't think he's hungry. His lips aren't moving. You can still rest. I'll carry him into the living room."

"No, wait." Her voice was pitiful, pleading, but she didn't care. "Wait."

"Yes, dear." His smile grew broader, as if to say "Anything for the tired, suffering mother of my child."

Clarie's fingers kneaded the covers in pure, hot anger. Yes, she was tired, but she was not mad nor suffering nor unreasonable. "You promised. The doctor."

Bernard swayed back and forth, trying to coax the baby into another sleep. "I promise, I'll get him. Tomorrow. First thing in the morning And I promise to ask him about hiring a wet nurse, even though my mother says—"

"What does your mother know!" Clarie didn't even care if her mother-in-law heard her this time. *What does she know. Or Madeleine, or Papa, or you!* What did they know? She began weeping again.

Bernard crooked the baby in one arm and sat down at the edge of the bed. "Tomorrow is Monday. I'm sure we could not get anyone before then. If that's the way you feel, then we must do it, I know we must. I know, my darling. Please don't worry so." He kissed her forehead as if she were a child, in the same way she saw him kissing Henri-Joseph's forever furrowed little brow. "First thing," he repeated. "First thing."

Henri-Joseph's cries began to subside. He was falling asleep again. Maybe that was good, Clarie told herself. After all, what did she know?

11

IT WAS A MOMENT OF rare quiet. Clarie and the baby were sleeping, Madeleine had taken Martin's mother to High Mass, and Giuseppe was sitting in the chair by the fireplace only half-awake, the newspaper hanging limply from his thick, callused hands. Martin tiptoed to the living-room window and was staring out, worrying about Clarie, when he caught sight of an unlikely threesome three stories below, in front of the Steins' shop.

He stretched his neck forward, squinting in disbelief. The man in the tophat was his colleague David Singer. Beside him, an elegantly dressed woman was engaged in an intense conversation with a shabby peddler, who stood holding on to the long extended arms of a wooden cart. In the middle of the cart was a stone wheel of the kind used for sharpening tools and scissors. Martin pulled back the heavy lace curtain and leaned to the side for a better view of the trio. The peddler's face was framed by a long, scraggly gray beard. He wore a tight-fitting cap without a rim and a long black coat that Martin could see had been patched over and over again. He did not look quite French. Was this one of those poor Jewish immigrants that Rocher had complained about? And how would Singer know him? Could it be that Israelites of all classes were on familiar terms with each other?

The one thing Martin did not want to believe was that Singer had come to see him. Such an unannounced visit would be too extraordinary, a sure sign that something was terribly wrong. During the last few tumultuous days, Martin had not thought about the courthouse. And if something had gone badly at the Palais, he certainly did not want to think about it now.

Suddenly Singer backed away from the other two; and when he did, the woman urged a package into his hands. Then she reached into a little sack hanging from her wrist, withdrew a coin, and placed it delicately on one of the wagon's handles. Singer quite abruptly turned and disappeared out of sight. Martin was sure that he had entered the building and was climbing the stairs. But he didn't know whether Singer intended to stop at the second floor to visit the Steins' apartment or was coming up another floor, to the Martins'. Troubled, Martin let go of the curtain. For a moment, he considered hurrying to the door and warding off the visit, if indeed Singer was coming to see him. Instead, he convinced himself, calmly and rationally, that his colleague was visiting the Steins. A tentative tapping on the door told him otherwise.

"I'll get it," Martin said, as he straightened out the curtain. He smoothed down his shirt, tucking it into his trousers, and went to the door.

It opened upon an abashed David Singer, gingerly holding up a large cake box wrapped in thin orange paper and crowned by a blue and silver bow.

"My wife," Singer said, as if that were enough to explain his presence, his red face, and the extravagantly adorned offering. It was almost comical enough to get Martin out of his bad humor.

"Come in, David. Pleased to see you," although Martin was far from pleased, and very perplexed.

"When she heard I was going to try to talk to you, she insisted on my bringing something for your family and your visitors." Singer lowered the cake to waist level and stepped into the foyer. "Oh, sorry, I don't know what's the matter with me. First I should say congratulations on your son. I. . . ."

Singer was not a man to countenance looking ridiculous for even a moment, which is why he kept trying to get Martin to take the cake box. Martin hoped that he was equally flustered by arriving unannounced.

"Come," Martin repeated and stepped aside. "I want you to meet my father-in-law."

Giuseppe had already risen from his chair, ready to offer his hand to the visitor. But the cake was still a barrier.

"Here, let me take that from you," Martin said. "I'll put it away."

As soon as Martin took the package from him, Singer gave out a sigh of relief and took off his black beaver tophat.

Martin carried the cake to the dining-room table and stood with his back to the living room, listening intently to the introductions for any ominous tones in Singer's voice. He placed his hand lightly on the box, to make sure it was steady. He was torn between apprehension and anger. No matter what had happened, Singer had no right to bring professional problems into his home, most of all not now.

Determined to keep his feelings to himself, Martin returned to the living room with a smile plastered across his face.

"Why didn't Mme Singer come with you? I'd like to thank her."

Singer scowled. "Oh, she came," he said, clenching his jaw. "She's still downstairs." After making a slight bow to Giuseppe, he shot a glance at Martin and gestured with this chin toward the window. "May I?" he asked.

"Of course." Martin hadn't dreamed that the mention of his wife would put Singer in a dark mood.

Singer pulled back the curtains, as Martin had done moments before.

Martin approached him. "What's wrong, David?" he asked quietly.

Singer swallowed hard and let the curtain go. "It's him. The tinker," he whispered. "The purveyor of old wives' tales and superstitions." When Singer turned away, Martin thought he heard his colleague mutter the word "Polaks."

"What did you say?" Martin asked in disbelief.

"That he's Polish or Russian, not French, not modern, not rational. He's the reason that so many people around here despise the Jews. Take a look. You'll see what I mean."

Martin peered out the window. Mme Singer was waving good-bye to the peddler as she headed toward the door. Suddenly, perhaps as a result of Singer's contempt, it occurred to Martin that the tinker was exactly the type of old-fashioned, traditional Jew that had inspired the dangerous fabrications of the wet nurse and Antoinette Thomas. Martin was certainly not about to voice this observation, or do anything else that might prolong this particular conversation. He desperately wanted to know the real reason for Singer's unprecedented arrival. So Martin merely shrugged. "He looks like a harmless old man to me. No different from other beggars and peddlers and water carriers you see on the street."

"Harmless?" Singer looked up at him. "Imagine if you had a fanatical priest visiting Mme Martin every week. This one comes to my kitchen and fills my wife's mind with fantasies of the way it used to be, when all the Israelites were supposedly happy and pious and poor. As if it were a good thing that we were forced to live in villages outside the city. As if it were a good thing that most of our grandfathers spent every week, like he does, wandering from town to town, selling cattle or pots or rags to Christian peasants." Singer closed his eyes and pursed his lips. "Sorry, that's not why I came. All this has nothing to do with you. It's just that I didn't expect him to crawl out of his hole on Sunday. Wherever his hole is," Singer added caustically.

Martin put a hand on Singer's shoulder. "Let's open the door for your wife."

"I'll do it." Although Giuseppe had not gotten far from the foyer, evidently he had heard everything. He went out to the head of the stairs to greet her. They heard his voice from the hallway. "You must be Madame Singer. I'm Clarie's father. And"—one could well imagine the pride swelling his chest— "Henri-Joseph's grandfather."

"Monsieur," a high, sweet voice responded, and its owner arrived at the door. Mme Singer was a very beautiful woman, perhaps made even more beautiful by the fact that her delicate oval face was flushed with some anticipated or recently experienced pleasure, for her hazel eyes glistened merrily as she entered the living room. Martin got the impression that she was also something of a fashion plate. She wore a crimson coat trimmed with a shiny sable fur collar and cuffs. Most of her thick chestnut-colored hair was hidden underneath a dark red velvet bonnet adorned with ebony feathers. If there was anything exotic, or Jewish, about her, like the slight upward slant of her eyes, it only added to her allure. She strode over to Martin with the confidence of a woman accustomed to wealth, station, and admiration. "Monsieur le juge Martin, David has told me so much about you. Congratulations on your son."

Martin reached for her black-gloved hand which, for just an instant, she hesitated to give to him. This barely perceptible gesture did not escape Singer. "This is how you act after five minutes with him," he bristled. "Martin is a modern man, not like your tinker. And you," he said pointedly, "are a modern *French*woman. You can touch each other." She let her hand drop to her side, and the glimmer in her eyes dimmed into a plea that her husband not ruin the occasion. Singer's angry reproof hung uncomfortably in the air, until Giuseppe offered to take "Madame's coat."

"No, that won't be necessary. I'm afraid we're intruding. We were just out for a stroll, and I thought—"

"The cake is lovely. Thank you," Martin intervened. At any other time, meeting Mme Singer might have been a pleasure. Not now. Not with Singer at his shoulder, waiting to tell him something.

Just then, they heard a thin cry from the bedroom.

"The baby," Mme Singer's face lit up again. "Your son."

"Noémie loves babies," Singer said, and this time he looked at his wife with pride and affection. "My Noémie is a wonderful mother."

"Then we'll see if Clarie and the little Prince are 'receiving,'" Giuseppe said, chuckling at his own mock pretentiousness as he scurried into the bedroom.

"Yes, you should meet Clarie and Henri-Joseph," Martin urged. He was bristling with anxious curiosity. He wanted Singer to himself.

"But we've intruded so much already," Noémie Singer demurred again, even as she bit her pretty scarlet lip and lowered her eyes.

"It would be a good idea." Hands behind his back, Singer bowed slightly toward his wife.

A second glance passed between them. This time it communicated the perfect understanding of husband and wife. David Singer had a professional duty to perform, and it was her role to find a way to let him do it.

The two men waited until she was beckoned into the bedroom before they began with the serious business. As if in accord, they returned to the window, which offered two advantages, being farther away from the bedroom door and giving them both, in the mounting tension, something to look at besides each other.

"I came to warn you."

"Of what?" Martin did not even try to hide his irritation.

"The possible consequences of your actions."

The nerve. *My actions.* What about Singer's actions, and Rocher's, and Didier's? Martin had thoroughly prepared himself for some grumbling about his release of the tanner, Pierre Thomas, who didn't have the money or the lawyer or the wit to get himself out of trouble.

"So I let Pierre Thomas go," Martin retorted. "I charged the wife with a *délit*, a misdemeanor, and left Didier to decide how long he wants to keep her in prison while I try to wring a confession out of her. I warned Thomas that if he repeats any vicious lies, I will prosecute him to the hilt. As far as I am concerned he is still an innocent man, and still mourning for his son."

"And *he* may also be a killer."

For a moment, Martin's mind went dead, silent, then his ears began to vibrate with a pulsating buzz. Could the fool have actually killed someone? Could this be a repetition of the nightmare he had lived in Aix-en-Provence, when he had had a murderer right before his eyes, and stupidly, tragically kept letting him off the hook? Martin leaned against the wall beside the window frame for support. Finally, he uttered, "Who would Thomas kill?"

"A mill owner, an Israelite."

Martin moistened his mouth with his tongue. "Why do you assume that Pierre Thomas did it?" Despite all his efforts, the buzzing in his head did not subside, and his chest was heaving as his breath got shorter and shorter. He stared into the room, away from Singer. He heard Singer's words as if they were disembodied, coming from an echo chamber. "The victim owned the mill where the Thomas woman worked."

Martin slumped, as his knees almost gave way. *This could not be. Not again.*

"But," Singer said, "we're not sure yet."

"Of what?" Martin whispered.

"That Victor Ullmann is dead—"

"Oh my God," Martin almost shouted, as he turned to Singer. "Then why did you come here?" he hissed. "Why did you—"

Clammy with fear, Martin welcomed the hot anger that shot through his body.

"Ullmann's missing. Reported by the maid on Friday. There's the slightest possibility that he went to Paris with his wife on a shopping trip, and he will arrive on the night train carrying her bags and hat boxes. But I doubt it. The maid insisted that he had stayed behind."

"Only missing since Friday?" Martin stepped around to Singer, forcing him back against the wall. He wanted to take his friend by the lapels of his elegant, expensive topcoat and shake him. "This Ullmann could be anywhere. With his wife gone, who knows where and with whom?" Martin prayed that Singer did not hear the desperation in his voice.

"No." Singer shook his head with maddening calm. "No. If he were here, he would have gone to the synagogue on Friday night. I know him. I know the family. He is a pillar of the community."

"That doesn't prove anything," Martin asserted as he stepped away, his hopes evaporating.

"He is one of our leaders, I tell you, a member of the Nancy Consistory. And if someone could kill him, they could kill any one of us." Singer's tone grew more agitated, as if he were taking the possibility of such a murder personally.

"If Ullmann is so important to you, then why don't you—" *What? Take the case back. Make up for my mistakes.* Martin had no defenses left.

"Didier was very clear," Singer said. "He told me it was your mess, and you are going to clean it up. He's furious. That's why I came. To warn you. You've got to see him as soon as possible tomorrow. We arrested Thomas late last night, and the police are looking for the body."

So Didier and Singer were already convinced that the man had been murdered, and that the killer was that drunken sot, Pierre Thomas.

"I'm sorry," Singer finally said. "I feel responsible for getting you into this."

The apology stopped Martin short, mollifying him. Of course,

Singer was no more responsible for what Martin had gotten into than the demonically clever Didier. Or that idiot Rocher, who had passed the case on to Singer as a cruel joke. Martin glanced at his friend who was staring at him, waiting for some response. He had no intention of ever telling Singer about his encounter with Rocher. He did not need to stir up the waters more. They were already roiling. In his chest. In his head. At the courthouse. Well, all of them could go to hell.

"I can't come in first thing tomorrow," Martin said, defiantly. "I've got to fetch the doctor for Clarie. I promised her."

"Get him today." Singer's voice was quiet, insistent.

"No, it's Sunday. It wouldn't be right. I'd only go if it were an emergency."

"No one cares about bothering me when it is my sabbath," Singer blurted out.

Martin was shocked that at this moment, this terrible moment, Singer had the nerve to be so sensitive about being an Israelite. Who cared when his sabbath was? Why couldn't he be like . . . Martin clenched his fists, pressing his nails into the palms of his hand, in an attempt to dam up the angry flow of his thoughts. He had always assumed that Singer *was* like everyone else. Like *him*, in fact. Now he was beginning not to know what to think.

"Bernard, listen. Maybe Ullmann is not dead. Or if he is, maybe someone else did it. But you've got to take charge. Your career depends upon it. And, perhaps, someone else's life."

Singer was imploring him, again. Not to take on the case this time, but to make Martin realize that he had no choice. At the very least Martin realized, his reputation at the courthouse depended on what he would do next.

Both of them were startled when Giuseppe came out of the bedroom. "They're talking. Your beautiful wife is giving Clarie some good advice," Giuseppe announced with a grin. "And you are watching the snow fall."

It was snowing. How could you stare out the window and not even notice the first scattered flakes of the season?

"We don't get enough of it in Arles. It makes everything new, don't you agree?"

"Yes, of course," Singer answered Martin's father-in-law. "New snow for new life. Although," he glanced out the window again, "it doesn't look like it's going to stick."

Having no interest in the weather or trying to be polite, Martin moved away from both of them just as Noémie Singer emerged from the bedroom. Martin thought he caught a look of alarm on her pale face, as she glanced at him before going up to her husband. "We must be going," she said to Singer, taking him by one hand, "dinner, the children." She took a big breath before turning to Martin. "You have a beautiful son and a lovely wife." Martin sensed something forced about this praise, something held back. It made him want to rush into the bedroom to see if Clarie and the baby were all right.

Instead, he stood rooted to the ground, watching as the lovely Mme Singer implored her husband with her eyes to follow. She had something to tell him, Martin was sure of it. Then as if in some slow silent waltz of perfect understanding, Singer looped his arm in hers and led her into the foyer. The ringing in Martin's ears grew louder. Could he be wrong about the baby too? Giuseppe and his mother had kept telling him that all new mothers worry, that all new babies cry all the time. Should he have been listening to Clarie instead?

For the next few moments, he felt as if he were pushing his way under water, desperately trying to emerge at a safe destination, at the very place where Noémie Singer smiled and cooed about his tiny son.

In the foyer he saw only the bowed heads of his guests. He swallowed hard and reached out to shake Singer's hand. "I think you were right," he said, keeping his voice steady, not wanting to alarm his father-in-law. "I will fetch the doctor tonight and come to the Palais first thing in the morning."

12

Monday, November 26

AT NINE O'CLOCK ON MONDAY morning, Martin marched into the courthouse, past the guard, past his chambers, straight to Didier's office. He did not want to deal with his ever-curious clerk. Nor did he have the slightest desire to talk to the esteemed Prosecutor of the Court at Nancy. But, of course, he had no choice. If Didier considered him a fool or an incompetent, all the better, Martin thought as he trudged up the stairs. Let him berate me. Let him try to demote me. Above all, let him reassign the case. For now, for the next few critical days, just let him leave me alone.

By the time Martin reached the second floor, he was gasping for air. He had spent the night desperately trying to get his tiny son to imbibe drops of water from the glass bottle contraption Dr. Pinot had brought them. Dehydration. Tiny Henri-Joseph was dehydrated. And infected. And jaundiced. Those were the words that Pinot kept repeating as he shook his head in bewilderment. He actually said that Martin's son could be "failing." Yet Martin knew this was impossible. Not in this day and age. Not his and Clarie's baby. They were strong. They were young. It simply could not be.

Before knocking on Didier's door, Martin pulled his scarf loose and tossed it, along with his bowler, onto the bench outside the prosecutor's office. He slowly unbuttoned his coat. His brain and mouth felt fuzzy and dry, as if webbed with cotton. He pressed his lips together, trying to moisten his tongue. To be speechless in front of Didier could spell disaster.

He tapped sharply, waited for a response, then stepped inside. As soon as he entered the grim green room, he sensed that something was amiss. His neck stiffened, setting his jaw on edge and his tired brain on alert. He had to move his head to look around the room, if only to loosen his taut nerves and to prove to himself that he could meet whatever dangers awaited him. His eyes roved first to Didier, who was standing up and observing him, then to the far side of the office where a fire roared. There, in an armchair across from the humble Roland's desk, was a heavily veiled woman, all in black. Having heard his entrance, she turned toward him and stood up.

"Ah, good. Monsieur le juge Martin, how fortunate that you have decided to come in this morning. I need to introduce you to the Widow Ullmann." After Didier delivered this bombshell in his most annoyingly arch tone, he lifted his long-fingered hand toward the small buxom woman, who bowed her head slightly acknowledging Martin's presence. His heart sank. So, they had found Victor Ullmann's body. This is what came from not nipping the libel against the Israelites in the bud. This is what came from Martin's foolhardiness.

Even as he absorbed the shock of a violent death and the role he might have played in it, Martin managed to return her bow and say, "Madame Ullmann, I am so sorry that we must meet under these circumstances." She did not respond. The only visible part of her not covered in black was the white handkerchief she was clutching in her right hand. Martin turned back to Didier, furious that the prosecutor had seen fit to ambush him in this most unseemly way.

Their eyes locked. "Monsieur le juge Martin," Didier explained in a loud voice, "will investigate your husband's tragic murder. And I am sure that he will take into utmost consideration your religious beliefs with regard to your husband's body and the burial. Won't you?" The prosecutor kept his piercing blue eyes on Martin's face while he spoke.

"Of course." What else could he say? The bastard Didier was carrying on as if he were in the courtroom, sadistically orchestrating the responses of the accused—in this case, the foolish, incompetent Martin—and enjoying every minute of it.

"Thank you," the little woman by the fireplace interjected, in a low raspy voice. When she lifted her veil to dab her eyes, Martin observed her gray hair, her red nose, and her despair. She was no longer the pampered, rich wife who had gone off to Paris to shop. She was a woman in full, sorrowful mourning. "He was such a good man," she whispered, "so observant. We must follow the laws." Her face collapsed around the handkerchief as she tried to suppress a whimpering sob.

Didier stared at Martin, waiting. "You have nothing to say?" he asked quietly.

Martin shot an angry glare at Didier before walking over to the widow. "I am very sorry about your husband, Madame Ullmann. I will do everything I can to bring his murderer to justice." Martin's body was tingling with a desire to flee. He didn't know which was worse, to be under Didier's malicious scrutiny, or to try to console a woman whose husband may have been killed because of his own mistakes.

"I've told Mme Ullmann," Didier said, with less obvious sarcasm in his voice, "that you will consult with Singer about appropriate Jewish burial practices and that the two of you will do everything you can to release the body as soon as possible. Therefore, if it seems like the most compassionate thing to do, perhaps you could plan to question Mme Ullmann in her home, later this morning, after things are arranged."

"Yes, of course," Martin answered as he helped the widow back into the chair. This is exactly what he would have done, with or without Didier breathing down his neck. Then again, Martin would have agreed to anything to get the torturous charade over with. At least he was beginning to understand the game. In front of the widow, in front of the world, everything should proceed in a normal fashion, with no hint that Martin might have let a killer out of jail, or had failed to get a full confession from a scheming, lying woman, or had never managed to uncover the reasons why her doltish husband would believe her in the first place. Above all, the courthouse must appear to be unified, efficient, and just. That was political. That was normal. But nothing felt normal. Not with Victor Ullmann dead, and Martin's own son "failing."

Didier shot a contemptuous glance at Martin as he walked past him to the widow. His long torso bent almost in half as he reached down to the little woman. "Mme Ullmann, if it is all right with you, I'll have my clerk take you to a police officer who will accompany you home."

"I have to send telegrams to my children." Mme Ullmann sniffled, trying hard to compose herself. "They must come immediately"

"Of course," Didier responded. Martin saw that, very much against his nature, the prosecutor was trying to be gentle. "Our officer will take you to the post office," Didier continued, "and to your home. And Monsieur le juge Martin will come to see you later this morning, if it is convenient."

"If it must be." She looked at Martin full in the face, scrutinizing him. Her cheeks were damp with tears, her mouth set against her grief with the innate dignity of a woman of status and breeding. A long marriage, grown children, even a family business: Martin could well imagine how many bonds between man and wife the killer had torn asunder.

Given the nod from Didier, the stooped white-haired Roland walked over to Mme Ullmann and helped her up. For just a moment her arms held on to his, as if she would fall back. Then, holding her head high and steady, she walked out of the room with Roland trailing behind her.

As soon as the door closed, Didier strode back to his chair, sat down and began drumming his finger against the desktop, waiting. Martin followed him at a pace which he hoped signaled neither fearful reluctance nor hurried obsequiousness, ending up in his usual position, at the front of the desk.

Didier leaned forward. "Now to you," he began quietly. "Why did you release Pierre Thomas?"

Hands clasped behind his back, chin jutting forward, Martin answered, "I did not think he was capable of violence." Then he added, mounting the only possible defense which might redeem his folly. "I presume that he has not confessed."

"No, not yet."

"And Jacquette—"

"Yes, he's been 'cooking' him, I can assure you. Yet Thomas keeps claiming his innocence, keeps repeating 'I did what the judge told me to do.'" Didier paused before asking, "Which was?"

"To keep to himself, not to repeat the lie about his son, not to get drunk, not to speak out against the Jews." Martin made sure his sigh was audible. *Let's get this over with.*

"Hmmmm." Didier leaned back in his chair. "And where have you been exactly?"

"I had no urgent business here. I had left Antoinette Thomas in the tender care of Jacquette, assuming that he would get her to confess. My wife delivered our son on Wednesday morning."

"Oh yes, of course," Didier pursed his lips, eager to dispense with the obligatory niceties. "Congratulations. I assume that Mme Martin and the child are doing well?"

"My son is very ill." As soon as the words came out of his mouth, Martin wanted to snatch them out of the air and bury them in secret place where no one would ever hear them again. To say them aloud made it real. *My son is very ill*, echoed in Martin's brain. He bowed his head to hide a grimace.

Didier took in a long breath. "I'm sorry to hear that. Usually these things pass, you know, with newborns. I am sure that Mme Martin has a maid or a relative, someone who can take care of this women's business."

"Yes." Martin's mother had put off her return to Lille. Rose had arrived early in the morning, and Madeleine would come right after school. If they were lucky, Dr. Pinot would be sending a healthy, healing, strong wet nurse. Martin's chest was quivering. This was not a conversation he wanted to have with the cold, cynical Didier, yet at the same time he longed for some indication that his colleague had an inkling of what he was going through.

"Well, then. Now to our business. You understand why I cannot hand this case over to Rocher."

Martin nodded. The moment had passed. Didier had already overspent his ration of sympathy.

"Or Singer," Didier added.

"No, I don't understand." Still stinging with the anger aroused by Didier's little ambush, Martin was in no mood to give in so easily. He desperately wanted to get back to Clarie and the baby. "Why not Singer? If I've already made such a mess of—"

"No, no, no." Didier waved one of his narrow fingers at Martin. "No. What would that say about our attitude toward the Israelites in our midst?"

"Singer's a good judge. He understands—"

"No!" Didier shouted. "I will tell you what that would say. That we, who are not of the Israelite race, do not care about the Jews. That the murder of a Jew is somehow their problem, not ours, not the

Republic's. While we, you and I and Singer, believe that in France everyone deserves equal justice."

A lovely speech, made less lovely by Didier's addendum: "There are many important Israelite families in our fair city. We do not want to alienate them. Nor do we want to encourage those who, because of their lack of republican values, scorn them. You and I know that there are red-hot embers, right below the surface, ready to burst into flames because of what is going on in Paris. We do not want to stoke them."

Dreyfus again. His mouth set in a grim line, Martin folded his arms and stared out the window behind Didier's desk. It was almost impossible to argue against a man who had a unique talent for wedding high principle to political calculation. Still, Martin was about to put up more of a resistance when Didier delivered the lowest blow of all.

"And surely you must see this as a way of saving your own skin. And perhaps, if you are lucky and Pierre Thomas is not guilty, making amends."

Martin blanched. Although at that very moment, he did not give a damn about his career, he knew that he might tomorrow, or the next day, or even the moment he left Didier's office. Silent acquiescence, as hard as that was to swallow, remained the only reasonable course of action.

"I've asked Singer to help you to understand the important community you will be dealing with," Didier said as picked up his pince-nez from atop a stack of papers and mounted it on his nose. He opened a file. "I expect a report by the end of the day tomorrow."

That was it! Dismissal. Oh no! He was not about to be treated like a servant or a child. Martin clamped both of his hands on the front edge of Didier's desk and leaned toward his tormentor. "Can you at least tell me what we know so far?"

With a sigh, Didier laid the papers aside. "Victor Ullmann's body was found late yesterday afternoon by a game warden in the woods just across the Meurthe."

By the river. A hot sweat burst over Martin's forehead. How close to Tomblaine? he wondered. But he did not ask. He was not about to invite another round of Didier's sarcastic recriminations. They both knew that if Ullmann had been killed near where the unfortunate little Marc-Antoine had been discarded, it made Pierre Thomas an even more likely suspect.

"Ullmann's horse was tethered to a pine tree several kilometers from his estate," Didier continued dryly. "That's what instigated the game warden's search. It seems Ullmann liked to ride for an hour after his daily visits to his office to look over the books. Last seen, therefore, Thursday at the factory, around four P.M. Cause of death, several blows to the head, the first of which probably threw him off the horse. Fauvet surmises that the weapon was a large tree branch, since he picked some splinters out of Ullmann's skull. Ground hardened by the cold, no signs of animal tracks, so we assume that he was attacked by someone on foot. I'm sure the details are in his report." Didier paused. "Anything else?"

By this time, their mutual desire to be rid of each other was so palpable that Martin was tempted to leave Didier's office without saying a word. Instead, he conceded: "I'll go to Singer immediately."

13

Martin grabbed his hat and scarf and headed down the hall to Singer's office. At least with David Singer he would be dealing with a human being. Oversensitive, perhaps; stiff, always; but human. Besides, Martin needed Singer's help. When he reached Singer's chambers and put up his hand to knock, he realized that it was shaking. He was shaking. He could not remember ever being so angry. He let his hand drop and took a few breaths, then he slowly turned the knob and opened the door. "David?" he inquired.

As soon as Singer saw him, he stood up at his desk and peered with concern into Martin's eyes. Singer knew, Martin was sure of it. Singer's wife had told him. There was something wrong with Martin's son.

Singer cleared his throat. "Monsieur Nisard," he said to his clerk, "Monsieur le juge Martin and I need to discuss something in private."

The tall, gray-bearded Nisard, whose age and professional demeanor lay somewhere between the old-style meekness of Didier's elderly Roland and the youthful presumptuousness of Martin's Charpentier, set aside the papers he was copying, nodded to both judges, and left.

"How is he?" Singer asked.

Martin shook his head. "I don't know."

"Sit, please."

There were three chairs lined up against the plain white wall across from Singer's desk. Martin sank into one of them. Singer came and sat beside him. He gently took Martin's scarf and hat away from him and set them on the empty chair. Martin stared into space. Singer's sympathy was harder to bear than Didier's indifference.

"I'm sorry. But we must hope for the best."

Martin hung his head and sighed. How ironic. Only moments ago, he had spoken words of consolation to the widow Ullmann. For her, all hope was gone. He squeezed his eyes closed. If only it would be different for little Henri-Joseph.

"And you just came from Didier."

Martin nodded.

"I'm sorry about that, too."

"You should be." The words slipped out before Martin could stop them. He turned to see how Singer was reacting to the involuntary rebuke.

One corner of Singer's mouth stretched into a bitter smile. "We've all been stung by him more than once."

This was firmer ground. A complicity of interest and principle between two like-minded judges. They didn't have to talk about Henri-Joseph. They could stick to "men's business." The courthouse, the case.

"You know," Singer said as he leaned forward and lifted himself out of the seat, "Didier is a good man. He's on our side. He wants to do the right thing. It's just that," Singer shook his head as he walked around his desk, "he can't stop being the prosecutor. It's in his blood."

"I thought you were angry at him for handing you the Thomas case."

"Yes. But when we talked last week, he admitted that he had made a mistake in originally giving it to Rocher. And then, this morning, he called me in to tell me about Ullmann and asked me to help you."

"You didn't want to take over?" Martin was stunned. He got up to face Singer. How much had been going on behind his back, while he was dealing with the birth of his son? He didn't know whether to feel betrayed or relieved.

"I agreed with him that you should keep the case," Singer said. "I can help behind the scenes, but it is better that in public we have a non-Israelite handling this. I trust you. And, for your sake, I hope to hell that Thomas didn't do it. But if he didn't, I know, in some ways, your job will be harder. Finding out who is inciting the anti-Israelites. Who. . . ." Singer paused. Martin could see his friend's mouth clamp shut in protest against uttering the words. Finally Singer continued. "Who would do this? Murder an innocent man just because he is a Jew. How is this possible in our day and age?"

As he listened and watched his friend, a wave of nausea overtook Martin. His mind and body protested against the turbulent sway of contradictory demands: Clarie, the baby, the courthouse, the idea that he, Bernard Martin, was to head an investigation with potentially explosive political consequences. Martin retreated a few steps and edged back into the chair, gripping its arms. What could he do? About Henri-Joseph, very little. About irrational, stupid hatred, probably even less. About a murder case—he looked up to see Singer waiting for a response—about friendship, at least something. Martin let go of the chair's arms. The only way to set himself aright was to move forward by doing what he did best: bring a killer to justice.

"We don't know yet, do we, how and why this happened?" Martin said. "But we'll find out." He sighed like a man facing an uphill journey without any notion of where and how high he would have to climb. He took the first, dutiful steps. "What can you tell me about Ullmann? And what do I need to know before talking to his widow?"

Singer slowly, patiently built a portrait of Victor Ullmann and why he was a leader of the Israelite community. It was not only the man's wealth, but also his philanthropy and his service. Ullmann had been elected twice to the Nancy Consistory, the body which administered Jewish affairs in the region and carried out the directives of the Central Consistory in Paris. Martin knew that these boards had been created by Napoleon at the beginning of the century to replace the traditional self-governance of Jewish communities and to tie Jewish citizens to the state, to make them French. That's all he knew. Singer seemed to admire the way the consistories had modernized religious education and made Jewish rites more dignified, all in line with Enlightenment principles.

Singer knew Ullmann only by his deeds and his attendance at the Temple, where he sat in the front row with the richest and most pious members of the community. Ullmann would expect and deserved that all the traditional religious laws be carried out: the washing by the burial society, being wrapped in a white shroud and his own prayer shawl, interment in a plain pine box as soon as possible; in Ullmann's case, as soon as his sons could be notified and reach the city.

"Evidently, Fauvet has completed his report," Singer concluded. "You could sign an order to release the body right away. That would demonstrate your respect of our laws, which might be helpful if you need to talk to more members of our community."

By the unemotional way in which Singer delivered this report, Martin suspected that he was not a very pious Jew. And yet he spoke as a member of his "community," whatever that was, and whomever it included. Singer said he had voted to elect Ullmann and he, at least occasionally, attended services. Martin could not even begin to fathom what being a Jew meant to his friend. Yet he was getting the sense that the colleague to whom he felt closest actually lived in a slightly hidden, different kind of France, a world apart, one he was about to enter.

14

IT WAS CRAZY. PURE SUPERSTITION. He had to interview Mme Ullmann as soon as possible, to fulfill his promise to her, and to sustain,
at least for a short time, the hope that he would uncover another
motive for the murder of the Jewish factory owner besides the
vengeful hatred of Pierre Thomas. Yet, despite all this, Martin felt an
even more urgent compulsion to go out of his way in order to pass
through the rue des Dom. Once he reached his block, he pushed
through a crowd of happy, chattering shoppers to the wall of the sta-
tioner's store across from his apartment and pressed himself against it.
He stood there, staring up at the windows on the third floor, searching
for a sign, any sign, of hope or disaster.

The dark green wooden shutters had been flung open and securely
hooked onto the white stucco wall. That was good, normal. Clarie

always insisted that they should try to capture every precious ray of morning light. Martin clutched his coat across his shivering chest as he scanned the windows to detect any fluttering of the heavy string lace curtains, any shadows moving behind them. But the glassed-in curtains hung resolutely still and mute, and Martin's longing to be with his wife and son overtook him with such keen force that for one insane instant he envisioned a spectral version of himself, crossing the street, unlocking the door and climbing the stairs. He blinked hard. He could not go home. If he did, he might never leave.

Holding down his bowler to protect his face from the swirling wind, Martin prodded himself onward toward the rue Saint-Georges, which cut across the width of the city and led past the canals to the river Meurthe. He jumped on the first horse tram that rolled by. Fortunately, since only three old women, hugging shopping bags from the market, sat on the one-car train, Martin did not have to worry about whether his appearance was appropriately professional or judicious. He could well imagine how haggard and scared he looked, caught as he was between two destinations each with its own surfeit of despair and desperation: his apartment, where Clarie lay with the tiny sick Henri-Joseph in her arms; and the Ullmann mansion, where the grieving widow awaited him. Standing by a pole, making sure his face was not on display to the sitting women, he watched impassively as the tram passed the mammoth eighteenth-century cathedral and the Saint Georges gate. Only the sight of the factories, workshops and abattoirs that lay beyond the dignified older sections of Nancy roused him from the blank grayness befogging his mind. Huddled near these big, stout buildings with their belching smokestacks were rows of dwellings, two and three stories high, leaning on each other for support. Houses inhabited by the likes of the wet nurse, the weaver, and the tanner. Homes crammed with the kind of people that Martin had always thought he would help.

Where had those ideals gone? Had they died with his youth? Or with Merckx, who had taught Martin hard lessons about injustice and exploitation? Merckx the anarchist, the army deserter, the closest friend who had always managed to get him in some kind of trouble until the final trouble, Merckx shot in the woods because . . . because Martin had not been decisive enough. Martin gripped the cold metal pole. Never again. He needed to be strong. For himself, for Singer, even for Clarie and little Henri-Joseph.

He glanced up as they passed the canals, built with great fanfare in the middle of century, links in a chain that extended for three hundred kilometers, connecting the river Marne to the Rhine. Built to encourage industry and commerce. Built for progress. Built, Martin also knew, to fill the pockets of the rich. But who were these wealthy men? And how many of them were Israelites? And who were the poor who were flooding the city, seeking work in the mills and factories? If Martin had been paying more attention, if he had been truer to his ideals, perhaps he would have understood the hatreds and resentments that could drive a man like Pierre Thomas to murder. If. . . .

A jolt brought Martin back to the present and the unhappy duty of confronting the Widow Ullmann. They had crossed a narrow branch of the Meurthe and were at the last stop, on a river island that formed the eastern boundary of the city. Martin stepped down, offered a helping hand to the remaining old woman, and then jumped out of the way while the conductor unbridled the broad-backed horse and walked it to the other side of the tram. Martin stood there for a moment, getting his bearings. Except for a large glass factory on his side of the tracks, most of the island was still thickly wooded. Across the way he spied the mansion, standing beyond a tree-lined path, on a rise above the narrow channel. Victor Ullmann had chosen to live in splendid isolation, yet near enough and high enough to watch over his factory. Near enough to see, but also to be seen. How many mill hands, Martin wondered as he began his ascent, would have resented the lordly pretensions of the Israelite's estate?

Martin panted as he walked up, using more effort than he should have, gulping air in his tense, taut chest. By the time he reached the house, Martin was out of breath and sweating, despite the cold. He paused at the door to pull himself together. No matter what was going on in his life, at least he knew how to do his job, what questions to ask, what tone of voice to take, how to make a compassionate, proper and expeditious exit. Fortified by these banal self-assurances, Martin took hold of the shiny brass handle in the middle of the thick polished mahogany door and knocked hard several times.

The first person who greeted him was a maid, wearing the kind of uniform—the black dress, white apron and white cap—that befitted a wealthy, confident household. She invited him in and took his hat. The second person Martin encountered as he entered the great hallway came as a surprise.

At first glance, Martin would have sworn that the portly middle-aged man was a well-fed priest. He had on a long heavy black cassock with small cloth-covered buttons running down the center, a wide black silk belt, and a small rectangle of white linen running from his circular collar to the midpoint of his chest. Behind him, near the staircase, on an end table where the maid had put Martin's bowler, lay a black felt oblong hat, a style nicknamed "the boat," the kind usually worn only by Catholic clergymen. But this could not be a priest, not in the Ullmann household.

The man held out his hand. "I am Isaac Bloch, the Grand Rabbi of Nancy."

Still confused, Martin shook the man's hand and introduced himself as "Monsieur le juge Martin."

The rabbi stepped back and scrutinized Martin. "You are surprised? You expected someone with a top hat and a long beard?"

"No, of course not." Martin also retreated a step. The truth, of which the rabbi seemed fully aware, was that Martin had had no idea what to expect. The pince-nez, the thick mustache and the goatee gave the rabbi a modern, almost rakish look. But he exuded an authority, a learning, a sense of his own worth that was far beyond that of an ordinary clergyman. He spoke to Martin, a judge, as an equal.

"I am here to comfort Mme Ullmann. I assume you will allow me to stand by her while you talk. Then we must arrange for the burial. Victor Ullmann was an important member of our community."

That word again. Community. Although it was certainly not his preference, Martin realized that he'd have to give in to the presence of the Grand Rabbi during his interview with the widow. Perhaps, in turn, he could get something out of him. "May I ask," Martin said, "what community you're speaking of?"

The rabbi paused as if weighing the question—and the questioner —as well as his answer. Finally, he spread out his hands and explained, "As a great industrialist Victor Ullmann was important to all of Nancy, of course. But I was thinking of our religious community. The rites we must carry out, the funeral procession. For us, he was a truly righteous man, a leader who served our people."

"You served with him on the Consistory?" Martin confirmed, hoping that the rabbi would reveal something about the way Victor Ullmann had dealt with his peers.

"Yes, yes. For four years. Fine man. Devoted."

This told Martin nothing. Before he could probe more deeply, the double doors leading to a salon burst open, and the maid and another woman hurried in carrying big blocks of black cloth. Without saying a word, they began to cover the portraits and mirrors that decorated the hallway.

"You see, it has begun," said the rabbi in a solemn voice, "the mourning. It is imperative that you settle your business with Mme Ullmann as soon as possible. Then she will enter into a period of seven days when she will see no outsiders."

"No one?" Was the poor woman going to be totally left on her own?

"No one but family and the members of our *community*," Bloch said, with the slightest glimmer of amusement in his gray eyes. As the chief representative of the Israelites in Nancy, he was undoubtedly accustomed to dealing with the ignorance of outsiders. "Come." The rabbi placed his hand on Martin's shoulders. "Let's get this over with."

Bloch guided Martin into the salon where the Widow Ullmann sat almost lost in a large armchair. As soon as she noticed the two of them, she put her hands on the arms of the chair and struggled to her feet.

"Monsieur le juge." She no longer wore the veil. Yet her eyes and nose were so swollen and red that Martin could not tell whether she was, or ever had been, pretty or sprightly or charming. He only knew she was middle-aged and grief-stricken. And that she was very wealthy.

"Please." The rabbi went over to her. "Sit for now." He gently lowered her into the chair.

Martin slumped toward the sofa and sat down. He hated what he had to do. If Didier and the widow hadn't insisted that he come immediately, he would have put it off. In the face of her raw emotions, taking a notebook out of his pocket to record her answers felt like a insult. *The very best thing you can do for everyone involved*, he goaded himself, *is to get it over with and get out*. "This won't take long," he murmured. "Just a few questions."

She folded her hands, staring at him, waiting. Rabbi Bloch did not move from her side.

"Can you tell me," he said softly, "everything you know about your husband's disappearance?"

A grim line worked its way across Mme Ullmann's mouth. "I've already told everything to Monsieur Didier."

"Is this necessary?" Just as Martin had feared, the rabbi was interfering, protecting her.

"I must," he insisted, feeling more and more like an intruder.

So she repeated the tale that Didier had told him. She had left for Paris early on Thursday. Ullmann always spent part of the day going over the books at the mill. He liked to ride in the late afternoon. She stayed in Paris Friday night to spend shabbat with her cousins. They urged her to stay a second day, which is why she waited until Sunday afternoon to take the train home. "I should have been here," she cried before sobbing into a white lace handkerchief.

"There was nothing you could have done," Martin said, trying to soothe her pain.

This brought a nod from Rabbi Bloch. Approval. Approval that Martin was demonstrating the appropriate degree of delicacy and compassion.

"No one wired me," she continued after wiping her face and blowing her nose. "My housekeeper told me she had gone to the police when Victor did not come home on Saturday night. She always comes in the morning. At first she had assumed that he was away on business Friday and had taken shabbat dinner with friends. Sometimes he stays on if he goes out of town. But when he did not come home by Saturday night and his horse was not in the stable. . . . She said she didn't want to worry me. After all," Mme Ullmann's voice cracked again, "what could I have done?"

"Yes, of course," Martin said encouragingly and waited for her to go on.

"I was frantic. I couldn't imagine what had happened. I wanted to go to the police. Mme Franc—my housekeeper—persuaded me to wait until morning. And by that time they had found my dear Victor, left to die in the cold and wet." The widow closed her eyes and breathed in hard. "I saw the body and called Rabbi Bloch, so that he could send the men to the morgue."

"It is our custom," the rabbi intervened, "to prepare the body for burial and dress it according to our faith. We have certain men from the synagogue who do this."

"Were these men intimate friends of Monsieur Ullmann?" Martin asked, ready to take down their names.

"No," again it was the rabbi, "they are always the same men who dress the dead, members of a *Hevra*, formed for this very purpose, that one get the proper Jewish burial."

Martin usually found any interference irritating. Not this time. He was fully aware that the rabbi was not only protecting the grieving widow from having to answer useless questions, he was also protecting Martin from asking them.

Martin rubbed a trembling hand across his moistened beard. The worst was coming. "Madame Ullmann," he began, "can you imagine anyone in your acquaintance who bore a grudge against your husband, enough to want to do him harm?"

Her body went stiff and her black eyes burned with fury. "No!"

"Perhaps," Martin prodded, "there was trouble in the business, or at the mill. Relationships with the workers."

"No!"

As her resolve hardened, Martin felt his hope fading that he would soon identify a suspect other than the tanner Thomas. Still, Martin went on. "Your husband was an important man, a rich man. Such men are often envied, even hated." He was thinking of his own walk up the hill to the crest and how the Ullmann house must look from the factory across the Meurthe.

"No!" This time she rose to her feet without faltering. "No, I say. What are *you* trying to say?"

"This is a murder investigation." How many times had Martin said this in his career, always attempting to calibrate the timbre of his voice to the needs of the moment, the sex of the witness, her status, and her emotional state? He immediately feared he had sounded too docile, for the tiny, angry woman approached him with fists clenched.

"My husband was a good man, a kind man. Because of the Germans he had to build his fortune twice. His grandfather and father traded horses and cattle, but when he was growing up the rabbis told him that trading was not 'useful,' that we Israelites must learn to be French, to speak French, to *produce* something. So he did. He became a Frenchman, a citizen, a philanthropist, and you say he had enemies?"

"Léonine, the judge is only doing is job."

She swirled around with unexpected force. "Then he doesn't know his job," she said to Rabbi Bloch. As she turned back to Martin, she no longer seemed diminutive or fragile.

"At this moment someone is holding my husband's cold feet and asking for forgiveness for any wrongs they may have done to him during his lifetime. Someone is closing his eyes. That should be his own eldest son. But it cannot be, because my husband died in a frozen woods, not, as he should have, at peace, in his own bed, with his children gathered around him helping him into the next world. We don't even know if he had the time to say the prayer to his God declaring his faith. We know nothing. And that is because someone murdered him and left him there, alone, while we were," she closed her eyes and began swaying back and forth, "while all of us were far away."

"I am so sorry," Martin said as he rose to his feet. The rabbi had already come behind her and was holding on to her shoulders, so that she would not fall.

She righted herself and pressed her two hands on her heart, as if to suppress a sharp pain. A pain communicated so nakedly to Martin that he had to look away so no one would see the fear and grief written on his face. *My son*, he thought, *who will be to blame if he dies?*

"Look at me!"

Martin forced himself to face her.

"Look at me," she repeated. "I know what you see, what you think you see. A frivolous woman, arriving from Paris with her striped hat boxes and frilly dresses. A spoiled woman." She stretched out her arms. "Do you want to know why? Because," she said almost in a whisper, "because Victor always protected me, spoiled me since I was practically a child. But now," she let her arms fall to her side and drew herself up to her full height, "that woman no longer exists. As soon as my sons arrive, we will bury my husband. I will follow him on foot to the grave. I will pour dirt upon his body. And when I return, all this," her eyes scanned the room, "all this will be black. I will sit on a low wooden stool for a week. I will eat hard eggs and drink water. I will wear a veil to cover my face and tear my dress to show my grief. But that will be nothing. The hard stool, the fast. That will not begin to express what is happening here," she pounded her chest, "in my heart. I will no longer be a beloved wife. Inside of me there will be an emptiness and a howling, a cry that will never, never end."

A howling, an emptiness. Martin wanted to sink back into the sofa, but he stood still, receiving the punishment he might well deserve. Neither the widow nor the rabbi yet knew about Pierre Thomas.

"Find my husband's murderer, Monsieur Martin, that's all I ask of you."

She turned and with a glance at Rabbi Bloch sat down again. All three of them knew the interview was over.

Martin's knees wobbled a little as he bent down toward the widow and bid his goodbye.

"I will see you out," the rabbi said as he followed Martin through the salon doors. After Bloch closed the doors behind them, he came up to Martin. "You can call on me if there is anything I can do to help," the rabbi said quietly. "I, too, want you to find Victor's killer."

"Yes, of course." Martin kept his head down. It had been a truly amateur performance from a presumably experienced judge.

"You can always find me at the synagogue, and perhaps I can help you with the community," the rabbi continued.

With the turbulent storm of Léonine Ullmann's emotions muffled and closed behind the salon doors, Martin was getting his wits back. "One thing," he asked the calm, compassionate clergyman: "will I be able to see the housekeeper before the seven days are up?"

"Yes, I'll see to it. I'll send her to you," Bloch said as he picked up Martin's bowler and gave it to him.

This time there was no confusion as Martin took the rabbi's hand and shook it warmly. Only gratitude and renewed determination. He was going to haul the tanner and the brazen Antoinette Thomas into his chambers, confront the brute with his wife's lies, and get both of them to confess their sins. He was going to find the killer.

15

AS SOON AS MARTIN OPENED the door to his chambers, he encountered the wispy gray tendrils and acrid aroma of Jacquette's beloved Blue Jockeys. Evidently Martin's inspector, who jumped up to greet him, had been waiting for a long time.

As Martin grasped the inspector's hand, he realized that nothing could have been more comforting at that moment than Jacquette, his cigarettes, and that deceptively lugubrious face. For the fact was, the forty-year-old inspector was anything but mournful, although his physiognomy—the long nose coming to a rather bulbous end punctuated by a thick tawny brush of a mustache—had, indeed, helped earn him the nickname "the hound dog." Martin knew from happy experience that this stationhouse sobriquet was also a tribute to the inspector's tenacity and investigative skills. He was every bit a cop in love with his work. The chin was always slightly grizzled, a seeming requirement of the job, and his features fittingly mobile. Martin had often observed with pleasure the way the bushy eyebrows above Jacquette's dark brown eyes arched in amazement or glowered with anger, depending upon what he hoped to get out of his prey. Yet Martin knew him to be essentially unfazed by stupidity, venality, cruelty, or gore. Jacquette credited this sangfroid to his peasant stock, firmly rooted in the soil of Lorraine—"all that dirt, shit, blood, and the squealing of pigs at the slaughter," he explained to Martin more than once. Yet he also admitted to being one generation removed from the country, and was as sophisticated an investigator as any judge could want by his side.

Martin had gotten himself into a mess, but, at least, he was not alone. The two men sat down and agreed upon a tried-and-true strategy. Jacquette would continue to press Antoinette Thomas to confess everything, while Martin had his way with the husband. Then they would bring them together and pit them against each other.

Two hours later, despite his questions, threats and specious offers of mercy, Martin had not gotten very far. Pierre Thomas was quite willing to own up to any number of sins, including the drinking and brawling that was par for the course where he came from. But he was not ready to confess to murder, to talk about his political beliefs (if, indeed, he had any), or to admit that he knew his wife had told a vicious, dangerous lie. It was time to send Charpentier to fetch Jacquette.

When the clerk returned, he headed straight for his desk with his nose in the air and his hands folded over his waist as if avoiding contamination. This was the irritating attitude that the fastidious Charpentier always took on when they were dealing with what he called "the lower orders." The stalwart Jacquette, who feared neither man nor contamination, soon followed, dragging a resisting and cursing Antoinette Thomas by the arm. "Sit and keep your mouth shut," the stocky inspector barked as he shoved her into a chair opposite her husband. For once she complied, crossing her arms defiantly. Even in relative stillness, she crackled with energy as she glared across Martin's wide desk at him, before shooting a contemptuous look at her husband.

"Why is she here?" Thomas asked, alarmed.

"To tell you the truth about your son. To make you see how useless your denials are." Martin softened his voice. "To make it easier for you to confess and get it over with. If you do, the judges might offer you clemency instead of the guillotine."

"I told you," the tanner shouted and leaped out of his chair toward Martin, "I did not kill anyone!"

"Your lovely wife has told me everything," Jacquette mumbled under his tawny mustache as he pushed Thomas back down in his seat. The inspector gave a nod of confirmation to Martin.

So Jacquette finally got it out of her, Martin thought. *This may be it.* He kept his demeanor stern and impassive, despite the turbulent crosscurrents of emotions swirling inside of him. It was Martin's duty to salvage some measure of justice for the Ullmann family. Yet what he should fear more than anything else is that Pierre Thomas confess to the murder. If he did, Martin would be implicated in the death of an innocent man because he had foolishly released the volatile tanner from prison. It could mean the end of his career. But then, every minute he spent with the lumbering tanner was a painful reminder of something else, what they had in common: a little son, ill or injured beyond anything a desperate father could do. If it ended now, today, perhaps Martin would be released too, to be in that other place that duty called. By his infant son. By his wife. The tension in his body was so keen that he realized he had bent his pen almost in two. Without moving a muscle in his face, he opened his hand and let it go.

"There's nothing to tell!" the miserable tanner insisted, breaking the silence.

"Ah," Jacquette gave Martin a crooked smile as he leaned over and, with his mouth close to Thomas's ear, spoke in a stage whisper meant to be heard by everyone in the room. "She told me how she found your son stone cold in the wet nurse's cottage, how she was afraid you would blame her for not taking care of him, how she plotted with the feeble-minded Geneviève Philipon to make up some story about a Jew." Jacquette paused before building to the climax. "Finally, how she took her own baby to the river bank, opened him up, and gutted him."

"No, she didn't," Thomas dumbly, stubbornly persisted.

Jacquette straightened up. "Ask her. And after you do, Monsieur Charpentier writing at his desk over there will take everything down and put it nice and neat in your dossier," the inspector said as he raised his index finger right in front of Thomas's nose and pointed in the direction of Martin's clerk. "And then," he continued, "the whole world will see that you are not only a murderer, but a fool who believes old wives' tales about fairies and witches and wandering Jews."

Martin held his breath as he observed Jacquette's well-orchestrated provocation. Martin's fate was as much on the line as Thomas's.

"It can't be. She wouldn't." The brawny blond tanner grasped the sides of his chair like a man ready to endure the most exquisite tortures without giving in.

"Did you hear what my inspector just said?" Martin asked, playing the role of the reasonable inquisitor. "The game is up. You've just heard that Mme Thomas has told us everything. So did the wet nurse. Now it is time for you—"

"Why did you do that?" Ignoring Martin, Thomas turned to his wife as his face collapsed into a grimace. "I would have never told on you. Never."

"Oh yes, after you beat it out of me, do you think I was going to let him do it too?" Antoinette Thomas leaned toward her husband as if she were about to spit on him. Jacquette grabbed her shoulder and set her back in the chair. As she twisted out of his grasp, the mass of wild brown curls swirled around her handsome, insolent face. For an instant, Martin imagined them slithering and hissing like Medusa's snakes. When she was through shaking off the inspector, she took on the judge. "You've got it all wrong if you think he killed Ullmann," she told Martin scornfully. "He ain't no murderer. He's too much of a coward. And who cares about that dirty old Jew anyway?"

For the first time, as her mouth turned down in hateful distaste, Martin saw how this seductive woman would grow into an ugly, bitter old harridan. Would Thomas still love and try to protect her then? Martin doubted it. Besides, by that time she would have eaten him alive.

"I didn't really beat her," Thomas explained to Martin, imploring him to understand. "I'd never hurt her. Maybe a slap or two and some yelling. But she hits me back. That's the way we are."

"Of course, I gave back what I got. You fool." Antoinette Thomas's lower lip stuck out as she scornfully turned away from husband.

"Toinie, Toinie," the big oaf pleaded with his wife, begging her to look at him.

"Stop it!" Martin shouted, disgusted with both of them. Then, catching himself, continued in a calmer tone, hoping that reason would finally bring the tanner around. "Monsieur Thomas, it is time to be a man and accept the terrible tragic mistake you have made. You killed an innocent man because you believed an Israelite murdered your child. You were," and for just an instant Martin's voice cracked as he mouthed the words, "a man maddened by shock and grief." Martin recovered himself and asserted for the hundredth time that afternoon that the court would understand and have mercy on a grieving father.

"Why are you blaming me? I didn't kill nobody. You don't understand what this has done to me. Seeing my little boy like that, all cut up." The distraught tanner stretched his two powerful hands toward Martin, pleading for him to understand. "A son. Someone who would look up to me. A little boy to show off to my comrades. A son to teach my trade to. Gone like that. My baby, dead." He dropped his arms, bowed his head and broke into loud, inconsolable sobbing.

The lies, the shouting, the stupidity. The possibility that Martin had made a fatal mistake. All that was bearable. But not this full-blown grief shaking a grown man to his very core. At first a protective numbness spread over Martin as he watched Thomas break down. Then he realized that the dull, anesthetizing tingling would soon dissipate and the pain would seep through, for, unbeknownst to everyone else in the room, he understood only too well what Thomas was going through. Martin pushed himself away from his desk. "That's all for now." A judge should show no weakness, no emotion.

Jacquette lifted his bushy eyebrows in surprise. The job was not done.

"Take him back to his cell. Do what you want with him." Martin waved his arm, pointing to the door. He had to gesture dramatically. It was beyond him to sound stern and righteous when all he wanted to do was to bury his head in his hands and block out everything he had seen that day and everything he feared to see that night.

"Yes sir." Jacquette was a good man. Loyal, smart, able to pick up on signals. *Thank God for that*, Martin thought. His clerk was a different story. That's why Martin had no intention of offering any explanations before rushing out of the courthouse to be with his own wife and son.

Only one ray of light greeted Martin as he entered the foyer of his apartment. He followed its narrowing path to the little dining room where the gas lamp, which hung over the round dining table, shone upon Martin's mother and father-in-law holding each other's hands and talking softly. At any other time, Martin would have found this scene, and the possibility that his snobbish, pious mother was succumbing to the charms of the burly blacksmith, heartwarming. Now seeing them in a tête-a-tête sent a wave of fear down to his belly.

"What has happened?"

Giuseppe got up and put his finger over his lips, signaling that

Martin should be quieter. "Nothing," he whispered. "The doctor is with Clarie and Henri-Joseph. They want to see you. First, though," he said as he squeezed between the wall and Martin's mother, "let me take your hat and coat."

Martin peered at his mother who was smothering her nose with an embroidered handkerchief. Her sniffling spoke louder than any of Giuseppe's words. Without taking his eyes off her, Martin let his father-in-law reach up and slip his coat down from his arms.

"Is there anything I should know?" Martin insisted.

"Clarie will tell you." His mother's blue eyes seemed to be imploring him to be patient and strong.

If only I loved this woman as much as a son should, Martin thought. Sadly, because of Henri-Joseph, he was beginning to understand some of the sorrows he had caused her. He laid his hand briefly on her shoulder, thanking her as best he could.

"We sent Rose home. She was exhausted. So Mme Martin and I plan to cook up a big fat omelet together, don't we?" Giuseppe said with false cheer. Adele Martin nodded as she bent her face into her handkerchief again. Only then did Martin notice that the table was not set for supper as usual. He could not fathom what his mother and father-in-law were conspiring about, besides providing him and Clarie with a comforting meal. Martin shook himself. What did he care about eating? His world was waiting for him in the bedroom.

As soon as he opened the door, he was assaulted by the effluvia of sickness and sour milk, and the sharp, vinegary scent of faithful Rose's efforts to scour and wash it all away. Dr. Pinot, in shirtsleeves and suspenders, sat reading the newspaper in one of the dining-room chairs that had been commandeered for the bedroom. He stood up to greet Martin. "We've been waiting for you," he said, like a man who had many other matters to attend to.

"I'm sorry. It's the case. The murder of an important man." Martin was in no mood to apologize to the doctor, a supposed friend, that somehow he held to blame for the illness of his son, even though he knew it was irrational.

"Martin?" Clarie's voice was weak. She lay, as he had left her in the morning, lifted up by the pillows, with Henri-Joseph in the crook of her arm.

Martin hurried to her side of the bed, sat down in a chair, and kissed her hand. It was to her that Martin owed all his apologies. And the explanation he daren't make: that in a case fraught with political danger, he had acted with a foolishness that might have had murderous consequences.

He touched her cheek. It was very warm. Someone had plaited Clarie's thick dark hair into a single braid, which peeked over her shoulder. Perhaps because of the shadows of fatigue that surrounded them, her eyes seemed unnaturally bright. "Bernard," she said, "I let them take Henri-Joseph."

Her words took Martin aback. "But darling, he's not gone," he said with alarm. "He's still here." Martin opened the blue blanket and examined his son. It took a superhuman effort to keep from gasping. It was like seeing Marc-Antoine Thomas for the second time. His son, who had come ruddy and screaming out of the womb, had faded and shrunk into the yellowish pallor of a wizened old man. Henri-Joseph's life force was all too evidently draining out of his weak little body. Was his wife also going mad? Martin smiled at her, in a feeble attempt to mask his growing dread.

And, almost miraculously, she smiled back and reached to shake his arm. "I know that. I know he's here, silly."

A little joke, almost bringing Martin to tears.

"I just don't want you to be angry with me. My father said it would be all right."

"What, darling? Tell me. I'm sure it was fine." Martin glanced up at the doctor who stood by, waiting to have his say.

"Madeleine and your mother convinced me that Henri-Joseph

should be baptized. That he was healthy enough to go to the cathedral." She raced on as if to forestall any questions or objections. "Papa said he would make sure that Henri-Joseph would be nice and warm. That not a flake of snow or drop of rain would touch him even in a storm. You know Papa's arms. So strong. So warm. So I let them take him."

Martin kept on smiling and holding Clarie's hand, although a flush of angry heat was rising up his face as he imagined what had gone into that little drama: Madeleine and his mother conspiring with each other to thwart Martin's will, talking about him as if his doubts about the Church were some kind of blind fanaticism, when of course he would have allowed his son to be baptized. He didn't hate God or true men of faith: he only hated authoritarian bigots, the kind that had brought him up and produced narrow-minded men and women like his own mother.

"Why should I be angry?" he asked. "It must have been safe. The cathedral is just around the corner." The smile was so firmly and falsely plastered on his face that he was sure she would see through it straight to his soul, as she always did.

"You know, sometimes you talk about the Church and the Republic and how they are against each other—"

He pressed her hand harder, trying to find the words to show that nothing she could do at this moment would upset him. They came to him in a flash of inspiration. "Clarie, when we first met, you told me that although your father was 'the biggest Red' in all of Arles, he sometimes liked to carry the holy statues in procession. You said that your father was big enough and generous enough to fight for the workers and love God at the same time. And," Martin continued, riding on the wave of this memory, "that his God was big enough to want justice for the workers too."

She nodded and smiled, remembering that happier time, in Aix-en-Provence, when she had spoken so proudly of her beloved father. She moved her own child closer to her breast.

"I know I'm not as big a man as your father. Yet," he added with sudden insight, "when I get older and wiser, I hope to be like him, a man of many worlds."

"You're not jealous of Papa, are you?" Even now, with her dying baby in her arms, she saw through him enough to tease him.

"Of course not," although, in truth, he was a little. More than anything except the life of his son, he wanted Clarie to admire him above all men.

Henri-Joseph gave out a weak little cry. Martin watched as his fingers wriggled with pathetic slowness.

"Here, here." Clarie placed her son on her chest and patted him on his back before turning to Martin, smiling. "You're every bit as good as Papa, and Henri-Joseph will be, too. Won't you?" she said to the top of her baby's head, then kissed the little wool blue cap that covered it.

"Of course he will," Martin said, although he was afraid that Clarie would see through this lie. Gazing at the inert tiny fingers splayed across his wife's breast, he knew. And he realized what he had hated most about the "secret baptism" was not the scheming—or the idiotic assumption that he would not have been willing to baptize his son into the Church—it was that Madeleine and his mother and Giuseppe Falchetti knew too. There was very little time.

Martin's mouth had gone completely dry. He could find no other words of comfort for his wife. He looked up at Dr. Pinot, who had put on his jacket and was motioning with his head that they had to talk.

Martin got up, kissed Clarie on her forehead and lightly rubbed his baby's back. It was very warm. Soon, Martin wondered, as chill ran down his spine, will it be very cold? "I think Dr. Pinot has to leave," he whispered to Clarie, "so let me show him to the door. I'll be right back." By this time, he thought the smile would crack his face open and all his falsehoods would come tumbling out. But Clarie's attention had once again turned to the baby. She was rocking him slowly on her chest, kissing the top of his head, trying, without being aware, to bring him to life.

With a nod from Martin, the two men left the room and hurried to the foyer. Pinot put on his coat, scarf and hat in silence before indicating that they should go out in the hall, away from everyone else in the apartment.

As soon as they closed the door, Martin asked, "Where is the wet nurse? I thought you were going to——"

Pinot grabbed his arm. "It's an infection. Something in the blood, coursing through his body. The wet nurse wouldn't have helped. It's over. You know that."

Martin wanted to argue, to deny, to plead. But he could not find the strength. "Yes," he finally said. "I know." He swallowed hard and waited.

"What you have to worry about is your wife."

"She seemed fine," Martin said in desperate hope.

"No, no." Pinot shook his head. "The maid told me that when they took the child to be baptized, she kept calling for him, wanting him near her."

"I suppose that's natural. She wants to hold him, feed him——"

"No!" Pinot took hold of both of Martin's arms. "You have to understand what is happening to her, in her body, in her mind. Childbirth is a shock to the female system. Her fluids are rushing through her, blurring her thinking, perhaps at this time even protecting her from reality. But when reality hits, she may go a little mad. I'll do what I can. But you may have to look for some other help."

"No, no." Martin backed up against the wall as tears began to flow from his eyes.

"That is what she does not need. Your tears. You must be strong."

"Of course." Did Pinot think that he would burden his wife with his own weeping?

"All right, then, listen to me." Pinot waited until Martin had straightened up and was staring into his eyes. "Tonight will be the night. I've left a bottle of laudanum on the nightstand. Make sure she drinks two spoonfuls. Then you must get the baby out of her arms. And when it happens, you must remove the baby and all his things as soon as possible." Pinot reached inside his pocket and handed Martin a card. "Here. I've worked with Monsieur Girard before. He can arrange a quick burial. And after that, all your attention must go to your wife."

Martin took the card. "Gustave Girard. Funeral Arrangements," it read in plain black letters. He wanted to tear the card into pieces and throw it down the staircase. To spit on it and stamp on it. Instead he crumpled it just slightly before placing it in the pocket of his suit jacket.

"I am so sorry, Bernard." These were Pinot's last words before he put on his bowler and headed down the stairs.

16

Tuesday–Wednesday, November 27–28

MARTIN AWAITED THE DAWN WITH dread. He hadn't slept all night. He lay, holding the baby, with his back to Clarie, listening intently for her every slow, steady breath. It had taken all of his powers to persuade her to get some sleep. He promised to wake her if Henri-Joseph needed her, to tell her if anything went wrong. Of course, he had no intention of keeping these promises once she fell into a merciful laudanum-induced sleep. So, during that long dark night, he lay as still as a sentry at his post, only daring to move once. At three o'clock he had slowly, carefully reached for his watch to record, in his mind, the moment of Henri-Joseph's death, although he had no way of really knowing it. His son's exit from their world had happened gradually, without a murmur, so unlike his bloody and glorious entrance into it.

Martin shifted a bit as the light began to pierce through the curtains. He pressed his son closer to him, not wanting ever to let him go. Why? That was the question that haunted him through the night. Why did his son have to die? When he had asked Pinot that question, the doctor had been judicious, clinical. These things happen. Martin was fortunate to have a strong, young wife who would bear him other children.

This told Martin nothing. It certainly did not explain how he had come to love so desperately a tiny being that he had hardly known. His son. Even the puerile words of Pierre Thomas came back to Martin during the night as he thought of all the things he would not have: my son, the dolt had shouted, someone to look up to me, to show off to my comrades, to teach. My son, Martin cried in his heart and bit his lip to squelch the sound, someone to love.

The worst was yet to come. How was he going to tell Clarie? Thank God Giuseppe is here, he thought as he maneuvered his stiff body to the side of the bed. Always, knowing how little Giuseppe could afford a hotel, Clarie and Martin had tried to persuade her father to stay with them. Only when he saw how much they needed him did he agree. Never had Martin needed him more.

Bit by bit, Martin managed to put his feet on the floor without making the bed creak. Then as he tried to stand, he lurched to the side, upsetting the lamp. He grabbed it with his free hand and glanced at Clarie, who moaned and turned, still sleeping. His body felt so heavy, as if a giant stone were crushing his chest, squeezing the life out of him. He had known grief. His father's death when he was twelve, the fatal shooting of Merckx in Aix. But nothing like this. Mme Ullmann had cried out from the pain of her howling emptiness. Martin didn't feel empty. Yet. He was so weighed down by what lay ahead that he could barely move. His only thought for the moment was Giuseppe: he had to reach him. The emptiness, the howling would come later.

He stumbled to the door, took a breath and opened it. It was beginning. He had to say the words.

Bleary-eyed, Giuseppe stood up immediately, as if he, too, had not slept. They met in the middle of the room. Giuseppe took one look at the still, little body and knew.

"He has a peaceful look on his face." These words shocked Martin, yet it was so like his father-in-law to try to find a way to bring Clarie and Martin comfort. This time he didn't succeed. Martin clutched Henri-Joseph to his chest and began to cry. Giuseppe reached out and enfolded them both in his strong, stout arms. "You are the son I have always wanted," he said through his tears, "a son I could never dream of having. And I know, I know, that you and Clarie will have more children. And I know I will live to see them and play with them. I know this. I do."

Martin slipped away from him and fell into a chair. Tears ran down his face. His father-in-law gently pried Henri-Joseph out of his arms and offered him a handkerchief.

"Clarie." That was the only word that Martin managed to say.

"Yes. My poor girl." The weight of what was to come pushed Giuseppe into another chair.

It seemed they sat there for hours in silence as the light inexorably announced the day, the hour, the moment when it must be done. Still they did not move until they heard her call.

Numbly, grasping the chair by its arms, Martin managed to get to his feet. He no longer felt weighed down, he was weightless, unreal, moving through the thick, resisting air that separated him from the bedroom.

Clarie was already sitting up when he entered. "Where is he?" she demanded. "Where is my baby?"

Martin tensed as the words shot through every fiber of his body, almost locking him in place. He willed himself to her side of the bed. He edged onto it, bent over and kissed her. "He is gone," he said. "Our little Henri-Joseph is gone."

"No, he isn't!" Her eyes flashed and her face, in the morning light was red and angry. "Bring him to me."

Martin shook his head. "He's gone. You were right. He was sick. The doctor said there was nothing we could do."

"No! No! No!" She slapped him across the face. And then she began pushing him, and making fists, and punching him.

Martin did not even try to ward off the blows. He wanted to feel the pain, to be punished. For not being there every minute. For not paying attention. For being a fool who had gotten himself tangled up outside their world. Only Giuseppe's strong arms stopped her. Her father had crawled across the bed. He held her close until her arms stopped flailing, and she began to cry.

Now, Martin thought with a start, would be the time for the tearing of clothes, the rending of garments. The vision of Mme Ullmann's dignified and righteous fury flooded Martin's mind. Yes, this is what Clarie would be like when the wildness had gone out of her, the futile, mad wishing to have her baby back. Burying his face in his hands, Martin knew that this was the most he could hope for.

In the end it was his mother and Madeleine who made the arrangements. Adele Martin got Gustave Girard to come to the apartment to talk with Martin about coffins and gravesites; Madeleine informed the other teachers at Clarie's school, the maid, and the Steins of Henri-Joseph's death; together they went to Madeleine's parish and found a priest to say prayers at the grave. Martin's mother, in an uncharacteristic demonstration of tact, even hired two carriages for the next morning, one for Martin, his father-in-law, and the tiny coffin; the other for her, Madeleine and the priest. Martin did little during that sad, long Tuesday, except to send a message to the courthouse. He lay in his clothes, on top of the covers, staring at the ceiling through eyes blurred with fatigue and the tears that dribbled down the sides of his face into the pillow. He held onto Clarie when she would let him. Yet he did not try, like Giuseppe or Madeleine or his mother, to console her with food, or words, or hope. The emptiness had begun to yawn open inside of him. It was Clarie who did the howling, crying out for her son, beating her fists on the bed, and sobbing. Martin marveled at the women. They did; they felt. The cynical Didier had said that birth and sickness was woman's business. So, it seemed, was death. Were all men as weak as he? There were moments when he thought, even prayed, that the emptiness would swallow him up and make his jabbering, impotent mind stop.

Was it right to let Girard take the body away, to put Henri-Joseph in a sealed wooden coffin? Was it right to remove every trace of his son from Clarie's sight? Benumbed and drained, Martin did not have the answer to any of these questions. He only wanted it to be over. And he knew only one thing, they could not allow Clarie to go to the grave, to see the dirt shoveled onto her son. Pinot had to be right about that. This is why they left her, screaming and protesting, with Rose and Mme Stein holding her down, trying to soothe her.

At eleven o'clock, on an obscenely bright and sunny Wednesday morning, Martin and his father-in-law took the carriage across the railroad tracks to the cemetery. They rode all the way in silence, gently swaying side to side, staring straight ahead, as if any sight, any word might breach the dam of their pent-up sorrows. When they arrived at the gate, the other carriage was waiting for them. So was a line of beggars sitting against the cemetery wall. Martin saw them as a drab, annoying blur. He could not imagine why they were there. Who could know about the death of such a tiny being?

He did take note of the priest clapping his arms and stamping his feet against the cold, as if he could not wait for it to be over. Martin and Giuseppe lifted the small coffin together, and put it down on the ground while they waited for the women to alight. Madeleine came out first, heavily veiled in full black mourning, as if she were securing her place in the Martins' tragedy. His mother also emerged in black, something borrowed? Something new? Before Martin could push these trivial thoughts away, the priest began to address him. "We've been watching them," he said as he gestured up the path to where a congregation of top-hatted men were standing and talking. "Israelites. They carried the body through the town in procession. Whoever it was, must have been important."

Martin had not even noticed the gathering of men near a thick high wall that marked one boundary of the cemetery. The first thought that ran through his mind was, why should anyone care? The second was: it is the Ullmann funeral.

"At least they separate themselves from us. I wouldn't want them in Christian burial ground." Madeleine's remark was muffled by the veil, but not enough for Martin's taste. He wanted to strangle her. Why were they talking this way? Why had he himself given one iota of thought to his mother's clothing? His son was dead. That's all that mattered. He was about to ask Giuseppe to join him in picking up the coffin when he saw that a man from among the Israelites had broken off and was walking toward them. Chin forward, the man was squinting as he strode down the path. As he neared, Martin recognized Singer.

Martin's colleague tipped his hat toward the women. Martin was forced to introduce them, even though, at this moment, attending to the pieties of politeness struck him as irrelevant and insane. "And you know my father-in-law," he mouthed as his heart began to flutter with a kind of hysteria, a need to get it over with. Singer put out his hand to Giuseppe, who took it gladly. "And Father—" Martin didn't know his name and the priest did not come forward to introduce himself. "Father Clermont," Madeleine mumbled. He did not offer his hand, but Singer, the ever-correct Singer, ignored the slight. He was staring at the little coffin.

When he looked up, Martin saw the sadness in his eyes. "I'm so sorry," he whispered to Martin. Singer's expression of sympathy hit Martin like a blow to the chest. When he staggered backward a step or two, Singer reached out to steady him, and kept holding him just above his elbows. Martin's every instinct told him that Singer was too formal to embrace him, too polite to presume or to intrude. Yet he was a colleague and a friend. As Martin began to weep, he heard Singer say, "I understand. I know." And then he caught himself, and with the humility of a true friend, he admitted, "but, of course, I don't really know." Then, with another slight bow, Singer turned and slowly walked up the hill, leaving them, in private, to perform their sad duties.

17

Thursday, November 29

STILL NO CONFESSION. MARTIN HAD come in late Thursday morning and was sitting across from Jacquette delivering his instructions. Question the Ullmann's housekeeper. Go the woolen mill to ferret out the discontents. Keep grilling Thomas.

Jacquette crushed the stub of his cigarette into the ashtray on Martin's desk. "I don't think he did it."

Martin eyed his inspector. In some ways he considered Jacquette to be better reader of men than he. Jacquette knew the streets. Jacquette used his instincts. Martin probed, reasoned, and analyzed his way to a verdict. Whenever the two of them, together, came to the same conclusions, they were invariably right. Martin sighed. He also was becoming more and more convinced that Thomas was not the killer; that, indeed, they had stepped into the kind of nasty conflict between man and wife that Didier had so dismissively labeled a "sordid lower-class drama."

Yet Thomas's presumed innocence brought no relief. Instead, it filled Martin with a new anxiety. Despite all their efforts to squelch the ritual murder libel, at least one man had gotten wind of it and had willfully turned a sordid little drama into a full-blown tragedy. But who? Without the tanner, the investigation threatened to become amorphous, unmanageable, fanning out to all the haters of the Israelites.

"You've made sure that he would not *know* anyone who did it?"

Jacquette nodded, his face more downcast than usual.

"Sir, I'm sorry about your son."

Martin was stunned. But he should not have been. He had rushed into his chambers, making it clear that he was only there to give orders, and had not let anyone else get in so much as a word of greeting. Now he knew why. He had been avoiding just this moment. "Thank you," he said, and pulled his chin in as if that would slow the trembling in his chest. "Thank you," he whispered again. "You understand, then, why I must get back as soon as possible."

Perhaps to cover his own emotions, Jacquette concentrated on patting his jacket down, searching for another Blue Jockey. "Yes," he mumbled, "and I'll keep nibbling around the edges of Ullmann's life."

"No!"

Jacquette looked up, startled.

"No," Martin said again, more quietly. "We need to do more. You need to keep your ear to the ground and use all your informers to look for anyone who might be talking about 'ritual murder' or who is speaking out against the Israelites in general. Then you must nibble around *his* edges. I'll pick up all the anti-Semitic rags I can find at the newsstand and scour them for local priests and politicians who might have developed an entourage." When Jacquette did not grunt his agreement, Martin added, "That's the direction that Singer and Didier wanted me to take from the beginning, and that's what we are going to do."

Jacquette had captured a cigarette and was tapping it on the desk. "But don't you think that we should first deal with someone who *knew* Ullmann, someone with a personal grudge?"

"That, too." Martin was in no mood to argue. "But we cannot ignore the possibility that Ullmann was killed simply because of his race."

Jacquette struck a match against the bottom of his boot to light his cigarette, then gave Martin a reluctant nod. Despite his own best instincts, Jacquette would make an attempt to carry out his superior's orders. It was a rare discordant moment between the two of them, and Martin tried to cover it over by asking his inspector if he had anything else to report.

"Well, of course, there's Mme Thomas." A grin grew on one side of Jacquette's face and eventually conquered the other. His tawny eyebrows arched expectantly.

"Yes?" Leave it to the trusty Jacquette to find some way to break the tension.

He took a long draw from his cigarette and blew it out with obvious pleasure. "A piece of work, that woman. Still shouting. Now she's complaining about the food. Not fine enough for her. No silver, no gold plate. At the jail they're all grateful that Didier has seen fit to keep her locked up for only six weeks. Although, if she were out and about she'd be my prime suspect."

"With both of them in jail, you think we're keeping the town safe?" Martin commented, continuing the joke.

"Let's hope so."

Martin got up to signal the end of their meeting. Jacquette quickly pocketed his notebook and stuck the cigarette in his mouth. He stood and reached to grip his superior's hand. In that handshake, Martin felt Jacquette's strength and sympathy. Neither of them had forgotten about Martin's son.

They agreed to meet again on Friday at ten o'clock. In the meantime, they could hope that they were, indeed, keeping the town safe.

18
Friday, November 30

THE NEXT MORNING, MARTIN ARRIVED according to plan exactly at ten. By ten-thirty he was drumming his fingers on his desk. *Where the hell was Jacquette?* It was not like him to be late, especially when he knew that Martin was in a hurry to dispense with business and get home.

"Are you sure Inspector Jacquette did not leave any message?" he asked Charpentier, who sat behind Martin doing whatever he did, copying, organizing, preening.

"No, sir. Should I go to the station and inquire?" Martin heard the eagerness in Charpentier's voice. Martin had been gone much of two weeks; his clerk was restless too.

"Good idea." Martin would love to be able to vent his impatience without his notoriously curious clerk around.

"Yes, sir." Charpentier jumped up to begin his leave-taking, which was never easy or straightforward. Martin did not have to look behind him to sense every movement: stacking papers in perfect piles, plugging the inkwell, lining up every damned thing on the desk to be parallel or perpendicular to something else. Martin closed his eyes and listened until he heard footsteps scurrying to the coatrack, then he watched as Charpentier wound his long red wool scarf around his neck no less than three times.

Ten minutes later, Jacquette strode into the room, panting and sweating. He swiped off his cap and plopped down in the chair in front of Martin's desk. "Sorry for being late," he muttered. The doleful look in Jacquette's face put Martin on edge. Every instinct in his body told him that Jacquette's lateness was about to be the least of his concerns.

"What happened?" he demanded. "Did Thomas confess?"

Jacquette shook his head and shifted uneasily in his chair. "We've found another body."

"No. It can't be." Martin sank back, hardly breathing. "Who? Man? Woman? Israelite?—"

Jacquette pressed his lips together, as if he were considering how best to break it to him. "This is where it gets sticky, sir. Another Israelite, Daniel Erlanger. The uncle of Judge Singer's wife. Killed in his own kitchen."

Martin's mind went blank. His mouth fell half open, but no words came out.

Fortunately, Jacquette provided them. "I know, sir, I know. Too close to home. We gotta get him. Whoever is doing this." He stared at the floor and began to turn his woolen cap slowly in his two thick hands. "Maybe I was wrong, sir, maybe we'd better start by tracking down some of those anti-Semites."

"Let's worry about that later." Martin had trouble absorbing the fact that someone so close to the courthouse had been murdered. *Incredible.* Martin got up and began to pace, which did not help. He stopped by Jacquette's chair. "What can you tell me?" Martin asked.

"How did it happen? When?" It was good to be able to get out these normal questions, in a situation that went far beyond any norm that Martin could have imagined.

And Jacquette seemed just as eager to answer them, to perform the duties that were well within his ken. "Erlanger's maid found him late yesterday afternoon when she came in with the shopping for dinner," he reported. "She thinks he was making some tea. Pot left burning on the stove. Blood fresh, but she was sure he was dead. She'd been gone two hours. She ran to find Singer, who sent for me. I went over the scene, looked for the weapon and talked to her for over an hour. She has no idea who could have done it and claimed there was nothing missing. The old man was a bachelor, a notary. She kept saying that everyone loved him. When I went over to the morgue this morning, Dr. Fauvet was still examining the body. He finally told me that a single wound to the heart was all it took. Came back here as soon as I could. Singer's still there, with—" Jacquette halted this rapid recitation for just a second before going on. "He wants to talk to you right away."

"Then he may have something to tell me, some idea about the killer?" Martin went back behind his desk.

"No, I don't think it's that, sir." Jacquette shook his head. "You'd better talk to him yourself."

Martin did not like the sound of that. He dropped into his chair. His desk, his papers, the pure white wall, all that had appeared in sharp relief just moments ago, suddenly blurred and curved, turning in on him. Could Singer be blaming him for what had just happened? Would he come to take Didier's part against him? No, Martin slouched back. That would not be the worst of it. Feeling responsible for the murders, losing Singer's friendship and trust would.

Jacquette cleared his throat, retrieving Martin's attention. "Right away, sir. That's what he kept saying."

"Yes, of course," Martin said, still staring, unable to focus on what was right in front of him. *Of course.*

Jacquette stood up and put on his cap. "All right, sir. Then I'll start making up the list of possible rabble-rousers for you."

Martin nodded.

"And—" Jacquette waited until Martin looked up. "I'd stop by Fauvet's office and talk to him first before you head down to see Singer and the body."

Their eyes met. Coming from Martin's trusted right-hand man, this was a warning.

Martin decided to go on foot to the Faculté de Médicine. He needed a brisk walk to clear his head, or so he told himself. Since it was not easy to speedily wind his way through the crowd on the busy rue Saint-Dizier, he had to acknowledge something else, what he was avoiding: the enclosed forced humanity of the tram, the onslaught of feelings that would assault him if he had chosen to take the shortcut past his apartment on the rue des Dom. Holding his bowler down with a leather-gloved hand, Martin strove for an anonymity as gray as the winter morning. He needed to be alone. This determination carried him almost past the central market, where he caught sight of a flower stall at the entrance. He stopped and stared at the bright, greenhouse blooms, remembering. Every few weeks he had made it a practice to surprise Clarie with a little bouquet, because this small, unimaginative gesture always gave her so much pleasure. When, he wondered, would those days return, the happy meals, the talk about their work and colleagues, their laughing together? No, Martin wasn't merely alone. He was lonely. Lonelier than he ever imagined he would be after he married Clarie and they settled down in Nancy, each to their own profession, joined in their own little home, both of them of one mind about what they held most dear.

Martin had to believe that this happiness would return, but he had no time for daydreams or wishing. He continued his headlong rush to the Faculté, even faster this time, as though something was chasing him instead of pulling him toward his duty. He would have missed the turnoff if it hadn't stood at the corner of the towering Saint Pierre Church. The short block between the broad Avenue de Strasbourg and the enclave that held the Faculté gave him time to catch his breath and take heed of Jacquette's warning to see Fauvet first.

Not wanting to alert Singer to his presence, Martin made a quiet entrance and went directly to Fauvet's office. He tapped lightly on the clouded window that comprised most of the top half of the heavy oak door.

"Come in." Martin found Fauvet ensconced, as usual, in a pungent blue-gray haze of tobacco smoke. He laid his pipe on a large, heavy glass ashtray before standing up and reaching out to shake Martin's hand.

"Another body," he said, almost cheerfully.

"Yes," Martin responded quietly as he sat down in front of the desk. He was always a bit unnerved by Fauvet. His delight in the grisliest aspects of his work was one reason. The other, Martin had to admit, was his all-too-apparent youth, despite his barely sprouting blond mustache and ever-present pipe. Fauvet's bouncy enthusiasm, his rosy cheeks and the gold-rimmed round student glasses always had the effect of making Martin feel old, although he was only thirty-five. Martin could not imagine that Fauvet, who seemed to work endless hours in his classroom, his office, and in the morgue, had a lover or a family, except perhaps for the mother he had spoken of, who told "old wives' tales" to her skeptical son. Fauvet treated the tragedies of life as interesting matters of fact, to be dissected, categorized and filed away. Martin doubted whether the avid scientist could tell him what he really needed to know, what Singer was thinking and feeling.

"Quite a crowd down there," Fauvet commented as he pursed his lips and raised his eyebrows with incomprehensible amusement sparkling in his blue eyes.

"Crowd?"

"Yes, Singer's co-religionists. He's the judge. I couldn't stop him from bringing them in. Although," Fauvet said as he picked up his pipe and tamped more tobacco into it, "he would like your permission before they clean up and carry away the body, since it is your case."

"Where are they taking the body?" Martin said, surprised by this request.

"To the victim's home, I think," Fauvet said with a sigh, then struck a match and lit up his pipe with the help of a few hard sucks. "They told me it has to be done as soon as possible. Don't ask me why," he said as he waved the flame into extinction.

Martin did not understand the need for such a hasty burial either. It sounded too much like a special favor. He pressed his fingernails into his legs, reminding himself not to show any emotion. If he was about to have a confrontation with Singer, he did not want Fauvet involved in any way.

"Do you have all the information you need from the victim's body? What can you tell me now?" There, Martin thought, rational questions. Answers that can provide a way to deal with Singer.

"Very simple, really," Fauvet said, laying his pipe down again. "One wound, almost directly to the heart. Although this Daniel Erlanger was a healthy man—portly really—in his sixties, it would not have taken him long to bleed to death. A big cut across the right hand as if he had tried to grab the knife and caught the blade." Fauvet imitated the motion with one of his own smooth, hammy pink hands. "Big knife and sharp. Tanning? Butchering? Or just cooking? No way to be sure. Strange thing, although he tried to save himself, there was a peaceful look on his face, not the shock or rage you would expect. Singer told me that was because he had time to say his prayers before dying. At least he hoped Erlanger had time. Singer almost broke down when he was talking about it. I didn't know he was that religious." Another shrug, sloughing off everything that did not have directly to do with the "science" of the case.

Martin realized that he had no sense of how religious his colleague was either, except that Singer felt that his Jewishness determined the way people saw him. Perhaps it was anti-Israelites like Drumont who made it so important, who forced David to think about being a Jew all the time. Yet here he was thinking and talking about his relative's final prayer with, apparently, as much emotion as the Widow Ullmann had. Martin shook his head. Now was not the time for philosophical questions.

"Anything else you could find out from the body?" he asked Fauvet.

"No. It was fresh when they brought it in last night, maybe only four or five hours after he died. It will all be in my report."

"Then you don't see any reason why——"

"No, I think I have everything I need. I've measured the wound. The best thing would be to find the weapon, but apparently Jacquette had his men search the house—that's where it happened—and the yard. Nothing."

"So I can release the body," Martin confirmed.

Fauvet waved his hand as he reached for a pile of papers on his desk. "I've nothing more to learn. I'll write up the report tonight and leave Singer and his friends to you."

As it should be, as it must be, although the thought of having to talk to Singer and deal with his special request filled Martin with dismay. He thanked Fauvet, put on his bowler, and left the medical professor reading and sucking on his pipe. As soon as Martin closed the door, he paused and leaned against it. It was his job to assure the relatives of the maimed and murdered that their loved one would get justice. With due process and time. To treat each victim, each family, as equitably as possible. His job, even if the victim was related to a judge.

Walking down the stairs, he heard the prayer before he reached the door to the morgue. Someone was chanting in a language that was neither French nor German. He knocked, giving warning, then went in.

Martin was shocked to find about a dozen men in the morgue, including Singer and the rabbi, all of them wearing close-fitting skull-caps and white silk shawls bordered by blue stripes and long fringes. Erlanger's body was covered with a sheet, except for his feet. A man holding these swayed ever so slightly back and forth in a kind of a trance, chanting. This was not right. The room should not be filled with strangers. No one should be handling the corpse. It was presumptuous on Singer's part to have allowed this. Martin coughed to get his attention.

Singer was standing by the dead man's shoulder. When he looked up, everything stopped for a moment, and all heads turned toward Martin. "Martin," he said, "I'm glad you have come at last."

Come at last? Martin had come as soon as he had heard. Thoroughly irritated, Martin made a slight bow of his head to the other men before opening the door and signaling to Singer to join him outside. He had no intention of carrying out any discussion in the midst of the Israelites. It was annoying to feel like he was the interloper when he was the one who had every right to be there.

As soon as Singer stepped into the hallway, Martin closed the door behind him.

"What's going on, Singer?" he asked.

"What do you mean?" Singer straightened up and gave Martin the supercilious look which had made him unpopular with others at the courthouse.

"All these men, in this—"

"We are practicing our faith." Each word clipped.

Martin could not take his eyes off the skullcap and the shawl. He had never imagined Singer in this guise. "This is not the place."

"Where, then? I am a judge. I have a right to be here. I made sure that Fauvet had full opportunity to examine my uncle. But I never had any intention of leaving him. We do not leave our dead loved ones alone. We honor them. That's why we need to take him home and get him ready for burial as soon as possible. Even so, we won't be able to do it before our sabbath."

"I don't understand. No one seemed so hurried about Ullmann." Martin was not sure if this came out as a question or an accusation, and realized it was both.

"Ullmann was different. They had to wait for his sons to come before they buried him. Moreover, the rabbi and his widow felt he should have a great procession. In my opinion, unwise, given . . ." Singer stopped and took in a breath. "Given the hatred," he continued. "Look what it has led to."

"I don't understand—"

Singer interrupted him. "Don't you see what can happen when we have the audacity to show ourselves, to be important, to praise one of our own?"

"Oh, David." It was so disheartening to see his friend like this. Martin simply could not believe that a funeral procession would drive someone to murder. A second murder.

"You say we are out of place here, in this room for the dead. What about the man who came into my uncle's home? Does anyone care about that?" Singer's grief and resentment were making it impossible to reason with him. He had gathered a full head of steam against Martin. And what if—sweat broke out on Martin's forehead imagining it—what if Singer began accusing *him* of being responsible for Erlanger's death? Because Martin had not pursued the anti-Israelites of the city. Because he had not taken the threat seriously enough.

"Of course I am sorry about your relative's death. But you are asking me to grant you privileges I would not give others." Martin wanted to make a truce, he wanted to understand, to accommodate his friend in his grief, but Singer had to offer him some explanation, some reason.

Singer stepped back until he hit the wall behind him. "I suppose," he began, "if the rules were made for people like me instead of people like you, then I would not be breaking them. We try to bury our dead within twenty-four hours; we wash them, pray over them, lay them in a plain pine box. All this, so their mortal remains will return to the earth as pure and as blessed as they came into it. This strikes me as supremely rational, if that is what you care about. And it is the way of my community."

Arguing about privilege and rights was getting nowhere. Martin realized that it would have been better, more human, to start with his sympathy. "David," he said softly, "you called Erlanger your uncle. I thought he was your wife's relative."

"He was." Singer bent his head for a moment, as if he were considering what to say. Then he looked straight in Martin's eyes. "You might as well know this, although there are some who might consider my wife's family to be *insufficiently patriotic*." Singer underlined these last two words with sarcasm. "Noémie and I knew each other as children, in Metz. After the war, her parents decided not to leave German Lorraine because of their business. They sent her to boarding school in France, but would have never allowed her to stay if her uncle hadn't moved here. They considered him to be her guardian. For both of us, he became the beloved bachelor uncle, invited to all the holidays, bringing the wine, the stories, the sweets for the children." Singer turned his face away from Martin to hide his emotion.

As Martin listened he thought of Giuseppe and how much Clarie's father meant to him. Martin reached out for Singer's arm, but was unsure whether or not he should touch the shawl. He withdrew it. "I'm sorry," Martin said again.

"Then will you let me do it?" Singer asked. "Let me have my uncle's body washed and prayed over properly. Allow us to bury him. You are the judge. This is your case."

Martin thought for a moment. What would it cost him? He'd have Fauvet's and Jacquette's report. Didier would surely concede that the funeral should occur as quickly, as quietly and as discreetly as possible.

Martin stole a glance at Singer, who kept staring at him, waiting. Despite his office and his duties, Martin always felt that holding the dead in the morgue as if they were merely scientific specimens was a kind of violation. Death should be a private, family matter, attended only by close and loving friends. Martin nodded his agreement. It was the least he could do.

Martin left the morgue weighed down by sadness and apprehension. A second murder. The realization that the jailed Pierre Thomas was likely innocent of Ullmann's murder gave him little consolation. If Singer and Didier were right, the task ahead would be daunting. He quickened his pace. He had much to do.

19

Saturday, December 1

WHAT ARE ALL THESE PEOPLE doing here? Clarie huddled into the plaid blanket. Even though she sat close to the fire, she could not get rid of the chill. The headmistress of Jeanne d'Arc, perched on a dining-room chair set right in front of Clarie, recited a supposedly amusing anecdote about one of their students. Elise Fremier settled into the nearby armchair, accepting a cup of tea from Papa. *Oh yes, Saturday. School ends at noon. The teachers have come to see me. But why? No one talks to me about what I need to know. Was my baby ever happy here? Is he cold now? Is he all by himself in that dark place? Or is he already up in heaven with the angels? What did I do wrong? Why doesn't anyone tell me?*

She surveyed the room. Madeleine and Bernard's mother stood in the corner, sipping tea with the school's youngest teacher. For once they weren't scrutinizing Clarie's every reaction.

Marie Dusseau smiled expectantly, waiting for a response. But Clarie hadn't heard what she said. The headmistress looked down at her teacup, embarrassed. Elise broke in: "How long is your father staying? I'm so happy to have met him."

"Until Monday, I think," Clarie mumbled. *Then the apartment will be even emptier.*

"And Monsieur Martin's mother?" Mme Dusseau asked.

Clarie had to think. They've told her all this, as if it really mattered. "Tomorrow afternoon."

"We'll have to say good-bye now. What a wonderful family you have." Approval from the headmistress. Clarie should be pleased.

"When school is out," Elise added eagerly, "we'll be able to visit much more."

No, I don't want to see you. Or anyone. I want my baby.

"Oh, dear," Elise said as she got up to comfort Clarie.

Clarie resisted her embrace. "I'm all right. Sorry." She couldn't help it if a few tears fell once in a while. It was nothing. Didn't they understand? Nothing compared to the emptiness. Clarie's hand groped under the blanket, landing on her stomach. *If only he were still there, safe and warm.*

Good, kind Elise retreated, biting her lower lip and frowning with concern.

Clarie managed a reassuring smile, thinking that if everyone thought she was "recovering," they would leave her alone. But recovering for what, for whom? Bernard just went about his business; Papa had to go back to Arles; and Madeleine and Adele Martin spent all their spare time praying. Maybe Madeleine and Mme Martin are right, Clarie thought, as she traced a line of the dark blue and green pattern with her finger. At least they were doing something.

20

Sunday, December 2

HE KNEW THAT SUNDAY WOULD be the worst day.

Yesterday there had been a glimmer of hope. The headmistress and the two other teachers from Clarie's school had visited after their morning classes and brought with them not only murmured condolences, but also flowers, bread, cheese, cakes, and news of their students. They had surrounded Clarie in the armchair that in the last few days, replete with a tattered tartan wool blanket, pillow, and padded stool, had become hers alone. Martin watched the teachers from across the room and saw Clarie smile.

But today was different. Barely had Clarie risen from her bed and made her way to her chair by the fire when, straight from High Mass and the fortification of the Body and Blood of Christ, Madeleine and his mother swooped in and down on her. Giuseppe greeted them at the door and gallantly fetched two wooden dining-room chairs so that the women could be as close to Clarie as possible. There they sat, smothering her with whispered pieties about God's mercy and the power of prayer.

Martin rattled the newspaper as he shot an irritated glance at the three of them. He wanted to leap across the room and grab his mother's hand as she smoothed back a strand of heavy black hair from Clarie's worn, pale face. For years his mother had disdained his choice in marriage because Clarie was a blacksmith's daughter and, worse, had become a public school teacher. But now, now, she and Madeleine were eagerly welcoming Clarie into the sorority of suffering womanhood and the narrow-minded righteous world of crucifixes, daily rosaries and dead babies magically transformed into little angels. Of babies dead and babies not born. Martin bit down on his lip and pressed his eyes closed. He had to try harder to be kind to his mother. All she had wanted in life was a family, and all she had gotten was him.

All Martin wanted at this moment was his Clarie back.

He felt a certain envy for his father-in-law who sat beside him in an armchair, glasses halfway down his nose, either reading or dozing over the Sunday paper, somehow at peace with the scene. Martin straightened and folded his section of the *Courrier de l'Est* before setting it on the end table between them. If only he had Giuseppe's gift for tolerating those with whom he so profoundly disagreed.

Martin got up and walked to the window, turning his back on the women. He stared at the scene below him. It was hard to believe that people were cheerfully going about their business in the cold, shopping, talking, scurrying home to make their Sunday dinner. It would have seemed so normal only a week ago.

Martin grabbed at the window frame to steady himself. *Only a week ago.* How could these simple words throw him off balance? *A week ago,* he saw Singer and the tinker from the same window. *A week ago,* Henri-Joseph was alive. *A week ago,* Martin, fool that he was, believed his son was well. Before Martin could straighten up again, he felt a strong hand grip his shoulder.

"I know," Giuseppe whispered. "But we must be strong for Clarie's sake."

Martin nodded, as he pulled a handkerchief from his pocket and undid it, fold by fold.

"Perhaps you and I should go for a walk," Giuseppe suggested.

Martin wiped his face and blew his nose. He nodded to signal that he was all right. "I'm taking Mother to the station soon; you are welcome to join us." Martin stood up beside his father-in-law's warm protection. The blacksmith's broad body kept his weakness out of Clarie's view.

"Oh, no, I would not intrude. That's a time for the two of you."

"And you're going tomorrow?" Martin confirmed, trying to suppress the dread in his voice. He didn't want to contemplate leaving Clarie alone with Rose and Madeleine.

"I must. I've left the forge for too long. But I promised Clarie I'd be back right after Christmas, and I'm going to bring her Aunt Henriette with me. That should help."

"Yes." Martin forced a smile. "It will be good for all of us to think about the old times, the restaurant in Aix." The place where he had met his beautiful, smart, headstrong Clarie. A girl bold enough to hide his secrets, and kind enough to put up with him. Martin glanced again at his wife. Perhaps by Christmas the dark rings would no longer circle her eyes. Perhaps she'd be out of her nightgown, out of the braids, into his life again.

"Take that worried look off your face. Clarie will be fine. She's strong. My little girl has always had friends who love her, who will take care of her." Giuseppe paused as a mischievous little smile spread under his white mustache. "Besides Madeleine," he whispered in Martin's ear.

"I'm that obvious?" Martin arched his eyebrows in mock dismay and slapped his father-in-law on the back. Martin was really going to miss him, even though he knew that he was being selfish. He could not expect the older man to sleep on an easy chair in their living room indefinitely.

"So, back to our papers, until your mother's ready to leave?"

Martin nodded, but stopped in his tracks when he saw his mother take a medal from around her neck and give it to Clarie. Adele Martin tenderly closed her daughter-in-law's hand around the religious medal, before bowing her head in prayer.

"Come," Giuseppe urged him again. "If this helps Clarie find consolation. . . ."

Consolation. As he watched the women, Martin realized he had little right to be upset. What had he to offer Clarie, except to assure her that it would get better, that they would try as soon as possible to have another child, that he loved her? Time. The future. Each other. That was his consolation. Perhaps she needed something stronger, something more tangible. At least for a while. Like his mother's most precious sacred keepsake, a medal dedicated to all true Children of the Virgin Mary.

He slumped back to his chair, about to reopen the paper when the bell rang. Giuseppe put up one finger and gave Martin a triumphant look. "I bet I know who that is. You'll see how many people love our Clarie."

Curious, Martin headed for the door, and opened it to find his land-lady, Esther Stein, holding a soup pot and her daughter, Rebecca, behind her, peering shyly above her shoulder.

"Oh, Monsieur le juge, I saw Monsieur Giuseppe when he went for the papers. I told him that I knew it was your sabbath, and that Rose would not come and could we—"

"Here, let me take that from you," Martin said as he reached to relieve his landlady of her burdens.

"Soup, soup is good," Mme Stein continued. "Always. For every-thing. Especially in the winter."

"Yes, of course. Thank you. Come in, please." The pot was heavy and still warm. Although they already had a shameful amount of food in a home where no one was prepared to eat it, he hastened to add, "This is going to be wonderful, for all of us."

"And Rebecca was wondering if she could visit with Mme Martin just for a little while. We don't want to—"

"Please." Martin stood aside. "Come in."

Although Mme Stein stepped in without hesitation, Rebecca held back, her hands clasped together below her waist and her shoulders rising up to her neck as a shy smile flickered across her face.

"I'm certain Mme Martin would love to hear news of the school," Martin assured her.

Bowing her head, she followed her mother into the living room, where the appearance of the landlady and her daughter brought the hushed conversations by the fire to a standstill. Staring at Martin, as if he had committed a breach of etiquette, Madeleine stiffly rose from her chair and stood a little apart from Clarie.

"Madame Froment, don't disturb yourself. We just came up to bring some soup," Mme Stein told her.

"How thoughtful," Madeleine remarked, and then turned to Martin's mother. "These are the Steins," she explained.

"Oh." Martin's mother eased her way out of her seat. "You two can sit here. I must go back to my hotel and pack."

Martin was relieved. This was polite and considerate.

"Really," she gestured toward her chair.

Mme Stein backed away. "Visiting in my apron. No. I must go back to the store."

Clarie observed the scene languidly until she caught sight of Rebecca, who, seeing that she had been spotted, immediately went to her teacher and knelt down at her feet. This time it was Clarie smoothing back Rebecca's curly black hair. Martin's heart leaped with hope. This is what Clarie needed. A reminder of her other life. But when he saw his wife put her hand back in her lap, like an awkward young girl who for a moment had forgotten who and where she was, he felt deflated. It was too soon for her to forget for more than an instant that she was in mourning for her baby.

While he was watching, Esther Stein took the pot from him and headed into the dining room. He followed her.

"There," she said as she set the soup on the table. "You'll have dinner. No worries. And anything else we can do. I know Monsieur Giuseppe is leaving too. We are almost always at the store, except during our sabbath. And then we are home." Her eyes were warm and moist, sympathetic.

"Thank you. And Monsieur Stein, how is he?" Martin expected that this conventional politeness would bring a conventional response. But it did not.

Mme Stein's face fell. She reached to the table for support and began to slowly shake her head. "At the funeral. A terrible thing has happened this week. You must know about it. Another man of our community has been murdered."

"Erlanger," Martin whispered, caught off guard by this unexpected reminder of his other life. He helped her into a chair and sat down himself, staring into space. *The funeral is today, going on right now. Singer's uncle.*

"Yes, Maître Erlanger, the notary. Such a kind man. No matter how poor a man or woman might be, he drew up their marriage contracts and wills, and gave advice to all of us. Always willing to help anyone. Who can understand it?" He could feel her eyes searching his face, waiting for some response.

The newspapers had reported the crime, but thankfully they had not yet mentioned Martin's name. Nor had they made the connection between the murders of Ullmann and Erlanger. But they would, inevitably. And Mme Stein already had.

"Two murders," she murmured. "Two of our best men. Why?"

Martin could not bear to look at her. He had no answers, although he knew he should. Two murders, his responsibility.

"Oh, Monsieur le juge," Mme Stein said, recovering before he did, "I should not trouble you with all this. Surely this is not your affair today."

"Surely." He mumbled the blatant untruth, and managed a weak smile.

"I must be going." Her face brightened a little, he assumed for his sake. "I'll get Rebecca."

He leaped up to pull out her chair and watched as she went over to Clarie. She said some consoling words that he could not hear, before she took Rebecca's hand. The girl looked eager to leave. He, too, needed to get out. Observing his Clarie, he hated himself for being so easily absorbed into his other life. But Esther Stein's words had filled him with a new anxiety. Did Jacquette know about the funeral? Certainly someone should be there to observe and protect the participants.

21

MARTIN'S MOTHER LOOPED HER ARM into his as they headed for the Hotel d'Angleterre. Usually Martin stiffened when she took possession of him in this way, but today was different. Today she spoke of his wife with tenderness and sympathy. His body relaxed as he leaned toward her, listening, and protecting her from the swirling wind blowing up the side streets onto the busy rue Saint-Jean. "And Giuseppe is a sweet man, a good man. He even reminds me a little of your father, because he is so kind," she said as they approached the hotel. When he tried to catch the expression on her face, she had already turned away. Of the three of them, Henri Martin had been the most gentle and yielding. Martin never doubted that his mother missed her husband terribly. Now he understood that she may even have missed the softening influence he had had over her. She patted his arm, to assure him that they could continue, and they entered the lobby of the modest hotel.

"I'll call you when I'm ready," she said with a lilt in her voice and headed up the stairs, hanging on to the banister with one hand and to her heavy skirts with the other. Martin noted that she had grown slower and thicker, even while still aspiring to a certain degree of fashion. The peacock feather in her hat, the matching blue coat trimmed with black velvet, must have been things she had scrimped and saved for. Things that allowed a poor widow to "keep up appearances" in front of the rich relatives. It was quite admirable, really, Martin thought as she disappeared around the corner.

Martin was pleased to note that the only other person in the lobby was a young clerk with his nose in a book. Behind him, the many hanging keys indicated that most of the travelers were out for the day. Or the hotel was empty. Being only two blocks from the railroad station, it offered a full array of the national dailies hanging invitingly on wooden rods. For the next few minutes, Martin could be anonymous. Neither judge nor mourner. He might be taken for a tourist, a salesman, a visiting relative. Or just a man at his leisure, waiting for a woman to do her packing. The lobby, including its three threadbare armchairs, was all his.

Martin took off his woolen overcoat, scarf, bowler and gloves, and laid them on one of the chairs. Rubbing his hands together, he examined the framed row of newspapers. He was about to reach for *Le Temps* when something in *Le Figaro* caught his eye. A guest, or the owner, or the clerk, had circled a story with dark, angry pencil strokes. The newspaper was an old one, from Wednesday, and yet it still lay folded over the wooden rod, as if by design. The article was about Dreyfus, reported on the day of Henri-Joseph's funeral. Something Martin had missed. Sucking in a breath, he grabbed the paper, rod and all, and sank down into one of the armchairs.

A stream of pain pulsed across his forehead as he grasped the full import of the circled article, which was much more incendiary than the rumors circulating in the cheap tabloids, rumors that could be dismissed or explained away as silly or speculative. By contrast, *Le Figaro's* information came straight from the top, from General Auguste Mercier, the minister of war. Martin could hardly believe what he was reading. The head of the army had offered his verdict, or at least an oblique idiotic version of it, even before the case reached his own military court. "The general staff," Mercier was quoted as saying, "has found out from very reliable sources that Dreyfus has been in contact for more than three years with the agents of a foreign government, which was neither the government of Italy nor the government of Austria-Hungary."

How coy, Martin thought with disgust as he slapped the newspapers into his lap. Neither Italy nor Austria-Hungary? Why not just say that he meant Germany, the country that had taken over the city where the Dreyfus family still owned factories? Why did he feel it necessary to insult in this stupid insidious way the great power whose guns were pointed straight at French Lorraine and its capital? Martin's home, Clarie's home. Mercier was a fool.

Martin had no sympathy for anyone who would betray his country, if that is indeed what Dreyfus had done. But what about other Israelites, like Singer and the Steins? This naming, but not really naming, this kind of insinuation, where would it lead? To painting all Jews from Alsace and Lorraine with the same dastardly brush? Martin angrily tossed the paper aside, letting it drop to the floor. His mind was racing. Worst of all, would further proof of Dreyfus's treachery and connection to Germany embolden the man or men who had killed Ullmann and Erlanger to try again?

The desk clerk cleared his throat and shifted his pimply bespectacled gaze from the felled newspaper to Martin's face. Abashed, Martin reached down and smoothed out *Le Figaro* before getting up to replace the rod on the wooden frame. If the clerk knew I was a judge, he would have been more polite, Martin thought ruefully. But Martin had no intention of revealing who he was. Keeping his back to the desk, Martin chose the monochromatic, staid *Le Temps* this time. He planned to hide behind it until his mother called.

Ten minutes later, she rescued him from the clerk's disapproving glances. She had taken a long time, because, Martin suspected, she preferred to spend the time in her room, checking and rechecking her belongings, rather than trying to fill the awkward moments of a prolonged good-bye on the train platform. Yet today, of all days, they could have talked. About Clarie. About his mother's newfound love for his wife. Adele Martin would never admit, of course, that she had been wrong, or that Clarie should have the audacity to continue to teach in one of the Republic's laic high schools. Still, for the first time in years he watched his mother with concern as she went over the room to make sure she had not forgotten anything. She was a head shorter than either he or Clarie, and more stooped than he remembered her. Since he had seen her last, her hair had become whiter, her face more wrinkled, her blue-gray eyes, the only feature they shared, a little dimmer. As she brushed past him, he realized at least one thing had not changed: her scent, lily of the valley. He wondered if she had been wearing the same perfume since the day he was born. He realized with a start that to him, that was a mother's smell.

When she saw him staring at her, she smiled. "Done!" she said brightly.

"You're sure?" He hoped she had not caught the irony in his voice, which amazingly even to him was filled with affection.

She nodded. "Come, my handsome son, take me to the station."

She took the hat box and left him to lug her heavy valise. They walked to the station in a comfortable silence. When they got to the platform and he put down her case, she remarked, "There are baby things in there. I knitted them. I'm going to save them for the next time. Don't tell Clarie. I just wanted you to know how much I was looking forward to. . . ." She grimaced as tears made a single trail down each powdery cheek. She reached inside her black velvet sack for a handkerchief.

"I know that; of course I do." Because Adele Martin had been able to have only one child, she had never kept her desire for grandchildren a secret.

"She's strong, you'll see. And you know that Henri-Joseph is in heaven, don't you?"

Martin did not know. Still, he nodded, avoiding her eyes, which were pleading with him to believe and to confirm what she believed.

Martin swallowed hard. "You've been wonderful, you know. To Clarie. And to Giuseppe. Thank you." If these were not the kindest words he had said to her in years, they were certainly the most sincere.

She reached up and touched his bearded cheek with her gloved hand, and then, for the first time in a decade, they pressed their bodies together in a real embrace. As if that was all she could hope for, she urged, "Go. The men can help me to my seat. You need to be home."

Churning with unexpected emotion, Martin backed away as a porter came to carry her bags. It was hard to believe that after so many years, he might have a mother, despite the fact that he had broken with almost everything she believed in. Adele Martin looked back one more time and waved before stepping onto the gasping train. He lifted his hand too, and smiled sincerely, even though he was aware that he hadn't been completely honest with her. He could not go back home, not yet.

As soon as his mother was out of his sight, Martin went to the front of the station and hired a two-seated hansom cab to take him across the tracks and up the hill toward the Préville Cemetery. This was an extravagance, but he needed to get to the graveyard in time to see the funeral procession. The chill wind battered him in the open cab as he remembered how he had felt at the morgue on Friday. Pushed aside. An outsider. Was it possible that he was childish enough to feel hurt or insulted by Singer's slights? Martin clapped his leather-gloved hands together impatiently. No! He was going to observe the funeral as part of his duty as an investigating magistrate, in case a killer might be bold enough to admire his handiwork. And to understand. He slouched back in the carriage seat. He had to admit that another part of him wanted to see the hidden side of Singer, and that this was why he did not intend to show himself.

When Martin descended from the carriage at the far edge of the cemetery, he knew immediately that he was not too late. Beggars were scattered along the stone wall that enclosed the huge graveyard, waiting, some talking among themselves, others in sullen silence. A few of the paupers, the more practiced and professional, had brought chairs; others sat on the cold hard ground or stood leaning against the equally inhospitable wall. All hoped that they would become the ben- eficiaries of the funeral-goers' charitable duties. How did they know that there would be a procession, Martin wondered as he shrank into his coat and hat, avoiding their eyes. He hadn't noticed any black-lined placards announcing the death. But then, he had not noticed a great deal in the last few days. What he could observe through his lowered eyes, as he hurried to the main entrance, was that some of the beggars had long scraggly beards and wore broad black hats. Jewish paupers, he thought, and so different from Singer and his family. Were they part of what Singer called his "community"?

As soon as Martin stepped inside the wall, he was overcome with a paralyzing fear, and his breathing quickened. How could he have for- gotten even for one moment? His baby's grave lay down a row directly within his line of vision. But—this is why the panic fluttered in his chest—did he even know which little mound was his? There were so many of them. The day they buried his son, that whole afternoon had passed in a blur. Martin pressed his lips together as he tried to calm his breathing. How silly, how womanly he felt. Of course, there would be a name above where Henri-Joseph lay. He'd come back later and fix the exact place in his mind, and prepare for the day when he would lead Clarie to the grave.

He closed his eyes, blocking out everything but what he had come to witness, and waited. When a hush fell over the beggars, he knew the procession was approaching. As soon as he spotted Rabbi Bloch turning the corner at the head of the line of mourners, Martin slipped over to the other side of the gate and flattened himself against the wall. To avoid being seen, he had to settle for observing the mourners from the back as they passed him on their way to the Jewish side of the cemetery, which was separated from the Christian side by a thick high wall. He could tell that Singer was one of the pallbearers holding up the plain pine box. Although the casket was humble, the entourage was quite impressive. About fifty men in black frock coats and black tophats hardly made a sound as they followed the pine box up the slight incline toward the graveyard set aside for the Israelites. Even Stein, the shop-keeper, appeared in a tophat. Then came the veiled women, also in black. Martin thought he recognized the trim figure of Noémie Singer, holding the hand of what must have been her eldest child. Martin was about to leave his hiding place after the women had passed until he caught sight of a few stragglers, humbler men, some in wide-brimmed round black hats, others in caps, shuffling along behind, mumbling prayers. All the mourners ignored the beggars, who would have to wait until after the burial rites to reap any rewards for their efforts.

When Martin was certain that everyone had passed into the Jewish cemetery, he left his spot to find a better observation post farther up the hill. Fortunately the open grave was only a few meters from the gate. Martin could see and hear everything. But he could not under-stand. Rabbi Bloch swayed a little as he recited a singsong prayer, Martin presumed, in Hebrew, the sacred language of the Israelites. Most of the mourners stood by without moving, frozen in dignified grief. A few of the stragglers, however, swayed even more than the cleric, bouncing their heads up and down with greater and greater force as the prayer went on. Martin saw Singer turn and was afraid he had been observed, until he realized that his colleague was moving back from the innermost ring of mourners to comfort his wife.

"Do you recognize any of them?"

Martin almost leapt out of his skin. He turned to see Jacquette.

"Sorry," the inspector said. "Looks like we're both on the job today."

Martin nodded, still conscious of not wanting to make a sound. Then whispered his response. "I don't recognize anyone but the rabbi, the Singers and my landlord."

Jacquette held a small notebook in his hand. He had been taking notes. Good man. Martin should have known he would be here.

"Look again to be sure," Jacquette mumbled. "I'd be particularly interested in anyone who doesn't fit in."

Martin shook his head. The men who were bobbing their heads had their backs to him. He did not think that the tinker, who had caused so much friction between Singer and his wife, was among them.

For the next few minutes, Martin and Jacquette stood, close together, watching in silence just behind the gate, their breath forming wispy clouds between them and the Israelites. When the pine box was lowered into the ground, the mourners lined up one by one to throw dirt over the dead man. Martin stepped away and stretched himself against the outer wall. He could not watch this. Only days ago, he had left his son's casket next to a hole in the ground. They had all left before the custodian had begun to drop shovelfuls of dirt over the tiny body. Even now he could not bear the thought.

Martin felt Jacquette's gloved hand on his shoulder. "I can take it from here."

"Yes," Martin managed to mumble, "I need to do something." Martin lurched away, down the sidewalk to the main entrance. He must have looked desperate. The beggars did nothing to hamper him.

When he found the mound marked with his baby's name, he did

what he could not do in front of Clarie, or Madeleine, or his mother, or Giuseppe. He wept, openly and shamelessly.

By the time he recovered, even the beggars were gone, and in the waning light, he staggered, drained and numb, into the Israelite cemetery. He had no idea what he expected to find as he walked among the gravestones and monuments. Perhaps respite in a place that was not his own, not his family's, where sadness and tragedy belonged to people he did not really know.

Without being aware of what he was doing, Martin began to read, or tried to read, the gravestones, until he realized that some of them were written in Hebrew script. On closer scrutiny he found that on the back of these same stones, the dead, their relationships and their accomplishments were described in French. For some reason this troubled him. Like seeing Singer in the white silk shawl, like being almost pushed out of the morgue as if he were the intruder. Martin scrutinized the gravestone of a dead lawyer. What did it mean to show two faces to the world, even in death? For the first time in his life, Martin found himself asking: to whom or to what did these Israelites owe their first allegiance?

22

Monday, December 3

FOR THE REST OF THE night, and early into the next morning, whenever Martin was not worrying about Clarie, he thought about Singer.
Who was he really, and why was Martin beginning to have doubts?
Like a good judge, Martin tried to weigh the arguments. There was a
"community" from which Martin was excluded. He hated feeling like
an outsider in his own realm, his own country. On the other hand,
hadn't Singer complained about not being invited to the du Manoirs,
about the fact that no one recognized *his* sabbath. As Martin attempted
to analyze the two sides, he realized that when he thought about his
recent encounters with the Israelites, he wasn't dealing with rational
arguments, but with *emotions*. How was it possible that he *felt* these
resentments over observing a praying "community" in the morgue or
reading gravestones? Why was he so uneasy about the ways in which

Singer seemed to be different from him? Was everyone as susceptible as Martin to this insidious wariness? Or was it just him, because he was not as firmly wed to his principles as he had always believed. The more he ruminated, the more Martin realized that what he was beginning to feel was something like shame. He needed clarification, purgation. He needed to know that he had nothing in common with the bona fide anti-Israelites who distorted, taunted and hated, and perhaps even killed. When he got to his chambers Monday morning, he was eager to confront the hatred head on, to make sure that he did not mirror in any way the prejudices of the kind of men he had always considered enemies of a just society.

Jacquette arrived early with the list of possible suspects that Martin had requested on Friday. But the inspector had something else on his mind. Even before he sat down, he asked what they should do with Pierre Thomas.

My God, the tanner. "I almost forgot," Martin admitted. To cover his embarrassment, he got up from his chair, took the sheet of paper from Jacquette with mumbled thanks, and handed it over to Charpentier. Martin was glad to have his back to his inspector as he gave his clerk the order to make a copy. The truth was that since Erlanger's death, since Henri-Joseph's burial, since the papers were no longer screaming about a worker wrongly accused, Pierre Thomas had completely slipped from Martin's mind. Keeping a poor man in jail because he had no one to stand up for him was unconscionable. Martin had to be more attentive.

By the time he sat down again, he was ready to deal with the tanner, and Jacquette had already lit up his first Blue Jockey of the morning. "Do you think Thomas is dangerous?" Martin asked.

"I could see him beating a man to death after too much drink, and not even remembering why the next day. Frankly I don't think he's smart enough to have stalked the mill owner, killed him and hidden the weapon. And besides, after Erlanger. . . ." Jacquette shrugged and yawned. He looked every bit as tired as Martin felt. He had been working all weekend, trying to identify vocal anti-Israelites and, apparently, questioning a number of suspects.

"Did you get anything out of Thomas? Any names?"

A grin took over the right side of Jacquette's grizzled face as he shook his head. "Doesn't go to church, doesn't go to many political rallies, and he'd never give up a comrade. He's got guts. Stupid, but guts."

"Do you have a man to keep a sharp eye on him every once in a while?"

Jacquette nodded.

"Then let's release him and get on with it." Thomas was not only presumably innocent of murder, he had also become a dead end in the investigation. They did not need dead ends. "And in what you gave me this morning, where do you think we should start?" Martin said, referring to the list Charpentier was copying.

Jacquette leaned back in his chair, inhaled deeply, and let out a stream of smoke. "That's a good question. Where *do* we begin?"

"Any local demagogue who blames the Israelites for society's woes. Look for those connected in any way to them or to the victims." Martin paused. "You know all that."

Yet Jacquette was shaking his head. "It's just that, after I started trying to outline the case, I realized that this approach is too vague, too much, despite what I said on Friday about going after the anti-Semites. For example," the inspector said, gesturing toward Charpentier's desk with his cigarette, "if we start at the top, we've got Barrès and Adam, both writers, both ran for the Chamber of Deputies on an anti-Israelite platform. Adam lost, Barrès won. He's the local prodigy, famous at twenty-five, big name. They're both in Paris. If they were campaigning, maybe we could go watch a rally. They only come back to get elected, so we have no way of knowing who their most rambunctious followers are. I skipped over the obvious, of course, our own Rocher in the courthouse." Jacquette gave Martin a meaningful look.

If the inspector thought his sarcasm would lighten the mood, he was wrong. Martin pressed two fingers against his temple, hoping to relieve the building tension. He was not accustomed to so much resistance from his inspector.

Jacquette continued: "I listed a few big army men, but my guess is that if we scratched the surface we could include half the officers in the garrison. And God knows how many priests, although not the bishop." The inspector spread out his arms in mock despair.

"The Thomases, their associates," Martin insisted.

"I put a few names at the bottom. I've already talked to them. Again, if you go down to one of the cafés off the rue des Tanneurs and press hard enough, you'll always find a couple of louts who will bleat out some nonsense about the Jew boss and the Jew banker. They might have known about the mill owner, but I can't imagine that any of them knew the notary. There's a lot of poison just under the skin, ready to ooze out. But no one's said anything about killing."

Scratch the surface. Poison under the skin. At least the good Jacquette seemed to know what they were dealing with: a disease. Martin was beginning to realize how easily one could be infected with it.

"Sir?"

"And the bookstores?" Martin recovered quickly. He did not want to give off even a hint of what had been lurking under *his* skin.

"One of my men took a little stroll. He picked out three that most prominently display Drumont's books and newspapers."

Jacquette let his cigarette dangle beneath his tawny bristle mustache for a moment. Then he took it out of his mouth and held it, clasping his hands in front of him.

Martin prepared himself, knowing his inspector was stalling. "Go on."

"Sir, the more I think about it, the more I worry that we're going about this in the wrong way. Or at least looking in only one direction. Why look only for those who hate men of the Mosaic faith? Why not someone who was close to the victims?"

"Do you mean a family member—"

"Or someone in their community."

Even Jacquette used that word, as if he were quite aware of what it meant. "Are you saying that we should interview all of the Israelites?"

"No, sir." Jacquette screwed up his lips as he often did when preparing to deliver a drollery. "Although I'll warrant there are fewer of them in Nancy than there are anti-Israelites."

Martin did not find this amusing. "Then what are you saying? What do you mean by their 'community'?" If the tone was sharper than he intended, it was because he wanted to make it absolutely clear that he was not about to disturb the Singer household during its mourning period. Or worse, force the best friend he had in the courthouse to feel compelled to stop the police at his door. It was bad enough that he had betrayed Singer in his thoughts; he was not about to do so in his actions.

"Sorry, sir, I was talking in the old way. In the village where my grandfather lived, there were only two communities, theirs and ours, the Israelites and us. Now I suppose it's different. We're all in the city. We're all divided in so many ways. So what I'm thinking is that there are two avenues to pursue. Either those close to Ullmann and Erlanger, professional men and the rich, who form a kind of clan around the synagogue, or those who might feel left out of it."

"Left out?"

"You know, the poorer types. Bumpkins just arrived from the old villages, foreigners. Like the stragglers yesterday."

Pursuing the poor, the enthusiasts who had been bobbing up and down at the gravesite. Or the tinker that Singer had so disdained. No, that wasn't the way that Martin was going to expend his energies.

"You want to investigate the Israelites, for a crime committed against them? A crime that followed the false report of a ritual murder?" A crime against a people, a *community*. After all, that's what Singer believed it was; so did Didier.

"Well, as we would do with any other——"

"The Singers cannot be disturbed."

"I know that." Jacquette took a long pull from his cigarette. This was the first real disagreement in their two-year relationship, and it was the first time that Martin had gotten Jacquette on the defensive. "Look, sir, my family's from around here. In the old villages, everyone lived cheek by jowl. They knew each other's customs. As a little boy, visiting my grandfather, I knew not to enter their homes at certain times, during their holy days or when they were in mourning. But at other times, I played with them and the grownups helped each other out. My grandfather said we wouldn't let them starve, they wouldn't let us starve. He even said he was saved by a Jew, the one who sold him two cows after his died, and loaned him the money, and then didn't collect until he knew my grandfather could pay. That saved his farm. Now that's all changed. The banks loan the money. And they don't wait. Believe me, me and my family have nothing against the Israelites."

"Yes, but with the Dreyfus treason case, don't you think those who do——?"

"That's exactly the problem," Jacquette broke in. "How do you investigate all of them?"

"You start." But how? That was the question. And what if Jacquette was right: what if there was something more personal in the motive of the killer? Martin rubbed his hand hard against the side of his beard. Two murders. There could be more. Should they leave any avenue unexplored? "Charpentier, are you done with those lists?" Martin barked, directing all his frustrations toward his clerk.

Charpentier jumped up, handed Martin two copies of Jacquette's report, and immediately retreated to his desk.

Martin glanced at Jacquette's report. The names swam in front of him, as if they had been written in foreign language, like the gravestones. He could not absorb them all now, in front of Jacquette. But he could move forward.

"All right. Keep a man on Thomas and the cafés he and his wife frequent. Talk to some of the people in the Ullmann factory. And here," Martin picked up one of the newspapers lying on his desk, "find out who this Titus is. He's filling the local *La Croix* with one story after another about evil Israelites."

Jacquette took the paper.

"And," Martin continued, "I'll go to the bookstores." Martin had made a decision. He had to be part of the action. He needed to confront a living, breathing anti-Israelite as soon as possible.

Jacquette's bushy eyebrows went up in surprise.

"I don't think they'll take me for a cop," Martin explained. "Perhaps they'll take me for one of them."

Jacquette pressed his lips together as he stubbed out his cigarette. Martin suspected he was holding back his glee at the notion of his superior becoming an undercover agent. That didn't bother Martin, as long as Jacquette did not argue against him.

When Jacquette had restored a serious and respectful mien, he asked, "And I assume it would be all right with you if I talked to Mme Ullmann?"

Tit for tat. "Yes," Martin conceded. "But be gentle."

"Of course."

Of course. Jacquette knew how to deal with every class of suspect or witness, but he had not yet met the flinty fierceness of the little widow. She would be his match. The thought made Martin smile for the first time that day.

An hour later, when Martin strode into the bustling, bright Librairie de la Gare, the big bookstore in the railroad station, he still believed that he could ferret out the political sentiments of the proprietor better than Jacquette or his men. After all, Martin did not look like a detective. With his trim beard, long gray coat and bowler, he would be taken for an ordinary, moderately well-off customer, distinct only for his interest in the works of anti-Semitic authors. He was even a little sorry that he had not borrowed a walking stick to complete the image.

In the end, even this appendage would not have helped. The middle-aged proprietor, sitting atop a tall chair near the cash register, declared he did not know who regularly bought *La Libre Parole* and had no interest in discussing its contents. When Martin asked him if he carried Drumont's books, the man gestured toward a pimply-faced young clerk, who then proceeded to dog Martin's path, staring at him, mouth half-open, every time he picked up a book. Martin had no idea whether he was simply hoping for a sale, or curious about a customer who had so effectively irritated his boss. In any case, he was breathing down Martin's neck, which had become increasingly hot and prickly under his scarf. Unable to carry on the charade, Martin made a quick exit, determined to do better at the next stop.

The unfortunate Royale, on a crooked medieval side street in the oldest section of the city, was one of those dark, dank stores higher than it was wide or long, with books, new and old, piled everywhere. The shelves, with their jumbled contents, reached up to the ceiling. Even the newspapers, sitting on rusty tin frames at the front of the store, seemed old and musty. Among them were several unsold back issues of *La Libre Parole*. As soon as Martin asked about them, the bent-over almost toothless owner clammed up, making Martin wonder whether the old man had ordered them for his own pleasure, of which, it would seem, he had very little. Had the man been younger or stronger, had he been able to employ even one assistant, Martin might have questioned him further. Instead he left him alone to tend to his failing shop. He could not imagine anything as vigorous as a killer emanating from it.

After the moldy smell of the Royale, the cold mist clinging to Martin's face relieved and refreshed him as he headed to La Librairie de Bonne Politique. His path took him north on the Grande Rue and through the bulging round towers of the Porte de la Craffe. When they first arrived in Nancy, Martin and Clarie had visited this famous city gate, which hundreds of years before had served as both a sentry post and a prison. But Martin had seldom gone north beyond the fortress-like gate to a section of the city that had little to recommend it beside wider streets and newer buildings. Still the name of the bookstore held out a certain promise. Martin did not know what the "good politics" of the title were, but he suspected that they were not his, and if he was careful, he'd find out.

This time, after delivering a polite "*bonjour*" upon his entry, Martin refused any help in finding what he wanted. He spent some time in front of the newspaper stand, perusing the headlines of *La Libre Parole* and *La Croix de Lorraine*, before searching on the shelves for the latest edition of Drumont's *La France Juive*. When he found it, he took the second volume down from the shelf and carried it to a table, where he loosened his scarf, unbuttoned his coat, and laid down his hat. With an air of profound engagement, he began to thumb through the thick paper-bound volume, which listed on the back cover all of Drumont's many works.

After a few minutes, the owner sidled up behind him. "A fine book, Monsieur, don't you think."

"The finest," Martin murmured keeping his gaze fixed upon the pages. "I have the first edition at home. I was just wondering if he's added more."

"Hmmm. Not much I believe. But he does have some others. You've read *The Last Battle*, of course?"

Martin turned to his interlocutor. Looking a man straight in the eye as you were lying to him was a ploy he had learned to use during his interrogations. "Of course."

"A good one," the proprietor continued, "one of his best." He was shorter than Martin, with a balding pate, covered by a few strands of neatly combed and oiled hair. He was clean-shaven and gave off the sweet, sharp scent of a cheap cologne. Everything about him was fastidious. The dark blue vest buttoned over the starched white shirt, a gold-rimmed pince-nez hanging on a thin chain over his chest, the paper wound around his cuffs to keep them clean. And, he was Martin's last hope.

"Oh yes, that came out a few years ago," Martin said, nodding sagely, grateful he had skimmed the back cover.

"Yes. Unbelievable, isn't it, that he predicted the whole Panama Scandal. The whole thing. And *their* role in it."

Eager to latch onto something he knew about, Martin demonstrated his agreement by reciting the slanders that had become commonplace during the Panama Company's calamitous failure. "Think of it. First, *they* mismanaged the whole thing, then they bribed the Chamber of Deputies to shore them up, and when it all collapsed," Martin pursed his lips in disgust, "they almost brought the country down."

"And, worst of all, think of what happened to the little men who they got to invest in the scheme. That's who our Drumont cares about. The little men. I hope you weren't one of them."

Martin shook his head. "I keep my money in the bank, and I chose my bank wisely." As soon as he winked, he feared that this exaggerated gesture had given him away. He was relieved to hear the other man react with a chuckle.

"Wise man. Especially since there are more and more places they control. *They are everywhere.* Just look in our streets. Have you noticed the Russian invasion, those beggars?" he said with vehemence.

"Surely there must be something we can do about it," Martin whispered, hoping that his nervousness at playing a part was not showing. He could feel the sweat under his armpits, but did not want to remove his coat, in case he had to make a swift exit.

The owner's eyes grew large. "Yes. We should do something about it. Especially when we know that they meet all the time, planning, plotting."

"The Rothschilds, yes," Martin murmured, giving the most obvious response he could think of.

"No, sir. Not just in Paris or in the great boardrooms, or on the international scene. No, sir, oh no. Right here in Nancy." The man began to punch one of the books on the display table with his finger.

Martin swallowed hard. This could be it. An entrée into a conspiracy. He had to find a way to keep egging the bookseller on.

"You haven't noticed?" The man stepped back and opened his arms in disbelief.

"Well, yes, you see them on the streets and in the shops." To his chagrin, Martin realized that ever since his involvement in the case, he had been *seeing* more foreign peddlers and noticing more Israelite names on storefronts. Is this how one comes to see "them" *everywhere*? Was this a symptom of the disease?

"Not only the selling and the cheating. Our cafés. They've taken some of them over, you know. And our theater, too."

"The newspapers, the Chamber of Deputies. It doesn't take many." Martin held Drumont's book to his chest and nodded vigorously, grasping for other familiar slanders.

"Yes, yes. But don't you think it is particularly dangerous, right here, in Nancy? Right on the border," the man insisted.

"Yes," Martin agreed with alacrity. "You're right. If only I could find a place or men of like mind, but I'm only a clerk at the courthouse—"

The owner interrupted Martin's lie. "But, my man, talk to Rocher. He's in here all the time," he said in a reassuring singsong voice.

This, of course, did very little to reassure Martin. Rather it confirmed everything he thoroughly disliked about his senior colleague. But he had to keep on playing a role. "I can't talk to him, he's a judge, and I'm just a greffier—"

"But you're at the courthouse. Then you must know the latest."

Martin shook his head slowly. He prayed that he was not about to hear a reprise of Antoinette Thomas's lies. But he had to find out what the "latest" was.

"You mean they've suppressed it there, as well as in the press!" the man stuttered a few steps away from Martin as if jolted by an electric shock. A happy shock. The man was eager to tell all.

Martin took in a short breath and held it. He dare not move, lest he give himself away. What should a greffier know about courthouse gossip? How far did rumors travel through the halls and cloakrooms? Martin had no idea.

Having built up the suspense, the proprietor drew nearer, suffocating Martin in the aura of his cheap cologne. "A boy. A Christian boy. Just across the river," he whispered. "Killed and drained of his blood. For one of their diabolical rites!" Since he had spit out the last words, Martin had leave to move away from the bookseller and his smell.

"When?" All the moisture had evaporated from Martin's mouth, which he had left slightly agape, as if a willing vessel of the other man's confidences.

"Just last week." The man paused. "Or the week before. Does it matter?"

"No, of course not," Martin sputtered with false anger, even as he reached down to the display table support. *How many people had that idiot Rocher told?*

"I see you're as shocked as I was." The vile proprietor had the nerve to lay his hand on Martin's shoulder. "I guess Rocher has kept it under his hat."

"Yes, I guess so," Martin mumbled, as he thought, *hardly.*

"Imagine, not even knowing at the courthouse," the man said, shaking his head in wonder. Suddenly, he clicked his fingers. "Why don't we show those big shots like Rocher. I've got exactly the thing that will bring you up to snuff and really impress him. We 'little men' have to stick together, don't you think?" he said as he moved toward the counter and the cash register.

Martin left *La France Juive* on the table and watched as the proprietor reached under the counter and pulled out a book bound in the soft beige paper that was the innocuous covering of hundreds of cheap editions. "I only have a few of these," the bookseller said, proudly holding it up. "I've been waiting for the final edition to come out, but somehow it's never happened."

Barely daring to breathe, Martin walked up to the counter and saw at once that there could be nothing innocuous about a book titled *Nancy-Juif. Jewish Nancy. Or the Jews at the Border and the War of Tomorrow.*

A spurt of heat shot up straight from Martin's gut. He was sweating even more than before. Staring, mesmerized, he asked if he could take a look.

For the first time since their conversation began, the man looked suspicious.

"You've never told me your name."

"Charpentier." Martin thrust out his hand, hoping to God, for more than one reason, that his clerk had never been to the store. Hoping, too, that Charpentier would appreciate having been given a stellar role in this drama when Martin told him about it. Knowing that in this instant, it was the only name that he could come up with.

"Villiers," the man said as he shook Martin's hand.

Martin withdrew his hand as soon as he could, and the man pushed the book toward him.

"This should tell you everything. He talks about who let the Huns inside the gates during the war and who are aiding them now. Not just Dreyfus in Paris, but here, here in Nancy. It could happen again. The occupation. The humiliation. And now we know who's responsible."

"So it's mostly about the war?" Once he had his hand on the book, Martin hoped not to let it go.

"Oh no, not just that. It names all the shopkeepers, all the officials. It's as if," Villiers's eyes grew bright with pride, "as if we had our own Drumont, right here. Instead of Jewish France, he's written Jewish Nancy. And we need to heed what he has to say."

189

"Have you sold many of these?" Martin could not keep the trembling out of his voice. He bit his lip.

"No, because it's still a work in progress. And look here," Villiers grabbed the book from Martin and opened it to the title page, "printed in Commercy, probably because they control all the presses in our fair city."

"May I?" Once more Martin held out his hand for the book, and when he got it, he began to flip through the folded, uncut pages. Even under the oppressively eager gaze of the book dealer, it didn't take Martin long to realize that *Nancy-Juif* was everything Villiers had said it was: a Nancien version of Drumont, a prescription for hate, a call to action against the Jews. Martin turned back to the cover. There was no author's name on the title page, only "a Lorrainer who has seen the war."

"There's no name here. Do you know who wrote it?" Martin asked, trying to keep his voice steady. By this time the sweat was sprouting all over his face. He kept telling himself, he had nothing to fear. What could the man do to him, even if he discovered that Martin was not who he said he was?

Fortunately, Villiers was too wrapped up in his enthusiasm to notice Martin's anxiety. "Oh yes. I've met him only once. A priest. I expected that he would come in with the final copies some time this winter, but," he shrugged.

"If he's in Nancy, I'd love to hear him." *And wring his neck.*

"Let's see," Villiers put on his pince-nez and took out a second copy of the book from underneath the counter. "I know he has a small parish way outside the city. That's probably because what he has to say, his truth-telling, is too hot for the bishop." This time it was he who gave Martin a wink. "The bigwigs in the Church are gettin' too cozy with the Republic, don't you think?" Without waiting for Martin's answer, Villiers opened his copy of the book. "See here," he pointed to the corner of the title page, "he signed mine."

Abbé Hémonet, Noviant-aux-Prés.

Martin committed this scrap of information to his memory, then asked if he could purchase a copy.

"I only have three." Villiers continued in a tone that was much too intimate for Martin's liking, as if from one "little man" to another. "You can have it for five francs, if you promise to take good care of it."

"I will, I can assure you," Martin said. This, at least, was not a lie.

23

As soon as Martin got to his chambers, he started to flip through Hémonet's book. He didn't take off his coat, he didn't sit, he didn't take the time to tear open the quarto pages. It was enough to see every page in eight to know that *Nancy-Juif* was a poisonous piece of propaganda. After he turned the book over to Charpentier to cut, he flung off his coat and jacket and loosened his cravat. It didn't help. Nothing relieved the heat of anger and anxiety. Not even the arrival of Jacquette.

Martin crossed his arms and jiggled his foot impatiently while the inspector gave a desultory report on his meeting with the Widow Ullmann. In sum, nothing new. At least Martin had *Nancy-Juif*. After giving a full report of his excursion into the bookshops, Martin concluded: "I'll read, you go find him."

Instead of jumping to obey Martin's curt command, Jacquette stood up and stared at him for a moment with a look of mock sorrow on his long face. "The priest really got to you, didn't he? Should I take the army to fetch him?"

Martin threw his pen on the desk and looked up at his inspector. Leave it to Jacquette to find an irreverent way to point out obvious logistical problems. It might not be easy to retrieve Hémonet from some godforsaken town more than an hour's ride away. After all, they had no idea how the villagers might react to a contingent of police from the city coming to arrest their pastor. Martin sighed and shook his head. "Right. How should we go about this?"

Jacquette placed both of his broad, callused hands on the desk. As he leaned forward, Martin caught a strong whiff of the Turkish tobacco that always enveloped the inspector. "Tell you what," Jacquette said. "I'll go by myself, if that's what you want. Look over the scene. And then we can figure out what to do. If it's easy, I might find a way to bring him back. If not," Jacquette shrugged, "we'll have to think about it." After straightening up, Jacquette reached across his chest and drew a Blue Jockey from his vest pocket. "Noviant-aux-Prés," he murmured as he patted his pockets, looking for a match. "You can be sure the bishop doesn't like this guy, or he wouldn't be out there in the middle of nowhere. At least that means we shouldn't have any trouble on that front."

This was the first reassuring opinion that Jacquette had delivered all day.

But what Jacquette gave, he immediately took away. "Of course, if the Monsignor does squawk," he continued with the satisfied sigh that always followed his first pull of tobacco, "you'll have to handle it." His closed-mouth smile did little to conceal his delight at the thought. "I don't think the Monsignor would deign to see anyone lower than a judge."

Martin snorted. It was enough to know the formidable Monsignor

Turinaz by reputation. The last thing he needed was to confront the powerful bishop about one of his priests. "Charpentier, are you done with the book?" Martin said, once again redirecting his impatience at his clerk. His greffier had been cutting the pages of *Nancy-Juif* with his usual finicky precision while Jacquette and Martin talked, and undoubtedly taking in every word they said.

"And how did you feel about the judge using your name, heh, Charpentier?" Jacquette's annoying jocularity had not abated. There was no better proof of that than his addressing, with collegial familiarity, a man whom he usually referred to as an over-educated dandy.

Charpentier stood up as if at attention, his *coupe-papier* hanging from his hand like a sword at his side. "As Monsieur le juge chooses, if it helps with the case. I will certainly know never to go there myself!"

Martin heard a touch of pride in Charpentier's high-pitched voice. The truth is that he had been pleased that Martin had used his name, for it was the closest the young man had ever come to being treated like more than a clerk. And now, even the sardonic, usually dismissive Jacquette was speaking to him.

"Good boy!" Jacquette nodded. "All for the cause, no? Let me have a look at that book," he said as he strode over to the clerk's desk.

Martin scratched his beard in frustration as Jacquette, still in inexplicably good humor, took an orator's position in front of him and turned to the first page of *Nancy-Juif*. He held the book at arm's length as he declaimed the first lines. "LORRAINERS! FRENCHMEN! The past leads to the future. What two Jews of Nancy did a hundred years ago, what five hundred Jews did again twenty-two years ago, fifteen thousand Jews in Nancy will surely do tomorrow!"

Martin knew the page practically by heart, knew that the priest intended to show how the Jews were responsible for the Revolution, for the humiliating defeat at the hands of the Prussians, and God knows what treacheries in the future. He watched as Jacquette mouthed the last words of the introduction to himself. "Get rid of those who hate Christians. Get rid of the successors of Judas. Get rid of the Jews."

Jacquette clicked his tongue as he winked. "He's a bad one, all right."

Martin held out his hand. He had had enough of the inspector's high spirits.

Jacquette relinquished the book and took a long draw from his cigarette, exhaling very slowly. He had suddenly turned serious. "Sir, sir," he whispered almost in a pleading voice, "you can't, *we* can't, catch them all. We can't bring in every person who shouts 'dirty Jew' to someone passing in the street. Or everyone who feels they've been cheated by an Israelite. Or every politician who thinks a little anti-Semitism will win them a seat in the Chamber of Deputies. We can't. All we can do is find one murderer in the best way we know how."

Suddenly, Jacquette's dark brown eyes turned soft with loyalty, and Martin knew why his inspector had made so many feeble attempts at levity. He wasn't just trying to warn Martin about Hémonet, or the possible uprising of devoted villagers, or the flabbiness of Martin's investigative plans. Jacquette was worried about *him*, Martin. They both knew that the cloud he was under was much thicker than the fog of Turkish smoke that wafted between them. Invisible, yet impenetrable. A potent mix of exhaustion and sadness.

Through the most seemingly futile and endless investigations, Martin and Jacquette had always been easy with each other. That's the way they worked. That's the way they succeeded. But this time Martin could not go along with Jacquette's attempt at cynical humor. His heart was too heavy. The stakes were too high. He was under pressure at home and in the courthouse, from Didier, from Singer, from the press. Yes, he knew he could not root out prejudice against the Israelites, especially now that he realized how widespread and deep it was. How apparent and yet how hidden. Even from himself, even— and this was so humiliating he would admit it to no one—*in* himself. Only he knew that finding the killer was his silent act of contrition.

"But, of course you understand," he insisted in an even voice as he tapped on the beige paper cover of Hémonet's book, "this one is certainly worth catching and dragging in."

"Of course." Jacquette knew when to back down. And he certainly was not going to express his concerns about his superior in front of Charpentier.

"In a few hours, then," Martin stood up. He hoped that the firm, lingering grip of his handshake would show his appreciation for what Jacquette had tried to do. The inspector met Martin's eyes, nodded, and, without another word, set out for Noviant-aux-Prés.

As soon as Jacquette left, Martin took out two sheets of paper. One he labeled "names," the other he left blank, to jot down any questions that arose as he read, questions to throw at Hémonet when he finally got him in his chambers. His fingers trembled a little as he opened the newly cut pages. He was not afraid to confront the usual charges against the Israelites: that they still practiced blood ritual; that they planned to take over the world through the machinations of the Rothschilds; that their Talmud taught them to despise Christians. These were the kinds of slanders that Martin had become all too familiar with in the last few weeks. No, what made him hopeful and fearful at the same time was that Hémonet would single out particular Israelites in Nancy, men and women who fell under Martin's jurisdiction and protection.

Martin skimmed through the early sections on the Middle Ages, the Revolution and the Prussian War. They demonstrated only too well how deeply the priest hated the Jews and how willing he was to blame them for every ill that had befallen the natives of Lorraine from time immemorial—plague, the Terror, betrayal, impoverishment, defeat, corruption, starvation. Well and good, Martin thought, his anger rising as he skimmed the pages. Let him bleat about the past. Most of the men the priest had named were probably dead anyway.

What concerned Martin was the present. Here the accusations were more scattershot, and more lethal. Martin's stomach began to churn as he read Hémonet's description of present-day Nancy. The priest described the city as a "little Jerusalem" infested by a steady influx of eastern and northern Jews who would someday, once again, betray Lorraine to the Germans. It was a ridiculous claim. Martin had never felt surrounded by Israelites. Before this investigation, he had never thought about how many shops were owned by Jews or taken note of which poor immigrants in the city were of the Mosaic faith. Now he was ever alert to the presence of men like the tinker, whom Singer had reviled, and the long-coated, black-clad mourners bowing and swaying at Erlanger's gravesite. Harmless types. He shook his head. The priest was raving. Yet after the murder of two Israelites, Martin could no longer dismiss *Nancy-Juif* as one man's madness. The book was dangerous. It filled him with disgust, but he had to read on. For clues. For collaborators. For potential victims. For some connection with Ullmann and Erlanger.

It came on page 117. A "true" story about a poor woman begging in the wealthy Place Saint-Jean in the bitter winter of 1892. She had made the mistake of knocking on the door of a mansion inhabited by a Jew. She was rudely rebuffed and sent back into the cold with nothing to eat.

Martin lifted his head and thought for a moment. "Charpentier!"

"Yes, Monsieur le juge." The clerk had been sitting quietly, fussing with whatever he found to fuss with.

"Can you go through Jacquette's report and tell me where Daniel Erlanger lived?"

"The Place Saint-Jean," Charpentier said, as though it were obvious. He prided himself on his memory for details.

"That's what I thought, " Martin mumbled as he circled the paragraph with his pen and bent down the corner of the page.

Fortified by having found one possible piece of tangible evidence, Martin took in a breath and plunged back into *Nancy Juif*'s vicious stew of hatred and paranoia. By now it was clear that the Israelites as human beings had no place in its roiling pot. Martin had already observed that the priest never once granted them the dignity of calling them Israelites. To him they were Jews or *youtres*, the "descendants of Judas," "the devil you can see," subhumans dangerous whether outside of society eager to get in, or, worse, inside. In one particularly nauseating passage Hémonet even suggested that they be treated as pigs had been in the middle ages, as too filthy to be allowed within the city gates. Or, in another nasty formulation, compared them to the wasps who swarm into hives so that they can "kill the bees, tear open their stomachs and suck the honey out of their entrails."

Pretty writing, this, Martin thought sarcastically. And all the more dangerous because Hémonet occasionally gave names to the pigs and wasps he claimed were "judaizing" the city. Martin's head was beginning to pound. There were enough factual details and real names salted into Hémonet's steady diet of slanders to convince the weak-minded. The priest named cafés where Jews supposedly conspired, listed stores and their owners on the main streets of the city, pointed a finger at a few prominent politicians, factory owners and jurists. Martin noted and read over these lists carefully to make sure that the Steins and the Singers were not on them. But then again, neither were Ullmann and Erlanger.

Martin shook his head in disbelief at the most preposterous claims. Jews spaced their houses throughout the city in such a way as to be able to take over Nancy when the time came. Richer Jews paid their poor, immigrant co-religionists to spy and report back to them. By the time he finished, Martin understood what it meant to hate an entire race. He thought of the Singers, of the Steins, of the Widow Ullmann and the rabbi. All of them, rich or poor, male or female, young or old, were the same to men like Hémonet: Jews, lepers to be stigmatized and cast out.

"In the past," the priest concluded, *"lepers were kept away from populated areas and lived in huts or leper hospitals far away from cities and*

villages. . . . They wore mandatory uniforms, known to all. If ever they were about to encounter someone, they had to warn them by ringing a little bell that they wore hanging from their necks. . . . The Jews are the lepers, the contagious of our society. . . ."

Oh, yes, Martin thought as he slapped the book shut, I am eager to talk to this priest. Eager to know everything about him. How often he comes into the city. How he finds the time away from his "investigations" to say mass, hear confession, comfort the sick, and console the dying. And what in hell he thinks he's doing. Martin shot out of the chair and began to pace; he stoked the fire in the grinning potbellied stove even though he did not need the warmth. In his need to move and clear out his head, he did not even care that Charpentier was watching him under lowered eyes. Finally, Martin was able to sit again and begin to formulate the questions that he intended to ask the Abbé from Noviant-aux-Prés.

Night had already fallen by the time that Jacquette returned to report that François Hémonet had been defrocked. "About a year ago. The vicar they left in charge seemed quite cowed. I guess the bishop has quite a temper and doesn't like insubordination. Whatever that means."

"Do we know where Hémonet is?" Martin asked, alarmed.

"Would you believe it?" Jacquette chortled. "Sent to his family, like a schoolboy. If he did what he was told, we should be able to pick him up tomorrow, in Laneuveville. I'll have two men and a carriage ready by eight o'clock. Want to come along for the ride?"

"Yes!" Martin wanted to lay his hands on the priest as soon as possible, although he was still taken aback by the unexpected turn of events.

Jacquette grinned. "Isn't it grand that the old Monsignor has seen fit to aid the 'godless' state by pinning our friend down in a place where we can just go and snatch him up?"

This time Martin returned the smile. It was good to end the long, chill day with a bit of republican humor.

24

Tuesday, December 4

THIS IS WHERE IT BEGAN.

Martin wrapped his scarf more tightly around his neck as he stared out toward the canals and the Meurthe. Through the morning fog, the buildings blurred and loomed like mirages, but Martin knew them to be all too real: the mills, the tanneries, Ullmann's majestic mansion across the river, and somewhere even further beyond, the hovel where little Marc-Antoine had choked to death. As the dampness seeped into Martin's bones, he began to rue his decision to sit beside Jacquette in the high driver's seat. The two armed men below them in the black police wagon did not have to endure the full lashing force of the wind. The sturdy Jacquette had protectively wound his knitted wool scarf over his mouth and mustache, but otherwise seemed undeterred by the elements. Clear-eyed and purposeful, he urged the horses down the road with a crack of his whip. Whether or not he agreed with the direction that Martin was taking, the inspector always found a way to move forward. Martin squeezed his eyes shut and took a long breath. *Let us hope we can track down the priest and that he'll have something useful to say.*

"How much farther?" Martin muttered, as he rubbed his gloved hands together to keep them warm.

Jacquette hooked one finger at the top of his scarf and pulled it down to answer. "Laneuveville devant Nancy is as its name says, the new town just in front of Nancy, if the southern boundary can be thought of as the front instead of the arse." The town's modest appellation seemed to amuse Jacquette, who let out a little guffaw. Then, much to Martin's relief, he let the scarf spring back over his mouth. Martin was not in the mood for pleasantries. He much preferred the hypnotic clipclop of the horses' hooves to words. Words too often expressed doubts and sorrows. Or said nothing at all.

Like the hollow civilities exchanged at breakfast between him and Clarie. The cool forehead offered for his kiss. The desultory pat on his arm as he left the table. Her thick, dark hair matted and braided. Their eyes never really meeting. The unspoken emptiness between them. Martin grimaced as he stared over the top of the horses' heads at the road rushing toward him. How futile it was to think of these things now. Or anything. Singer, the Thomas baby, his baby, Ullmann, Erlanger, Clarie. In his dreams, in his thoughts, they had become intertwined, inseparable. Yet Martin knew this was not so, it should not be so.

After they passed through a woods they emerged into the outskirts of town. Martin held tight to the back of his seat as the wagon jolted to a stop in what appeared to be Laneuveville's center. Or, better, appeared to be like any of a thousand towns in France with its inevitable stone church, attached shops fronting the main road, and narrow unpaved streets crisscrossing it. And just as in every main street, when trouble or spectacle marched by (and certainly a big black police wagon ranked high as both of these) heads popped up at the windows of butchers and bakers and sundry stores to see what was going on. Although he and Jacquette were prominently perched atop the wagon, Martin sensed that they were not the main attraction. With his respectable gray bowler and coat and well-trimmed beard, he could have been any boring bourgeois type from the city. No, the eyes behind the windows focused on the police and their rifles.

Jacquette turned to the bigger of the two policemen. "Vincent, climb out of your nice warm seat and get directions to the Hémonet house."

Martin hoped the inhabitants would not resist the inquiries of the red-headed cop who put down his rifle, descended from the wagon and lumbered into the *boulangerie*. Squinting hard through the window, Martin saw the female proprietor and her customers shrug their shoulders and consult with each other, until finally one man escorted Vincent out of the bakery to point and gesture as he described the way. Once Vincent delivered the directions to Jacquette, they set out again. It seems that the Abbé François Hémonet was a country boy, living in one of the outlying districts.

Here, too, most of the one- and two-story stone houses were pushed up against each other or attached to wooden stables painted in a variety of colors. All of them stood several meters from the road. In the long front yards, carts rested for the season along with neatly stacked piles of farm tools, wood, and manure. A trusting, traditional community, Martin thought. No fear of thieves, everyone knows each other. Except for us. For in contrast to the town's center, the wagon's arrival seemed to have made the rural inhabitants disappear. "They're afraid we're here to collect their taxes," Jacquette said, observing the resolutely opaque windows. "They have so little, who can blame them?" Martin responded. Although he wondered what the farmers had to hide. Many of their most precious possessions were already on display, stewarded with the utmost care. "Let's make sure they know why we're here."

Jacquette ordered Vincent out of the wagon again, to start knocking on doors. They were lucky on the first stroke. Once the old man understood that the police had not come to take stock of his worldly goods, he was eager to talk. Without even putting on a coat, he hobbled straight to the carriage. "Third house from the end," he said, pointing, as whiffs of chilled air curled and swelled in front of his reddened nose. "Can't you tell? That's the house that needs a real man, not someone in skirts," he snorted, referring to the priest's cassock. Jacquette gave Martin a wink. They had probably found the neighborhood's reigning anti-cleric.

Or not, Martin thought. How many more in this tight-knit community held Hémonet, who had been defrocked and sent home to his family like a troublemaking schoolboy, in total contempt? The faithful would have as many reasons for mocking a disgraced priest as an atheist.

Jacquette thanked the old man and started the wagon again. They stopped in front of a wide two-story house, its yellow stucco façade stained and peeling. Attached to neither house nor barn, it seemed isolated from its neighbors in the misty cold that tinctured everything with gray moisture. "I think we can do this alone," Martin said to Jacquette as they descended from the driver's seat. He saw no reason to invade a house with rifles drawn unless absolutely necessary. His boots crunched down on ridges of frost-hardened mud as he walked around the wagon. In unspoken agreement, he and Jacquette stood for a moment, observing a scene that was deplorably chaotic by the standard of other neat, well-tended yards. A cart disabled by a missing back wheel; a few broken old tools set against the wall; manure, presumably used for fertilizer, strewn all around. What they did not know was whether this disarray had been caused by neglect or hostility. Martin took in a long breath to prepare himself, and was grateful that the cold had damped down the pungency of scattered cow and horse dung. Still he stepped carefully as he followed Jacquette, who, in his role as police inspector, took the lead, striding up to the thick green door and giving it a few authoritative raps with his bare knuckles.

At first there was no answer, although Martin signaled to Jacquette that he had seen a curtain move. The inspector began to accompany his knocks with shouts of "Police." Finally the door creaked ajar. A bent-over old woman peered out, suspicion burning in the dark eyes of her wrinkled face. The hair sprouting from under her faded floral kerchief and on her chin was snow white.

"What do you want?" she demanded, holding on to the door with her gnarled hands.

"We are here to see François Hémonet. I am Police Inspector Jacquette and this is Monsieur le juge Martin from the court at Nancy."

Her eyes widened, and she shrank back a little without letting go of the thick wooden door.

"Why do you want to see him?"

"We don't have to tell you why. The judge is with me. That's enough. Let us in!" Jacquette's voice had risen to a shout. Gone was the bonhomie of Martin's travel companion. This was the official Jacquette, and he was very good in the part.

The old woman stuck her head out to survey the street, to see if anyone behind the curtained windows was watching them. After glancing again at Jacquette, she focused on Martin, who returned her stare with a stern face. That's all he had to do to assert his authority, for she immediately stepped back and held the door open. Even a farmer's wife knew the powers of an examining magistrate.

Martin removed his bowler and bowed his head slightly, as if he were greeting any other mistress of a household. And, indeed, she deserved this sign of respect, for the polished neatness of the large rectangular room they entered belied the disorder into which the family's lives had been thrown. At one end, a fire roared. Above the fireplace stood four shining silver candlesticks and a clock framed in gilded porcelain. On the other side of the room, a large mahogany cupboard, filled with dishes and cups, had been rubbed to an auburn sheen. The stairs leading to a second floor, not all that common for farming families, confirmed that this had once been a prosperous household. And a pious one. In front of Martin on the walls were three familiar pictures, the Sacred Heart of Jesus, the Virgin and Child, and Saint Joseph. There was a table set for three on the right near the cupboard and, to the left, four armchairs by the fire. A young woman, in a flowered flannel dress, got up, laid down her knitting and stood to face Martin and Jacquette. She was as plain as her mother, albeit taller and straighter. Her skin was rough, almost swarthy, and her hair, pulled back in a careless, loose bun, was mousy brown. It occurred to Martin that if she did not already have an ardent suitor, her brother's scandal could condemn her to spinsterhood.

"Anne-Marie, go get your brother," Mme Hémonet said as she leaned her hunched body against the wall.

The young woman tiptoed toward the stairs, never taking her eyes off the intruders. No one had taken his hat or offered him a seat, so Martin leaned against the door and observed the young woman mounting the stairs. Even though she had been glowering at him, he watched her with a twinge of pity.

As soon as her daughter disappeared, the old woman began clutching at her white apron as if in prayer, walking back and forth in front of Martin and Jacquette. "It's good my husband's too dead to see this," she said to everyone and no one. "He never thought his boy should become a priest."

"You are a widow, then?" Martin asked. She was in a dire situation. Neighbors who scorned her household, a son incapable of cleaning up the yard.

His mild comment roused her again, to defiance. "Yes, yes, I am. A poor widow who needs a son. So why do you want him? He's a good boy. A priest. He's never done nothing wrong."

There was much Martin could have said in response: That her son might have committed a murder or incited someone else to kill. That he was, at the very least, a slanderer and hatemonger. That he certainly was no longer a boy. But Martin clamped his mouth shut. The mother was not responsible for the sins of the son. Nor was the sister, who was taking her time getting the brother downstairs.

Jacquette had already begun to pace, and stopped at the first sound coming from above. They heard murmured voices, then shouting, finally quick footsteps descending the wooden staircase.

It was the girl, in an agitated state. "He doesn't want to come. He said that you have no authority over him. He is studying." Her chest heaved up and down as she spoke.

"We'll see about that!" said Jacquette as he tried to pass her. She grabbed him by the arm. "Don't," she cried.

He shook her off and went up the stairs.

"It's about that book, isn't it?" the mother asked Martin. "It's a brave book. That's what he told me. Brave and true. Anne-Marie has read it. Tell the judge about it."

"Don't you know that some people don't agree with us? People who—" She stopped herself in time.

People who what? Are friends with the Israelites? Are somehow beholden to them?

She glared at Martin. Whatever sympathy he had felt for her dried up. Martin tightened his jaw and ignored her. Instead, he began to worry that he either should be upstairs helping Jacquette or calling in the police. Making a decision, he bounded past the women to the stairs, but before he could shake off the girl's desperate grasp, he saw a hulking figure heading down toward him. Without taking his eyes off Hémonet, Martin stepped away to avoid a collision. Jacquette had twisted the man's arm behind his back.

"Here's your priest." he said, as he gave his captive a shove.

"I'm not anyone's priest any more," Hémonet slurred. This was certainly true. He was a wreck. His half-buttoned cassock was stained with whatever he had been eating or drinking. Greasy clumps formed little peaks in his thick brown hair and beard. As he lurched forward, Martin caught a whiff of more than liquor, a rotten unwashed smell. Jacquette grabbed him by the arm again and held him back. Hémonet peered at Martin through bloodshot gray eyes, then gave out a laugh. "I suppose some Jew subprefect sent you after me. Or are you one of them yourself? They're all after me. I know that."

"Do you want to change?" Martin said coldly, facing him down. "Or should we take you back to Nancy in your cassock?" He meant to cut Hémonet short, and to the quick. Defrocked priests were not allowed to wear the vestments of their lost office.

"Oh, judge," Hémonet gave a snort, "this isn't a cassock. It's a bathrobe. I'm a sick man. You want to take a sick man into one of your *youtre* jails. I could contaminate the Jews. Contaminate them! That's a laugh." And he continued to snort and chortle shifting his head this way and that.

Was the defrocked priest mad, or merely stinking drunk? Even in this unwashed state, Martin perceived that Hémonet did not take after the women in his family. He was strapping and handsome. Perhaps even a charmer. The brightest hope of a family that had launched him into his holy vocation. Now he was only contemptible. "Why don't you get dressed. Show respect for your mother," Martin said, as he walked away toward the door.

"Oh, Monsieur le juge, Maman likes me here," Hémonet shouted after him. "She likes having her boy at home. That's what she tells me every day." He dropped to his knees, almost taking Jacquette with him. "I'm not going anywhere. I can't preach, I can't teach. I can't do anything any more. You must know that. It's against the law." Then he started to giggle, as he swung his arms open in a wide arc. "But is it your Jew-Republican law or canon law? I don't even know." Then he stopped laughing. "What does it matter, after all. I'm stuck," he spit out, barely missing Martin. Jacquette cuffed him on back of the head and sent the priest sprawling to the ground.

The Widow Hémonet clasped her apron to her mouth to shut off her moan, while her daughter knelt on the floor and tried to help her brother up. These were the scenes that Martin hated most. The pain of the bystanders, the wailing, the recriminations, the accusations that the justice to which he had dedicated his life was harsh and cold. His stomach was tied in painful knots of disgust for the man and pity for the women. They were the ones who were stuck.

Before Martin turned to leave and call in the men to help Jacquette, he decided to perform an act of mercy, whether Hémonet and the women recognized it or not. He told Jacquette to make sure that the priest changed out of his cassock. Martin knew that if Hémonet entered jail as a defrocked priest he would be subject to the endless ridicule and taunting of prisoners and guards alike. For Martin republican justice meant that everyone should be granted the dignity of being treated as a man like any other. This was, of course, more than Hémonet granted the Israelites. Whether his acts of indecency had become crimes was what Martin would determine in his chambers.

25

Wednesday, December 5

ON WEDNESDAYS AS ON SATURDAYS, school ended at noon. No meal was served. Everyone was on her own. Well, Madeleine Froment thought she as stood inside the school entrance staring out the window, in truth only she was on her own. The students had their families to go to, and so did the other teachers. Indecision swirled in her mind as turbulently as the wind outside, which was coughing up papers and dust in the street. Should she return to her cold empty room? Or visit a bright, warm café, which she could ill afford? Or go to the Martins'? Madeleine blinked to hold back a tear. Wednesdays used to be her favorite time with Clarie. They could linger over a modest lunch without fear of being interrupted by the judge. Even then, although Clarie invited her, Madeleine sometimes felt she was imposing. And now, no one invited her, because Clarie didn't really talk any more.

Madeleine clutched her heavy school bag to her chest, going over everything that had happened in the last few days. And then she knew. She must go to Clarie. In a few hours it would be exactly a week since they had laid her baby to rest. Clarie needed distraction. She needed someone who could help her back to life. She needed her, Madeleine.

With that resolve, Madeleine set out, lowering her head against the elements and thrusting herself forward through the few blocks that separated the Lycée Jeanne d'Arc from the Martin apartment. By the time she reached the entrance beside the Steins' drygoods store and struggled up to the third floor, she was sweating and panting. She took a moment to catch her breath and straighten her hat. Then she tapped lightly on the door. Madeleine never announced herself with a clamor.

The Martins' day woman arrived almost at once to greet her. Madeleine noted with satisfaction the relief on Rose's face as the maid bent her knee ever so slightly in an awkward version of a curtsy. At least she understood how necessary Madeleine had become to the household.

"How is Mme Martin today?" Madeleine asked as she put her bag down and handed over her gloves and scarf.

Rose shrugged and shook her head sadly. She was an unattractive, thin-haired little creature, wearing a threadbare cotton floral dress ill suited to the winter weather. She was, Madeleine knew, all the Martins could afford. The kind of help Madeleine, in straitened circumstances since her father's death, barely managed to keep herself. With a sigh she let Rose take her coat. In her youth, Madeleine never dreamed that her closest friend would be the daughter of a blacksmith. Or that she would be devoting herself to someone who was neither her own husband nor her child. At least there would be some kind of beef stew— Madeleine could smell it already—and warmth.

She hurried into the living room, where she found Clarie wrapped in an old maroon woolen shawl, huddling in the big, soft chair by the fire. This was the same chair Clarie used to offer to her almost every afternoon at teatime. For just an instant after Madeleine glanced at the chillier spot to which she would be consigned, she thought of retrieving her scarf. But she shunted this desire aside. She did not want to appear to be criticizing her friend during her travail.

"Darling," Madeleine said, as she reached down to take hold of Clarie's hand, "are we feeling any better today?"

"No. How could I?" Clarie, who had always been so cheerful, had become relentlessly mournful. Her large, brown almond-shaped eyes, always her best feature, were now rimmed with red and circled in the gray of her fatigue. Her nose, a bit long even though it tipped up at the end, seemed even longer now. As did her oval face. She hadn't even bothered to put her hair up. Instead it hung in one thick dark braid, lying dormant on her shoulder. Clarie could not go on like this.

"My poor sweet, try to take solace in the fact that you can always have other children." Madeleine crossed both hands over her heart as she sat down. "I have every faith that you will."

"It won't be Henri-Joseph, my baby. And why do you keep saying that, you and Bernard's mother? How do you know?"

Clarie sounded genuinely angry. This was so unlike her.

"Because, my dear," Madeleine said gently, "we both have faith in you, as does your doctor. You are young. You are strong." Madeleine caught her breath before going on, for she could not help thinking, *You are married to a man who loves you. A judge who is making his way up the ladder, who will some day provide you with all the comforts.* Sometimes Madeleine felt a little impatient in spite of herself. Didn't Clarie understand that she had so much more than Madeleine could ever hope to have? At least Martin's mother, an impoverished widow with a son who had never taken her wishes into account, understood this.

"Why did this happen to me and my son? Why?" Clarie blurted out, and then drew the shawl around herself more tightly as she folded in on herself and turned her head away.

Madeleine sloped forward, grasping the arms of her chair and staring at her friend as she tried to think of what to say. She was not so fanatical as to believe that Clarie was being *punished*. She could have repeated what everyone else was saying, "These things do happen. No one knows why." But deep in her heart Madeleine believed there was more to it. That everything happens for a reason. That maybe this was the way God intended to purify and save Clarie's soul. And maybe Madeleine was the humble instrument of His Divine Plan. She bowed her head. How could she have forgotten, even for an instant, that she had the one thing that Clarie did not have: faith. A truly generous person would want to give this gift to those who needed it most.

"Did I do something wrong? Was I a bad person? Did I not do everything I should? Didn't I love him enough?" Clarie began to weep.

"No, no, dear. You did nothing wrong. But—"

"But, what?"

Was this the moment? Madeleine clasped her hands together and pressed her eyes closed. *May I have the wisdom and courage to find a way to fulfill Your Wishes.* "There are ways for you to find solace," she began carefully. "In faith and in prayer. We baptized your little Henri-Joseph. He is happy now. He is an angel. You know that, don't you?"

"That's what Bernard's mother kept telling me," Clarie whispered as she turned away again, as if dismissing Madeleine's words.

"He is an angel," Madeleine insisted. "Pure and happy. He'll be waiting for you in heaven."

Tears streamed down Clarie's cheeks. "All I can think of is that he was never well. He was always sick. He was always suffering. I tried so hard to feed him and hold him and comfort him. He suffered so. He didn't deserve to suffer."

"Oh, my dear, my poor dear." Madeleine searched frantically inside the pocket of her skirt for a handkerchief. Retrieving it, she went to Clarie. "Here take this." She watched as Clarie dabbed her eyes and blew her nose. "You are right, his life was too short. But eternity is forever. He will never suffer there. He's probably looking down at you right now, wanting to touch you with his tiny hand and comfort you.

Wanting you to smile again. And he is not the only one. Remember how the Blessed Mother suffered for Her Son. She understands what you are going through. She can help you."

Clarie rolled the handkerchief into a tight fist. "Can you really believe that?" Her shawl fell open, revealing the crumpled white flannel nightgown she had been wearing for days. She was so angry, so aggressive, so unlike herself.

"Yes, I do," Madeleine said quietly, inspired enough by her own words to hold her ground. "The love of Jesus and Mary is there for us, offering comfort and grace, if only we allow them to come into our hearts."

If only she could get Clarie to look at her, to see her faith, then she might believe, she might get better. Madeleine scanned her surroundings for some aid, some support. Nothing. Windows looking out upon a street where Jewish and profane goods were bought and sold. The lamps, the end chairs, the shelf of books, undoubtedly secular books. Not one sacred object in sight. It was as godless as the Republic Bernard Martin represented. She needed to get Clarie out of here. If not today, then tomorrow.

Rose's sudden appearance interrupted Madeleine's thoughts.

"The stew's ready, ma'am," she said, with eyes so wide they seemed to be pleading, inviting Madeleine. Had she found an ally? In silent agreement Madeleine and Rose entered the dining room.

As soon as they got there, Rose whispered, "See if you can get her to take a bite. This is from last night. She didn't eat a thing."

"Of course," Madeleine said, before pressing her hand against her own rudely rumbling stomach. She could see the tiny kitchen and the steaming pot on the stove. And smell it. "Do you think we should eat in here or by the fire?" she asked, treating Rose almost as an equal in their struggle to help Clarie.

"Makes no difference to me, ma'am," Rose said as she reached for an envelope lying on the dining-room table. She gave it to Madeleine.

"Maybe before lunch you can get her to read this. Maybe it will cheer her up."

Madeleine stared at the letter. It was from the head of their normal school at Sèvres. The itch of curiosity made Madeleine almost forget the growling in her stomach. Unlike Clarie, she had never been a favorite. Mme Favre only deemed to write her to answer her pleas for a placement. Madeleine ran her finger over the return address. She was dying to know if the letter mentioned her. "Mme Martin hasn't opened it yet? When did it arrive?" Madeleine asked, trying to keep her voice down despite her excitement.

"This morning. She's afraid. . . . She said her headmistress did not know. . . ."

"I'll read it first," Madeleine assured the maid. "I'll make sure it won't upset her. You set up the table in here." She wanted nothing to disturb her examination of the letter.

She walked back into the living room. "My dear, I see you've gotten a letter from Mme Favre."

Clarie hadn't moved. She stared at the floral pattern on the dark carpet that covered the center of the living room. "Yes," Clarie answered. "I thought Bernard should read it first. He says that I shouldn't do anything that will upset me."

"You never know. It could just be a bit of gossip about our old comrades. Why don't you let me have a look?" The letter trembled in her hand as she perched on the edge of her chair.

Clarie shrugged. "I don't want to hear anything about the baby," she murmured.

"Then you won't," Madeleine said, as she unsealed the letter, trying hard despite her eagerness not to tear the envelope. She lifted the first page up to the light. It was all about the baby, wishing Clarie continued good health and an easy and safe delivery. Then Mme Favre, in her self-appointed role as the adviser to her favorites, counseled Clarie that whether she decided to be a "Rousseauist" who breast-fed her child, or hired a wet nurse, or used the modern glass bottles, she would make the decision that was right for her and her child. It was love that made children thrive.

Madeleine let out a humph.

"What?" Clarie looked up.

"Nothing new, dear, not yet," Madeleine said, protecting Clarie from Mme Favre's pieties. She made a show of going on to the second page. First, she skimmed through it looking for her name, which was not there. Then she saw what may have been the real purpose of the letter, and gasped.

"What? Tell me!"

If Clarie hadn't been so insistent, Madeleine might not have revealed the letter's astonishing proposal. She might have kept it to herself, at least for a little while, until she figured out what it meant to *her*.

Madeleine set the letter on her lap, still clutching it in her right hand.

"She says, my dear, that there is a post in literature and history opening in Paris next year, and she wants to recommend you for it."

"Oh." Clarie turned away, indifferent.

"Is that all you have to say? She's asking you if you want to apply to teach in the best school for girls in all of France!" Had Madeleine had time to collect herself, she would have suppressed the disbelief and envy that raised her voice above its usual well-bred, calm timbre. But her mind was astir. What *did* this mean for her? If Clarie left, could Madeleine claim her post in Nancy? And why, why, when she had been the eldest student in her class at Sèvres, one of the most experienced, one who had taught for many years in private boarding schools, why hadn't she been asked?

"It doesn't matter. I don't care."

"But Paris!"

"And Bernard?" Clarie sighed, as if she were bored with the whole discussion and wanted to put an end to it.

Madeleine scoured the letter again. "She says to wish him well for her, and that perhaps he, too, could find a post in the capital."

Clarie shook her head. They both knew this was virtually impossible. Getting on the list for the Palais de Justice in Paris took years. And connections.

"Well," said Madeleine, somewhat recovered, "it must be nice to know that Mme Favre thinks so highly of you." She willed her hands to refold the letter exactly as it had come out of the envelope, and she slipped it back into its cover.

Before the birth, before Henri-Joseph, such an unexpected boon for Clarie would have served as a reason to commiserate with Madeleine about how unfair life had been to her. There was none of that now. Only that blank stare, the sighs, the withdrawal. This could not go on.

"Ma'am, the dinner's ready."

Madeleine heard Rose's irritatingly timid voice behind her. She got out of her seat and offered her hand to Clarie. "Come, dear, let's get some food inside of you."

She looped her arm into her friend's as they moved slowly toward the kitchen. "Would you like me to write Mme Favre and tell her about Henri-Joseph?" Madeleine reminded herself why she had come, to help.

Clarie shook her head. "Bernard is going to do it. He promised." She sat down at the table and watched as Rose set a steaming bowl of beef, potatoes and carrots in front of her and Madeleine. She gave a weak smile to her guest as she picked up the spoon. "Like old times," she said.

Clarie was remembering her manners. There was hope.

Madeleine put down her spoon, forsaking the first mouthful. She reached over and placed her hand over Clarie's.

"I'll tell you what we must do, my dear. We must make a plan. Get you out of here. Tomorrow when I come at four, I expect you to be fully dressed. We'll take a walk, look in the shops, and go around the corner to the cathedral. Then we'll light a candle for Henri-Joseph and pray to the Virgin together."

Clarie picked up her spoon and stared into the bowl. All Madeleine had to do was to turn her indifference into acceptance.

26

MARTIN SWORE THIS WOULD BE his last session with Hémonet. He had spent a day and a half questioning the priest and going over police reports. During that time, Jacquette and his men had grilled ten of the most vocal habitués of the working-class cafés. None had a particular motive for stalking and killing Ullmann and Erlanger. Neither did the venomous bookseller, Villiers, whom Martin had placed in the tender inquisitorial care of his inspector. As for Martin's witness, by late Wednesday afternoon, Hémonet had deteriorated into a shaking, red-eyed mess, reeking of his own vomit. "Drink," Jacquette told Martin. "Give him a few days and he'll get over it." But when? Martin wanted answers now. Did the priest have associates? Had he incited anyone in his parish to do violence against the Israelites? Or did Hémonet possess the cunning and nerve to stalk and kill two men on his own?

As before, their encounter threatened to end in a shouting match:

"What do you know about the incident in the Place Saint-Jean?"

"Nothing! Like I told you, I heard it from another priest."

"A priest you claimed died last year."

"Yeah, yeah, yeah," voice more tremulous, as the head of clumped brown hair lolled this way and that, like one of the hysterics in Charcot's famous asylum photographs. The torn and stretched-out sweater, undoubtedly the product of his mother's or sister's knitting needles, added to the aura of madness, which Martin suspected the cunning priest was knowingly spinning around him.

"Don't pull that act on me!"

"What?" a smile oozed across Hémonet's lips as saliva dribbled from one side of his mouth into his filthy beard. "See these?" The priest raised two impotent, trembling hands. "Who could I kill? I'm a sick man." His laugh ended in a sneer.

A sneer Martin had seen all too often. Are all Israelites the enemy? he had asked last time. Even women and children? Children grow up to be cheats, exploiters, traitors, the priest answered, and women are their breeders. We should drive them all out, let them crawl over the border with whatever they can carry on their backs, and keep the rest where it belongs. Here, for real Frenchmen.

"Look at you," Martin hissed in exasperation, despite his knowing that the priest was beyond shame. "You've ruined yourself with drink. You've dishonored your Church, your country, your mother, whoever has been good to you."

"Look at you, Jew-lover," Hémonet spit out, "you have no idea who they are and how they have you and everyone else in this court-house on a string. A string, a string," he intoned, "idiot little marionettes on a string—"

"That's it. Get him out of here." Thank God Martin had taken the precaution of always having a brawny guard in his chambers. He would not have to wait long to get the priest out of his sight. With little effort, the young blond policeman lifted Hémonet out of the chair and yanked one of his quivering hands behind his back.

"Jew-lover, Jew-lover, Jew-lover, Jew-lover." At first the epithet blared out as sharp as a trumpet call, but by the time the policeman had dragged Hémonet into the foyer, his words had slurred almost into a snore. Martin closed his eyes and clenched his teeth until he heard the door slammed shut.

"Charpentier, a summary today. Then we'll let him rot in a cell until I can figure out what to do with him."

Martin hardly needed to give this order. His clerk had been diligently taking notes and just as certainly taking in the inefficacy of the interrogation. Martin pulled his cravat away from his stiff white collar and scratched at the beard under his chin. Not only had he failed to find any connection between the two murder victims and the priest, he had not even come up with a list of associates to hand over to his inspector for investigation and surveillance. Instead, Martin had become convinced that Hémonet had acted alone and that his only weapon had been his pen. Martin could well imagine how it had been, the once-ambitious priest stuck in a shabby country parish, imbibing the communion wine by candlelight as he spewed his hate and paranoia into his notebooks. Only the bishop's interdict had stopped him from causing more damage. Jacquette assured Martin that there were no more copies of *Nancy-Juif* in the bookshops. As for the ostracized Hémonet, he had become so isolated that he had, according to his repeated, invective-filled testimony, not even read a newspaper for months and had no knowledge of the Thomases, or their pitiful wet nurse, or the ritual murder rumor that seemed to have started it all.

Martin put his elbows on his desk and rubbed his eyes. There had to be a connection somewhere. How else could it be that Ullmann and Erlichman were killed so soon after the death of the Thomas boy? Martin reached for the pile of reports he had pushed to the side of his desk. He tapped his fingers on top of them while he settled his taut

stomach to the task of reading through them one more time. He had
to squeeze some clue out of them, just one tenuous connection
between the victims and the anti-Israelite invective. Martin's fingers
stilled as he stared at the white, blank wall in front of him. If he didn't
find connections, if the killer was still out there, would other Israelites
be in danger? Was it even remotely possible that he would lose another
friend, that David Singer might be danger? That once again, his
actions had not been swift enough, decisive enough.

He lifted the first sheet, written in Jacquette's firm strong hand, a
report on a tanner who worked and drank with Pierre Thomas. Martin
had to focus on what he was doing. Forget the disgust that Hémonet
aroused in him. Put Clarie and the baby out of his mind. She'd understand, some day.

And if he found nothing? He'd concede that Jacquette had been
right all along, that they should be looking for a murderer closer to
home. Contrary to Didier's views, against Singer's expressed wishes,
he'd order a full scale investigation of the Jewish community, whatever that meant. Even though Singer had exhorted him not to excuse
the haters and accuse the Israelites. *If I do it, Singer,* Martin thought
to himself, *it will be to keep you safe.*

An hour later, as Charpentier was floating around Martin's chambers
turning up the gas lamps, a sharp knocking at the door startled both of
them. It was Jean, the Palais's concierge, announcing that the Grand
Rabbi of Nancy wanted to speak to the judge in charge of the Ullmann
and Erlanger murders.

"Please ask him to wait a moment," Martin said as he stood up and
hurriedly straightened his cravat. Although he had no idea what had
inspired this sudden visit, he felt little apprehension about meeting the
gracious Isaac Bloch a second time. Perhaps he had even come with
some useful information about the two dead men.

As soon as Martin caught a glimpse of the rabbi's grim face, however, he understood that the cleric was in no mood to take on the kindly intermediary role that he had played in the Widow Ullmann's house.

"Rabbi Bloch, good to see you again," Martin said as he offered his hand.

Bloch's grip was cold, not only because of the weather.

"Shall I ask my clerk to leave while we talk?" Martin kept his eyes fixed on Bloch's. Martin did not pose this question merely out of a polite respect for the Grand Rabbi's station. He knew all too well that his clerk would like nothing better than to report such a unique confrontation to his peers.

"That would be best," said the rabbi as he stepped back from the desk.

Both of them stood in silence while Charpentier slipped out of the room and closed the door.

"Please sit down."

"That won't be necessary." With slow, precise movements, the Grand Rabbi unbuttoned his heavy black coat, took it off, folded it in half lengthwise, and hung it over the back of the proffered chair. He did not take off his hat. When he straightened up, Martin noted that he had pinned three medals, of the kind the French Republic bestowed in appreciation of exceptional service and accomplishments, to his cassock. Well aware that rabbis and priests were used to putting on the performances that were part of their sacred rites, Martin was beginning to grasp that he was about to be witness to one.

"I am angry," the rabbi announced. "Angry. I have just returned from grieving with another of our families. The Singers, whose uncle Daniel Erlanger, a good and innocent man, was felled in his own kitchen. So I come here with a question. An important question, Monsieur le juge." He held his right fist aloft. "One question. Today is Wednesday. Will we find another body of an Israelite tomorrow? Frozen in the fields or hurled down in his very own home."

"There's no reason to believe—"

"Who would have believed it two weeks ago, even a week ago, that two leading members of our community would be dead, slaughtered like sheep?"

"I repeat, we have no reason to believe that anyone else is in danger or has been hurt." Martin hoped that the quivering inside his chest did not resonate in his voice. He could not let on that only a short time ago, he had been torturing himself with fears about Singer.

"Oh," Bloch spread his hands over his chest and threw his shoulders back in a theatrical pose. "You have no reason to believe that anyone is in danger? Is that because you have the police protecting their homes? Because you have placed a guard in front of the Temple? Do you even have a list of leading Israelites who may need to be protected? Of the three remaining Consistory members?"

"I can assure you we are doing our best, questioning all suspects, every day without cease. Using all of our men. We are getting closer." A blatant lie. The kind that always made Martin's mouth run dry. The kind one tells during the worst moments of every investigation. "We'd be glad to accept any help you can give us," he added, employing the old judicial trick of turning the tables in order to go on the offensive.

"*My* help! But that is *your* job. The job of the Republican courts and the Republican police." Bloch's voice crescendoed, higher and louder.

"Why don't we both calm down." Martin did not want to spend his time matching wits with the rabbi or standing on ceremony as a judge who had the right to ask all the questions. He wanted desperately to catch the killer before anyone else got hurt. "Please sit, Rabbi Bloch. And tell me anything you can to help me."

Bloch blinked a few times, considering. Then he walked to the chair in front of Martin's desk and sat down. Martin followed suit.

"What can I tell you? I have received no threats. I am not personally acquainted with anyone who hates us enough to kill us."

Martin took up his pen. "Let's start here," he began quietly. "Can you think of any way the two men and their deaths are connected?"

"Besides the fact that Thursday, tomorrow, seems to be the killing day?"

Martin wanted to say two days do not make a pattern, but he bit his tongue. "Please go on."

There was a movement under the cassock as the Grand Rabbi crossed his legs, and thought. "They were both members of the Consistory. Well, not exactly. Erlanger volunteered to be our secretary. But Ullmann was fully elected."

Martin nodded. On the day after Ullmann's body was found, Singer and Martin had discussed the factory owner's membership in the Consistory, the small committee comprised of the rabbi and leading Israelites, which regulated everything that had to do with their religion in the region. There had been no mention of Noémie Singer's uncle. "Who would know about Erlanger's participation?"

"His name would be on all the decrees, because he signed them."

"And what would these decrees be about?" At last, a possible connection. Anyone reading the decrees might believe that Erlanger was a full member of the Consistory. Martin sat up, alert, his fingers gripping the pen. Then the thought that he should have already known about Erlanger's role in the "community" punctured his momentary elation. Clarie. The baby. That's why he was so tardy in finding out about the kinds of decisions the two victims might be identified with. He slumped back. There really was no excuse. He should know. At this point in the case, he should know so much more.

The rabbi did not seem to notice Martin's embarrassment. Rather, he acted as though there was something impertinent about trying to make any connection between the followers of his congregation and the murders. "I don't see what you are getting at. What we decide only affects the Israelites."

"Please."

The Grand Rabbi sighed and sat back, letting his eyes wander over the ceiling. "There is nothing remarkable in what we do. We are mostly charged with carrying out reforms ordered by the Central Consistory in Paris. You can come to my office and get a full list if you need them."

Martin made himself a note. He would do that. The governance of Judaism, like that of the Protestant sects, had been centralized in the French capital since the beginning of the century. He circled the word "consistory." Would everyone in Nancy appreciate following edicts emanating from Paris?

"And you agree with these reforms?" he asked. "Everyone agrees with them?"

"Yes, yes," Bloch waved away the irrelevance of the question.

"Are there any financial issues? Do these men control a great deal of money?"

"Control money? The men of the Consistory *give* to the community, they do not take from it. We provide charity for our poor. We educate the young about our faith. We preach love for family, religion, and country. Just as important," Rabbi Bloch tapped the desk with his finger for emphasis, "we have worked hard in Lorraine to bring our rites and ceremonies into the nineteenth century. We are modern while upholding a great tradition."

"And no one objects to that?" Martin could not imagine that many Catholics would accept changes in the ritual of the mass, or that women like his mother would willingly give up their pilgrimages and rosaries, and their belief in miracles and the intercession of the saints. He wrote down "changing religious practices."

The rabbi shrugged. "There are those who might object to the fact that we let women enter in the same door with men and have an organ in the Temple, but none of these things are worth killing over. Jews argue. It is part of our heritage. We've disputed everything about our religion for centuries, as recorded on the very margins of our greatest books. We are men of free minds and strong hearts."

A lovely rhetorical flourish, which would have been more effective if the rabbi's words had not evoked the image of Mme Singer's reluctance to shake Martin's hand and Singer's angry reaction. Martin suspected that some disagreements were more acrimonious than others.

"What about the issue of women? I don't know your traditions, but—"

"Monsieur le juge, you are barking up the wrong tree. As you may recall, there was a false accusation of ritual murder made in this city a little over three weeks ago. Who did that incite?"

"This is where we are looking, I can assure you." Martin was not about to tell the rabbi of the debate that kept his own mind abuzz, between Jacquette's sage advice to look "closer to home" and the political sensitivities of Didier and Singer, urging him to leave the Israelites alone. Ironically, even the Grand Rabbi's attempt to chastise Martin played into Jacquette's side of the argument. By unwittingly offering an important connection between the victims, he had underlined an obvious strategy. Martin was beginning to suspect that it was time for him to look into even those possibilities that meant stepping on some sensitive toes. "The issue of women strikes me as one of the more controversial issues of the day, and—"

"And what?" the Grand Rabbi was out of his chair again. "What? How do you see us, Monsieur le juge Martin?"

Martin laid aside his pen, considering what to say. If he didn't have so much respect for the rabbi as a man and a leader, he would not have deigned to try to answer his insulting question. But he did, and he stumbled: "As good citizens, as Frenchmen, as . . ." What could he say, *as Frenchmen and somehow different?*

His hesitation left room for suspicion, and, just as he had learned from his recent dealing with Singer, the Israelites had a talent for sniffing out any doubts about them.

"French, but a little exotic, perhaps, Monsieur le juge Martin? A bit 'Oriental' for your taste?"

Martin shook his head in angry denial. "Of course not." Those were not the words he would have used to describe Singer or the Steins. But what of this man standing before him in priestly robes, orating like a prophet of old? What was his lineage? Where did he come from?

"I can assure you, Monsieur le juge, that we are just as French as you are. Where are you from? The north? The south? I am from Alsace. My family lived there for centuries. And when the Germans took over, I crossed the border back to my beloved country. And your colleague, Monsieur le juge Singer and his relative, Maître Erlanger, their family lived here in Lorraine for centuries. They are of the very soil of Lorraine, the true blood of Lorraine. No one can deny them that."

Martin shifted in his chair impatiently. Perhaps this was the penance he had to pay for his moments of doubt in the cemetery and his fear that somehow Singer was not as French as he thought him to be.

"Or what about Monsieur Osiris, the businessman?" Rabbi Block asked, then paused dramatically. "Ah, his name rings of the Levant, does it not? But did he not build the statue of the Maid of Lorraine for our fair city? Have I not preached that that lovely martyred maid, Joan of Arc, is as much the Jews' national heroine as any Catholic's?" He shook his fist for emphasis. "This is the blood that flows through our veins. French blood, defeated blood, blood that will someday be victorious against the Germans *and* the anti-Israelites. Blood that fights to fulfill the dream of liberty, equality and fraternity. For everyone. Even ourselves."

Quite a speech! Although Martin had never liked being preached to, he did have to admire the oratorical power and fervor of the man who was the moral leader of his people and the guardian of their reputation. Martin picked up his pen again and opened his notebook to a clean page. It was his turn. As long as the rabbi had come to his chambers, he could very well answer Martin's questions about the other members of the Consistory and what decision they had promulgated. In exchange, Martin would give the Grand Rabbi something he wanted: policemen to guard the Temple and the homes of the remaining Consistory members, tomorrow, Thursday.

27

Thursday, December 6

THE NEXT MORNING, CLARIE STOOD in front of the armoire, surveying her dresses. She was going out for the first time in weeks. They all said it would "do her good": Rose, Bernard, Madeleine. Bernard wanted her to take long walks through the park, by the shops, in the square, anything to take her mind off Henri-Joseph. Madeleine expected that she'd find solace by lighting candles in front of a holy statue. Clarie didn't know what "going out" could possibly accomplish, although part of her wanted, truly wanted, to feel herself again, and to feel for others too. Sighing, Clarie reached forward to pull the dresses apart, one by one, as she tried to remember what life used to be like when she had worn them.

"Darling, have you seen the weather?" Bernard came into the room carrying his bowl of café au lait. "The sun is shining. It's going to be clear with blue skies just like in Provence. Your beloved Provence."

When she did not respond, Bernard set his bowl down on the dresser and drew the curtains back even further. "A perfect day for you to go out."

She did not have the heart to tell him how little false cheer became him. So she kept staring at the clothes.

"If you'd like, I could take off part of the morning, and we could go while the sun is so bright."

She turned to inspect Bernard. He still had a very nice face, the face of a gentle man with a good heart. A face she used to love. No, she shook her head slightly as she turned away, half-shocked by the formulation. The kind, intelligent face she *still* loved. But she could not tell what he was thinking or feeling any more. Was there more gray around the edges of his beard and his head of slightly wavy brown hair? Had he shriveled up inside like she had? In his white shirt, open at the neck and cuffs, he still looked like the near-boy she had fallen in love with and who had fallen madly in love with her. But she was no longer the girl he had met in Aix. She was tired of seeing that look in his eyes, pity. Her back almost burned with the burden of his gaze. He was waiting for an answer. "I know you have your work to do. The case. Besides, I promised Madeleine," she said.

"By that time it might be getting dark again." Bernard was sipping his coffee. It would be such a relief when he put on his cravat and jacket and became a judge again. This is what she and Madeleine had agreed that men did best. Deal with the world outside.

"Where are you and Madeleine planning to go?"

In other words, whose prescription for my well-being am I to follow—his or Madeleine's? Even though she knew he would not argue with her, she did not tell him. She intended to make her own decision about what she needed.

"Do you think I can get into the corset again?" she asked, without turning around, changing the subject.

"Does it matter? You'll have your long winter coat on." Suddenly he was behind her, reaching his arms around her waist and pulling her close to his chest so that she felt his soft beard on the back of her neck. "You'll be beautiful, no matter what you wear."

Even though she felt far from "beautiful," Clarie turned and smiled. The look of absolute relief on Bernard's face confirmed that this is what he so desperately wanted: to have her back again. Still, she could do no more. She began sorting through her clothes again. The most somber dress was the black and gray wool that she often wore to school. She took it out and threw it on the bed. The lace-trimmed linen collar and cuffs that she and Rose had conspired to keep immaculately white seemed obscenely cheerful. She had nothing appropriate for a mourning mother. And for that ridiculous reason she let out a sob, which she covered with her hand.

"Clarie." Bernard took her to him, hugging her face to his chest and swaying gently back and forth. "It will get better. I promise."

When? How? And why was Bernard so willing to comfort her, to hold her until he thought she had fallen asleep, when she knew that he'd often slip out of bed and go into the living room to pace, perhaps even to weep? Why did he leave her? Why had he taken Henri-Joseph into the living room that fateful night? Didn't he know that if he had kept their baby in their bed he might be alive? If she still had Henri-Joseph inside of her, he would be safe. Despite all her efforts, she began crying again. These were insane thoughts. Was she going mad?

She pulled away. "Silly me," she said.

He kissed her cheeks and forehead. "Never silly. I've never known you to be silly."

That's why, he once said, he loved her so much, because she was reasonable and intelligent and strong, willing to take risks, to do something new. Was she still that person? Would she ever be that person again?

She wiped her eyes with the handkerchief she kept beside her bed. "You'd better hurry. You'll be late. I know you're worried about this case." Even though he hadn't said anything about it for days, she could tell. Whenever someone was murdered, somehow Bernard felt responsible. Did he even feel at all responsible for the death of their child?

She plopped down on the bed, horrified again by the words invading her mind.

"Dear, what is it?"

"Nothing." She smiled again. She'd never reveal to him how she was betraying him in her thoughts. "I'm better already. Every day. As you say."

"I'll tell you what." Bernard sat down beside her and kissed her on the forehead again. "Tomorrow night we will go to one of the cafés on the square for supper, just like we did when we first arrived. Then we'll walk and see what is happening in the theater and the shops. And all those handsome army officers will look at you and want to take you away from me. But I won't let them."

Clarie pulled away. Really, he was making too much of an effort, treating her like a child or an invalid. "Your coffee's getting cold," she murmured as she went back to the armoire. "Do you want me to pick out a cravat for today?" He used to like her to choose one in the morning and tie it under his collar. There was no reason why he had to know what was going on in her mind.

During the hours between Bernard's departure and Madeleine's arrival, Clarie tried to read, to sew, to think of next week's menu and shopping list, all to no avail. Finally, at three o'clock, Clarie started to dress. Rose helped her with the corset and pinning up her hair—things Clarie always did for herself. But for some odd reason, her fingers were incapable of finding the clasps. Clarie knew that Rose loved doing these things for her, but it didn't seem right. Clarie towered a head above the older woman, and yet Rose was doing all the work.

"There now, look at you," Rose said as she pinned back the last errant strand of dark hair. "You look lovely."

And useless, Clarie thought as she sat staring in the dresser mirror. That must change. She reached up to pat Rose's hand. "Thank you," she said. "I'm sorry you've been working so hard."

"Oh, no, ma'am. Not so hard." The maid leaned down so that their faces reflected back at them. They both looked ashen and worn out.

"Well," Clarie said as she got up, "tomorrow you will have the day off. Monsieur Martin is taking me to dinner."

"Lovely." Rose clasped her hands together, smiling. "But I can still come to help," she hastened to add. Her gray hair was so thin, it was always falling out of the pins. Her plain features seldom came to life, except in response to something happening to Clarie. When had Clarie stopped worrying about what Rose's life was like? It was unfair.

Unfair, too, that she was releasing Rose tomorrow less for Rose's sake than for her own. She wanted to be alone. She didn't want to be hovered over. "No, do take some time to rest," Clarie insisted as she went to the armoire to get her coat.

Madeleine was always on time. Even so, when the bell rang, Clarie's heart leapt in her chest. She swallowed and started to button her long blue coat, which fit her rather loosely. She hadn't needed the corset. She had no idea what was happening to her.

She hurried out of the bedroom, through the living room to the foyer. She wanted to get this over with. She needed to learn to go out on her own, do things on her own.

She greeted Madeleine with a kiss on each cheek and said good-bye to Rose. Then they stepped into the hallway. When Clarie heard the door close behind her, flashes of fear pulsed through her body. She grasped the banister. She should have gone, they should have let her go to the grave. That's where she should be going now, she thought frantically as she looked down stairs that heaved and ebbed like ocean waves before her. She took the first step. Then the second. Madeleine was slow and patient behind her, encouraging her forward whenever she stopped.

When she got to the ground floor, she flattened herself against the wall, panting despite the slow descent. The wall was cold. Everything was cold. When Madeleine opened the door, it was colder still. Finally, Clarie stepped outside into the street and gazed around her at people going to and fro, pointing at shop windows, hurrying home, greeting each other. This was normal life. Sooner or later she had to become part of it again. Clarie took in a few deep breaths. She felt as if the cold was painting her alive, in pink and rose. It did feel good, to be here, among strangers, among people who did not know what had happened to her.

"Let's see what's in the gallery," she suggested, and Madeleine took her arm as they crossed the street, skirting past the other pedestrians and a peddler's cart, to look at the prints in the window. Clarie especially loved examining the street scenes and the pictures of old buildings, which took her to other times and places. She drew Madeleine closer to her as she felt her body relaxing. She could do this.

"Watch out," they heard a man cry behind them. When they turned they saw Rebecca Stein barely avoiding a collision with a portly gentleman and a carriage as she ran across the street toward them. She had obviously run out of the Steins' drygoods store without her coat.

She landed in front of Clarie. "Madame Martin," she said, still panting. "Madame Froment." She curtsied to both of them before going on. "I saw you from the window," she said to Clarie. "Maman says that I mustn't bother you. But I know that your maid does not come in on your sabbath, and I am learning to cook, and I . . ." she gulped hard, the look in her dark brown eyes eager, almost pleading, "I could bring you some lentil soup and bread from the baker."

"Your mother is right, no one must bother Mme Martin."

"No, wait," Clarie said, ignoring Madeleine's stern admonition as she laid a gloved hand on the girl's arm. "That would be very kind, Rebecca." How could one refuse a young girl, especially one who reminded Clarie how much she loved all her students and of what she had been to them. "Now, run along, or you'll catch your death. And be careful of the street."

"Yes, Madame Martin, yes." Rebecca was on her toes with eagerness, before she scampered across the street, taking more care this time not to run into anyone.

"Humph. Always interfering."

"I don't think so. Why do you say that?"

"They are always getting into everyone's business. Don't you know that?"

"They?"

"You know."

"Madeleine, come." She wasn't in the mood to have a dispute about the Israelites, but at least her companion was acting herself, not like the nursemaid to an invalid.

"Yes, let's go to *our* church," Madeleine said, steering Clarie down the block.

But when they rounded the corner and came within sight of the cathedral, Clarie froze. She felt as if someone was squeezing her heart, wringing all the blood out of her. The episcopal church was so overwhelming. All she could think of was that they had bundled up Henri-Joseph and brought him there to baptize him, that they knew, they had suspected. And that she had let them take him out of her arms. She had not gone to mass for months, and she could not imagine finding solace in the massive, princely building. Clarie shook her head. "No, I don't think so. Bernard said I should walk."

"You're sure?" Madeleine asked.

Clarie nodded and turned the other way, toward the rue Saint-Dizier, away from the cathedral.

"Shops, then? The market?"

"The market, yes. Flowers. Good."

The Central Market was only a few blocks away. Women were coming out burdened by sacks filled with the preparations for dinner.

They looked so happy, so ordinary. When Madeleine started to go inside, Clarie stopped her. "Let's stay outside with the flowers." She didn't want to smell the meat or the cheeses or see the hanging flesh. Red and pink-tipped white roses, fiery orange gladiolas, brave little violets in the waning sunlight, that was enough. Clarie leaned over to smell a white rose. When the vendor was busy with a customer, she touched its soft petal. Bernard used to bring her flowers. Perhaps he would today. "Where do they come from in the winter?" she asked dreamily.

"Greenhouses, you know that."

Clarie blushed. Where had her mind gone?

They kept on going down the broad, busy street. Clarie had a feeling that Madeleine was guiding her, but she didn't care. Walking, seeing people, this is what she needed.

"This is my parish, maybe you would be more comfortable here."

Clarie paused a moment and looked up at the single tower of Saint Pierre. The church was beautiful. Even though it was much smaller, bone-white and new, it reminded her of Notre Dame in Paris. It, too, had an ornate façade which soared over its three doors. And inside, she knew, the arches would reach almost to the sky, and everything would be light and airy. It might not press down on her, it might allow her to pray for her son and find a bit of peace.

She took Madeleine's hand as they walked up the four low steps to the main entrance. They had only penetrated a few meters into the interior of the church when Clarie knew where she had to be. A flood of memories propelled her to a side altar with its two humble, familiar plaster statues. It was, Clarie knew, Our Lady of Lourdes, the youthful virgin in white and blue standing on a rock just as she had appeared many times to the other statue, the kneeling peasant girl, Bernadette. Clarie's mother had loved to tell her this story. For Clarie's mother, the apparitions and the pilgrimages they inspired were proof that miracles could happen and would continue to happen in her lifetime. Then her mother had died. And Clarie, submitted to the discipline of the unbending nuns, no longer had any reason to believe in miracles or apparitions. But the statue seemed to be smiling at Clarie so sweetly. Even if the vision had cured no one, even if miracles did not exist, she had made the sickly Bernadette happy. She had made Clarie's mother happy.

"Maman, Maman." The altar became a blur as tears filled Clarie's eyes. Could it be possible that her mother was in heaven watching over her, praying for her, sheltering her son? Clarie swiped her hand across her nose and cheeks, and began to search frantically for a coin in the little sack hanging on her wrist. When she found it, she dropped it into the vertical slot of the tin box beneath three rows of candles flickering in their blood-red glasses. Madeleine steadied her hand as she took a straw and transferred the flame from one burning candle to a fresh wick. Still sobbing, Clarie fell to her knees in front of Bernadette and the Blessed Virgin, and Madeleine Froment knelt beside her.

28
Friday, December 7

EARLY FRIDAY MORNING, JACQUETTE ARRIVED bearing two gifts. The first was expected. Still, Martin received the good news with a sigh of gratitude. The rabbi had been wrong: Thursday had passed, and no one had been murdered or even threatened with violence.

"And what else?" Martin asked, impatient. His sense of relief had evaporated before he could sustain even the slightest pleasure from it, leaving a hard, leaden taste in his mouth. The reality was that Martin did expect that, sooner or later, on Thursday or Monday or any other day, unless they caught the murderer, there would be more killings. They desperately needed a break in the case.

"I believe we have an informer."

"Here? Now? A witness?" Martin got out of his chair, as if ready to go to the door himself.

Jacquette held up his hand. "Not exactly."

"Well, then?" Martin stopped short. "Who?" It wasn't like Jacquette to be coy.

"I just want to prepare you to meet him before we think about how we can use him."

"I'm perfectly capable of deciding how to use a witness." Martin threw himself into his seat, thoroughly annoyed.

"They call him Shlomo the Red Dwarf."

Martin slumped back. *A dwarf? A red dwarf?* His frustrations would have gotten the better of him if he hadn't noted how eagerness, triumph and anxiety were vying for dominance in Jacquette's usually placid face. Obviously the man thought he had found a treasure, and he was groping for a way to convince Martin of its worth. The police, of course, relied on any number of degenerates and small-time crooks to help them solve the tawdry crimes that were their stock in trade. But to use one of them to solve the murder of two prominent men? "Sit," Martin commanded, giving in. He'd hear Jacquette out.

Jacquette reached into his pocket for the comfort of a Blue Jockey as he bent into the seat. He held the cigarette suspended between two fingers as he began. "I wanted to prepare you because at first sight you might think I picked him up at the circus or off the street for begging." With the deft thumbnail of his left hand, Jacquette struck a match and lit up. "In fact, one of my men caught him trying to filch a pen and paper from the Papeterie by the railroad. Our dwarf claimed that he needed supplies for the 'translations' he does for his community. 'His community.' Those words caught me, I'll tell you. And the reason that François thought I would be interested in the first place was that this little fellow speaks French as well as German, and apparently all the other languages of the Israelites. And, what is better, he loves to talk, willing to tell you everything he knows. He's the kind of guy who for a few sous or a little 'consideration' can keep us informed about certain 'types' for years." Having rammed through his argument, Jacquette took a well-deserved pull from his cigarette.

"What makes you think he knows anything about Ullmann or Erlanger?"

"I'm not sure he does," Jacquette conceded as he emitted a line of smoke from the side of his mouth. "But you know, sir, I think it's time to look the other way. To see if there is some reason that the Israelites might have for killing their own."

And go against the wishes of Didier and Singer. And deny the righteous anger of the rabbi and the Widow Ullmann.

"He told me—I swear this fellow cannot keep from talking—that he would be our guide to the 'other half' of the Israelite community. He says unless you know these Jews, you don't know what a Jew is. Maybe we can pick up something from him. Some hate. Some resentment. Maybe, for a little 'consideration,' he can help us hire a few other sets of eyes to be on the alert as they go out on the street with their carts, selling and begging."

How ironic, Martin thought. The mad priest Hémonet accused the poor Jews of spying for their rich co-religionists. Now Jacquette wanted to turn them into police informers. Martin ran his fingers through his hair, wondering, not for the first time, if it had not grown thinner and grayer in the last few weeks, if this case and his own suffocating sadness had not aged him and made him dull when he needed to be sharp. Jacquette wanted to do some real police work, the kind he and his men thrived on. The inspector didn't give a jot for the politics of the courthouse. Neither had Martin, before this case. What if this case was no different from any other? Envy, greed, humiliation: Isn't that why people usually killed?

Martin relaxed back into his seat and crossed his arms. "What have you asked him so far?"

"Nothing about the murders. I thought I'd let you put a scare into him. That might guarantee that he's not just telling us stories, once we get him talking."

Martin liked that. That he would "put a scare" into someone. Evidently he was not so far off his game that his subordinates would notice. And, if Jacquette was so sure that his find could be of value, why not? "Let's take a look at this Shlomo."

While Jacquette bounded out of his chambers, Martin straightened out his desk and asked Charpentier to be ready to take notes. Martin wanted to leave no doubt that he was in command, official, and quite possibly threatening.

When the door opened again, Martin understood why Jacquette had prepared him. Barely a meter tall, Shlomo the Red Dwarf rolled in slowly, swaying from side to side, with the aid of a cane that looked like someone had sawed it in half to accommodate the man's shrunken legs. At least he was not really red, for his skin, or what little Martin could see of it, bore merely the yellowish pallor of the poor and the sickly. Clearly it was the hair that endowed him with his strange nickname. The unkempt frizzy beard that covered most of his face was blazing orange. Once the man had limped halfway into the room, he planted his cane to give him momentary balance and used his free hand to swoop off his dented, broad-brimmed black felt hat. He moved this oversized dilapidated headgear to his heart as he bowed. "Monsieur le juge, I am honored to be in your presence." The hair that jutted out in all directions from the top of his head looked like it had caught on fire.

Martin glanced at Jacquette, who towered behind the witness. The inspector could not suppress a mischievous grin. Martin could well imagine what Charpentier was thinking behind him. He hoped he wasn't smirking.

"Monsieur—" Martin remained seated. This was not the kind of witness that one rose to greet.

"Shlomo, Simon Shlomo at your service." The man's outsized head and hands seemed to dominate his diminutive body. His face was so broad, it was as if it, like his shrunken legs, had been compressed by some terrible accident of birth. Across this wide expanse, his mouth stretched into a perpetual smile. Martin knew the expression well. It was the smile of the ugly and the deformed, whose very existence depended upon their ability to please and keep on pleasing. The pleasers were not always the most dependable witnesses. Anything this man said would require corroboration.

"Monsieur Shlomo," Martin said evenly, "would you like to take a seat?"

The dwarf advanced a few steps, eyed the chair, and shook his head. Martin saw then that for the dwarf getting up on the chair might be a difficult, even humiliating venture. But, like so many of the world's unfortunates, who suffered more than their due of humbling experiences, Shlomo had the wit to disguise his embarrassment.

"In front of Your Eminence, I prefer to stand," he said with another bow. The high singsong voice, like the man, was not fully grown. It emanated from somewhere behind his large, hooked nose, and floated out through his yellow-toothed grin. Martin could well imagine the dwarf speaking in rhythms and tongues, telling jokes, or performing tricks before a crowd, and then laying the dented hat on the ground, like a wishing well, waiting for the coins to fall.

Martin had every reason to be wary. "May I see your identity card?"

"Of course, Monsieur le juge, of course. At your service." The man hobbled a little closer. Leaning against the desk, he reached into his patched brown wool coat and pulled out a tattered leather wallet, thick with documents. He laid it on Martin's desk and nudged it forward, as if aware that His Eminence, the judge, would not actually want to touch him.

Martin stood up and flipped through it, amazed by what it contained. The man had crossed the borders of the Ottoman and the Russian Empires, he had sojourned in Austria-Hungary and Germany, Belgium and Holland. And somehow they had let him into France.

"*Lebn vi Got in Frankraykh*," Shlomo declared, as if explaining his impressive travels.

"What?" Martin looked up sharply.

"Lebn vi Got in Frankraykh. It is one of our sayings in Russia. Live like God in France. I feel I have come to the end of my journeys at last."

"You do?" Martin could not imagine why.

"Here, in the land of liberty, equality and fraternity, we hope to be free, to gain an honest living."

"And yet that does not seem to be what you have been doing." Martin wanted to make it clear that he was not the kind of man to be charmed by flattery or cleverness.

"Ah, Monsieur le juge." The little man shrugged his arms and his shoulders in a wide gesture before deftly replanting his cane on the floor. "As one of your priests might say, a mere venial sin, and all for the greater good. I spend my days helping my countrymen become your countrymen. Helping them find jobs, get into schools, learn a trade. I feel every man must use the talents he has to fulfill God's purpose. My talents are my tongue and my pen." Martin noticed the dwarf's blue-flecked gray eyes for the first time, as they grew large with the need to explain away his crime. "Someone stole the instruments of my trade. So I had to find more." He simpered as he added, "I do not live in a mansion."

There was little doubt of that. Nor did Martin believe that Shlomo the Red Dwarf's purposes had much to do with God.

"And how is it that your tongue and your pen became so talented?" The dwarf's French was remarkable if he had, indeed, only recently arrived in the country. He was obviously a sharp-witted, slippery creature.

"As God wills it, as God wills it. I killed my mother when she bore me. I broke my father's heart with my ugliness. And yet the good man, my father, believed God has His reasons, and somehow I would become a blessing to him. And so he carried me on his shoulders, everywhere. Borders in the east are not so important when all our people speak the same mother tongue. My dear father hoped they would pay to hear a little genie tell stories and do tricks. But other villagers came to watch me too. Having ears and eyes, I learned their tongues, many of them, until finally the Lord willed that I would come here, to help my people become your people." Another bow.

"In doing God's work," Martin asked, wondering if the dwarf was capable of giving an answer without embellishment, "did you ever come across a Monsieur Ullmann or Erlanger?"

"No, no, although I am sure they are very fine gentlemen." The fiery head shook a denial, while the man's giant hands gripped the cane and his hat.

This answer had been quick, too quick and definite. "Be careful." Martin held up a finger. "If you do not tell the truth about this, you will pay for more than the 'venial sin' of a petty theft. We are talking about two murders."

The dwarf stumbled a few steps backward, almost bumping into Jacquette, who had stayed behind him, silently observing. He reared his head up to look at the inspector. Martin read shock and betrayal on the little man's face. But the trickster recovered almost immediately. "What I meant to say, Your Eminence, is that I know the names. I attended the funerals. A good place for . . . collections. One has to make a living, of course. And I will admit, from time to time, I've sent women to Monsieur Ullmann with letters explaining that in Russia they had worked in the mills, that although they speak only the old common language of our people, they know how to weave and operate the machines. He even hired one of them, a poor widow with children. This shows his kindness." Shlomo paused. "That is what I know."

"Then why didn't you say that in the first place?" Martin kept his voice loud and severe to indicate that he expected straight answers.

"Because," the dwarf bowed his head so low it almost touched his rounded chest, "I know that they were murdered. Shlomo and his friends know nothing about murders. Jews do not kill other Jews."

"Is that so? You mean to say that you don't know anyone that might envy or hate these men?"

"Oh no, sir, no." For the first time fear crept into Simon Shlomo's eyes. He had come here as a petty thief, and all of a sudden the judge, this powerful man, was talking about murder.

In the silence that followed, Martin made a show of examining the dwarf from head to toe. He ended by focusing on the preternaturally large hands, which well might be capable of becoming a weapon. Deep down, Martin doubted that this rascal had violence in his blood, but he had to keep the pressure on if he were to wring any valuable information out of him. He kept staring until Shlomo put his hat behind his back, as if rescuing his fingers from being scorched by the judge's scrutiny. Then Martin added, "Would *you* resent or envy these men?"

"No, no, no. I am sure they were good men." The dwarf swayed a bit as if he were about to lose his balance.

"That's what you said. How can you be so sure?"

"They were good Jews. Good Jews are good men." Shlomo thrust his foreshortened chest forward to demonstrate that whatever else he might have been embarrassed by, it was not by his race. Although the little man held his breath and his stance with admirable self-control, Martin did note a certain quivering in his chest. He had him.

Martin swung around his desk and approached the dwarf, forcing Shlomo to twist his neck upward in order to see his face. Once again, the dwarf almost fell against Jacquette's strong, sturdy legs.

"Your rabbi tells me that you Israelites have a tradition of disagreeing with each other. Doesn't that cause problems?"

"Your rabbi, my rabbi, whose rabbi? They argue, we argue." The dwarf sidled away from Martin and the inspector, grinning widely in an attempt to make light of his fears.

"He's not your rabbi?" Martin arched his eyebrows as if he were shocked.

"We have many rabbis, just as you have many priests."

"I am speaking of the Grand Rabbi Bloch."

"Yes, and grand he is." The grin grew wider, as he tried to signal his agreement with Martin's assessment. His little feet shifted back and forth in agitation. Despite his shrunken legs, it was obvious that Shlomo the Red Dwarf was accustomed to dancing away from threatening people and dangerous subjects. He had probably spent his life fleeing stones thrown by thuggish boys and the contemptuous glances of women.

Martin shot Jacquette a frustrated glance. He did not enjoy pounding down on a man who barely came up to his waist. A creature who, if he were not so clever, would certainly deserve any man's pity.

The inspector cleared his throat. "I am sure if we could forgive Monsieur Shlomo's crime this one time, he would keep his ears and eyes open for us. He could listen. See if anyone had bad things to say about Ullmann or Erlanger."

"Listen." Martin nodded sagely and strolled back behind his desk. It was all play-acting now, trying to figure out what degree of threat and mercy would elicit the most information. "Do you really think that 'listening' is enough of a payment for a crime? A few weeks' hard labor—"

"Better yet," Shlomo eagerly interjected with another sweeping bow, "let me show you. The inspector said he wanted to know more about the poorest Jews of the city. I can be your guide. I can translate. Tonight is a good night. Everyone is returning for the sabbath. You will see, Monsieur le juge, you will see we are all honest men, religious men, God-fearing men."

Martin glanced at Jacquette again. This is what his inspector had wanted, a chance to wade into the underside of Jewish life in the city. Martin lowered himself into his seat, considering, or at least making a show of working it through. The truth was that nothing else had worked. The truth was, too, that he was curious. He wanted to know more about the stragglers and the beggars whom he had seen at

Erlanger's funeral. He wanted to understand why Singer had talked about the tinker with such anger and contempt.

"How will you do that? How can you show us?" Martin asked, rubbing his beard, as if in deep thought.

"The men come to the café to warm themselves before going to the *shul*; you can talk to them then."

"The shul, their place of worship, I believe," Jacquette explained to Martin.

"You know our people, our language!" the dwarf exclaimed. "No wonder you are such an admirable inspector!"

"I know enough to know when I am being fooled," the inspector muttered under his mustache. "Where is this shul, and why don't you go to the Temple?"

Good! Jacquette was keeping up the pressure too.

The Red Dwarf sighed and hung his head. The smile disappeared. Martin got the impression that the little trickster finally understood what he had gotten himself into, caught between a powerful judge and an inspector who might be able to see through his tricks. "The Temple, Monsieur l'inspecteur, is not for our kind," he explained sadly. "It's for men who go home on Friday and put on their fine black tophats and the prayer shawls kept glistening white by their maids. It's for men who bathe in their own homes and do not give off the odors of their daily labors. Men who actually pay a fee to sit in a chair designated only for them. Men who speak your language and can understand the Grand Rabbi when he gives his Grand Sermon in French. This is a language many of my brethren do not yet understand. Where is our shul, you ask? What is it? It is a shoe shop that we make holy every Friday and Saturday with our candles and with our songs."

Martin stared at the dwarf. Had he revealed something new, something real? Or was this the way he ended all his performances, as if he were throwing himself and his sincerity at the mercy of the crowd before he collected their money?

The dwarf took Martin's silence as a kind of consent, or at least as the magical moment of weakness that proceeds reaching into one's pocket and throwing out a coin. "I should go ahead and tell them you are coming," Shlomo said, shifting from one foot to another, his eyes wide with eagerness. "They need to be prepared. In Russia everyone is afraid of the police and soldiers, because"—this time his bow was so low, his fiery orange mop almost skimmed the floor—"we are not accustomed to living in the land of liberty and justice. My friends, they will understand this as soon as they see Your Eminences."

If the man had not been so pitiful, Martin would have kicked him out of his office with his own boot. The dwarf had no right to make bold assumptions about whether Martin planned to jail him, or fine him, or just send him packing. Certainly not the right to believe that Martin was going to follow his lead.

And yet, what alternative was there, really? It was Friday. Another week had passed with no new clues to the murders and every possibility that the killer would strike again. All that loomed before Martin was another weekend, in the apartment, with the women, with the sadness, with his failures. Jacquette was waiting. Jacquette believed that the little showman might actually have something to show them. There were even times when Martin felt he could have nipped the whole affair in the bud, even prevented the murders, if he had understood at the start what had gone on in the minds of the Thomases and the Philipon woman, if he had seen with his own eyes what life was like for the poor and disinherited of the world. This is what his dead friend Merckx had always cajoled and urged him to do. To remember always that justice belonged to all people. And, Martin would remind him, so did murderous intentions. A visit to the dwarf's café might be instructive.

Not wanting to reward the eager witness for his brazenness, Martin turned away from him as he asked his inspector to make the arrangements.

29

HOURS LATER, MARTIN AND JACQUETTE set out through the Pépinière Park on their way to the immigrants' café. They had decided to walk, because arriving on horseback might seem too threatening in the slums where Shlomo lived. Besides, it was a rare sunny, windless day. Unfortunately, Martin had forgotten that he'd be able to see Nancy's zoo from the path. It reminded him of the little boy that he had once hoped to bring there. He put his head down and focused on the gravel crunching beneath his boots.

Jacquette breached their silence with the sheepish admission that he had given the dwarf the fare for the tram. "I couldn't see him walking all that way on those legs," he explained. Martin smiled to himself and grunted. Jacquette had a soft spot for society's strays. He was often bemused by their stories, quirks and alibis, all of which

Martin tended to perceive as evidence of misspent lives or unavoidable misfortune.

How much easier life would be, Martin thought, if he could find some amusement in the endless parade of humanity that marched through his investigations. He had always been too serious. Perhaps it had to do with his father dying when he was twelve years old. Or his Jesuit schooling. Although he had come to reject so much of what the priests had taught him, he had thoroughly imbibed their notion of life as a moral mission. But did he have to make such grim work of it? Martin kicked a dirty abandoned ball which had somehow found its way in front of them. Clarie, it was Clarie who had been making him a better, fuller, happier man. And now she seemed to be slipping away from him.

"Sir, you understood why I gave Shlomo—"

"Of course. I was just thinking about what we're going to find at the café. I like our plan."

It was Jacquette's turn to grunt. Although he admitted he would not really be able to understand the dialect the immigrants spoke, the inspector was going to ask the questions and act as if he could discern whether Shlomo was rendering an accurate translation. Martin would observe, standing aloof, the dispassionate emblem of official France. They would make it clear that they had not come to arrest anyone or to check their papers, that all they wanted was the truth.

"I'm wondering if it's going to be like what my grandfather used to tell me. All the peddlers coming from God-knows-where on a Friday evening, to eat with their wives and kids, and then run off to the shul."

"Jacquette, do you want to go back to the village?" Martin teased, knowing full well the answer. Even if he could not find amusement in common criminals and woeful victims, he always took a certain manly pleasure in being with his inspector, whose experiences were so different from his own.

"Oh, no, sir. I like my toilets indoors and sleeping without a farting cow by my side, thank you very much. But there's something about working so hard, barely scratching out a living, and then coming home, one night a week, with meat in your stew and your family and friends all around. My grandfather used to say the Jews were the poorest beggars in the village, but, at least on Friday night, the happiest."

Happy? Martin dug his gloved hands deeper into his pockets and shook his head. He had never thought of Singer as happy. In fact, except for his suspicion that Singer had higher ambitions, Martin had always thought that his Israelite colleague was much like him. Grave and dedicated, and oh-so-correct. Happiness. Were they going to a poor immigrants' café to see happy men? Martin doubted it. He sniffed the air as they continued in companionable silence, letting himself enjoy the way the crystalline cold lit up his cheeks and nose, awakening his senses. If he had any hope of picking out of a crowd a man with enough resentment and hatred to kill, he was going to have to be alert.

As if by tacit agreement, both men shrank into their coats and scarves as they entered the crowded neighborhoods between the canals and the river. Martin did not have to look at the signs to know that these were the mean, filthy streets that housed the Thomases and their ilk. The rotting fleshy smells of the abattoir and tanneries combined with the smoke of the factories to make the air thick and rancid. It was as if dusk had fallen long before the sun decided to fade into the evening. Scantily dressed women had already begun to strike poses in the doorways, waiting for the night trade. Jacquette and Martin hurried to ward off their pitiful carnal offerings and moved just as quickly past a working-class café which might issue, at a moment's notice, drunks engaged in a fight, or just looking for one. Jacquette led the way deftly, until they reached a line of low buildings, shops and clapboard houses holding each other up against the cold. Shlomo was waiting for them at the corner.

The dwarf hobbled toward them, using his cane as an oar. "I've gathered a few of my God-fearing countrymen," he announced between large gulps of the tainted air. "Of course, you know that some would not see you or have you see them. Ehud the Anarchist and his friends don't trust any policemen, even ones as kind and just as Your Eminences. But I can tell you where they work if you need them."

Jacquette winked at Martin over the dwarf's head. He was still hopeful that he had found a first-class informer. Just then a woman, with a bawling child by her side, rounded the corner. "Herr Shlomo," she said with surprise as she spotted Martin and Jacquette. "Liebe Madame Noa," the dwarf bowed, "Gutes Shabbes." She did not respond, for the presence of a man in a fine woolen coat and bowler had left her opened-mouthed and silent. Even the child stopped in midsquawl. "The boy is looking good," Shlomo said as he patted the youngster on the head. Martin was shocked. A boy, with two long curls falling from either side of his face? Without realizing it, he had stepped away from the child in distaste.

"And so it is with us," Shlomo grinned, still patting the boy on the head as he took in Martin's discomfort. "And so it is."

Martin was embarrassed. How was he to be the authoritative, dispassionate observer if he made himself so obvious? In compensation he tipped his hat to the woman, which only made her draw her heavy brown knitted shawl more tightly around her head and neck. Pulling her son away, she murmured "Gutes Shabbes" and hurried down the street.

Jacquette cleared his throat. "Let's go in, shall we? Let's meet your friends." Once again, Martin knew why it was his inspector who went out into the world investigating, and not him. Nothing seemed to faze Jacquette.

"Yes, yes. The women are hurrying home to keep the fires burning and make the *cholent*, and the men must be home before sundown," Shlomo observed as he pushed aside the thick curtain that served as the only door to the café. If indeed, one could call it that. The room was only large enough to hold two benches, one long wooden table, and a counter. No bottles of wine or beer or spirits lined the walls. No rich aroma of steaming coffee. Instead, there was a giant metal urn on the counter. Five men, two in broad hats and three in caps sat on one side of the table, the tallest in the middle, as if they had purposely arranged themselves in a pyramid. They were sipping hot amber liquid from glasses and eating little squares of white, spongy cake from chipped dishes. Although Shlomo hastily announced their names as each of them stood up in greeting, for Martin the only thing that distinguished one from another was their age, eloquently expressed in the hues of their untrimmed beards, which ranged from snowy white to pitch black.

"Moshe, would you like to give our guests a glass of tea?" Shlomo asked the man behind the counter.

Martin was about to refuse, when Jacquette accepted, and sat down beside Shlomo on one of the long benches. Martin edged onto the other end and studied the men across from him. They looked so foreign. They gave off an unbathed odor of onions and sweat, an intimate pungency that reminded Martin of his first visit to a working-class café. When he was fifteen years old, Merckx had taken him to a larger but equally humble miner's tavern outside of Lille. Martin had been frightened and awed by Merckx's father and the other colliers, by the eyes that glared out of their soot-coated faces, and by the dank, dark smell that clung to them. It was if they were spirits emerging from the netherworld, unable or unwilling to shed the mud that encased and shaped them. They swore and drank hard, celebrating the light of day, and cursing the heat and blackness of the pits. They spoke in a language that Martin could understand, the language that Merckx had taught him about the exploitation of bosses and the hypocrisy of priests. And, of course, they spoke in French.

Martin squinted in concentration as he heard Jacquette's quiet questioning voice and Shlomo's high whining translations begin. He was trying to see if he recognized any of the men from the funeral procession. He felt both intrigued and repelled by their bushy unkempt beards, their suspicious glances, their gesticulations, and their language, an incomprehensible dialect of German, with neither its authority nor its precision. When they began to respond to the dwarf, their words circled round and round, wheedling, disagreeing, complaining, questioning. Like Shlomo, they did not seem to be men of straight answers. Martin examined the glass that had been slapped down in front of him before he lifted it, with some trepidation, to his lips. Hot strong tea. A simple innocent pleasure for men who may or may not be innocent.

When Jacquette asked them their opinion of Ullmann, one of the younger men, with a curly black beard and sharp dark eyes, opined that Ullmann was a good man who opened a school for his workers' children. In response to this, the tall man in the middle, who wore a broad black hat, slammed his fist on the table, rattling the glasses, and complained that he would not allow his wife or daughter to work in the factory because the mills ran on Saturday. He'd rather starve in order to keep the sabbath. Martin noticed that Shlomo's translation sounded much less adamant than the original. He began to suspect that the dwarf was trying to please both the talkers and the listeners. Still, whatever grudge or praise they had for the mill owner seemed distant and impersonal.

As for Erlanger, those who knew of him had only praise. He was kind, he distributed alms, he helped people in trouble. "That's why we prayed for him," one of them exclaimed. Martin recognized the word said almost in chorus, "Amen."

The question of why they didn't go to the Temple got a much less reverential response. Who could afford it, one of the younger men asked, and complained that the rich pay for their fine seats. And who would like to sit like them, cried the tall graybeard in the middle of the table, who clamped his arms by his side, stiffened his body, and raised his eyes to heaven. The oldest man thumped the table in pleasure as others laughed. And Shlomo had to stop several times to hold his oversized hand over his giggles as he tried to translate the mimicry of his countryman. "Sometimes *we* dance while we pray," he told Martin and Jacquette.

As Jacquette smiled in appreciation of the mockery of the bourgeoisie, Martin wondered what his inspector had thought of the exaggerated swaying and bowing at the edge of the crowd surrounding
Erlanger's grave. Singer, and all the others in tophats, had stood up
straight, speaking their prayers softly, and had lightly thrown a
handful of dirt upon the dead man. Singer had told Martin that the
Consistory had made the Israelite services more "dignified." Did the
immigrants feel left out? Or were they content to have their own services in a shoe shop on Friday evening? Contrary to what the dwarf had
claimed, it did not seem like his friends wanted to become French at
all. It was almost as if the foreign and the French Israelites were
leading parallel lives which seldom intersected. And when they did,
was there enough friction to drive a man to murder?

Martin had seen one of these collisions and the angry reaction of
Singer to the tinker's influence on his wife. Martin leaned over the
table toward Shlomo. "Ask them if they ever go into the homes of men
like Ullmann and Erlanger, if they know their wives and children."

The question evoked a pantomime of shrugs and head-shaking.
"Monsieur le juge," Shlomo explained, "I think all these poor honest
men are out in the cold every day, selling on the streets, or in their little
shops. They do not enter the homes of the rich."

"What about the tinker with the sharpening wheel?" Martin
pressed.

"Ahh," Shlomo said, and nodded. He repeated Martin's question to
the men. Suddenly the dark eyes of the young man who had praised
Ullmann lit up. "Jacob, Jacob," he said through a set of strong, white
teeth and began to laugh. Then he said something which set off an
argument among the immigrants.

"What's going on?" Martin asked, irritated.

"They are disagreeing, as Jews will, about Jacob, who we call Jacob
the Wanderer. This one," Shlomo said, pointing to first speaker, "says
he is *meshuge*—crazy—and our elder on the end says that he is a holy

man, the holiest of men. And this one," Shlomo pointed to the tallest of them, the one who had refused to send his women into Ullmann's mill, "agrees and says that Jacob is not crazy." Martin could see that the defender of the tinker was not finished. The man in the broad black hat kept raising his fist and pounding it on the table, punctuating the thuds with the name "Jacob."

The dwarf held up a finger, signaling for Martin and Jacquette to wait, and listened intensely. When the speaker had exhausted his arguments, Shlomo summarized. "It is Jacob who urged him not to send his women into Ullmann's factories, who said it was a *shanda*, a shame, that a Jew should work people on Saturday; Jacob who said we must keep the old laws, as they did in Russia, as they did in the countryside, even here; Jacob who wants to make righteous Jews of every one of us." Shlomo ended with a flourish.

"Meshuge, meshuge," muttered the younger man beside Jacob's tall defender. He was the one who had praised Ullmann. He spread out his arms, lifted his head, and chanted the saying that Shlomo had declaimed in Martin's chambers: Lebn vi got in Frankraykh. Martin did not even need Shlomo to tell him what came next. He was able to surmise from his knowledge of German and from the vehemence with which the young man was pounding the table that he was insisting, "We are here. Now."

Martin rubbed his hands on his legs. He could hardly sit still. Holy or crazy, this Jacob might be the link between the two worlds of the Israelites. He leaned toward Shlomo. "Ask why he is called the Wanderer, and why he isn't here."

Suddenly the jabbering stopped and all five men across the table looked askance at Martin. Was it the urgency in Martin's voice that had alerted them and sapped all the joy out of their disputations? Yet Martin persisted. He was a judge. He had a right to know. "Ask them," he repeated.

But a judge of France was a frightening specter to these men and just as foreign to them as they were to him. Martin realized from their

silence that he should have stuck to his plan of letting Jacquette ask the
questions in his friendly and matter-of-fact way. They were not about
to say anything to get one of their own in trouble with the law.

Caught between their "Eminences" and his friends, Shlomo
repeated the question about the Wanderer, and suddenly, rather than
offering any real response, the eldest of men let out a low cry and a
string of lamentations.

Martin shifted uneasily in his seat, as he noticed tears spring from
eyes so old and blurred he could hardly distinguish their color. Shlomo
listened and prepared to translate.

"He is saying," Shlomo began, "why do we ask about Jacob only.
We have all been condemned to wander. Why must we wander?
Where is our homeland?"

Suddenly one of the younger men got up from the other end of the
table, went over to the old man, and held him, repeating over and over
again, "*nu, nu, nu.*"

"Shlomo?" Martin inquired. The scene was getting out of hand.

The dwarf stretched back from the table, with a sadness in his eye
that Martin would not have expected from the trickster. He kept
staring at the whitebeard and the younger man.

"They are father and son," Shlomo reported. "They had to leave
their town because someone set fire to their shop. Abraham did not
want to leave. He misses his *rebbe*, his rabbi, who guided their life in
everything. Everything. It is not like the laws here. We do not have
our own judge, we have you."

There was no hint of accusation in Shlomo's words, only resignation.

"*Dos iz a fremder platz, dos iz a fremder platz,*" the old man moaned,
before wiping his nose on his sleeve. Suddenly the old man broke from
his son's embrace. "*Jacob iz frum, frum,*" he insisted to his friends.

Martin reached out and tugged at Shlomo's sleeve. "Tell me what he
is saying."

The dwarf shrugged and sighed, looking down at the floor between his two short, swinging legs. "He says he's unhappy here, he can't be comfortable here. It's not like it was in his village where everyone obeyed the laws, our laws, together. That's why he says Jacob is holy, *frum*, because Jacob wants everyone to remember, to obey." Shlomo heaved his body in the bench, as if reminding himself that he must continue to be ingratiating to his important guests. "Please, Monsieur le juge, you can be sure most of us like your laws, we like coming to a place where we can have the full dignity of our manhood and not worry about the Czar's army. He's just lonely and old."

Abraham was sobbing, clinging to his son. Martin heard the word rebbe again, and suddenly his heart went out to the old Jew. In Martin's short lifetime he had gone from one corner of France to another, to escape his past and to build a future. Even knowing the language, believing in the laws, having a status and a place, Martin had been utterly lonely in Provence. But this Abraham was a stranger in a strange land with a strange tongue and too old to want to change. He had lost everything. Martin watched as the tears abated and the white-beard leaned against his son's chest. Abraham sighed and stared at the table. Was he embarrassed by his outburst or simply too sorrowful to face his companions? Martin almost wanted to reach out and touch the father's withered hand to say he understood. But he knew that his gesture would not be welcome. Martin stood up. It was time to leave. He signaled to Jacquette, who was observing the father and son. Then Martin thanked the men for talking to him.

Jacquette nodded as he too rose and tipped his cap to the immigrants. It was over. They had no hope of gaining any more information.

"Wait, wait. Let me walk out with you." The dwarf used his arms to help him pivot around the bench and hop to the floor. He had not lost his desire to make Jacquette his meal ticket. He had more to say.

After they had closed the heavy curtain behind them, Shlomo whispered what he knew, or what he was willing to tell, about Jacob. Apparently he lived like a hermit in the countryside and was called the

Wanderer because he had traversed the continent many times, more times than even Shlomo himself.

"Is he holy or insane?" Jacquette asked as he pushed his fingers into his leather gloves.

"I think both, perhaps, maybe. I am not a doctor or a holy man. You might think of him as like me, a bit—" the dwarf hesitated while searching for the right word—"a bit of an eccentric." The shrug, the evasions were back. So was the yellow-toothed grin. "Where he is crazy, I think, is when he tries to convince everyone that they should obey the old laws. We no longer live in the village. We are here in your beautiful city."

Martin shot Jacquette a skeptical glance. Shlomo, the pleaser, was again saying what he thought they wanted to hear.

Jacquette preferred to play along. He patted Shlomo on his shoulder and said that they would talk next week. He had many more questions and—the inspector moved his head toward the curtained door—this was not the place to ask them.

Shlomo clapped his hands together, warming them, and nodded. "And now we must all go," he announced as he pointed to the waning sun in the dusky sky. "Shabbas comes quickly on a winter's day."

Yes, night was coming, and the weekend. Martin owed it to Clarie to be on his way. As soon as they were out of hearing, he apologized to Jacquette for having made a mess of their "conversation."

"Don't worry, sir. As soon as Shlomo mentioned 'Ehud the Anarchist,' I realized I might be more interested in who wasn't there than in who was. After all, we don't have enough men to follow everyone. But an anarchist and an industrialist?" Jacquette made a clicking sound with his tongue. "Sounds like a lethal combination to me."

Martin grunted agreement as they quickened their pace through the garbage-strewn streets. He, too, was interested in who had not been in the café. Interested in an "eccentric" who somehow had bridged the gap between the rich and poor.

30

Saturday, December 8

MARTIN WOKE UP IN A cold sweat, clinging to the side of the bed. He gulped for air as he tried to recapture the dream. He was back in Aix, in the cavernous basement of the jail where they did autopsies. The mounds of a body were under a sheet. The corn-yellow hair of his oldest friend, Jean-Jacques Merckx, stuck out at the top. Two unidentified hands pulled back the white shroud, revealing a precise, pointed black beard, and a knife in the corpse's chest. Martin protested. Merckx was clean-shaven. He had been shot four times, not stabbed. Suddenly Martin was overcome with joy. This was not Merckx. Maybe he wasn't dead. Maybe he had made it to Switzerland after all. Martin looked again at the pale body on the table. And saw that it was Singer.

No! Martin reached his arm across the bed to touch Clarie, not wanting to wake her, only to feel her warmth. But her place was empty.

Martin gasped as he sat up. Clarie! Did she get up in the night and walk the floors as he did? Had he not heard her, when he should have gone out to her, taken care of her? He swung his feet over to the side of the bed. His mouth was dry all the way to the back of his throat. He needed water. Just as his feet hit the floor, Clarie walked in.

"Oh, I'm sorry. I didn't mean to wake you."

Martin was stunned. Clarie was fully dressed. Was he still in the dream?

"I'm going to Mass with Madeleine, I need to put up my hair. I can't go to the cathedral with a hanging braid."

Martin was so groggy and parched that he barely managed to choke out a response. "My God, is this Sunday already?" Had he slept an entire forty-eight hours?

Without waiting for an answer, Martin staggered out through the dining room to the kitchen. He shook his head hard, as he poured himself a glass of water. He gulped it down, closed his eyes and swallowed. He felt the cold floor under his bare feet. He saw that the cupboards, the sink, and the stove were exactly where they should be. He was awake. He must talk to Clarie.

He returned to the bedroom and watched as she sat in front of the mirror and wound the braid in a ring in back of her head. She didn't ask for help in putting up her hair, as she sometimes did. She was intent on her task, hardly noticing his reflection.

When she was done, she turned to him. "It's not Sunday, dear Martin. You didn't sleep that long."

"Then why—"

She swung back to the mirror to scrutinize her face and pin back a few strands of stray black hair. "It's the Feast of the Immaculate Conception," she murmured. "A Feast of the Virgin. Madeleine tells me that the Virgin who appeared at Lourdes *was* the very vision of the Immaculate Conception. That proves it's true. That Mary was conceived without sin. That miracles do happen. My mother loved the Virgin at Lourdes."

Her voice was as toneless as if she was giving a lesson in simple logic. But none of this was logical. Her mother, the immaculate conception, miracles. This wasn't Clarie.

Now she was staring in the mirror, watching him, waiting for his reaction.

"You're sure you're ready for this?"

"Do you mean because little Henri-Joseph was baptized there?"

Her voice was so soft, so distant, it was as if he was hearing her through an echo chamber.

"Yes." Although he hadn't really thought of that.

"Madeleine says the Virgin will protect me. That she comes in many ways to many people if they pray hard enough, and eventually I will find the Virgin, who will protect and forgive me." Her lower lip began to tremble.

Martin ignored the irrationality of these propositions. He heard only the cruelty. He put his hands on Clarie's shoulder and kissed her cheek. "Clarie, my Clarie, why would you need forgiveness?"

She moved her head away from him as she whispered, "I don't know."

Martin got down on one knee. "Clarie, look at me. Please. There is nothing to forgive. Our little boy died. It's a terrible tragedy. We didn't deserve it."

She gently removed his hand from her waist and stood up, looking down on him. "I can imagine many things that need to be forgiven. Not going to church for years on end. Not taking seriously God's laws. Teaching girls a Protestant philosophy in a Catholic country."

This was Madeleine, fanaticism, speaking, not his Clarie, who had never expressed anything but respect and admiration for her teachers at Sèvres, no matter what their beliefs. If she went on this way, she might start complaining about the "godless Republic," the Republic to which both of them had devoted their talents.

Martin got up from his foolish position and sat down on the bed, staring at the blue woven carpet. Except for the squeezing pain in his stomach, every part of him had grown numb. He did not want to argue with Clarie, he wanted to talk to her. To tell her about his dreams and fears. It was selfish, he knew. But he could not help remembering. Sitting on a bench near the Hôtel de Ville in Aix, telling her about Merckx, crying, feeling her reach for him, pull him to her, embracing him, holding him, understanding. Because she had lost her mother. Because he had lost his father. She was the only one who knew his deepest, most dangerous secret. That he had broken the law by letting his friend desert the army. More, she was the only one who knew the depths of his remorse and his pledge never to be half-hearted again when someone he was close to needed him.

But now he didn't know how to help Clarie. Perhaps it would be best to let her find her own way for a while. In the meantime, Martin had to do everything he could to protect his friend, to make sure that they would never find Singer with a knife sticking out of his chest.

"What are you thinking about?" Clarie had on her coat and was standing over him.

"Us, the baby." It was a lie. But he thought that was what she wanted to hear.

"Not about your work?"

Was there resentment in her voice? If so, Martin thought with a sigh, he deserved it for being away so much. "That, too. I didn't tell you. Another man was killed last week. A relative of David Singer."

"Was he old?" She was putting on her gloves, one finger at a time, right in front of his face.

"In his sixties, I suppose."

"Oh," she said. "I must hurry."

He watched as her skirts disappeared through the bedroom door. Was Daniel Erlanger too old to command her sympathy? Or too distant? Too Jewish? Where had his generous-spirited Clarie gone? He had never dreamed that she would so casually dismiss the death of a kind, old man.

He was still in a nightmare.

31
Monday, December 10

THE SNOW BEGAN VERY EARLY Monday morning. By dawn, the skies had thrown a diaphanous veil over Nancy. By the time Martin left for the Palais, the streets were covered with a slippery silver carpet. Hours later, snowflakes floated down as big as feathers. They kept falling, layer upon layer, muting the sounds of the city and clogging its roadways. It was as if the world had stopped.

Martin stood at the window, staring out, remembering. When he was a boy, a day like this had thrilled him. He'd wanted the world to stand still while he ran free, free from school and the Jesuits, free from his father's clock shop and his mother's worries, free to roam, to flap his wings and make his mark in the snow. He'd open his mouth as wide as he could and catch the floating flakes, savoring their delicate melting on his tongue. Martin turned away from the sight of the snow-covered

Place de la Carrière. Children feel so powerful. They think they can swallow the world in a few gulps when, in truth, it is the world that will swallow them.

Martin slipped quietly back to his desk, past his clerk, who was busily transcribing the morning's interview. Martin no longer wanted the world to stop. He needed to push it forward. If the world stood still now, he would feel hollow inside forever.

He closed his eyes and prodded. *One thing at a time. First the case, then Clarie.* She was finding her own solace. Her own way. Eventually they would find each other again.

He opened his eyes to the sound of his clerk's scratching pen and his own fingers drumming on the desk. Martin needed to find some new way, some sure way of investigating this case. Not Didier's or Singer's or Jacquette's. He was going in too many directions at once. He angrily pushed aside a folder filled with newspaper clippings. In the last three weeks he had become an expert on the hatred of the Jewish race. And where had that gotten him? This morning's interrogation of a local reporter, who had written a particularly vituperative column on the coming Dreyfus trial, had ended with a fine speech on how judges thought they could quash the freedom of the press. No new names, no new leads. Only the problem of what to do with the maddening defrocked priest whose detainment might become public any minute.

"Charpentier, the fire!"

Yet as his clerk was about to get up to stoke the potbelly stove, Martin said, "No, let me do it. You keep writing." Too many directions. Just then, another came knocking on the door.

"Charpentier!"

This time his clerk moved quickly, before Martin could change his mind and go to the door himself, an unseemly proposition for a juge d'instruction.

Martin was still poking at the coals, when Charpentier came scurrying back to him. "It's Doctor Bernheim, sir," he whispered. Charpentier's eyes were arched so high they almost touched the descending waves of his auburn hair. The famous Hippolyte Bernheim!

Martin winced and groaned. How could he have forgotten? Frustrated to the core with the antics of Hémonet, he had sent Jacquette to Bernheim to explain the investigation and ask if a consultation might be useful. Martin hadn't imagined that the great expert in psychotherapeutics would answer the call on a day like today.

Martin laid down the poker and buttoned his jacket. He motioned with his head to Charpentier to invite the doctor in. Martin was at his desk by the time the surprisingly diminutive Hippolyte Bernheim entered, shaking the glimmers of snow off his cloak and bowler, and stamping puddles from his boots. He did this with a mixture of embarrassment and delight. Like a child.

After Charpentier took his coat and hat, Bernheim extended his hand to Martin. "It's about time we met. I like working on cases. Especially intriguing ones." The hand was cold, even as the doctor exuded confidence and warmth.

"You've already met my greffier, Guy Charpentier." Martin gestured behind him.

Bernheim nodded and sat down, rubbing his hands together. "I haven't seen a day like this since I left Alsace. And you know how long ago that was."

Martin did, of course. Over twenty years since the end of the war, when the University of Strasbourg had passed into German hands.

"In Paris we never had such snow. That's where I went first after the treaty. But this," Bernheim extended his arms, "this is glorious, like a holiday."

"Yet you are here. I'm so pleased you could see me so soon." This was more than politeness. Already Bernheim had brought a burst of new energy into Martin's somber chambers. The doctor was a robust middle-aged man, with a thick, dark mustache that stood out against his pale, cold-reddened face like a permanent smile set upon his upper lip. He still had a fine head of hair, a mix of black and gray, parted down the middle, and a trim gray beard. The clothes, a high collar, cravat and frock coat, added to the air of celebrity. Here was the leading light of "the school of Nancy," the great rival to Charcot's Parisian school of psychology.

"Anything I can do to help. I read the papers, you know. This is a nasty business. I say this as an Israelite, but more importantly as a Frenchman and a republican." Chin thrust forward, Bernheim said these last words as if he were about to raise a toast. He had opted to be in France, to add his achievements to his country's scientific and intellectual glory. His enthusiasm was infectious.

"Thank you. Of course you don't mind if Charpentier takes notes."

Bernheim grinned even more broadly. He liked being recorded. And, of course, Martin knew, his clerk would certainly want to be a part of anything to do with one of Nancy's most famous citizens.

"Well, then, let's get down to business, shall we?" Martin said, attempting to mirror Bernheim's easy professional confidence. "I have two types of questions for you. First, I'd like to ask you to see one of our suspects. And then—"

"Do you think he did it? Would you like me to try to get a confession while he is in an hypnotic state?" Bernheim's dark eyebrows lifted as his face brightened up even more.

Martin's mouth fell open. "Do you think you could do that?" A confession would get Didier and the press off his back. For the moment. But if it were false, it would only make things worse. And, more dangerous, it would leave the killer still out there.

Bernheim's ebullience was not allayed by Martin's alarmed question. "If you know my work, you know that most people can be 'suggested' into doing all kinds of things they would not normally do: for example, committing a crime or acting like an hysteric."

"Even admit to something they did not do?"

"Yes! Or, telling a truth they dare not tell with their conscious mind. This is the very basis of my argument with Charcot, and why our methods are being debated across Europe right now. Charcot claims that only hysterics can be hypnotized. Then he takes these poor women, puts them under his spell and invites his colleagues and friends to the asylum at Salpêtrière to watch them. He even photographs them in that state." Bernheim stuck out his lower lip with distaste. "I don't like that. Anyone can be hypnotized, if they are willing. Suggestion and hypnotism should be used to cure people, not display them like animals in a zoo."

Bernheim's cures of mental and physical ills were so famous, some thought of him as a miracle worker. Martin began warily to shake his head. He needed assurance that the doctor did not intend to "perform a miracle" on his prisoner. "Of course, you would never *induce* a false confession."

Bernheim crossed his legs as he sat back in his chair and gazed at Martin. "I can see I've perturbed you. Whether I could or not would depend on the willingness and character of the subject. But I'll leave confessions up to you if you'd like. You just tell me what you believe about your suspects and what you want me to do."

Martin had to smile in spite of himself. He should have known that his dismay would not get past a famous mind doctor.

"The suspect," he explained, "is a priest, recently defrocked, and a drinker. I haven't been able to find any connection between him and the victims, but I am not sure that anything he's telling me is true. His behavior and speech are utterly erratic. But he may be acting a madman just to throw us off course. I need to know if he is really mad and how dangerous he might be."

"Oh, yes, Hémonet," Bernheim nodded. "Jacquette told me about him. But what about the tanner?"

"So you have been keeping up with the case."

Bernheim shrugged. "Yes, and I am sure, as the two murders go unsolved, more and more people will be interested."

This was not what Martin wanted to hear. He cleared this throat. "I released Pierre Thomas. I'm sure he's innocent of everything but gullibility."

"That can be dangerous too," Bernheim interjected.

"Yes," Martin agreed, bending his head forward, trying to keep his focus on what he needed from this important man. He had eliminated Thomas. He did not want to revisit that line of inquiry.

Bernheim seemed to sense his resistance. "Tell me more about your priest," he said quietly. "What makes you think he might actually be unbalanced?"

"His ravings. His eyes, the way they seem to signal a mind going in and out, as if sometimes he's not here. Sometimes he seems some-where else entirely." Martin struggled to explain. "Even though he knows that everything he says could be used against him, he can't stop himself from raging against the Israelites. He may not be a murderer, but he certainly sounds murderous."

"You don't know how long he's been this way, or if he was any-where around the victims?"

"After we brought him in last Tuesday, I sent Jacquette out to inter-view the neighbors. Apparently when he became a priest they were all proud of him. Now they hold him in contempt because the bishop gave him the boot. Yet they swear he could not have committed any crime, because no one saw him leave the house. On the other hand," Martin added, "as you know, villagers often stick together. They could be covering for him."

"Of course," Bernheim agreed. "What do his former parish-ioners say?"

"One of Jacquette's men went back to his parish last week after we took Hémonet in. Those who would talk only said that his sermons against the Jews were getting more violent, but otherwise. . . ." Martin shrugged.

"Otherwise he was normal?"

"I think so."

"But, of course, that is not 'normal.' Jacquette told me about the book. This hatred he holds against the Israelites is a sickness, a disease. It has nothing to do with the rational mind. The so-called truths such people proclaim are delusions. They make the Jew the bogeyman for everything that is wrong with the world."

The bonhomie had drained from Bernheim's face, reminding Martin that the doctor was, indeed, an Israelite. Martin had not meant to imply that Hémonet's hatreds were "normal."

"However," Bernheim said, as if to allay Martin's discomfort, "this kind of delusion has become so widespread, it might appear to be in the realm of normality. With the Dreyfus trial coming up," he sighed, "I expect worse. In fact," the doctor leaned forward eagerly, "I've seen far worse, in a case that might be of interest to you."

Good God, not another one, Martin thought, as a sudden spurt of anxiety heated his neck and face. "Go on, please," he said, dropping each word with purposeful evenness, as he tried to appear pleasantly engaged in what Bernheim had to tell him.

"Well," Bernheim sat back and smiled, "just last year, I saw a soldier, a young corporal with an old noble name, but no money, and filled with overblown ambition. Yet he could no longer even lift his rifle to aim and shoot. Every time he was ordered to do so, his arm became as stiff as a tree trunk, and his fingers cramped like withering branches." Bernheim held up his hand, crooked forward, to demonstrate. "As you can imagine, to bring such a case to my attention would have been an embarrassment for most of our army men. But his commander was an enlightened fellow, who had some affection for the lad and had heard about my so-called cures. So he forced him to come see me. That young man was hostile, I can tell you! So I called upon my old colleague, Dr. Liébeault, to take a look at him. Ambroise has the manner of a kindly country doctor, which he was, but the mind of a brilliant diagnostician, which of course he is, for he is the very creator of our psychotherapeutics through hypnotism. In any case, as soon as he got the boy to cooperate and go into a 'sleep,' that young officer began to spout all kinds of anti-Israelite nonsense. It turns out he could not shoot at a target because he had been ordered to do so by a Jew, the very lieutenant who brought him to me." Bernheim chuckled. "You can imagine what he thought about being sent to someone named Bernheim. The Israelite conspiracy! Now, there's a case for you."

Was it? Was it a case for Martin? He had to clench his teeth together in order not to groan. *The army*. He grimaced before asking, "Is this young corporal here, now, in Nancy?"

"I should think not. Given that he had developed a severe hysteria with full psychosomatic symptoms, Liébeault and I recommended that the lad either submit to our treatments or be sent home for a long rest."

Martin suppressed a sigh of relief. "And the lieutenant, the boy's superior? Do you remember his name? Is he still around?"

"I never saw him again. I'd have to find his name in my notes."

"Please do. We'll look into it." Martin wrote down "Jacquette. Jewish officer?" If some discontented soldier had seen the Israelite lieutenant with Ullmann and Erlanger, would he have assumed there was a "conspiracy"? Martin's mind was racing so fast, it tripped over itself. He winced at the possibility that *he* was beginning to think like an anti-Israelite. Why did he assume that a Jewish officer from another region knew the victims? He etched nervous circles around Jacquette's name, and wrote "a connection?"

He had to ask the next, logical question. "Do you think that there are other men in the garrison prone to this kind of hysteria?"

"Well," Bernheim pursed lips together, considering, "certainly not to the extent of displaying such dramatic physical symptoms. But I am sure there is seething resentment, especially now, with the Dreyfus accusation fueling the flames. When someone thinks he has a right to a certain status, a certain command, a certain *superiority*, and all of a sudden he is passed by in favor of someone he thinks is unworthy, unlike him and everything he's known, well, then, he feels he's lost something. It's been taken away from him. That causes resentment."

Bernheim watched as Martin scrawled "army, resentment, loss." "Yes," he said, approvingly, "and that brings us back to your man."

"The ex-priest." Martin looked up.

"Yes. I think, given his attitudes toward the Israelites, we had better ask Liébeault to look at him, although we'll have to drag Ambroise in from the country."

This time Martin could not suppress a sigh. More delays. More complications. "You have no opinions, no—"

"Yes, I do," Bernheim broke in. "I would say that the physical symptoms you describe go beyond mere resentment. They seem to be either the result of an addiction to drink, or the result of a great loss, a kind of mourning. Or a very lethal combination of the two."

"Loss and mourning?"

"Yes. My guess is, whatever seeds of madness he harbored in his soul are blossoming because he has lost the one thing that was most important to him."

"You mean the priesthood," Martin whispered. The words *loss* and *mourning* had pierced him like a knife, transporting him elsewhere.

"Yes. He cannot teach or preach or succor. He cannot perform the rites that give him, according to his beliefs, supernatural powers over a congregation. He no longer has any station in life. Yes, loss. Loss can drive you mad."

"That would be enough?" Martin stumbled over the words. Clarie, too, was not always present. Her mind seemed to wander whenever they talked. She had lost the thing that was most important to her, their son. He could not keep from asking, "Is indifference also a sign of going mad from loss?"

Bernheim straightened up, surprised. "This is not the way you described the priest."

Martin could hardly breathe. "Is there no cure?"

Bernheim peered into Martin's eyes. "Is there someone else you are thinking of?"

Martin turned away, not wanting Bernheim to read his thoughts. He didn't want to discuss Clarie. He couldn't. So he prevaricated. "I was thinking of the many unfortunates whom I have interrogated. Women who've lost their children, men who've lost their homeland."

"All right, then."

Martin should have known that a man with Bernheim's talents would immediately perceive a private pain, and, as an equal, respect it. But he was also kind enough to reassure Martin.

"Often," Bernheim continued, "such madness is merely temporary. It passes with time."

With time.

The doctor waited, as Martin could imagine him waiting with his patients. Finally, Bernheim said, "Is there more?"

The question broke through the trance-like pall that had fallen over Martin, snapping him back to the issue of the defrocked priest and his vile works. "Yes, there was a second reason I wanted to see you. I've read your work on suggestibility. Do you think books or sermons that spread hatred of the Israelites could inspire someone to kill?"

Bernheim traced his smiling mustache with his finger as he thought. "That's a very good question, the kind I ask myself all the time. I suspect that a sermon, given with great flourish and emotion, would have more impact than the written page, but," the doctor shook his head, "I don't know. I know that a rousing speech to a crowd can make men act in abnormal ways. Rioting, marching off to certain death in times of war. Why would any rational man do any of those things? As for the Jews, from the time of the Crusades up until this very day in Russia, there certainly are instances of mobs being inspired to kill them. But whether a single man would be motivated to commit murder *in secret* because of a book, this I do not know."

"And, if, as you say, he is insane?"

"If I find that he could not help himself, that the *suggestion* to do evil was so strong that he was forced into action by what I call *irresistible impulse*, then you cannot send him to the guillotine. He is sick."

Martin did not know how he felt about this new way of looking at guilt and innocence. From his point of view, Hémonet had committed an unforgivable crime long before he had suffered a maddening loss. Martin opened his drawer and withdrew *Nancy-Juif.*

"There are some names and addresses in the book—"

"The victims?"

"No. At least not yet. We've taken the precaution of keeping the existence of the book out of the press. We don't want anyone to go looking for it."

"May I?" The doctor held out his hand.

"Certainly." Martin watched as Bernheim flipped through the pages. He did not react, even though he was an Israelite.

"Unfortunately," Martin continued, "this kind of writing is not a crime. If it were a newspaper column directed against one particular man, perhaps he could sue for libel, or even fight a duel for his honor. But this kind of libel that throws its poisonous net everywhere with hints and insinuations, there's no good way to stop it."

"Yes," Bernheim murmured, still thumbing through the pages. "One of our great liberties, freedom of speech. Where would science be without it?" he concluded as he closed the book. "But if neither victim was named in it, we still don't know why these two particular men were killed."

Bernheim was raising the same question Martin had asked himself many times. Pierre and Antoinette Thomas claimed they had reason to hate her boss, and there may be others like them who felt exploited by the mill owner. But who had reason to hate *both* Victor Ullmann, the rich industrialist, and Daniel Erlanger, the presumably lovable old notary?

The doctor stood up. "If I may have this for a while, I'll think about it, and I'll show it to Liébeault before he sees your suspect. I'll let you know what he tells me."

Martin got up, ready to escort him out the door.

Bernheim waved him off. Charpentier jumped up to retrieve his cloak and bowler. "I can find my way," he said as he reached for Martin's hand and shook it warmly. Then, taking his things from Charpentier, the celebrated doctor thanked the wide-eyed clerk and left the room.

Martin sank back into his chair. He'd have to wait for more concrete results. He could bear the waiting, as long as no one else was hurt. He could even bear the thought of taking a closer look at the local garrison. After all, that perilous venture had loomed as a possibility ever since that first terrible confrontation with Didier. What he could not bear was the lesson that Bernheim had just imparted: loss can drive you mad.

32

Tuesday, December 11

JACQUETTE REPORTED EARLY ON TUESDAY, eager to make up for time lost because of the snow. He wanted to set out immediately to search the clogged, narrow streets between the canals and the river for the man who called himself Ehud the Anarchist. But Martin had other plans for him.

"The army," Martin said, after summarizing his meeting with Bernheim. "How shall we proceed?"

Jacquette sighed, sat down and repeated his plaint: "We can't do everything." Then he shook a cigarette out of the sky-blue packet which occupied a permanent residence in his vest pocket.

"Bernheim will send us the name of the Israelite officer. If he's been transferred, then all we have to do is nose around the edges, and *only* the edges." Martin did not want anyone in the garrison to know that it was under judicial scrutiny.

"Umm," Jacquette grunted wearily as he rubbed his eye with the palm of his left hand. "Close to home. That's what I say." He seemed too weary even to light up.

Martin could not repress an affectionate smile as he sat back, clasped his hands over his stomach, and waited. They were all over-stretched, which is why he had expected some resistance. But Jacquette would come around, not because Martin was his superior, but because in all the tough cases they had always been loyal partners. He watched as his stalwart inspector stuck the Blue Jockey in his mouth, lit it, sucked in, blew out, and sighed.

"All right," he said. "If the Jewish officer is still around, we can ask him in nice and friendly-like. Make sure he knows we know he's done nothing wrong. Then see if he's noticed any particularly outspoken anti-Israelites among our warriors. If he's out of the picture, we make inquiries about the off-duty rotation of the officer corps. Your man Charpentier can do that. A clerical inquiry, a civic matter. Nothing suspicious. As for surveillance, I could put Barzun on it. Good man. Watchful. Quiet. Discreet. Notices details. In his old bowler, he could fade into any crowd. He can keep an eye on the soldiers while they strut about town. If there's a connection, Barzun will see it."

To recover his strength after that lengthy disquisition, Jacquette took another long draw and waited for Martin.

"I'll take care of the Singers," Martin said, as he stood up, ready to send Jacquette on his way.

"Good," Jacquette muttered. He had no desire to tangle with a judge or his family.

"Of course. Charpentier is waiting at the entrance to catch Singer as soon as he arrives." *Of course.* So absolute, hiding all the uncertainties, as well as what he was not telling Jacquette: that the case had driven a rift between him and Singer, and that he hoped to get Noémie Singer to talk about matters that might go far beyond the criminal investigation.

As he bid his inspector good-bye, Martin also did not say that he had asked Charpentier to leave Singer and him alone. There was so much of that these days, clerks being sent out of chambers. By now the whole courthouse must know how politically charged and difficult the case had become, Martin thought with chagrin.

Moments later, Singer arrived, looking none the worse for wear after the mourning period, his beard, his fashionable fedora, his expensive tweed wool coat as neat and precise as ever. Martin immediately walked over to greet him.

"David, good to see you back. I hope this last week wasn't too hard for you."

As their eyes met, Martin hoped that the anxious distraction that portends a mountain of unattended work explained the limpness of Singer's handshake. "Sorry to catch you like this," Martin continued. "I know you have a lot to do, but I need to talk about something."

Singer neither removed his hat nor started to unbutton his long coat. He just stood there, forcing Martin to fill the space with banalities. Well, then, Martin thought, we'll get to the point.

"I'm going to interview your wife."

"What!"

"I need to ask her about her uncle and—"

"Why not ask me?"

Despite its curtness, Martin was grateful for the interruption. He realized at once that bringing up the tinker would set Singer off even more.

"There are things she might be able to tell me about Maître Erlanger's domestic life. Besides, Singer, I'm only telling you as a professional courtesy. And," he stressed, "as a matter of our friendship." When Singer spurned this obvious appeal, Martin walked away and stood behind his desk, his lips grimly pressed together as he tried to quell his irritation.

When he looked up, Singer was tugging at the point of his beard and breathing hard. "You mean that there are no more anti-Israelites that you can talk to? No Dreyfus-haters, who now assume that we are all traitors? You have to disturb my wife during her period of mourning?"

"I've waited seven days," Martin said quietly. "I've respected your customs."

"*Our customs!* We are talking about human decency here."

"You know I must treat your wife as I would anyone else," retorted Martin.

Singer began to undo his coat, from top to bottom, with such violence that Martin expected a button to pop off. "So this is where you've come to. Two of our best men dead, and you have to invade our homes." He stopped short. "I am assuming you are not intending to drag Noémie in here."

"Of course not." Martin waved the suggestion aside. *Your customs, our best men, our homes.* Hearing himself, listening to Singer confirmed how much they had grown apart since Erlanger's death, since Singer's unspoken accusations that he had not worked fast and effectively enough, since Martin had seen the double-sided gravestones. This is not what he wanted. Martin wanted to believe that Singer was like him, that they were colleagues who agreed on the most basic philosophical issues.

"I assume you've made no progress?" Singer was flattening out his mustache with one finger, even though every hair seemed pasted in place.

"Why would you assume that?" said Martin. Now they were both thoroughly in a huff and not doing anything to hide it.

"Because if you had, I assume you would have had the courtesy to tell me."

Courtesy? When Singer had the nerve to imply that a colleague was not acting in good faith, doing everything he could? When he interrupted, refused to clasp the hand of friendship? The only courtesy that

Singer seemed to recognize was the stiff, prissy attitude he marched around the courthouse, ever sensitive to what his colleagues might be thinking or saying about him.

Martin caught his breath and sat down. Before that fatal November evening, before the Thomas boy's mutilation, before the killings, Martin had never noticed or, if he had, cared about these qualities in his friend. David Singer was an imperfect human being like every other. The question—one Martin had never given much thought to—was whether Singer's particular imperfections stemmed from having suffered real slights and insults. Despite the growing feeling of being intentionally excluded from an important part of Singer's life, in some ways Martin had become more sympathetic with his colleague. After all, Martin had suffered through the idiotic assertions of Rocher, had read and heard the testimony of scores of anti-Israelites, and, above all, had confronted Hémonet and his scurrilous book.

Martin took the risk of calling Singer by his first name again. "Look, David, we've both been going through a very difficult period. I'm working as hard as I can on the investigation. You must know that." *Despite Henri-Joseph.* Martin was not going to debase himself and their friendship by having to remind Singer about his dead child.

He did not have to. "Sorry, I do trust you are doing everything you can. And I should be helping." Martin was not sure what the sadness in Singer's eyes meant. Was he aware of the wall that was separating them, or finally remembering Martin's terrible loss?

"Then sit and tell me about the tinker. Why does he make you so angry?"

"I don't know that this has anything to do with—"

"Neither do I. But we are looking at rifts in the Israelite community."

Martin could see Singer bristle at that suggestion, and, at the same time, make every effort to control himself. When Singer took the seat in front of the desk, Martin felt that his colleague was relenting. After all, Singer was an investigating magistrate as well as an Israelite. He knew that when two murders are committed, no stone must be left unturned.

"If you must know, if you think you can understand, men like the tinker are holding us back. They look like," Singer pursed his lips in distaste, "like our ancestors from the village, like people imagine we still are, despised wanderers and peddlers, homeless, landless, nation-less. Not citizens, Frenchmen, republicans, but," Singer drew in a breath and let it out with exasperated force, "but superstitious peddlers living in hovels."

Martin thought back to the old Jew with tears in his eyes. For him, homelessness was having left the place that Singer scorned.

"And when," Singer pushed his collar out a little, "and when one of them tries to influence your own wife and bring her back to the old superstitions, then any man has a right to be angry."

"Yes," Martin nodded, listening, thinking of Clarie, and Madeleine's growing influence over her. He began to turn his ink bottle round and round very slowly. "Superstition, going backwards," he murmured, "I do understand." He hated thinking about what was happening to Clarie while he was away, investigating, trying to under-stand other people's lives.

"Good! We are both modern men, who want modern wives." Singer caught himself, as if he had suddenly perceived Martin's drift away from him. "How is Mme Martin?"

Martin shook his head. He didn't want to talk about her.

"Sorry." Singer got up to leave. He picked up his fedora and fin-gered the rim, allowing a moment for Martin to recover. When Martin met his eyes, Singer said, "Can you believe it, we have one of those modern contraptions, a telephone. Let me call Noémie and tell her you are coming. And if you could give her time to put the house together, arrive around two?"

"Of course." Martin stood up. Joining with Singer to lighten the mood, he remarked, "A telephone. That *is* modern."

This time the handshake was warm and firm.

The Singer apartments occupied the first and second floors of a building only four blocks away from where the Martins lived. Yet it was a different world. As he approached the building, Martin wondered where the money had come from, his family or hers, or both. A telephone. He had to smile. A very modern and very expensive contraption. He was not at all surprised when a maid in a black dress and starched white apron and cap answered the bell. She took his coat and hat and led him into a large salon to wait for "the Madame."

Alone, Martin took the opportunity to warm his hands above the white tongues of flames leaping from the fire in the impressive pink marble fireplace. Then he turned his back to the heat and perused the intricately woven Persian rug that ran along the center of the rectangular room. Around it on three sides were sofas and chairs in the curved, ornate Louis-Fifteenth style, their cushions and backs covered in silken, brocaded pastels. At the other end, a grand piano was on display. Moving away from the fire, he made a quiet survey of the mahogany side tables. Their gas lamps bore cloudy globes decorated with delicate rose patterns. Martin scrutinized the small photographs: Singer, his wife and their children. On the walls, in oil, were sterner portraits, ancestors.

Martin sighed as he gingerly took a seat on the sofa. The Singers had healthy children and wealthy parents. They did not, like the Martins, live three flights up a narrow staircase above a drygoods store on a busy street in a cramped apartment. They lived in a muted, spacious residence appropriate to the office of a juge d'instruction. Who, then, was the odd man out at the courthouse? Martin thought ruefully. Was it the Israelite held in contempt by a few bigots, or the son of a watchmaker married to the daughter of an immigrant blacksmith? Or both, by people who considered themselves their betters?

"Monsieur le juge Martin, how good to see you."

Martin stood up as Noémie Singer entered the room in a rustle of taffeta. She wore a skirt and waist-length matching jacket in mourning black that, in the light of the fire, gave off a silvery luster as she moved toward him. Her blouse was made of a soft, white accordion-pleated material and topped by a large bow. Her elegant outfit would have been very solemn, if it were not for the jacket's sleeves which puffed out in the whimsical leg-of-mutton fashion of the day. She brought with her the smell of spring, of flowers that Martin could not identify but found pleasingly feminine. Her heavy chestnut-colored hair was pulled back into a chignon, but not too tightly, and not without license to leave a frame of little curls around her face.

"Madame Singer, please accept my condolences."

"Thank you." Her eyelids fluttered downward, as she sat in the chair across from the sofa. She was a very beautiful woman. Shorter and rounder than Clarie. Softer too. Soft enough, he hoped, to allow him to probe into matters that caused tension between her and Singer, and perhaps between other Israelites. In order to lead her into that dangerous territory, he would have to proceed very carefully. So he began where she might expect him to begin.

"As you know, I asked to speak with you about your uncle."

"Why me? Why not my husband?"

Although a bit surprised by this early resistance, Martin had no trouble coming up with a plausible response.

"Certainly, you've known your uncle longer than Monsieur Singer. But it is more than that. I find that in order to understand how a crime could have taken place, you need many perspectives. Often it is the unexpected comment that will lead to the solution."

She was not convinced. "I don't know what I could possibly tell you."

"Many things," Martin said with an eagerness that sounded false even to his own ears. "For example, you know something about how your uncle lived. Can you think of anyone who held a grudge against him—his servants, his clients, his friends, someone at the Temple?"

"He only had one servant, Rachel. She managed the household and was devoted to him. He was always absolutely honest in all his business dealings. And generous, charitable. As for someone at the Temple . . ." She stopped short and lifted one dark, well-shaped eyebrow, as if to signal her dismay at Martin's impertinence. Then she shook her head. "No Jew would kill another Jew."

"Of course," Martin murmured. This is the same objection he had heard from other, very disparate, quarters—the dwarf and the rabbi. He took another tack.

"I've read that there was an incident on the Place Saint-Jean— where your uncle lived—a poor Christian, a woman, begging for bread last winter and turned away—"

"It could not have been my uncle." She sat straight up, offended. "He was too kind to turn away anyone, Christian or Jew. You must be thinking of someone else."

At least she had not asked him the source of the accusation. He did not want to tell her about Hémonet. Martin took a small pad and pen out of his pocket. He made a note to confirm that the police had gone door-to-door in the square where Erlanger had lived.

"We know why my uncle was killed," she said, when he was done writing. Her posture remained on alert, ready to defend the old notary.

"Why is that?" Martin asked quietly, eager to hear what she had to say.

"Because they hate us. That's what my husband says. There is no reason. They just hate us because of who we are. Especially now with this scandal about a Jewish officer committing treason. My husband won't even let me read the newspapers. He says I would find them too upsetting. He also told me that you should be looking for the killer among the anti-Israelites, among those who hate us."

She paused. Her words, which afforded no easy answers, echoed her husband's. But Martin heard in her voice a bitter resignation that was all her own. It was the voice of a woman who had lost a member of her family. The voice, Martin realized with a jolt, of a mother of three small children who might someday be taunted and despised just for "who they were."

He fumbled with his pockets, putting back the pen and notebook. The wood in the fireplace crackled and sputtered, punctuating the awkward silence that filled the space between them. How could he possibly tell her how widely he would have to cast his net if he were to entangle and interrogate all of "the haters"?

Fortunately, he did not have to, for Noémie Singer was not a woman accustomed to expressing her anger so openly, particularly to a man she hardly knew.

"I'm sorry," Noémie Singer whispered as she examined her hands in her lap. "It's just that I loved my uncle. He was so good to me."

"I didn't mean to imply—"

"I know. Sometimes David tells me about his work. What he has to do." She forced a smile as she looked up at Martin. "It's what men do, I suppose."

If not all men, Martin thought as he bowed his head, certainly judges like himself who consider it their right to manipulate, bully, and lie for the sake of justice.

Suddenly Mme Singer got up and started for the door. "I should call Béatrice. I didn't even ask if you wanted tea or coffee."

"Please, Madame Singer," Martin was also on his feet. "Don't bother. I won't stay long." He had not expected such fervent resistance from this coddled and protected woman. He could not imagine how he was going to get her to talk about the tinker. When she turned back to him, he stammered, "I'm sorry, I really am."

That's when a rosy blush of recognition and compassion flooded her face. "Yes, and I am sorry too," she said in a hush. "Do forgive me.

How could I have forgotten? You have suffered a far greater loss than any of us."

The blow was unexpected. Martin sank back into the sofa. Tiny, dead Henri-Joseph. Noémie Singer had known what was going to happen before he did. Soon she was on the sofa, beside him, so close that he could feel the heat emanating from her small, compact body. He dared not look at her as she tried to comfort him. Her beauty, her sympathy thrust him into a whirlwind of contradictory and violent emotions, sadness vying with the appalling apprehension that he could be attracted to another woman.

He watched with lowered eyes, as her fingers came within a few chaste centimeters of his flattened hand. He pulled it away as if saving it from a burning fire.

"How terrible it must be for you," she said, in a low and soothing voice. "I can't imagine. I love my children so much. And—" she paused as she withdrew and settled back into the other side of the sofa, "I know you are a good man. That's what David—my husband—has told me many times. You are not one of those who hates us just because of who we are. I know that, Monsieur Martin, I do."

With each of her words the dull ache in his chest spread and pressed upon him, as he understood not only how lonely he was, but perhaps also how angry. Shame reddened his face at the very thought that he could want the alluring Mme Singer to keep reassuring him. He *did* prefer Clarie above all others. Because Clarie was a rational woman. Because she believed in the same things he did . . . or used to. Without realizing it, he had pushed himself further into his side of the sofa. He had to banish any doubt that Clarie might not become again what she once had been. His true companion in life. The one he must cherish forever because they had conceived and lost a son together.

Martin clenched a hidden fist. The worst was yet to come. Noémie Singer had given him an opening. He was about to use the death of his own child to try to find out what he needed to know.

He forced himself to meet the gaze of Noémie Singer's large hazel eyes, which were glistening with tears of sympathy. "Madame Singer," he implored, "thank you for your kindness. I don't mean to impose, but I need your help."

"Of course." She drew a handkerchief from the pocket of her silk jacket and wiped away a tear.

"Not the usual help," he said in a humble voice, his determination shot through with pangs of guilt as he exploited her sympathy. His mind was racing, trying to calculate how best to get at any animosities that might exist in the Israelite "community," between rich and poor, between men and women. Acrimonies that might fester into murderous impulses. He began again, "I need help in understanding about your religion."

Her mouth fell open slightly, parting her full red lips. She seemed puzzled, and a little shocked. Undoubtedly she had expected him to speak about his loss, his own life.

"Please, let me explain." Martin leaned toward her, his tense, rigid fingers boring into his thighs. "I have found that women sometimes understand these things better than men. That they are more devoted, are closer to the traditions and the meanings of their faith."

She had begun to shake her head ever so slightly. "Not in our tradition," she said. "The men know the meaning. They study it."

"Then it is different," he agreed eagerly, sensing that if he could say something, anything about himself, he might still have her on his side. "In my tradition, many men, and I will admit I am one of them, reject the Church they were raised in, because they disagree with some of its doctrines and practices. We feel we must do this if we are devoted to the Republic. We baptize our children in church, marry, and get buried there, but we no longer call or think of ourselves as Catholics. We have given it up."

She kept staring at him, waiting. He could feel nervous sweat sprouting under his beard and mustache. He could not imagine, at this point in time, having a similar conversation with his Clarie, whose return to the Church seemed to be leading her away from him. He cringed at the thought that Noémie Singer would report his intrusion into their intimate life to her husband. Still he had to forge ahead.

"For David, for Monsieur Singer, it seems to be different. And for your uncle, too, who worked with the Consistory. I know David is as thoroughly devoted to the Republic as I am, yet his faith seems very important, being an Israelite seems—"

"You really do not understand."

"I know." It was his turn to wait. And hope.

Martin watched as she bowed her head and bit down on her lip. Finally she nodded to herself and began. "You don't have to go to your church every Sunday to exist as a French Christian. What you believe, what your history is, is everywhere. It is the sea that we all swim in, Catholic or not. You can reject it, because your rejection will not make you responsible for making those beliefs disappear. Your traditions will survive, with or without you. We don't have that luxury. We must struggle to keep ours alive. We are French, yes. All the men I know are devoted to the Republic. It emancipated us after all. Yet we are also Jews. Why can't some people accept the fact that we can be Jews and French at the same time?" Red patches of emotion spread on each cheek as she talked. When she was finished, she fell back into the corner of the sofa as if exhausted.

"I don't know," he mumbled, abashed at the reminder that even he had begun to question the first loyalties of Noémie Singer's husband. Yet when he glanced at her, it was she who seemed embarrassed. It took him a moment to remember where he had seen that look before—when Singer had chastised her for talking to the poor tinker. Perhaps she was a woman afraid that men like Martin would not take her beliefs or her ideas seriously. If so, she might be encouraged to say more, if Martin assured her that he did. This should not be hard, he thought ruefully; she had already proved herself to be an intelligent and articulate woman.

"Madame Singer, you are being very kind. And very helpful. May I ask more?" He was still leaning in her direction, wanting to show how interested he was in what she had to say.

She lowered her eyes and nodded. He sensed her reluctance and, despite the display of modesty, her pride.

"Are you saying that there are no non-believers among the Israelites, that they do not disagree about matters of religion?" *That your husband is not at odds with someone like the tinker.*

"We have our disbelievers, but they cannot stop being Israelites even if they wanted to. Who would allow them to forget? Especially now." She looked down and began to twist her handkerchief. She did not have to state what they both knew, *especially because of Dreyfus.*

"And the believers? Do they have disagreements?" Martin pressed.

"Of course. Just like you. Among the men. But it's not about killing each other," she hastened to add. "It's part of our tradition. There are books of debates that go back centuries." She shook her head, smiling at the foolishness of it all. "The men study these books and carry on the debates even today."

"And the women?" If Singer was right about the tinker's influence, how had he gotten to her?

"We go to Temple, of course, but mostly we take care of the traditions in the home: serving dinner, lighting candles on the sabbath, teaching our children. We carry our religion in our hearts."

"And this never causes conflicts between husbands and their wives?"

Noémie Singer stiffened. "There should be no reason for conflict; each has their role, their place."

"And yet—"

She sprang up and walked to the fireplace, her taffeta skirts crackling defiantly. She stood there for a moment with her back to him. Then she swirled around. "Is that why you came here, because you saw me and David argue?" She was very angry, as she had every right to be.

"In part," he admitted.

"It's important to your investigation?" Her chin was tilted upward, challenging him. Whatever glimmers of coquettishness and sympathy had shone through her eyes had dimmed into a dark storm of anger and hurt.

Martin stood up. "It may be. I know that men and women often disagree on religious matters; it's true in my experience," he said, once again bartering a piece of his own intimate troubles. "Please, believe me, I don't want to intrude on the kinds of things that should be kept within families. I just want to understand the ways in which the tinker is different from the men in the Temple." As soon as he said that, he felt foolish. Why had he beat around the bush? Why had he decided that he could not talk to this intelligent, astute woman as he would have to a man? He bowed his head, waiting for her judgment.

She began to pace, twisting her handkerchief between her two hands. "I don't understand what Jacob could possibly have to do with any of this."

"Jacob the Wanderer?"

She stopped and eyed Martin. "How did you know?"

"I have talked to some of his friends, immigrants like him. But that's all I know. This strange nickname."

"Not so strange, really." She began pacing again, considering what to do. Martin could imagine her turmoil, her shock at having been led into a place of conflict between her and her husband vying with her womanly impulse to be accommodating. He dare not move a muscle as he waited.

Finally she stepped in front of him, about a meter away. "He is a holy man. He has led a tragic life. He came here when he was a little boy, traveling with his father who was a trader and a teacher, a rabbi. When his father was thrown from a horse and died, a poor, childless young widow took Jacob in and raised him in a village not far from here. She took care of him until he was old enough to find his way home. That's when he began to wander, over borders and rivers, avoiding soldiers and anti-Semites, asking all the time in our villages, Jewish villages, where his home might be. Finally he found it, in Russia, in Podolia. Isn't that a beautiful name, Podolia?"

Martin nodded, not wanting to break the spell of her storytelling.

"Well, Monsieur Martin, it is not a beautiful place for our people. For one night, when he was away, trading, the others, the Christians, raided the town, setting fire to the houses. Jacob had married and had children. When he came back, all of them were dead. Everything he owned was a charred ruin."

Martin nodded again. He knew about the pogroms in the east, which may well have been the reason why old Abraham had fled his homeland. He watched as Mme Singer moved away from him. Surely she could not believe that Frenchmen were capable of such. "Why did he come back here?" he asked.

She shrugged and murmured into the fire. "To find his mother, the widow."

"And?"

Noémie Singer sighed and turned back to Martin. "She was destitute. The village was mostly deserted, after being partly destroyed during the war. People had come to the city to work. That's why . . ." She stopped herself.

"That's why?" Martin urged.

"Because of his foster mother, because of his dead wife and children. That's why he feels it is his duty to keep the old ways alive, as they are today in Russia, as they were here long ago."

"The old ways. How does he do that?" Martin whispered his questions through the thrumming of his mind that was as taut as a violin string repeating one refrain, *go on, go on, go on. Help me to understand.*

Her gaze seemed to fall everywhere but on his face, as if she were in another place, or wanted to be. "He survives by selling odds and ends, and fixing things. He comes every Thursday."

Martin caught his breath, remembering the rabbi's warning. "Thursday?"

"Yes, Thursday," she glanced at him. "Is that important?"

"No, I'm sorry," Martin lied. "You were about to tell me how—"

"He keeps the traditions alive, yes." She smiled to herself, as if remembering. "He comes to the kitchen and talks to me and Béatrice, tells us the stories of our people he has learned on his travels. What our true customs are. What men should do and women should do. He uses his wheel to sharpen the knives he says we must use on our special days. He remembers for us how there used to be joy and dancing when our people worshiped. And sorrow, too, of course."

"Is that different than—"

She faced Martin with a look of defiance on her face, the same look that he had seen on Clarie's when she told him that she must make penance. "He was too humble to enter the parlor during the shiva," Noémie Singer said. "But when Béatrice told him that my uncle had been killed, he stood in the kitchen and showed his grief by keening and crying out loud, and by ripping apart his poor white shirt, just as they did in the old days." She turned away to hide the emotions that trembled in her voice. "That is, before we had become so 'civilized' that we could not show what we felt inside."

Martin did not know what to respond. He could not help but think of how he had hidden his tears from Clarie in order not to burden her. To do otherwise would have seemed undignified, unmanly. But Noémie Singer admired this Jacob because he did express his rawest emotions. What if Martin had torn his shirt and howled his grief and anger? Would that have made a difference? Is that what Clarie wanted?

The clock on the fireplace sounded three strokes. They both stared at the mantle, as if it had sent out a command.

"Monsieur, I think it is time for you to go," she said as she headed toward the door and called out for the maid.

She did not offer him her hand. She kept her head down as he went past her into the doorway. When he expressed his gratitude, he got only a nod in return. After the door shut behind him, Martin paused on the steps to think about their encounter. On that fatal Sunday, Martin had seen how supercilious Singer could be when he disagreed with his wife. And, in a sense, through his duplicity, Martin had proved no better. No wonder Noémie Singer had fallen under the spell of a holy man unencumbered by the pretensions of status, the demands of position, or the veneer of modern "civilization." A man true to the traditions that she held most dear, and to his own deepest emotions.

Martin strode away from the Singer apartment resolved to bury his remorse about the interview. People got hurt in murder investigations, even kind and innocent people like Noémie Singer. There was only one way to make amends: find the killer. By now, it should all be clear, the pieces in place. Yet this entire case was filled with dangerous, jagged edges, like a mirror under too much pressure, cracked and jutting at him from a hundred places, distorting his vision. Politics, religion, race hatred, his growing alienation from David Singer. He needed to pick his way past the demands, past the emotions, to the fragments that offered real clues. Certainly opportunity and knowledge of the victims' movements had to be first among them. But Martin was still not sure whether the motive for the murders was hatred of the Israelites in general or some more personal animus toward Ullmann and Erlanger. He had found no reason why Hémonet would seek out these two *particular* men. Nor did it seem likely that a non-Israelite soldier, born elsewhere, had learned enough about the local Jewish community to stalk and kill two of its most prominent members. Thank God the army had no idea it was under surveillance, Martin thought, as he slumped his shoulders and pulled in his head against the stinging cold. As for the bishop, having thoroughly washed his hands of the priest and his anti-Semitic propaganda, the Monsignor was raising no objections to Hémonet's continued imprisonment. At least Martin felt no pressure from these important quarters *yet*.

Soon he would get reports from Barzun on the soldiers and Bernheim on the defrocked priest. Either they would help to indict a suspect or eliminate one. That's what Martin had to do too: indict or eliminate. The rabbi's warning about Thursdays lodged in the back of Martin's mind like an untended itch; so did Bernheim's admonition about loss and madness. But these did not constitute a theory of the case. Martin stopped and, for an instant, thought about going to the Temple to ask Isaac Bloch about the divisions among the Jews of Nancy. Instead, he continued on toward the Palais with even more determination. There was someone to whom he could address his questions with no need for apology or explanation: the clever and very talkative Shlomo the Red Dwarf.

33
Wednesday, December 12

SHLOMO DID TALK, ADDING FUEL to one of Martin's theories, while other aspects of the investigation remained in frustrating, low-burning latency. The Jewish lieutenant Bernheim had spoken of had left the regiment, eliminating one possible source of information on the army; and Barzun had just begun his surveillance of off-duty officers. Liébeault could not come until that afternoon to examine Hémonet, who had gone into a state of semi-delirium. And so, on Wednesday morning, there was Shlomo.

Arriving with Jacquette, who had found him begging on a busy street corner, the dwarf entered Martin's chambers with the air of a performer invited for an encore. He once again declined to climb up on a chair, choosing instead to rove "the stage" in front of Martin's desk as he answered the judge's and inspector's questions. It did not escape Martin's notice that the dwarf took ample opportunity to sidle over to the potbelly stove where he warmed his hands, and his back, and even, once or twice, lifted a thinly shod foot up toward the fire. The man was cold, hungry and poor.

That is why Martin held his impatience in check as he listened to labyrinthine commentaries on every subject from the orthodoxy (or lack thereof) of the Grand Rabbi's sermons to the role of the Tsar (possibly or not) in the suppression of the Jewish people.

Unfortunately, there was much about Jacob the Wanderer which did not fall under the aegis of Shlomo's vast and eclectic knowledge. He knew the tinker as an eccentric, an outsider who, because of his youth in France and manhood in Russia, did not really seem to fit in anywhere. Yet this Jacob had an overweening desire to preach his ideas on tradition and religion, thus irritating many of his fellows.

"And you didn't agree with these ideas?" Martin asked.

"Agree, disagree. Who likes to be told what to do, over and over again by the same mouth? How could he expect to make us what we can no longer be?" Shlomo pleaded, opening his arms as wide as they could go.

Whether Jacob said the same things to the rich as he did to the poor, Shlomo could not know. He had seen less and less of the tinker in the last few months, but he did think that Jacob usually came to town on Thursdays.

"Does he stay in town to worship at the Temple on Fridays?" Martin asked.

Shlomo shook his head. He didn't think so.

"What about your shul?" This was Jacquette.

Shlomo shrugged. "Only once or twice. Long ago."

"Why?" Martin interjected. "Didn't you ask why he didn't join you? Where does he worship?"

"Ahh." Shlomo raised both of his gigantic hands to heaven. "I forgot. This is why. He said he had to go home to worship with his mother, the widow who took him in when he was a child. She is alone and sick. That is what he said. A devoted son he is."

If that is the case, Martin thought, why did the tinker choose to stay in or come back to Nancy the very weekend that Ullmann's body lay in a field? "And you don't know where this mother lives?" Martin pressed his fingers against his tired eyes, praying that the dwarf would come out with something useful.

"Lives. Barely." An ironic opinion, not a fact, delivered by the dwarf who would not dream of keeping his opinions, or his wit, to himself.

Still, Martin calculated with a sigh, if she had been a widow long before the war, which took place twenty-four years ago, she *must* be very old indeed.

"Her name?" Even as the words came out of his mouth, Martin knew he was going around in empty circles. It was becoming apparent that neither Shlomo nor his friends knew much about the Wanderer except that he was holy—or crazy.

"All right," Martin leaned back in his chair and crossed his arms. "I think that is enough for now." He reached in his pocket and drew out a five-franc note, which he nudged over to his inspector. Out of the corner of his eyes, Martin saw how hungrily the dwarf watched the transaction.

That's when Martin got the inspiration to ask his last question. "When did this Jacob tell you about his sick and lonely stepmother? How long ago?"

"Months ago. In the summer. The last time I saw him. He was worried. She must be very cold now."

Or dead. Martin made sure not to move a muscle on his face. He did not want this thought to register in front of his witness. If it were true, he had to think through all the implications. "Thank you, Monsieur Shlomo. You must understand that your value to us depends on your discretion," Martin said, with little real hope that the dwarf could keep his mouth shut. "And now you can wait in the hall."

Shlomo bobbed and bowed his way out of the room, never turning his back on his benefactors, fawning and thanking them for their kindnesses, Their Eminences. All the while, Martin wondered, *Where does a man like Shlomo the Red Dwarf end up? Or old Abraham? Or Jacob the Wanderer, for that matter?* It was a relief to see the door finally close, to get down to business.

"Well, what do you think?" Martin asked Jacquette.

"Your idea that the tinker might be a suspect is plausible," Jacquette remarked as he settled into the chair in front of Martin's desk and lovingly licked the tip of a Blue Jockey before lighting up.

Martin leaned forward. "Certainly he's as good a suspect as the priest or the tanner or some unknown soldier."

"Yes, but the motives: 'they are playing an organ in the Temple, *which is against the old ways*; the rabbi gives sermons in French, *which is against the old ways*; they don't allow us to sing and shout when we are filled with love for the Almighty, *which is against the old ways*.' The dwarf is probably right that some of the immigrants resent the tophats who go to the Temple for looking down on them. Still," Jacquette shook his head. He took a long drag from his cigarette and blew a cloud of smoke, as if to indicate how vaporous these motives seemed to him. "I'd like something closer to home, some slight, some passion, something more personal. Or an anarchist." He ended with a chastened smile. He had already reported to Martin that Ehud the Anarchist had turned out to be a toothless wonder with one feeble-minded disciple.

"But the only connection we've found between the two victims *is* the Temple, the Consistory."

Jacquette puffed out his cheeks and nodded a reluctant concession.

Martin sat back and rubbed his aching neck. "I think we are looking for someone who is fanatical or mad or both. This Jacob could fill the bill."

"So might our little Shlomo out there."

"Mad, perhaps, but not fanatical," Martin retorted, and sighed. If he could not convince his inspector, how was he going to convince anyone else? He boosted his weary body out of the chair and began to pace. Jacquette had not been witness to Singer's contemptuous scorn for the old peddler. He had not seen the light in Noémie Singer's eyes when she talked about him, nor heard the trembling in her voice as she described the way the "holy man" rent his garments in grief when told her uncle had been killed. Martin had reported these incidents to his inspector, of course, but he had not described how deeply they had affected him. To express those feelings, revealing what should best be left between a man and his wife, seemed too intimate, almost like a betrayal of Singer. Or himself.

Martin could only imagine how devastated Noémie Singer would be if it turned out that Jacob's emotional outburst had not been an authentic expression of sympathy and grief, but a measure of his guilt. Another jagged edge in the distorted mirror of the case.

Martin gave his inspector, who was thoroughly enjoying his Blue Jockey, a light pat on the shoulder as he passed by and began to think out loud.

"He might be trying to get to the women of the men he hates and to influence their children through them. And not succeeding, or succeeding with only a few of the wives, he becomes frustrated or even desperate." Martin took in a breath before adding, "Perhaps the 'old ways' are all he has left. This Jacob feels that the only thing which sustained him through all his tragedies, all that he had lost, is his faith, and that the rich Israelites of Nancy are destroying it."

There, he had said it. Faith sustains. But what happens when faith becomes distorted, unyielding, intolerant? Martin winced as he tried to banish an image of Clarie with Madeleine from his mind's eye. "After all," he continued, if only to hear the sound of his voice making his case, "men have killed and wars have been fought over such matters." Martin paused. Or was it only Christians who killed over such things?

The Crusades, the heretics, the witch-burnings. Maybe he was barking up the wrong tree, again. He shook his head. He was not about to express his doubts to Jacquette. Not yet.

"Well, if we're talking about fanatics, what about our defrocked priest?" Jacquette said, then stretched out his legs and yawned. "We haven't found any evidence that he ever left Laneuveville, but. . . ."

"We should have a report on Hémonet tomorrow," Martin said. Things were moving too slowly. "In the meantime, we've got to make sure that people are protected." He stepped back to his desk, invigorated by being able to pursue at least one effort about which he had no doubts. "I know your men have been stretched thin, but we must make sure that they are watching the homes of the other Consistory members, the rabbi and Singer. And I want the tinker followed as soon as he is spotted. So have them out in full force tomorrow, Thursday."

"Yes, sir!"

Martin searched Jacquette's face to see if he was being mocked. His inspector was smiling impishly, holding his cigarette between his front teeth. This is what Jacquette liked, Martin knew, action, progress, anything that moved forward.

"And I'll have to talk to Singer," Martin said as he slumped down into his chair.

Jacquette's smile evaporated and his lower lip drooped so precipitously that Martin feared he was about to lose his cigarette. The inspector masterfully rescued it before asking why.

"He's asked to be kept informed, and he's offered to help." What Martin did not say was, *because he is my friend.*

"Are you going to talk to Didier too?"

Martin shook his head. Definitely not. He'd inform the supercilious prosecutor only when he was absolutely sure.

"Then why Singer?" Jacquette asked. "You yourself said that he wants the case to go a certain way. Won't he just argue and try to convince you that you're wrong? I'd wait until we had a chance to grill the tinker."

Martin surveyed the piles on his desk. He had plenty to do. The dossier for the case would include all the interviews with the anti-Israelites of Nancy as well as reports on the immigrant community. "All right, let's keep our heads down until we have a chance to talk to this Jacob," he said quietly. "I'll bury myself in these papers and send Charpentier to the Prefecture to see if he can find a surveyor who knows something about abandoned or near-abandoned villages. Hopefully someone can come up with a map, in case we have to chase the tinker down."

Jacquette stood up to leave. "And should I give our friend out there a nice warm cell and good meal? I hear it might snow again tonight."

Martin smiled as they shook hands. They both knew how much the dwarf liked to talk. "Good idea. Let's keep him under lock and key until Friday," Martin agreed.

Until Friday. Only forty-eight hours. If only it would be over by then.

34
Thursday, December 13

THE DARK-BLUE-AND-GREEN tartan. That would do, Clarie thought, as she pulled the dress out of her armoire. She hurried to the mirror and held the thin wool dress against her at the waist and by its stiff white collar. She hadn't worn it for months. It used to be her favorite for teaching. But that was before—

Rose's timid tapping on the door did not save Clarie from thinking *Henri-Joseph.* She froze, afraid again that her heart and chest would turn to stone, and that she'd be dragged down into a place so dark and deep she'd never return. Clarie took a few breaths, filling her lungs, assuring herself that she could go on. She had to. For her husband. For her father. For everyone. That's why she had to visit the church today, the one that Madeleine had told her about. She needed some reason to hope. For her son, and for herself. "Just a minute." She sat down on the bed and pulled the dress up over her flannel petticoat and bodice. She wanted to show her maid that she was perfectly capable of doing things by herself. "Come in," Clarie called as she began to fasten the tiny cloth buttons that ran down the front.

Rose stepped into the bedroom. "I heard you moving about. I wondered if you needed help."

"Oh, that," Clarie said dismissively, trying to smile away the worry on Rose's face. "I was just searching for my gloves. I had trouble finding them." She knew this did not explain why she had been slamming the drawers, or why she could not overcome the feeling that everything was somehow out of place.

"Are you going out, Madame Clarie? Alone?" Clasping her hands together, Rose ventured closer.

"Yes." Clarie got up and went back to the dresser. She picked up her brush and attacked her dark tangled hair with brisk, long strokes.

"Does Monsieur Martin know?" Rose asked meekly.

Clarie put down the hair brush and stared in the glass. Should she feel guilty about not telling Bernard, or angry that Rose was interfering, watching over her as if she were an invalid?

"I'm sorry, it's not my place to ask about Monsieur." Rose lowered her head as she backed away from Clarie's still reflection. "It's just that you haven't eaten any lunch, and with the snow coming down so hard, you could catch the grippe or—"

Assaulted by the same inexplicable impatience she had felt while searching for her things, Clarie swirled around ready to object. But when she saw the motherly concern furrowed across her maid's careworn face, her irritation evaporated.

"You walked here, didn't you?" she said gently. "You came through the snow just to dust our rooms, and light our fires, and make our meals. And I'm certainly stronger than you, younger too. Oh, you are such a dear." Clarie reached out and drew Rose to her. She rested her cheek on the shorter woman's head and pressed the maid's soft body close to hers. When she pulled back, she noted how thin the gray hairs were that Rose always pinned back into a tight bun. And that she was still troubled. "Don't worry about me, Rose, really. I'm just going for a walk," she explained, although this was not quite true, "and then I'm going to meet Mme Froment for tea in the square. School is out for the season, and she wants to celebrate."

Rose glanced at the window. "But it's still coming down. Monsieur le juge was so discouraged this morning, he almost didn't go to work."

"Discouraged. That's funny. It's going to be so beautiful," Clarie said, trying to sound cheerful. "Let's open the curtains even more and let the light in." *Let the light in.* That's what all of them kept telling her. They hadn't dared to add "Bring some life into this room," for that's what the room would lack forever after Henri-Joseph's death. For a moment Clarie feared that the paralyzing weight would descend upon her again. She lurched toward the dresser, hoping that Rose had not noticed her panic. She started again to brush her hair, harder and harder, until the air began to flow back into her throat and lungs.

Now it was Rose who stood paralyzed by the windows, gazing at Clarie. It was stupid, of course, but Clarie felt that if she did not play the part of a healthy strong woman, Rose would try to stop her from leaving the apartment. Even though Rose had no power over her. No right. Rose was like everyone else, "trying to help," hovering. Clarie had to keep on acting.

"Can you help me with my hair? I think I'll wear it up today," Clarie said as she lowered herself onto the wooden stool in front of the mirror.

Out of the corner of her eyes, Clarie saw Rose raise her hands to her mouth as if a prayer had been answered. The maid hurried to her side. "Let me help you find your pins," she said eagerly.

It was working. If she gave up the braids they might begin to leave her alone. Braids were for the sick, for women who stayed in bed all day. A fashionable hairstyle, piled on top, with little curls coming down over the ears. Well, that was a sign of health, recovery. What they all wanted. "Rose, do it so it's pretty. Monsieur Martin would like that," Clarie said, although she couldn't care less about being "pretty." As Rose lovingly began to wind her hair, Clarie stared ahead, hardly recognizing herself. Would she ever be the same woman that Bernard had fallen in love with? Should she even try?

"It doesn't have to be perfect." The impatience again, the fear. "I'm going to wear the hat over it anyway."

"The one with the little red feathers?" Clarie heard the lilt in Rose's voice, anticipating that her mistress was finally consenting to wear something with a bit of color.

"Yes, of course, it's warmer." Clarie hoped Rose did not notice that her chest was beginning to heave. She swallowed hard. It took every bit of control to remain gentle and patient as Rose put in the pins, carefully and slowly, making sure not to poke her.

When Rose finally stepped back to admire her work, Clarie wanted to leap up and throw on her coat. Instead she gripped the sides of the stool while she waited for Rose to retrieve the hat and attach it to her hair. The black Persian lamb's-wool hat, with the dead bird's wings, in obscenely festive red. Bought to match the ruffled black woolen cuffs and collar of her gray coat, which at least was sober enough and normal enough to wear out walking with no one taking notice. Clarie closed her eyes and sighed when Rose stood back again. Finally. She went to the bed and pulled on her boots while Rose left to fetch her coat. When Rose returned, Clarie shoved her arms into the sleeves, pushed on her gloves and, with a parting smile, headed for the front door. Just as she reached for the doorknob, Rose came running with her lamb's-wool muff.

"No, the gloves will do." Clarie did not plan to mince about like a lady. She was on a mission. Seeing the disappointment on Rose's face, Clarie leaned over and kissed her on the forehead. "I'll be fine. If Monsieur Martin returns before me, tell him I'm at tea." Then she gave

Rose one last smile, lifted her skirts, and scrambled down the three flights of stairs, the black velvet pouch hanging from her left wrist bouncing up and down with each step. At the bottom, she yanked the outer door open and stepped into freedom.

A strange kind of freedom it was! She gulped the fresh clean air as she peered up and down the rue des Dom. Only a few brave souls were out, holding the ends of their scarves over their mouths as they trudged through the heavy snow. The shops that remained open glowed with the flickering light of gas lamps and candles. This was not the busy, chattering Nancy that Clarie loved. Yet somehow a muffled, solitary city suited her purpose. Fighting the wind and snow would make her feel more like a pilgrim setting out on a sacrificial journey for her son.

By the time she reached the market place she was breathing hard. The damp was seeping into her boots, and her nose and cheeks stung with the cold. For a moment she thought of turning back. Or waiting for a tram. She heard one coming up from behind, the bells around the horse's thick neck jingling a warning. She stood aside and watched. The hooves of the great gray horse made only muted sounds in the thick snow and it was panting hard, snorting out bursts of warm air like vaporous apparitions. Poor beast. Her gaze moved to two shoppers leaving the market. Poor women. Heads bowed, they hugged their filled string bags against their chest as shields. Maids who had to work, Clarie thought, otherwise why would anyone be out here—anyone without a reason.

I have a reason. Clarie clenched her jaw. *I must pray for my son.* She plunged forward, becoming as oblivious as the others to anyone in her path, looking up only to measure her progress. At last, the Saint Nicolas Gate. Then, the graceful steeple of the Saint Pierre Church, unfettered by snow, rose to touch the sky, giving her hope. She was halfway there. She had only to march on, straight ahead even though the Avenue de Strasbourg widened before her into an eerie emptiness.

Her skirts were beginning to weigh her down, in spite of her efforts to hold them above the layers of white flakes. To keep up her spirits against a wind that had begun to blow against her, she recited what Madeleine had told her. *This is the miraculous Virgin who saved Nancy from wars and plagues; the Virgin worshiped by royalty; the Virgin to whom the faithful run and pray in times of trouble.*

Then Clarie saw it. Unlike other churches, Notre-Dame-de-Bon-Secours did not face the street. The broad avenue ran along the east side of the church, leaving the entrance right in front of Clarie as she walked along the sidewalk. She blinked away the snow and slowed her pace.

Notre-Dame was a bit forbidding. It did not soar. It was heavy and narrow, as if built to fit between the road and the priestly residences attached to its west side. She knew, because Madeleine had told her, that they built the church on this very spot in order to house the miraculous statue of the Virgin where it had always stood. Even the great Duke Stanislas insisted on being buried there under this Mary's protection. Yet, Clarie was suddenly assaulted by doubt. She almost heard Bernard's voice in her head. There are no miracles. And, if there were, as her dead mother and Madeleine believed, what miracle could the Virgin grant her? She would never get Henri-Joseph back. She let go of her skirt and covered her mouth to smother a cry. She would never see him again. Why had she come? What would the prayers of a sinner mean?

Was she a sinner? Was that why Henri-Joseph had been taken away from her? Then she remembered. Hadn't the nuns always said that to the Blessed Virgin the prayers of a sinner were the sweetest of all? Couldn't she make sure that her little baby was not suffering somewhere, in limbo, alone? She gathered her skirts and struggled through the snow, almost tripping as her feet tried to find the steps leading up to the door. Desperately she grabbed one of the door handles. She had to get in. Frantically pushing the snow away with her foot, she grasped the handle and pulled and pulled until it opened wide enough to let her squeeze into the pitch-black vestibule. Clarie stamped the snow off her boots and swiped it away from the sleeves of her coat. She took a breath, straightened up, and pushed through another door to the inside.

She saw the Virgin at once because a light from above burst upon Her through the center of a marble cloud over the main altar. It took Clarie a moment to realize that the sun had come out, and that its rays shone through a window purposely cut into the dome above the Holy Mother. This was God's light. The rest of the church was empty and dim, hardly illuminated by the rows of stained-glass windows and votive candles, which lent a comforting, familiar waxy odor to the chill air. Shivering from the cold, Clarie tiptoed toward the communion rail. The closer she got, the more her heart pounded with fear and hope. She didn't like the elaborate carved statues and gold-leaf curlicues and luxurious marble that surrounded the Virgin. This was not her kind of faith, if, indeed, she had any real faith.

Before the main altar, she took hold of the icy cold brass rail with her gloved hands as she bent to her knees, never taking her eyes off the Virgin. Clarie saw then how old and humble She was. Like a mother. Like Clarie's mother. The Virgin held out her arms to spread her great mantle over the supplicants that knelt before her, embracing them with her compassion. She was not fancy or majestic. She was plain, simple, an alabaster white statue, yellowed ever so slightly by the countless candles that other desperate souls had burnt before Her. "Blessed Mother," Clarie whispered, "take me back. I will be humble. I will obey. I will be worthy." Clarie bowed her head. To be truly worthy, what would she have to give up? Not Bernard, surely. Some of his ideas, yes. And teaching? Had she sinned in leading her students to believe that they could make the world a better place? Now she knew that the world was filled with tragedy. That Madeleine was right, there was pain and sin everywhere. "I know that now, Mother, I do." She bit her lip and squeezed her eyes closed. She did not want to cry again. She was tired of crying.

Then something, the sound of a voice like that of her own dear dead mother, made her lift up her eyes, toward the light, toward the cloud above the Virgin's head. She gasped. She saw that the marble cloud was carved with cherubim and Henri-Joseph was among them. Steadying herself on the altar rail, she rose up and peered hard above her. It was him. She could tell because unlike the carved statues, her baby had a fringe of black hair, just like he had when he came out of her womb. But he was older now, healthier, with fat cheeks like the other smiling marble angels. Her son, in heaven, smiling down at her. She clutched her hands together and raised them up in gratitude. The miraculous Virgin had given her a sign, Clarie was sure of it. Her baby was in heaven, her mother was taking care of him, and both of them would be waiting for her there forever.

If the Virgin had given her a sign, had she been forgiven for the sin that took Henri-Joseph from her? If only she knew what she had done, she'd never do it again. She knew then that she needed to confess. She stumbled down away from the altar to the side of the church, searching through the dark for a confessional. She found it, but of course no one was there. She was alone. Weeping in frustration, she knelt down and laid her head against the polished wooden confessional. She began to pray, for her son, for her mother, and for herself. When she had exhausted her prayers, she put her hands against the confessional to steady herself as she rose to her feet. She dried her cheeks and nose with a handkerchief and squinted at the cloud of cherubim above the Virgin. She let out another sob. Henri-Joseph was no longer there. He had gone back.

Although she was still trembling, she managed, by holding on to the chairs along the aisle, to begin her journey back. The shadows cast by the stained glass windows swirled before her on the floor in dizzying patterns. She steadied herself at the door leading into the vestibule before pulling it open. The entryway no longer seemed so dark, and the more she pushed at the outside door against the resisting snow, the stronger she became.

Panting, her breath preceding her in wispy little clouds, she began the walk back to the center of the city. A light hopeful blue had pushed away the gray in the sky. The snow had stopped. Instinctively she knew that she must keep her vision a secret. She did not want Bernard to think that she had gone mad.

35

MADELEINE DRIBBLED THE LAST TEPID drops from the pewter teapot. She hoped the waiter would not notice and ask if she wanted more. Reaching her hand under the table, she pressed and pinched the brown satin sack on her lap, feeling for coins. She had barely enough to pay for the tea and the biscuits that lay in waiting upon a little silver platter in the middle of the table. She was saving them for Clarie. Where was she?

Madeleine frowned as she opened the watch that hung on a gold chain around her neck. Three-thirty. It was unlike Clarie to be late. Or to forget. Unless? Madeleine shook her head slowly as she remembered their last conversation. Clarie couldn't have gone to Notre-Dame. Not today. The poor girl wasn't well enough to trudge through a storm.

Well, Madeleine thought, as she pretended to sip from her cup, if Clarie had gone all the way out there, she should be happy that they were meeting in the Café Stanislas. It was warmer than either of their apartments. And more festive. Madeleine replaced her cup in the saucer with a sigh. Except for today. The tables were almost all empty. In the late afternoon they were usually filled with fashionable women in threes and fours, chattering away, their feathery hats bobbing with each bon mot. Madeleine missed the hubbub and the fun of grading them on their taste and imagining what they were saying to each other. Even the great steel coffee machine behind the bar was mute, for there was no need for anyone to pull down its levers and hiss its delicious, exotic vapors into the air. All because of the snow.

Madeleine shrank back into the warm corner she had chosen for her observations and glanced to her side. Three tables away a man in a drab suit sat, like her, with his back to the mirrored wall, nursing his lonely glass of beer with the same care she was taking with her tea. She clucked disapprovingly. He hadn't even bothered to take off his bowler. He seemed to be staring at the soldiers who stood at the bar, talking and laughing. Undoubtedly the poor little man was envying their easy camaraderie and obvious gallantry. He was not worthy of her attention, but the officers, downing their little glasses of whiskey and cognac with manly briskness, certainly were. They did make a handsome trio in their blue jackets, aglitter with gold buttons and braiding and epaulettes. *Our protectors*. Her chest swelled with pride. They'd show the Huns one of these days. She was sure of it.

Without warning, an unbeckoned image sent a rush of blood throttling through her veins from head to toe. What if the tallest of them decided to take her in his arms and sweep her away? What would his pointed black goatee and hot breath feel like against her cheeks and neck? Her hand flew to her mouth as if it was about to blurt out these ridiculous, sinful thoughts. She slunk back again, deflated, and stared at the cuffs of the ready-made dark blue jacket that covered her prim shirtwaist. Anyone with eyes in his head would take her for a spinster schoolteacher or, worse, a worn-out shopgirl. Oh, how she wished Clarie would get here. Full or empty, cafés weren't festive when you were alone.

Suddenly Madeleine felt a burst of cold air and watched with relief as Clarie spread apart the heavy black velvet curtain that separated the interior from the outside door. Immediately a white-shirted waiter, carrying a tray of glasses, came to greet her. "Madame, you would like?" he asked. Before Clarie was able to answer, one of the officers had bounded toward them. "May I take your coat, Madame?"

Madeleine twisted herself around to get a better look. Was Clarie blushing? Or flirting? Even from across the room Madeleine detected the lowering of Clarie's almond-shaped brown eyes. Surely she must know these were her best feature. Madeleine heard her demur, "No, I'd like to keep it with me. Thank you. I'm looking for—"

"I believe she is there, Madame." The waiter gestured with his free hand toward Madeleine.

"Yes, yes. Thank you." Clarie gave the waiter and the soldier a wan smile as she moved between them toward Madeleine.

Two men at her feet. The handsome, mustachioed officer, whom Madeleine had picked out as the youngest of them all, followed Clarie with his gaze. Clarie had no idea how easy life had been for her. Until two weeks ago. Madeleine bowed her head remembering Clarie's tragedy. That's why she had to find ways to help Clarie, to get her to accept and understand what had happened to her. And, of course, to cheer her up.

"Madeleine, I am so sorry I'm late. I didn't know how long it would take to walk through the snow."

The troubled look on Clarie's face and the urgent sincerity in her voice forced a smile to Madeleine's lips. How could she be angry with the dear girl? They both fell silent as the waiter, who had come up from behind, helped Clarie into her seat.

"So, you went to Notre-Dame?" Madeleine raised her eyebrows. She didn't know whether to be disapproving of Clarie's foolishness at venturing out into the storm or happy that her friend had sought out the miraculous Virgin.

Clarie nodded as she took off her gloves and laid them on the table. Her face was red from the cold and she was panting a little. She rubbed her hands together.

"Some hot tea, Madame?" the waiter asked.

"Yes, please." Clarie began to unbutton her coat.

The waiter flipped open the top of Madeleine's teapot and saw that it was empty. He swept the pot away, leaving them alone.

"You went on a day like today?"

Clarie kept nodding as she pulled off her coat.

"And?"

Clarie bit her lip, as if thinking of what to say. "The church was lovely inside," she offered. "A little florid for my taste. Baroque, I guess, and the statue was very moving, just as you told me."

"And the tombs."

Clarie hesitated. "The tombs, yes, impressive."

Obviously she hadn't taken any time to study them, even though the tombs of Duke Stanislas and his consort were famous. But that was neither here nor there, Madeleine thought as she straightened up eager to hear all. The important things were spiritual.

She put her hand on top of Clarie's. "And you prayed."

"Yes," Clarie whispered, "I prayed." She withdrew her hand. Clarie took one of the tea biscuits from the plate and began to chew, avoiding Madeleine's eyes.

"Is there something wrong, my dear?"

"No." Clarie shook her head. "I'm really feeling better. Every day. Thank you for suggesting this. It's nice to be out."

"Even though the place is half-full."

She shrugged.

Madeleine sighed. Half the time she tried to talk to Clarie, she seemed to be in some other place.

"Your infusion, Madame." The waiter again. "Anything else?"

"Yes," Clarie sounded eager for the first time since she had entered the café. "Some more of those," she said, pointing to the silver plate in the center of their table. After the waiter left them, Clarie actually did brighten up. "I'm starving. Madeleine, I'm actually hungry!"

"Then the walk did you good." Madeleine hoped that Clarie would remember that it was she who had suggested this pilgrimage.

"Yes, I wanted to walk back too, but by the time I got to Saint Pierre, I realized how late I was, and I hopped on a tram. I was the only one." For just an instant Clarie seemed like her old self, but then the tumble of words slowed to a trickle. "What a strange day this is." She paused and reached for Madeleine's hand. "I really am sorry. Bernard gets so irritated with me when I'm late."

Him again. How was she going to save Clarie's soul if everything was about her husband the judge and his godless Republic? Still, Madeleine found it in herself to return Clarie's grasp. "It's all right, dear, I was only worried about you. But you're here all in one piece."

"Yes, I suppose." They let go of each other and Clarie flipped the lid on the pot to see if the tea was ready. "How was school?" she murmured.

"The same. Every day the same." Madeleine was searching for some amusing anecdote to relate about the students or the head-mistress when a flash of fear shot up her spine. "Are you thinking of coming back?" She had counted on staying the rest of the year.

"No, no." Clarie poured a little tea in each of their cups. "I don't know if I'll ever go back." She acted as if pouring the tea took all of her concentration.

Despite her relief, Madeleine was puzzled. Clarie loved teaching, and her students loved her. Surely Clarie did not think that is why Henri-Joseph had been taken from her, that her teaching was some kind of sin. Or, if it was, it didn't have to be. As long as she did not fill her students' minds with radical ideas, as long as she understood that it was her mission to raise the wives, mothers, and teachers of a God-fearing France. This is what Madeleine had always done, and would do until the end of her days.

Eyes downcast, Clarie sipped the hot tea.

"And Paris. You may never be asked to go there again. It's such an opportunity, especially at your age." *At any age.* Paris was the most coveted assignment, if only because it was the one place where a female teacher could make more than a pittance. The thought of it made Madeleine's pulse race.

Clarie had the nerve to shrug, and then mumble, "I don't know."

Madeleine slumped back in her chair. They were at an impasse. Another one of those lapses in conversations that used to be so lively. Clarie must be thinking about the baby again. It was so hard to get her to concentrate on anything. Madeleine's gaze wandered around the room hoping to find something to remark upon, when a chill wind blew into the café. Two portly men, dressed very smartly in coats with mink collars and beaver tophats came into the café and, each taking a side, held the velvet curtain wide open for their women. The first pranced in wearing a coat adorned with rings of expensive black sable, one around the collar, two around her cuffs, and three rows of the exquisite, expensive fur rimming the bottom of her outfit. The other wore a garish hat spiked with what looked like peacock feathers. Madeleine was about to comment on how inconsiderate it was of these couples to keep letting the cold air in, when she realized who they were: Jews, rich ones.

She bent toward Clarie and whispered, "Look who's coming. Don't turn around. Watch in the mirror." She tilted her head so that Clarie could observe the foursome.

Clarie peered into the mirror, but did not react.

"You can't tell?"

Clarie shook her head. The man in the bowler barely moved. He didn't seem to know either.

"They can." Madeleine caught a glimpse of the young officer with the curled mustache as he turned from the bar to face the two couples. He stood, legs apart, as if ready for a fight. "The soldiers," she whispered.

Clarie shifted her gaze in the mirror.

"Give them the best seats, why don't you," the officer growled as the waiter went up to greet the newcomers.

The two couples froze. The women looked to their men apprehensively.

"Messieurs, mesdames," the waiter, trying to ignore the soldier, started toward a table.

"Ask them about Dreyfus. Ask them if they speak German. Ask them if they just got here from across the border."

"I think he's drunk," Clarie said. Her mouth fell half open and her brow furrowed with worry or fear.

One of the other officers put a hand on the combatant's shoulder. "Come on, now. We need to finish our drinks and get back to the barracks."

This attempt to mollify him only made the young officer more aggressive, for he shoved his companion's arm away and took a step toward the four newcomers. Squinting hard, Madeleine saw that the women were tightening their grip on the men's arms. Afraid and, Madeleine hoped, ashamed. She straightened up to catch every word and every gesture. This could be a thrilling confrontation.

"It's enough you ruin all the little people with your banks and financial schemes, but now you think you can take over the army," the officer said as he took another step toward the two couples.

Suddenly Clarie, still staring into the mirror, rose out of her seat. "This isn't right."

Madeleine grabbed her arm. A young matron had no part to play in such a confrontation. Besides, how could Clarie dream of turning against a man who had been so chivalrous to her?

Fortunately, no one noticed Clarie's reaction, because at that very moment the two men, with their fur-collared coats and leather gloves and expensive hats, escorted their women back through the velvet curtain and out the door.

"Dreyfus!" the officer shouted, "Dreyfus!" and his two companions laughed. "All right. You told them. Let's drink to that," one of them said as he pounded on the bar and asked for one more round.

Clarie stopped peering into the mirror and slumped back in her seat. "That was terrible."

Terrible? "Terrible is when they ruin your life."

Clarie did not respond. Madeleine knew why. She didn't want to argue. She undoubtedly thought Madeleine was wrong to hate the Jews, to believe that they had no place in a truly Christian country. What with Clarie's immigrant father and her republican husband and the teachers at Sèvres—Protestant, most of them—she would never understand, never. Madeleine reached down into her sack and took out a lacy handkerchief to dab her eyes. Her best friend, and she had forgotten why Madeleine was a spinster, condemned to be forever alone and penniless.

Clarie stared as Madeleine dabbed her eyes. "Didn't you think it was terrible," Clarie said quietly, "making them leave like that?"

"They didn't have to leave, you know. The two of them could have stood up like . . . like men." Madeleine blew her nose defiantly. She didn't know whether to feel hurt or angry.

"Against three soldiers?"

Madeleine shrugged. "Please don't let it upset you; it's all over," she said, hoping it was all over and done with as she jammed her damp handkerchief back into her sack.

But Clarie persisted. "How did they even know?"

Sometimes Clarie was so naive. "The noses, I suppose, or the ostentatious clothing, or maybe they just knew who they were."

"And you, you knew."

"Yes. As I told you." Why did she even have to explain?

Clarie stared down at her lap and shook her head. "I never look at people that way."

"Hmmm," Madeleine sighed, "perhaps you have never had to. But when you grow up, as I did in Bordeaux, where some of them are as rich as the Rothschilds, you notice, believe me, you notice. And when your father dies because of them." How many times did she have to explain to Clarie about losing her dowry in the bank crash and then the way the Panama Canal scandal totally wiped out her family's fortunes?

"I've spoken to Bernard about what you've said about the Union Générale failure, and he said it was the Catholics who were incompetent, and the Israelites had nothing to do with the bank's failure." Clarie delivered the judge's verdict with gentleness, but this did not hide the fact that she was taking his side.

Madeleine clenched her jaw. "I believe differently. After all, it was my dowry that was lost. Which is why I was forced to go to Sèvres, hoping that somehow I would earn a living that would give me a position in life and some dignity. But," Madeleine said with clipped words, "as you see, my dear, it has not happened." She stopped. Clarie looked distraught and pale, despite the rosy chafed marks on her cheeks. Even though worried about Clarie's pallor, Madeleine could not resist a final plea. "How could you take their side?"

"I'm not taking anyone's side." Clarie was so subdued that Madeleine hardly heard her.

"Then you should." Madeleine made an effort to keep her voice low, so that no one else would overhear them. "You know that they brought down the Union Générale because it was a Catholic bank, and they just couldn't stand that. They are against the Church. Our Church."

Clarie frowned. Her eyes were blinking. As if, for once, she was trying to understand. "I just don't know," she murmured. "The soldier. . . . It didn't seem right."

"Our Blessed Mother. You know they will attack Her when they get more power."

Clarie began rubbing her forehead. "My mind feels so fuzzy. There's so much I don't understand." She put her hands on the table and pushed herself up. "I'm getting cold, my feet."

Madeleine got up and looked down at the dark wet stain circling the bottom of Clarie's wool dress. She had been dragging her skirts through the snow, unmindful of her fragile condition. Her boots must be soaking wet. "Of course you're cold," said Madeleine, alert to the fact that she needed to care for her friend's body as well as her soul. "Come here, my dear, let's button up your coat and get you home. We'll put your feet up right by the fire."

She placed Clarie's gray coat around her shoulders and waited patiently as her companion fastened it, one thoughtful button at a time. Madeleine noticed that the man in the bowler was writing in a notebook. Coward! He had done nothing to help Clarie or the soldiers. Madeleine sighed and put the last of her coins on the table. At least she knew what she had to do.

36

Friday, December 14

"TODAY IT'S SUNNY AND CLEAR," said Martin bitterly. He was bouncing on his toes with impatience as he began the morning's planning with Jacquette. What Martin managed not to say is that all the way to the Palais he had been cursing yesterday's storm for bringing down two plagues upon his house. He was sick with worry about Clarie, who had gotten the grippe because she had ventured out into the snow, while it was obvious that the murderer had not. Thus Martin had no way to prove or disprove his suspicions about the tinker. Nor could anything come of Barzun's observations of a certain Lieutenant Toussaint with Thursday leaves and an aggressive hatred of the Israelites. No trained officer would murder on an afternoon when he could so easily be tracked, and no judge in his right mind was going to haul in a soldier on the eve of the Dreyfus trial, unless he had concrete evidence. The snow had blocked the investigation as profoundly as it had clogged the roads.

"Sir," Jacquette tapped his knuckles on the desk to get Martin's attention. "No one got killed. That's good news."

"If you like waiting for the other shoe to drop," Martin grumbled. He knew, he could feel it in his bones, that if they did not catch the killer soon, someone else would be murdered. Worse, the next victim might be someone they knew, like Singer or the rabbi or, God forbid, even a woman or child. According to Hémonet, all Jews, of any age or sex, should be expunged from society. They still hadn't found any disciples of the ex-priest besides the bookseller Villiers, but who was to say there was not another madman, a third viable suspect, lurking in the streets?

"May I?" Jacquette pointed to the chair.

Martin nodded.

The inspector sat, crossed one leg over the other, and lit a cigarette. "What about our mind doctors? Any report on Hémonet?"

Martin tapped on three folded sheets of paper lying in the middle of his desk. "From Bernheim," he said. "Apparently he enjoyed yesterday's weather as much as you did. It trapped Liébeault in town and allowed them to spend the night reminiscing about old cases in front of a roaring fire." Casting his sarcasm aside, Martin added, "I haven't had time to go over his report. I'll send you a copy as soon as Charpentier transcribes it."

Jacquette screwed up his mouth so acutely that his tawny mustache ended up, for one instant, entirely on the left side of his face. "I didn't say I *liked* the weather. In fact, it has made my problems worse. The men. If we don't get them off this watch duty, we'll have a revolt on our hands. Standard-issue boots and coats aren't holding up in all this wet and cold, and neither is their patience."

Arms spread, palms down on his desk, Martin leaned toward Jacquette. "I thought that was their job," he said, emphasizing each word.

"Yes, but so is interviewing everyone in Ullmann's mill, his business associates, Erlanger's clients, keeping an eye on the workers' haunts *and* the entire regiment. To say nothing of the fact that there are other cases," Jacquette added as he pulled a drag on his cigarette. He did not meet Martin's heat with his own. Instead, he calmly laid out the reality of their limitations.

Martin crossed his arms and surveyed his desk. Piles of testimonies, slanders, and dead-ends. He opened the latest edition of *La Croix de Lorraine* and held it up for Jacquette to see. "Have we identified this Titus?" he asked, as he pointed to an article in the newspaper.

"Near Epinay, about forty kilometers away, some priest in a rural parish. I could get him for you if you really—"

"No." Martin shook his head. "He's far enough away, and you have plenty to do." He sighed and slumped into his chair. "Let's put a different man on a rotation every day," he suggested. "Make his presence in front of the Temple and certain homes visible, as a preventive measure. Then next Thursday—"

"Again?" Jacquette asked skeptically.

"Again," Martin confirmed, "unless we come up with a better idea. Or, if you like, someone is murdered on Monday or Tuesday or Wednesday." Martin should have bit his tongue. He needed to be alone. He was too frustrated to be fit for human company.

"We'll find the killer. Sometimes it just takes time."

"If we've got time," Martin retorted.

Jacquette arched his eyebrows and gave a half-mocking, fully friendly salute as he got up to leave.

Martin could not repress a smile as he held up his own hand in response. *Thank God for Jacquette*, he thought as he watched his inspector leave the room. Then, settling in, he unfolded the report that Liébeault had made to Dr. Bernheim.

My Dear Hippolyte,
The patient François Hémonet was brought to the clinic at 2 P.M.

on Wednesday 12 December in great distress. He showed all the signs of addictive inebriation: involuntary twitching, slurred words, raging temper, residues of vomit on his clothing. Since he kept saying that the only medicine he needed was a "good bottle," I was able to question him on what he meant. As I suspected, ever since leaving the priesthood, he has become a slave to the "green fairy" supplied to him by a "devoted" family. We can only hope for his sake that his absinthism *has not yet reached the point of causing permanent physical damage.*

There was no question of my putting him into a hypnotic sleep. As you know, it is useless to try to do so with an uncooperative patient, and I doubt if I could have effectively relieved his symptoms. God willing, time will do that if hereditary weakness does not lead him once again to try to ease the pain in his tortured soul with drink.

As to whether he is telling the "truth," I cannot say. Perhaps he is insofar as he can in his present despairing state. He told me, no, shouted at me, that he believed in Jesus Christ Incarnate, and all who did not belonged to the Devil. I kept trying to soothe him by telling him I have nothing against his religion, being a Christian myself, and suggested that he try to pray quietly to his God for comfort. I did not tell him what I truly believe, that he has distorted and twisted his faith into an instrument of hate, and there may not be a God that can help him. If he ever becomes willing to be put to sleep, perhaps we will find out the true source of his hatreds and help to expel them from his spirit. For now, I conclude Hémonet is a man maddened by despair, an absintheur, *and an extreme anti-Israelite. (I am grateful, dear friend, that you did not have to suffer his venom against your race.)*

As to whether he is capable of murder, you may tell the judge what we have always said: anyone is capable of doing anything, despite the teachings of religion, morality, and family, if the suggestion of the crime is forceful enough. If he did commit the crimes, then we will have to ask, what was his state of mind? Could he help himself? Was he mad or fully culpable? We cannot answer these questions until the poison of absinthe has drained from his body.

Yours, Liébeault

Martin refolded the pages and rubbed his aching forehead. *Nothing*, this is what the report amounted to, *nothing new*. Martin's eyes fell on the latest column by the man who called himself Titus, the one he had waved before Jacquette. What would it be today, another report of a ritual murder committed by the Jews in some exotic corner of the world? Or a peasant being cheated, once again, by a "circumcised one"? And why Titus? Was the *nom de plume* an homage to the disciple of Saint Paul or to the Roman Emperor who had so triumphantly destroyed the great Temple in Jerusalem? If both, the two together—the apostle and the conqueror of the Jews—how clever of him, thought Martin, unable to shake off the cloud of apprehension and irritation that was enveloping him.

Little did Martin know that Madeleine Froment was having exactly the same thoughts as she glanced at Titus's latest column. However, what she was experiencing was a kind of elation. How clever! How learned! And, of course, confirmation that she, too, had enough of a *Christian* education to understand the dual meaning of the pseudonym. She intended to read Titus to Clarie when she woke up. Madeleine had also brought, deeply hidden in her school bag, Grignion de Montfort's *Traité de la vraie dévotion à la Sainte Vierge* on the True Devotion to Mary, the Mother of God, and Drumont's *La France Juive*. Sitting patiently by Clarie's bedside, Madeleine set aside the newspaper and took out her rosary to pray for her friend.

37

Monday, December 17

DURING THE LONG WEEKEND OF Clarie's illness, Martin tried desperately to get her to enjoy the things that used to give her so much pleasure. He read stories by de Maupassant to Clarie and brought her expensive greenhouse roses from the market. He even transported hot chicken broth to her bedside on a tray with the mock flourish of a snobbish Parisian waiter. She was polite, grateful, but remote. Through it all, she seemed to find more comfort in Madeleine's company. Sitting alone in the living room, listening to the murmurs coming through the bedroom wall, Martin imagined them talking about miracles and angels, sin and repentance. He wanted to shout, *Our son is dead! We did nothing wrong!* But he held back. At some point the pious Mme Froment was bound to leave to visit her relatives for the holidays. When that finally happened, Martin would win Clarie back and make her whole. They'd go to mass together, if that is what she needed. Nancy was a big city. They'd find a parish led by a priest who shared their republican ideals. They could even clasp their hands together and pray to the God in whom each of them believed.

"Twisted." "Distorted." Martin had dismissed Liébeault's report because it gave him no proof, because it had told him nothing he did not already know. Yet certain words kept coming back to him. Was the faith that Madeleine preached to Clarie "twisted and distorted"? Was his dear wife absorbing beliefs and ideas she never would have accepted if it were not for her "despair," for her terrible loss? Martin could not stop his mind from roving between his private sorrows and public duties. Somewhere, somehow they seemed connected. At what point did despair become madness, did distorted faith become murderous fanaticism? When did the *suggestion* that Bernheim so firmly believed in become the *irresistible impulse* to mad action? And why? Alone, by his own hearth, filled with uneasiness about his future, Martin also kept coming back to Jacquette's refrain, that murders are usually instigated "closer to home."

He had to fit the pieces of the puzzle together. And so on Monday, he did not head straight to the courthouse. Instead he took off in the opposite direction toward the hospital by the Faculté, speeding through dreary sidewalks lined with mounds of black-speckled, graying snow. By the time he got to Bernheim's famous clinic, about a dozen men and women were already in the waiting room. Some of them sat straight up, staring into space; others exhibited their anxieties by holding themselves in with crossed arms or shuddering with involuntary tics. Martin knew at once that this was not a place he wanted to be. Fortunately, he spotted the white-winged wimple of a hospital nun bobbing above one of the patients. She seemed to be offering comfort and counseling patience, both of which Martin had in very short supply. He strode over to her and told her who he was and who he wanted to see. With only a slight bow of her head, the gentle-faced, middle-aged sister said she would find the doctor. Standing against the wall by the entrance, Martin fixed his eyes on the floor, refusing to take in more misery.

He barely heard the nun's return before he caught sight of her long black skirts. "The doctor will see you now," the sister said, and she led him through a door to an office lined with books and file cabinets. As soon as Martin entered the room, Bernheim placed his pince-nez on a pile of papers and rose from his desk. "Monsieur Martin, so good to see you again!" he exclaimed as he held out his hand. He wore a white cotton coat and had a stethoscope hanging from his neck. The nun floated away as both men sat down, soundlessly shutting the door behind her.

"I don't mean to keep you from your patients."

"No worry, the good sisters will see that none of them becomes desperate."

Martin fingered the rim of his bowler. He hated laying out half-baked theories. "Something you said last week caught me," he began, "your statement that 'loss can drive one mad.' I've wondered since how it could fit into the case."

"Go on." The jovial doctor folded his hands over his slight paunch.

"If a man has suffered terrible tragedies throughout his life, why should he suddenly turn to violence?"

"You're thinking of someone specific, then?" Bernheim sat up straight, eager to hear more.

"I'm not sure."

"Tell me. Tell me what you are thinking."

Martin slumped back. "What if Ullmann and Erlanger were not killed by an anti-Semite? Even though we managed to keep the false accusation of ritual murder out of the press, we believed, at first, that the slander precipitated the murders. After all, people do talk no matter how you threaten them. It would take only one man with a special hatred for the Israelites to carry out the murders."

"And you don't believe this tanner, the father, did it?"

"No. And even if we suspected one of his friends or associates, or someone else, why Ullmann *and* Erlanger? Why choose them?" Martin paused, letting the question hang in the air before going on. "Usually we look for personal motives: passions, envy, thwarted ambitions. The only connection we have found between the two men was that they went to the Temple regularly, and they worked with the Consistory. Both seemed utterly devoted to their families and got most of their pleasures within their intimate circles, which, as far as we can see, did not overlap. As for their professional contacts, and any connection between them, it seems unlikely that someone who worked in Ullmann's mill or the tanneries would have sought out Erlanger's services." Martin swallowed hard. "One possibility is that we are dealing with a crime within the Jewish community." There, he used that word, in spite of his dim conception of what it meant to the people who lived in it.

"No." This was less an objection than an expression of astonishment. "How can that be?" Bernheim asked.

Martin got up and lay his bowler on the chair. He began to mark the small space left by the encroaching books and files with measured steps. "Suppose, just suppose, it's about fanaticism or irrational fanatical hatred of a group of people, just because of who they are."

"Now, Monsieur Martin, you are describing anti-Semitism. But Jewish fanaticism?" This time Bernheim could not hide his skepticism. Yet the scientist in him remained willing to consider any hypothesis.

Hands behind his back, Martin continued his slow, circular march. "My inspector and I have made some forays among the Hebrew immigrants. All of them seemed to have suffered terrible *losses*, like being rooted out of their homes. Wouldn't it be possible that one of them could become so unbalanced by his own tragedies that he would lash out at a man or men who threatened his deepest-held beliefs about Jewish traditions and faith?" Martin stopped and looked at Bernheim. "In a way, that is what the Consistory is doing, isn't it? Changing the way people worship, making things French."

By now, Bernheim was shaking his head. "I don't see this as a motive."

Martin picked up his hat and sat down again across from Bernheim. "But what if he felt insulted? What if he felt that the last connection to all he loved was being destroyed?"

Bernheim pressed his lips together. "From the way I understand it," he said quietly, "the immigrants have a community intact, right here, in Nancy. Their own shul. Their own schools, albeit supported by the Consistory. No one is forcing them to change. The Consistory is only trying to help them adjust to modern society."

Bernheim's assessment made sense. There was an immigrant community separate from the Temple community. Martin had seen how much they shared, in the present and from the past. But Shlomo had averred in the last interview that the tinker didn't really fit in anywhere. The tinker did not go to the shul. Martin spread his hands before him, as if pleading his case. "What about someone who is unusually isolated?"

"Do you have a right to think of him as a fanatic? Does he have any relationship to the victims?"

Good questions, the kind Martin had been asking himself on and off all weekend. Martin could almost count off on his fingers what he would need to make a case: a precipitating event, resistance to change, a deep and fanatical religious faith, opportunity to commit the crime, and *some* connection to *both* of the victims.

"Religious faith can be a wonderful thing, you know. It provides solace at times of the most dire need." Bernheim smiled. "I work with the nuns. Their ethos of selfless charity is totally admirable. However," he put up a plump, short finger, "fanaticism, that's something else. You Christians have a great and bloody history of that. We don't."

From the impish look on Bernheim's face, Martin knew the doctor was only being playful with someone he must have presumed was a committed secularist. But Martin could not enter into the humor. What the Israelite may not have understood was that men like Martin became secular, in part, because of the kind of fanaticism they had seen among some of the practitioners of their own natal faith. The kind of fanaticism Martin read in *La Croix* and that Madeleine Froment was bringing into his own home.

"I do know," Martin said, "that the man I am interested in railed against Ullmann for running his factories on Saturday, that he even seems to have convinced some immigrants not to allow their women to work there."

Bernheim nodded. His patience and tolerance, unlike Martin's, seemed to have no limits.

"I also know that he has tried to influence the wife of a judge to follow the Mosaic traditions in a stricter way."

"And Erlanger?" Bernheim inquired.

That, of course, was the essential, annoying question.

"Can you think of a reason why anyone, who might have antagonistic feelings toward certain people, would suddenly become violent?" Martin returned to his first question.

Bernheim shrugged. "You mean like an immediate tragedy that could push him over the edge?" The doctor shook his head, unconvinced. "You know," he folded his hands in front of him on the desk as if he were about to prescribe a harsh remedy to a recalcitrant patient, "we Jews are accustomed to persecution and displacement. These woes are woven into our tragic history. Until now in France," he added before hastening on. "The point is, we have learned to bear it. You have your occasional martyrs; we, as a people, have suffered. All because we insisted on keeping our traditions, our God."

Bernheim seemed to have forgotten the dictum that his friend had written into the report on the ex-priest: that anyone is capable of doing anything if driven far enough. Instead, although Martin assumed that Bernheim was every bit as secular as he, the psychotherapist had fallen back into a sense of "we." Did it come from perpetuating a tradition, or from being scorned and despised by others? We Israelites, We French. Who belonged? Who was left out? Questions Martin had to thrust aside, at least for the moment. Homing in on a viable suspect was a much more urgent matter.

"Another factor," he explained, "is opportunity. Both murders were committed on Thursdays, the very day the suspect comes into town."

"Then you seem convinced."

"No. I'll need further evidence. I thought you might—" Suddenly Martin realized that his suspicions about the tinker were only part of the reason he had come to consult with the brilliant and kindly Dr. Bernheim. What Martin really wanted was to understand more about how the human mind dealt with tragedy.

"If you bring him in, I'd certainly talk to him. I can see that is what you are intending to do, and I can't see that it would do much harm if you did it quietly and discreetly."

"Yes, that is the plan, the hope," Martin mumbled, his thoughts turning to Clarie. "One more question. This grief, mourning, how long does it take? How do you know when it would drive a person to . . . if not madness, to radically change their beliefs about the world?" The last words came out in a stumbling whisper.

"You've lost a child."

Martin looked up, stunned.

"News travels around the courthouse and the Faculté. I'm so sorry."

"Thank you." Martin bowed his head.

"You are doing the right thing. Continuing your work. Accomplishing something. But I can imagine it's much harder for your wife."

Martin barely moved his head in agreement. He avoided Bernheim's kind gaze.

"If she has any physical symptoms that you find disturbing, perhaps I could help."

"No, no, nothing like that," Martin said quickly. *Nothing like that.* A numbing, immobilizing heaviness spread from his mind through his heart into his limbs. He could not speak about what most troubled him: that he could not seem to reach her.

"Time," the doctor said. "Time. The pain may never completely go away, but you will learn to bear it, to take it in as part of your lives. You are both young; there is much to come to fill your hearts, to make that void seem smaller."

"Yes, thank you," Martin mumbled. He was appalled at the effort it took to rise out of the chair, and that everyone, even this famous psychotherapist, gave him the same advice and offered the same assurances.

Bernheim came around the desk and patted him on his shoulder. "If I can help, please call on me." Martin put on his bowler and thanked the doctor again. Then he left, through the waiting room, past the entrance, into the cold air. His restless longing to escape his troubles and to "accomplish something" carried him forward to the next stop, halfway between the Palais and the Faculté, to the comforting atmosphere of the Café Stanislas.

He took a small square marble table in the corner and ordered a café au lait, hoping its warmth would help his benumbed heart believe what Bernheim had told him. He watched the lumps of sugar dissolve as he stirred them into the steaming creamy liquid. He would find a way back to Clarie. If he was right, he'd be rid of the case before Christmas; then he'd concentrate on making the holidays bearable. Lifting the thick white cup to his lips, he imbibed the smooth, sweet drink of his childhood, of today, of a better tomorrow.

At eleven o'clock, when he was sure that Singer had left for the Palais, Martin went to ask the barman to use the telephone. The man kept wiping the tiny glasses he was setting up for his regulars, as he told Martin the price. After Martin placed the coins on the zinc bar, the man led him downstairs where a black wooden contraption, with two bulging eyes and the horn of a mouth, was fixed to the wall. The barman showed Martin how to crank up the little arm on the left side and unhooked the longer conical horn hanging on the right, handing it to Martin. Then he left.

As soon as Martin began to turn the crank, the eyes, which were indeed bells, began to clang until he heard a voice asking him whom he wanted. Holding one horn to his ear and shouting into the phone's mouth, he told the exchange to connect him to the Singers.

The maid answered and agreed to get Madame.

Noémie Singer's voice was tentative, worried. She had not expected anyone to call at this time of day.

Martin explained that he telephoned instead of visiting in order not to disturb her more than necessary.

At first he feared that he had been cut off, but he persisted, shouting her name into the horn, until she finally responded. "How can I help you?"

"It's about the tinker, Jacob."

Again no response.

"Did he ever tell you the name of the village where he lives?"

"No, Monsieur Martin, no."

"Did he ever talk about his stepmother?"

Martin imagined her biting her lower lip, hesitating. So he asked the central question before she could put him off. "Do you know if she is well or ill?"

Her answer did not surprise him. "Monsieur Martin, Jacob's mother is dead."

"When did she die?" he asked eagerly.

"I really don't know." He could imagine her arching her eyebrows with impatience, perhaps even anger.

"Recently?"

"I believe, a few weeks before my own dear uncle." Even through the static he heard the ice in her voice.

"Do you know—"

"Monsieur Martin, I understand your Republic believes in the freedom of religion. I do not have to speak to you about these things, and I do not want to."

Martin wondered if "his" Republic included her husband. He did not press.

"Thank you, Madame Singer. Sorry, again, to disturb you."

He heard the phone on the other end of the exchange click.

It was time to talk to David Singer.

Passing the guard at the entrance to the Palais with barely a greeting, Martin galloped up the stairs two at a time, warding off the loss of his nerve. He had not seen Singer since his interview with Noémie the week before and had no idea what she might have told him. Martin knocked, and entered Singer's chambers to a decidedly chilly reception. After exchanging perfunctory greetings they stood, arms stiffly at their sides, until Singer's greffier, with the kind of discretion that Charpentier seldom showed, got up and left the room without being asked. Then they sat: Singer behind his desk, Martin in front of it, lowering themselves with watchful care, like two cats, nosing each other out.

"You have something to tell me?" Singer asked, his lips between the perfectly fashioned black mustache and beard barely moving.

"I wanted to talk to you about this tinker, this Jacob."

Singer took in a deep hissing breath. "Yes, so I've heard, and I also understand that you have no compunction about coming between a man and his wife."

"That certainly was not my intention, I was only—" Martin stopped himself just in time. He realized that Singer wanted to say more, and he wanted to hear it.

"Only what? Prying? I suppose she told you what a holy man this Jacob is, how gentle, how good."

"Yes." Martin nodded, the hair on the back of his neck bristling ever so slightly. *Yes. And you. What do you think?*

"She undoubtedly did not tell you about the time he shouted at her, told her our kitchen was unclean, told her that she was breaking all the old laws, and how she and Béatrice then turned the house inside out, as if that's what defined us as Jews, obeying archaic laws that make no sense in the modern world."

As he listened to these complaints, what Martin really wanted to know was how Singer defined himself as a Jew. But, at that moment and with what was to come, he dare not ask.

"You can see how upset all this makes me. Did you really have to dig into our affairs?" Singer continued, evidently taking Martin's silence as a kind of contrition.

"Yes, I did." Martin's response was quiet and insistent. "This is why I have come to see you first, before Didier. To tell you of my suspicion that this Jacob may be the murderer of Ullmann and your uncle."

"That's ridiculous." Singer slapped his hand on the desk, before getting up and moving away from Martin, who understood very well that his colleague did not want to face the possibility that one Jew had killed another. Certainly Singer realized, or should have, that Martin would prefer to accuse any anti-Semite of the crimes, if for nothing else than the irrational hatred he spawned. But despite what Didier or Singer wanted, suppressing the anti-Israelites was not Martin's most urgent duty. He had to find the killer before he killed again.

Martin got up and went around the desk to face his friend. "Do you believe this Jacob is some kind of fanatic?"

Singer stared at the floor, twisting his mouth in distaste. "He's just a fool."

For a long, tense moment, Martin resisted the temptation to take Singer by the arms and force him to meet his eyes. Finally, Singer did, in anger. "Do you even read your local Catholic press, see some of the hate columns, the vile accusations?"

"More than you know." Although he was shaking inside, hurt and resentful that Singer did not trust in his good faith, Martin had to persist, logically and calmly. It could be crucial. "Do you know if Jacob made it a habit to come to your uncle's house? Did he talk to the housekeeper?"

"How would I know?"

"Is it possible that Erlanger threatened him in any way?"

Singer opened his arms in exasperation. "Do you have any idea what you are talking about? Noémie's uncle using threats? He was kind to a fault. Charitable to everyone, Christian or Jew. He gave coins to any poor person he met, patted them on the head, and talked to them."

"About what?" Martin asked eagerly. Singer, the most polished of interrogators, may have slipped into the very trap he was trying to avoid: a connection between his uncle and the tinker.

"About how to improve their lives. Urging urchins to get an education, beggars to find useful professions. And, through the Consistory, providing the means for them to do so."

"Urging immigrants, then?"

"Of course, immigrants. They can't remain as they are, beggars, peddlers. They have to come into the modern world. Do something for their families, for themselves, for this country, if they want to live here. Be men." Singer's spoke so vehemently that he sprayed specks of spittle on his precise black beard.

Martin understood from this that above all Singer, and perhaps the kindly Erlanger, did not want these eastern Jews to become an embarrassment. "And Jacob is not a man?" he asked. *Like you. Like me. Even though he doesn't want to be like either one of us?*

"I told you, he is a fool. Which is not yet a crime. So I hope you will not bandy this preposterous story around the courthouse." Singer sat down again at his desk and crossed his arms. They were at an impasse.

Martin walked back to his chair, picked up his hat, and said, "I won't say anything until I have more proof," knowing full well there was only one way to get it: find the tinker. Jacquette's men were already on alert, and they would be out in full force on Thursday.

38

Thursday, December 20

MARTIN CURSED HIMSELF FOR COMING in early. Tuesday and
Wednesday had been bad enough. But today, Thursday, he could not
possibly sit at his desk and write reports when out there, somewhere in
the city, the endgame was in play. Martin threw down his pen and
began to pace. He scratched at his beard in frustration. He should be
with Jacquette and the others. Doing . . . what exactly? The question
deflated him, giving him pause. He'd be useless. He could not see himself wrestling a weapon from a suspect or shooting a revolver at him.
Martin's duty was obvious and galling: he had to stay put, wait, and
hope he was right.

Martin went over to the potbellied stove and poked at the sparking
bits of wood with unwarranted fervor. He slammed the door of the
stove shut and walked to the map that Charpentier had pinned to the

wall on Monday. Martin had ordered two gendarmes to start searching through the depopulated hamlets once inhabited by Israelites. He let his fingers trace the distance from the Palais de Justice to each of the six villages identified by the departmental surveyor. So far, Martin had reports on three of them. Could the tinker just be starting out from one of the others? Or was Jacob the Wanderer in the midst of making his weekly rounds, going from town to town, like the peddlers of old? Or had he set out stealthily in the dark of night to take up a hiding position from which to stalk his next victim?

The map told Martin nothing. All he could do was march back and forth until Charpentier pranced in, his long red scarf flowing behind him. The young man's obligatory, cheery "Bonjour, Monsieur le juge," was Martin's signal to settle down and look judicial. He had no desire to share his excitement, or his anxieties, with his clerk. Martin flipped through the papers on his desk until he heard Charpentier's pen scratching out a summary of their interrogations. Then he quietly opened his top drawer and took out the watch that his father had made for him decades ago. He wound it up and set it on his desk far enough away so that its ticking did not pluck at his already taut nerves, but near enough so that he could keep track of how long it was taking.

After an hour had passed, Martin slouched forward, mesmerized by the minute hand's excruciatingly slow march from one number to the next. By ten o'clock, he was convinced that one of his men must have spotted the tinker. Five minutes later, he could almost see Jacquette tramping into his office, dragging the Israelite by the collar of his long, filthy black coat. In the next ten minutes, as the second hand relentlessly ticked one tock at a time, Martin had created two opposing scenarios in his mind. Jacquette would arrive in a jolly mood, murderer in hand, eager to congratulate Martin on his perspicacious investigative powers. Or, standing in front of Martin's desk, the inspector would be shifting uneasily from one foot to another, attempting to explain away his superior's folly and pointing out that, because of it, they were back where they had started.

Ever the realist, Martin knew that neither one's longings nor one's fears ever materialized full-blown. But nothing could have prepared him for what took place at exactly 10:33 when the door to his chambers flew open.

A ghostly, pallid David Singer staggered in with blood running across his chest. Martin's heart leapt to his throat. The worst had happened. Singer was dying.

Yet the specter kept marching toward him and was not gasping or groaning. It began to speak. "Jacquette's been wounded. I heard yelling just as I was leaving my house. Someone put a knife in him."

Martin jumped out of his seat and bounded over to Singer. *Jacquette.* This wasn't possible. Martin's mind raced back to the scene in the quarry near Aix-en-Provence, where another gallant man lay with a knife in him. But Jacquette was not foolish like Westerbury had been. Only overconfident, almost cocky. Had his inspector not taken precautions before approaching the peddler? Or had he been assaulted by someone else entirely, someone they hadn't even suspected? *Was Jacquette, his good and faithful comrade, dying?* Martin's mind overflowed with questions and bloody images.

"Jacquette, is he all right? Where is he?" Martin shouted. Ignoring him, Singer stared down at his coat with a horrified look on his face. Charpentier, who had also leapt out of his seat, offered to take it. Singer nodded and hastily unbuttoned his bloody vestment, allowing Martin's clerk to slip it off this arms. Then Singer examined his suit coat and pants for stains. He held up both hands and scrutinized the thin, rippled red lines on his shirt cuffs. "I left my gloves at the Faculté," he murmured. "They're covered in blood." Martin watched all this with growing concern and impatience.

"Is Jacquette alive? Where is he?" Martin repeated as he helped Singer into a chair.

"Yes, of course he's alive. That's why I'm here. He told me to get you." Singer talked as if he were making all the sense in the world.

"Where is he?"

"At the Faculté de Médicine, with my gloves. I told you."

The Faculté? Singer's gloves? Martin realized that his friend was in a state of shock. He forced himself to breathe slowly and calm down, even though all he could think about was whether his inspector was dead or alive.

Singer sat docilely in the chair for an instant, and then shot out of it. "I must get to my family. Charpentier! Give me back my coat!" Singer's attempt to give an authoritative order came out in a strangled rasp. "The carriage is outside," he continued, explaining to everyone and no one.

Charpentier stood nearby, gingerly holding Singer's coat by the collar. His eagerness to help had been replaced by startled apprehension. He looked to Martin for direction. Martin motioned with his head, indicating that Charpentier should help Singer put his coat back on.

"David," Martin asked, "do you want to see a doctor? Are you cold? Are you hot? Are you dizzy?" He clenched his teeth, in order not to ask again about Jacquette.

"No, no, no. I need to get home. To protect my wife and children from a murderer."

Martin nodded. "We'll go together," he declared. It was useless to argue with anyone in Singer's condition. Once he got Singer tucked into the back seat of the carriage under a blanket, he'd find out more.

Singer calmed down in the carriage and was even somewhat abashed by his behavior. "Jacquette wants to talk to you as soon as possible," he explained. "He's got the weapon."

Jacquette can talk, and he's making sense. At first that was all Martin could take in. But the questions swarmed back. How badly was

Jacquette injured? Had they captured the assailant? What had Jacquette told Singer? He glanced at Singer. He'd have to go easy.

During the short carriage ride, Martin did manage to draw out the essential sequence of events from Singer's jumbled brain. He had heard the first cry just as he was getting ready to leave for the Palais. He ran out of the foyer, but not in time to see the struggle or the assailant. The cut on Jacquette's left arm was so deep, it looked like someone had tried to slice it off. Singer's face took on a greenish cast as he described how he pressed his gloved hands against the wound, trying to stem the blood. Fortunately, his maid, Béatrice, was more quick-witted. She grabbed Singer's scarf from his neck and tied it tight high on the injured man's arm. All this time, despite his distress, Jacquette begged to be taken to the Faculté de Médicine, so that Fauvet could sew him up and examine the weapon at the same time. He also asked Singer to get Martin right away.

"And the assailant?" Martin sat straight up, staring at his friend, willing him to have an answer.

Singer gave Martin an apologetic half-smile as he placed a friendly hand on his arm. "He said to tell you it was the 'damned tinker.'"

Martin hunched back, relieved. He had been right. But there was no time for triumph or vindication. The man was still out there somewhere. Martin had to find him. The blood drained from his own face as he calculated, once again, the dangers and complications of that hunt.

"I'm getting out here," Singer said, pulling Martin back into the present. "I've got to be with Noémie and the children." Then he did a wonderful thing. He broke out in a scornful laugh, revealing the ironic sense of humor that had not been evident for weeks, as he shook his head and added, "Although I don't know what good I would do, after that performance."

Singer was back. Their friendship was possible. That was the thought that cheered Martin as he watched his fellow judge descend from the carriage. "We'll protect you," he called out to Singer.

"That's why Jacquette was there. When I get back to the courthouse, I'll send two policemen, one to stand outside your door, and one to escort you to the courthouse. I may need your help."

Singer waved his assent, and Martin waited until he got inside before urging the driver to go as fast as he could to the Faculté de Médicine. As soon as they got there, Martin leapt out of the carriage, paid the driver, and ran downstairs to the morgue, praying that he would find Jacquette alive and alert.

The first thing he saw when he pulled open the door was the back of Dr. Fauvet's pudgy, white-coated body.

Martin called out for Jacquette

"He's right here," Fauvet turned in a cloud of pipe smoke and patted a blanket-covered leg, "ornery as ever."

Jacquette lay on an iron table, his head on a folded sheet. His heavily bandaged left arm was tied high up on the back of a wooden chair. Someone, probably Fauvet, had nested several chairs together as a way of keeping the inspector's arm lofted above his head and heart. As Martin approached, he saw that Jacquette's mustache was dripping with sweat, and his ashen face was damp and creased with grimaces. He was alive, going to live, but in obvious pain. In a flash, Martin's relief turned to anger at the madman who had done this to his friend.

The inspector managed a smile. "I hope Fauvet's as good at sewing up bodies as he is at cutting them," he said before wincing again. "*Merde*! I want to be there when you catch that bastard."

"We'll catch him," Martin assured his wounded inspector, as he stepped up to the table. He prickled with a desire to start asking questions, but Fauvet had moved between him and Jacquette's face.

"I think we can take this down now," Fauvet remarked calmly, as he began to untie Jacquette's hanging arm. The young doctor seemed to bring the same imperturbable delight to treating the gruesome wounds of live victims as he did to examining those inflicted on the dead.

"Your man here wouldn't go to the hospital. Lucky they only nicked the belly, didn't penetrate."

"And the arm?" Martin asked, irritated at Fauvet's unhurried demeanor.

"That will take a while, got some muscle," the doctor pronounced through the clenched teeth that gripped his pipe as he worked.

"*Merde!*" Jacquette yelped, when Fauvet gently placed his left arm at his side.

"He tells me he has a fine wife," Fauvet said removing his pipe from his mouth. "Take him home and make sure she keeps him in bed for a while, will you? But first, you'll have to listen. He's eager to talk."

"I don't need a nursemaid," Jacquette barked, although his grimaces and sickly pallor suggested otherwise.

Fauvet stood over him, puffing out his sweet-smelling tobacco, while shaking his head. "Rest," he repeated to Jacquette. "And get him to drink some water," the doctor told Martin, pointing to a pitcher and cup on a nearby table. Then he lifted up and separated the three piled chairs, placing one on the floor near Martin and inviting him to sit in it. After shaking hands, he finally took his leave.

As soon as the door closed, Martin asked, "So, it was him?"

"Yes, your damned tinker." Jacquette gritted his teeth in pain.

"What was he doing, how did he—"

"I was a fool. I didn't take him seriously. He looked like an old man, but he's stronger and younger than he looks. I marched up to him, asked if his name was Jacob and before I knew it, he had a butcher knife aimed straight at my heart. When I put my arm up, he took a big slice instead. I managed to grab his wrist with my right hand and wring the knife from him. When it fell on the ground, he took off, pushing that damned cart of his. By that time, I was kneeling on the ground, trying to stop the blood. Thank God Singer came running out."

Jacquette's chest was pumping hard up and down by the time he had finished his story.

Martin poured some water into the cup and lifted Jacquette's head. "Drink, and then we'll get you home."

"No, no." Jacquette managed to raise his right arm a few centimeters between swallows. When Martin placed his head back on the folded sheet, he continued. "You have to know what's out there. I have two men at the homes of the Consistory members and two at the rabbi's." Jacquette grimaced in self-disgust. "I thought I could take care of the Singers myself."

"You did," Martin said, trying to figure out how to get Jacquette to see that he needed quiet and rest.

"Now you might have to go to those old villages. You have to root him out." Jacquette's labored breaths were coming closer and closer together.

"As soon as I get you home, I'm going to Didier and ask for more men. We'll find him."

"Fauvet has the knife."

"Fine. Now be quiet. That's an order. And I'll go find two strong medical students to carry you out."

Jacquette's head lolled to one side as he closed his eyes and crunched his face in pain and frustration. He had miscalculated, almost fatally. Now it was up to Martin.

Didier was not happy. Glaring at Martin, the lanky, clean-shaven prosecutor leaned across his desk and shouted, "And what exactly are we supposed to tell the press? That one Israelite is killing other Israelites?"

This time Martin did not cringe, equivocate or apologize. He stood with his hands comfortably entwined behind his back and tried not to smile at the obvious discomfort of his arrogant colleague. If Martin had ever hoped to derive one moment of pleasure from the difficult and drawn-out investigation, this was it.

Didier tapped a long tallow-like finger on the desk. "You do know, don't you, that Alfred Dreyfus is on trial this very minute in Paris, that there are some who are insinuating that all Israelites born in our region may be traitors."

Martin nodded, his silence fueling Didier's distress.

"You're sure about this, this 'Jacob the Wanderer' then? You're really certain?"

The slice taken from the worthy Jacquette's arm would seem to be incontrovertible proof. "As certain as one can be before we catch him. That's why I need all the men I can get."

Didier turned a decidedly petulant profile to Martin and began to stare at the ceiling. "And the Jewish community, what am I supposed to tell them?"

Perhaps more people should understand there was more than one "Jewish community" in Nancy. More than one kind of Israelite. But this was not the time for such lessons.

"You'll tell them that you believe that the killer is a madman, and madmen are to be found in every race," Martin said. "You'll tell the press that this has nothing to do with Dreyfus's alleged treachery in any shape or form." He crossed his arms, almost daring Didier to contradict him.

Didier pinched his lips together in a straight grim line. His steely blue eyes began to rove around the room. Martin watched, fascinated, as the prosecutor's mind shifted gears, like the well-oiled political machine that it was. "At least this tinker is not 'one of *ours*,'" he offered.

"You mean 'one of us,'" Martin corrected him, assuming that Didier was referring to those Israelites who were Frenchmen, who possessed what the Grand Rabbi called the "true Blood of Lorraine."

"Ours, us, what does it matter? The important thing is, we can label him a foreigner."

"Indeed, what does it matter?" Martin muttered. Anything to get the courthouse off the hook, keeping the bishop happy and the rabbi happy and the prefect happy and all those good citizens of Nancy who felt they were truly, oh so truly French, happy. The only reason Martin bit his tongue was that he knew Didier was on the same side, the side of equality of the races. He also knew that the prosecutor was not one to tolerate ambiguity or complications. If there was anything that Martin had learned in the last few weeks, it was that life is not so simple, that some Frenchmen were both equal *and* different, all at the same time. And then there were those, whom the Republic should care about, who were less than equal. "We should not stigmatize the whole immigrant community," he declared, thinking of the Abrahams, and the Shlomos, and the women working in Ullmann's mill.

Undoubtedly pleased with his new characterization of the suspect, Didier blithely ignored Martin's last remark. "We can worry about *that* later. Perhaps you and Singer can figure out what to say to the press when we catch him."

"Ah, yes, Singer. Since it is an *Israelite problem*," Martin said, making no attempt to hide his sarcasm.

Didier responded with a scowl. He was not liking this conversation. "Let's catch him first and worry about everything else later. What do you need?"

"More men, not only to protect the most prominent Israelites in our city, but to go out to the countryside so we can track the tinker down."

"Yours. You can use Singer's inspector to organize more police. Whatever you need. Do it. And talk to Singer, get him on board."

Talk to Singer. Didier assumed he was leaving the most difficult task to Martin. By now, Singer's worst fear, that the killer was a Jew, must have hit home. Of course Martin was going to talk to him.

39
Friday, December 21

BY EARLY FRIDAY MORNING, THE police had fanned out across the city in twos and threes, watching for the tinker. Martin had also sent an inspector with the gendarmes scouting the remaining depopulated villages. Now all there was to do was wait, Martin in his ground-floor chambers, and Singer above him, undoubtedly pacing, distraught at the turn of events.

Martin had tried to temper the blow, by talking about madness and loss, about the things that tragedies can do to someone. A conversation, Martin realized as he listened for signs of his colleague's distress, that he dare not yet have with Clarie. He could not imagine when he would be able to tell her how disturbing her behavior had become. With a sigh, he went back to work, shuffling papers, giving orders to Charpentier, and beginning to outline a dossier of the case. He was just going through the motions. He felt eerily suspended between apprehension and hope. His body tingled on alert, and his ears stayed attuned to every sound in the courthouse. They had to find the killer. He had to get on with his own life.

Finally, at one o'clock, Franchot, Singer's inspector, arrived with the news that he believed they had found the place, but not the man. Someone was living in a stone hut, where they had discovered several long benches, a stove with wood in it, a single tin cup and bowl, and books. Inspector Franchot, grayer around the edges than Jacquette, bigger, and much less talkative, handed a black leather-bound volume to Martin and commented that it had lain open on a bench. He added that the engraved arch above the doorway bore the same kind of writing.

A tremulous wave rolled down Martin's chest as he watched the book fall open to a much-used passage. He recognized the script he had seen on the gravestones in the cemetery, Hebrew, the ancient language of the Israelites. His first instinct was to send Charpentier for Singer, but he caught himself in time. Ordering the brawny veteran officer to wait for him, Martin ran up the stairs himself. He paused before the door to collect himself, and knocked.

"David, I think we have him," he announced as he entered the room. He told Singer about the occupied hut in the abandoned village and handed him the book. Singer opened it to where it had been creased and worn. The blood drained from his face as he read the passage. "This is our Torah, our most sacred text," he said quietly, as he closed it and carefully laid it on his desk, his attention and fingers hovering over it. "Do you want me to go with you?"

"Of course: we may need you. Your wife said he speaks only the old common language."

"Most of our men know at least two languages," Singer mumbled as he tapped on the book with his finger.

Then, without saying another word, Singer went over to a clothes tree to retrieve a black wool coat, less grand than his usual tweed but untainted with Jacquette's blood. He threw it on, saying "If this is where Jacob lives and he is truly observant, he will want to be home before sundown. If I am right about the script above the door, it is the old shul of the village."

They rode hard, single-file, for forty-five minutes, Franchot in the lead, Martin between him and Singer. Their panting horses sloshed and spattered the mud of the narrow, rutted road. Melting snow lay in sullen, ashen-edged patches on the floor of the forest that surrounded them. The tall trees, sturdy pines and skeletal oaks, tattered the waning rays of the afternoon sun, obscuring their vision. Martin hoped they would be done with their work before nightfall shrouded them all in darkness.

Franchot held up his hand. They slowed down as they approached the village. Martin patted the head of his horse to quiet its labored snorting. At first they heard nothing; then an anguished cry split through the forest, and the inspector whipped his horse into a gallop.

By the time Martin and Singer caught up to him, Franchot was in a muddy clearing, standing beside a bonfire, warming his hands and talking to the uniformed men. He broke off from them and came up to Martin. "Your tinker's in there," he said, pointing to a hut that was slightly larger and more substantial than the other buildings near the clearing. Although it was doorless, it seemed in good repair and very clean, as if recently washed down. Beside it stood the cart filled with old pots and pans, and the thick round knife-sharpening stone. As if confirming his presence, the man inside the hut began to drone a lamentation.

"They think he's going crazy," Franchot explained. "I told them to wait if they spotted him, so they hid until they were convinced he wasn't coming out." Martin was about to dismount when Franchot added, "There's something else you should know, sir. While they were hiding they came across a mound, maybe another body, buried in the woods over there." He pointed in the opposite direction from which Martin and Singer had come. "They could dig it up, if that's what you want, sir."

From the puckered look of distaste on Franchot's face, Martin was certain that that was not what *he* wanted, uncovering a body that had lain in the ground for God knows how long.

Martin explained to Singer, "Probably the stepmother. To think he may have buried her himself in this place." Martin shook his head, imagining the scene. Then he told Franchot that they would not have to uncover the body tonight.

In the meantime, Singer maneuvered his horse toward the building and read the inscription above the open doorway. He slid down off the steed. "It is the shul," he told Martin. "I'd better go in."

"No, you won't!" Martin shouted. This time the blood on Singer's coat could be his own, oozing from a fatal wound. But before anyone could stop him, Singer had stepped under the inscribed archway to the inside.

Martin swung his leg over the saddle, landed on his feet and lurched toward the doorway. Franchot stopped him before he could step inside. "If it's their holy place, sir, I'm not sure we have a right to arrest him there."

"Singer!" Martin called and stopped, knowing that he had to respect a sanctuary and sensing that Singer wanted to do this on his own.

Martin leaned his back up against the outer wall by the arched entrance, breathing hard, and listening. Anxious sweat ran down his forehead. He tried to assure himself that a religious man would not defile his place of worship with violence. The singing had stopped. Soon he heard Singer shouting in French, accusing the tinker of humiliating and betraying his people. Martin turned to observe what was going on inside.

As Martin's eyes adjusted to the dark within, the tinker spread his arms wide and began to circle around the middle of the floor in a kind of ecstatic dance, ignoring Singer. Then he began to chant again. In the shadows, Martin could see that Jacob the Wanderer was a slight man, of medium height. His shoulders, long bent to the wheel of his heavy cart, caved inward, concealing the strength or the rage that allowed him to kill and to wound.

Martin and Franchot watched as Singer, still shouting, raised his hand to smite the tinker, and then, as if stayed by a supernatural force, let it fall by his side. He dropped down on a bench, his elbows on his knees, his head in his hands. For his part, the tinker began to weep, raising his hands to his face and then toward the ceiling. For a moment, all of them, the uniformed men by the fire, Franchot and Martin at the doorway, and the two Israelites locked in a shadow play of pain and grief, were suspended in an eerie calm.

Suddenly, horribly, the tinker rushed to one side of the room and began to beat his head against the wall. Martin was about to order Franchot to go in and stop him, when Singer got up, went to the tinker, and pulled him away. Singer began to speak to Jacob, hesitantly, as if searching for words, in some version of what Martin had come to know as "the common language." Gradually, Singer's sentences became more fluid, as if he were recapturing the sounds of his childhood, and as he did, he seemed to regain his composure. Singer and the tinker sat on one of the benches; the judge questioning and prodding, the killer sobbing and wailing. Martin whispered to Franchot that they must go in if there was a chance that the suspect might hurt Singer. The inspector nodded and gestured to the gendarmes to draw near.

Martin stood at the threshold, listening intently. He ran his tongue around his lips to moisten them. It took a tremendous act of will to hold back, when every instinct, every muscle in his body was poised to intervene. Once more he felt cut off from Singer, divided from him now by a stone wall and a language he did not understand. He watched anxiously as Singer became more "foreign" to him.

Or, was it that, foreign? Standing against the outer wall of the shul, Martin surveyed the ancient village. How long had it existed? When had it been built? Centuries ago, no doubt. Before there was a Republic. Before there was a France as they knew it, a France filled with citizens, not abject subjects. The inhabitants of this village, like the ancestors of Jacquette and Fauchet, had sustained the place they called Lorraine. More than the distant kings and dukes and emperors who once ruled it, they were its life's blood. And yet David Singer had kept this past buried deep inside, out of public view, out of the regard of non-Israelites. Because . . . because of men like Rocher, Hémonet, and countless others, who hated anyone who they thought was not French enough. Even, Martin realized, because of someone like himself, who had once assumed all men of good will were like him, or would be if given a chance.

Martin glanced at his friend, still and listening now, as Jacob the Wanderer wailed and explained. And then Martin understood something more about Singer. He wanted to be a French Israelite, not this poor, unkempt, despised Jew. Just as Jacquette did not want to be the peasant his grandfather had been. This was Singer's right, and yet— the words of Noémie Singer came back to Martin—in the sea of Christians and nonbelievers, Singer had an obligation to sustain the most ancient part of his past, or it might die forever. An obligation and a community, something which gave him strength while at the same time marking him, among other men, as different. Martin's heart reached out to his friend, with all his self-protecting correctness and aloofness, and his pride. How complicated it must be.

After about a quarter of an hour, the men inside had quieted down and were standing. Singer laid his hands on the tinker's shoulder and back and pushed him out of the shul. Martin, Franchot, and the other men stood by, ready to pounce. "Tie him up," Singer said, "but with his arms in front, so he can pray." For just a moment, Singer was the man that Martin knew so well from the courthouse. He examined the bottom of his coat, his fine shoes, and his pants and tried to wipe the mud off them. He soon realized it was useless.

There could not have been a greater contrast than that between the calm, methodical Singer and the trembling, humble Jacob the Wanderer. Martin stared at the killer, a man of indeterminate age who swayed from side to side to a persistent rhythm heard only by him. The tinker had the same wiry beard, aquiline nose, and battered round black hat as the men in the immigrant café. What was familiar, however, was overshadowed by what Martin would never forget: the watery blue eyes raised to heaven and the parched lips moving in an unending silent prayer.

"Martin." Singer signaled that he wanted to talk.

The two of them moved outside the circle of the others. "He did it. I knew as soon as I read the passage in the Torah. It was about a righteous Israelite killing other Jews because they were desecrating our religion. He was wrong, of course. He had no right to commit violence against our people. We will all suffer from the shame of it."

Singer barely got these last words out. He grimaced, his face dissolving in sorrow and grief. Martin reached out to take hold of his arm. He almost said, as Singer had said on the fateful day they buried Henri-Joseph, "I know." But Singer did not know then, and Martin did not know now the depth of what his friend was feeling. So Martin just said, "He is insane. He is mad. Madmen do mad things. That is what we will say over and over again."

When Singer did not reply, Martin let his hand drop to his side. "What else did he tell you?"

Singer sighed and stared at the ground. "That anyone who tries to teach the old ways, the right ways, is humiliated by the rich, the powerful, the ones who are changing everything. That His God curses us. And yet," an ironic smile crept across Singer's face, "he asked me to apologize to Noémie for her pain, for she is one of those 'who understands.' Heh," Singer's voice took on a bitter edge, "I probably have much more than that to apologize for."

"No, you don't. You have tried to make life better for men like him, for everyone. We all have." Martin grasped at these Republican straws, these half-truths, in an attempt to assuage his friend's pain.

"Really? I tried to make life better? Did I ever listen, ever want to hear his story? How he was left here as a boy, wandered far to find his home as a man, had everything taken from him by force and violence, and when he came back," Singer lifted his arm in a weak gesture toward the hut, "everything here had changed. Noémie tried to tell me, tried to explain why we should be kind, but all I saw was dirt and superstition. And my poor dear uncle," Singer turned away as his voice broke, "all he saw was a simple-minded man who needed to be reformed, remade in our image."

Martin struggled to come up with a comforting reply. Singer should have been kinder, more patient and less righteous with his wife. But Singer did not want Martin's sympathy, he wanted something else.

"I have a request. I want to walk back into town with the tinker."

"What?" Martin was stunned. "Even if we go at a gallop, we'll be lucky to make it back before dark."

"Not tonight. Tomorrow."

Martin's head hunched toward Singer. He did not believe what he was hearing.

Singer stepped back. "This will be his last shabbat evening in this place, where he grew up. He does not want to ride to town on his sabbath. He's begged me to let him stay and walk into town, and I am willing to do it."

"Singer, the man is a murderer, and mad. I can't let you—"

Singer threw his hand up, signaling for Martin to stop. "It is the one mercy I can show him, letting him obey his old religious laws before he becomes completely subject to ours."

"No," Martin shook his head.

"Martin," Singer argued, "how many times have you told me about your fears that becoming a judge robbed you of your youthful ideals, of your willingness to help, really help, *and to understand* the poor, the less educated, those left behind by the Republic?" Singer snorted. "Even those who do not have the slightest desire to become like us, upstanding bourgeois servants of a bourgeois state."

Martin kept shaking his head in disbelief as Singer spoke. This was not the time for philosophical discussion or self-recrimination. They had a killer. A madman. Their duty was to bring him in.

"I agreed with you," Singer continued undeterred. "*In the abstract.* As long as we were talking about ignorant peasants or desperate workers or young girls led terribly astray. I agreed with you as long as I did not see myself in those who came into my chambers. As long as they were not my people," he whispered hoarsely. "I wanted them to be better, because we have to be in order to survive."

Martin made a move toward the other men as he pleaded. "Come on, David. Let's go."

"No! Listen," Singer said, not letting Martin back away. "Tomorrow is the beginning of one of our holidays. It celebrates a victory of the ancient Hebrews over those who wanted to paganize us, to make us like everyone else in the classical world. In other words, to 'civilize' us. But our warriors resisted and rebuilt the great Temple in Jerusalem, the one the Romans destroyed. I could use this time alone to think about what it means to be 'civilized,' and what it means to be a Jew."

When Martin raised his arm in protest, Singer grabbed it. "Please. Ask Franchot or the gendarmes to stay with me. I'll be safe. You can tell Noémie what I am doing and why, and that she can prepare the Hanukkah candles for me to light tomorrow night, when I will be worthy of them." His grip got tighter as he waited for Martin to look him in the eye. "Ask them," Singer repeated.

Then Martin understood. Singer did not want to explain his actions to the others, only to Martin—and to Noémie Singer. He had just revealed the most private part of himself, the pain and shame of

Jacob's crime, and perhaps even his need to repent for his disdain and indifference toward the tinker and his ilk. Martin nodded his assent. If this was something Singer needed to do, who was Martin to deny him? Singer had opened his heart to him. What more could one ask from a friend?

"If I can get someone to stay with you."

"Please."

When the stalwart Franchot agreed, without asking any questions, to guard over Singer and the prisoner, Martin hastened to leave. They had the killer, he would be in jail by noon tomorrow. Martin's job was done. All he had to do before getting home was to stop by the Singers to deliver David's message. Martin and the gendarme took off for Nancy as fast as they could against the threat of total darkness.

Except for the crackling of a waning fire, all was quiet when Martin opened the door to his apartment. He called out and, getting no response, tiptoed into the living room. One gas lamp gave off a dim circle of light on an end table. He saw the top of her head above the back of a chair. He sighed. She was sleeping, or thinking, remembering, mourning, staring at the flames.

"Clarie?" he said softly.

She stirred.

He hurried to her place. Her hair was unkempt, and she huddled under a plaid blanket, as if she were incapable of stoking the fire or taking care of herself.

"Clarie, I have good news."

"Me too," she murmured, not taking her eyes off the sputtering flames.

"Yes, what?" He pulled up a chair beside her.

"Papa is coming with Aunt Henriette right after Christmas. They'll be here for two weeks."

"That is good news! Henriette will take care of you and cook, and fill our home with delicious smells." Even as he said this, his encouraging words disintegrated into cinders floating uselessly between them. He had no idea how to help Clarie find joy in anything.

"And you," she finally looked at him. "Your news."

"We have found the murderer. The case is over. You and I can spend more time together." Somehow he knew that this would not be cause for joy either.

"Oh," she said, turning away uninterested. "So who did it?"

"A tinker, a poor Israelite, a kind of madman."

She arched her eyebrow. "Just an old Jew, then."

Martin jerked away from Clarie as if he had been struck.

She covered her mouth. She had heard the contempt and sarcasm in her own voice. How could Bernard not be shocked? Two good men had been killed. An unfortunate was facing the guillotine. And she had chosen to think first of their race, with scorn.

He reached for her, for her cheek, for her temple.

For an instant, she was afraid. She shrank back into her chair, but his touch was gentle.

He rubbed her cheek lovingly with his thumb. If only he could erase those deep circles of exhaustion and grief from her beautiful eyes.

"Don't tell Papa, please," she said through tears.

"Clarie, my beautiful Clarie, I know this isn't you." This was the price of his abandonment.

"You won't tell anyone?"

"No, darling."

"I'm so ashamed."

They looked into each others' eyes.

How did this happen to us? he thought, holding back the tears.

How did this happen to us? she cried in her heart.

She finally said, "If I don't think about Henri-Joseph and pray every minute, if I don't do what is exactly right, what I've been told to do, then I am abandoning him, I'm letting him go. I can't do that. He's my baby." She began to sob. "But why would he want a mother like this?"

"Listen to me, Clarie, please," he said as he moved her chin so that she looked into his eyes. "He will be with us forever, in our hearts. There will be pain, a void, but we will have so many other things in our life to help fill the emptiness and make his memory sweeter. First of all, we have each other."

"I'm so sorry," she said as she turned her head away again. "What's happened to me?"

He took both of her hands in his. "Darling, we should get away from here. Leave this place. We could go to Paris. You could teach there. It would be so good for you. And me, I'll become an *avocat*. I'll do what your Papa keeps saying I should be doing, plead for the oppressed, for the working man. We'll be poor, but we'll be happy again. I swear it." *Please, please, I'll do anything.*

His face was bright with hope, but she could not understand what he was talking about. Leave. Paris. Teaching. Offering all this to her, when all she wanted was Henri-Joseph.

"Oh, darling," he said, "I wish I could take away the pain."

He knew.

He stood up and lifted her out of the chair.

She let him lift her up. Even under his official suit and shirt, she could feel the essence of him, and smell the scent of her sweet, good man. She could not imagine why she had fled from this comfort.

He felt the softness of her breasts. Her hair tickled his nose, almost making him want to laugh aloud with joy. He was here now. Nothing could keep him from getting his Clarie back.

They held on for dear life.

Epilogue
A New Year, 1895

BY THE END OF THE first week, Henriette Choffrut's wide bustling body had replaced the solemn presence of Madeleine. Tante Henriette arrived with Giuseppe bearing a huge straw basket stuffed to the breaking point with dried olives and preserved fruits, newly pressed oils and canned tomatoes, wild herbs, and home-made tartes. She filled the air with news—of the restaurant in Aix, of Clarie's six half-brothers, of the equally rotund and beloved Oncle Michel. And when silences fell, she hurried to embrace her beloved niece, holding Clarie tight to her ample breasts.

Every morning, Tante Henriette shooed the men away to go about their business. She sent Giuseppe to the cafés to read his newspapers, and Martin back to the courthouse to complete his dossier on the two murdered Israelites. She made Rose her ally in bringing cheer and the smells and tastes of Provence to the Martin apartment.

Giuseppe willingly fell into the role of Martin's ally as they debated whether or not the young couple should move. Could Martin afford to give up his safe career as a judge? Could Clarie pass up the opportunity to pluck the plum of all plums, a teaching position in the capital? The men amiably changed sides on a daily basis. When they finally got an exasperated Clarie, eyes shining with the thought of living in Paris, to join them, they knew they had succeeded a little.

On Sunday, January 13, 1895, the afternoon before Tante Henriette and Giuseppe planned to depart, a peaceful warmth pervaded the apartment. Martin settled down in an easy chair near the fire to start Zola's newest novel. Clarie and Henriette were behind the closed kitchen door, preparing a final feast. Giuseppe was on his way from the railroad station with the latest editions of the weekend newspapers, obvious fodder for a last political debate. Martin put his book aside and smiled, savoring the moment. He was, at last, part of a large, loving family; Clarie was getting better; and his role in the case was over.

Suddenly, Martin heard yelling in the street below and got up to take a look. About a dozen men and boys stood across the street, throwing stones at the Steins' shop. Even through the closed windows, Martin could make out the shouts of "dirty Jews" and "youtres" and "traitors."

He was about to get his coat and scarf to see what he could do to stop them, when he saw his father-in-law sauntering toward the fray. Realizing that he did not have a moment to spare, Martin charged out the door and down the stairs. On the second-floor landing he came upon Rebecca and Esther Stein. "Papa said we should go upstairs for safety," the girl told Martin breathlessly. "May we?"

"Of course. Go," he urged. "The door is open." He didn't have time to say more. He had to get downstairs before his big-hearted, impetuous father-in-law got involved.

With one pull, he swung the outside door open. By this time, Martin's landlord had splayed his body across the shattered shop window and was already bleeding from his forehead. Giuseppe stood by his side, waving his roll of newspapers at the ruffians.

"Stop," Martin shouted to the men across the street. "I am a judge at the court of Nancy, and if you do not desist this very instant, all of you will spend a week in jail."

Even in his shirtsleeves, Martin had what Giuseppe teasingly called the whiff of the bourgeoisie. The motley crowd of men and adolescent boys in winter jackets and caps caught enough of whatever official odor Martin exuded to pause, at least for a moment. Martin flashed hot and cold with anger and fear. What if they didn't believe him? Would a small riot break out, with him, Giuseppe, and Stein outnumbered? Martin was so much better at words than with his fists. That's why he decided to take a firm stand, hands on hips, glaring at the men across from him.

"Why should we believe you?" someone behind the front row of stone throwers shouted.

"Because it is true. I want your names," Martin yelled back with as much authority as he could muster, even though he had no pen, no paper, no policeman to back him up.

But they had no masks, no charcoal on their faces, no guile, only irrational hatred and pure drunken stupidity. Heart pounding against his chest, Martin stared them down, eying them one right after another, as if he were recording their individual features in his brain. First one, then another began to pull the brims of their caps down over their eyes. One by one rocks fell from flaccid fists, clunking and rolling on the cobblestones. Finally a tall blond middle-aged man, his nose and cheeks ruddy with drink and pent-up rage, said, "Come on, let's go," and they began to disperse. Whether Martin was telling the truth or not, this thug knew enough not to take a chance with someone who called himself a juge d'instruction. The last to leave, a mere lad of about fifteen, was the most audacious. He swaggered to the corner and when he reached it, he called out "Jew-loving Judge" before speeding away.

Martin tried to disguise the huge sigh of relief he expelled. He stared at the emptied street in front of him, taking in smaller and smaller gulps of frosty air, until he felt calm enough to deal with his injured landlord. By this time, Giuseppe was already dabbing Stein's bloody forehead with his handkerchief. "Those bastards," he kept repeating.

"It's nothing, Monsieur Falchetti, nothing," Stein said, even as his widened eyes riveted upon the blood on his fingers. Martin put a steadying arm around his landlord's waist.

"Mmmm." Giuseppe, no longer excoriating the hate-mongering cowards, examined the wound with the skill of someone used to working with his hands and dealing with injuries. "You're right. A glancing blow. Once we get you taped up, you'll be fine." He patted the frightened shopowner on his shoulder and handed him the hand-kerchief. "Let's cover those windows."

"Monsieur Falchetti, Monsieur le juge, you don't—"

"Let's get inside." Martin was freezing. The wind rippled his shirt sleeves, converting his sweat into pinpricks of ice.

"Why? why? I want to know why." Stein moaned as the three of them moved into the narrow hallway and shut the door behind them.

"I'll show you why." Giuseppe reached for the newspapers wedged between his upper arm and broad chest. He unrolled a copy of *Le Petit Journal Illustré*, revealing a full-page engraving of Captain Alfred Dreyfus, the first Israelite appointed to the General Staff of the French Army, being stripped of his rank and his saber in front of a jeering crowd. The heading in bold letters read THE TRAITOR.

Stein silently mouthed the word "traitor" and closed his eyes. "The shame of it," he whispered. "The shame on my people."

Martin grabbed the paper and stared at it, almost rending it in two with the force of his grip. Everyone knew about the verdict, but this kind of instigation, this rubbing it in, could only sow more hatred.

"It's not your people," he muttered. "It's Alfred Dreyfus."

He looked up to see Giuseppe solemnly nodding his agreement.

"I have to get Esther and Rebecca. We have to repair the window," Stein said weakly.

"Come, then." Martin started up the stairs and noted that his father-in-law had taken the precaution of walking behind the frightened, injured shopkeeper in case he stumbled.

When they reached the apartment, they found Henriette Choffrut sitting beside Esther Stein, listening to her with grave attention and shaking her head in sympathy. Rebecca was clinging to Clarie, muffling her tears on her beloved teacher's shoulder. They swayed slightly as Clarie cooed consolation.

"I'm fine, I'm fine," Stein declared as soon as he caught the attention of the women. "No bother. No worry. Just a broken window. We can fix that with a little paper until tomorrow."

Esther Stein broke off from Henriette and embraced her husband. "Papa, Papa," Rebecca cried as she joined her mother.

"We're fine. We're all fine. Isn't that true, Monsieur le juge?" Stein insisted again.

Martin knew that his landlord wanted desperately to assure his wife and daughter that the crisis had passed. He managed to get out a yes, even though nothing that he had seen or heard in the last ten minutes could qualify as fine or good or decent or even bearable.

After the Steins left, Giuseppe showed Clarie and Henriette the headlines and the picture of Dreyfus, the traitor, being stripped of his honors.

"Do you think there will be more attacks on people like the Steins?" Clarie asked, her brow wrinkled with worry.

Martin shook his head. "They've done everything they could to Dreyfus. The papers have had their day. Those thugs have enjoyed their little cowardly confrontation. Now everyone should let the Israelites alone."

When Clarie did not look convinced, he repeated, "It's over."

25

But it wasn't over.
Not for Clarie or Martin.
Or Captain Dreyfus.
Or France.

Reader's Guide to the History
in *The Blood of Lorraine*

THERE IS A VAST HISTORICAL literature on the case of Alfred Dreyfus. Most of it focuses on what is known in France simply as "the Affair" (of 1898). However, the first trial did have important consequences for Jewish history. Dreyfus's court-martial and public humiliation in front of a mob screaming "Death to the Jews" inspired the Austro-Hungarian journalist Theodor Herzl to found the modern political Zionist movement. Having arrived as a foreign correspondent eager to live in the land of liberty, fraternity and equality, Herzl left France convinced that the Jewish people needed to establish their own homeland.

To promote his anti-Semitic agenda, Edouard Drumont's newspaper, *La Libre Parole*, gleefully exploited the bribery scandals surrounding the Panama Canal fiasco as well as the discovery of espionage in the General Staff of the French Army. His *La France Juive* (1886) went through more than two hundred editions. The illustration from his weekly described in the first chapter of this book and the famous illustration depicted in the Epilogue can be found in *The Dreyfus Affair: Art, Truth, and Justice* (Berkeley: University of California Press, 1987) edited by Norman L. Kleeblatt.

No one knows how many copies of Abbé François Hémonet's hard-to-find *Nancy-Juif* (1892–93) appeared. Although information on the author is also scarce, we do know that despite its 308 pages, the priest claimed the work was "unfinished." He also asserted, before a church court, that the book was the true cause of the charge of insubordination that eventually led to his being forced out of the priesthood. *Nancy-Juif* excerpts several articles by the "Titus" mentioned in the last few chapters.

Hippolyte Bernheim is another "real" character. The leading light of the "Nancy School" of psychotherapeutics, he used "suggestibility" during hypnosis to cure his patients and disagreed strongly with the methods of the now more famous Jean-Martin Charcot. The young Sigmund Freud visited and was influenced by both of these pioneering psychologists. Bernheim's mentor in the techniques of hypnotism was the kindly old country doctor Ambroise-Auguste Liébeault who appears briefly in this book

The most relevant books on the history of Jews in France for this work are Françoise Job's *Les Juifs de Nancy du XIIe au XXe siècle* (Nancy: Presses universitaires de Nancy, 1991), which includes a sketch of Grand Rabbi Isaac Bloch, and Freddy Raphaël and Robert Weyl's *Juifs en Alsace. Culture, société, histoire* (Toulouse, Edouard Privat, 1977), which discusses the scorn for "Polaks." There is a fine Jewish collection in Nancy's Musée Lorrain. The biblical passage about a zealous Jew killing another Israelite that so startled Singer could well have been Numbers XXV, in which Phinehas saved Israel from a "moral plague." Almost nobody in the past or the present would interpret this as a rationale for disobeying the great Mosaic prohibition against the taking of life.

Finally, two books can serve as background to the lives and work of the fictional Bernard and Clarie Martin. Benjamin F. Martin's *Crime and Criminal Justice Under the Third Republic* (Baton Rouge: Louisiana State University Press, 1990) is an excellent introduction to the French legal system at the end of the nineteenth century. Jo Burr Margadant's *Madame le Professeur: Women Educators in the Third Republic* (Princeton, NJ: Princeton University Press, 1990) describes the training and travails of the women teachers who taught in the innovative public high schools for girls.

All translations included in this work are the author's.